come X break

♥ my ♥

heart X again

C.W. FARNSWORTH

For Farley.

PLAYLIST

Video Games ♥ Lana Del Ray
Where's My Love ♥ SYML
Anchor ♥ Novo Amor
when the party's over ♥ Billie Eilish
Ceilings ♥ Lizzie McAlpine
I Found ♥ Amber Run
loml ♥ Taylor Swift
Space Song ♥ Beach House
would've been you ♥ sombr
Fluorescent Adolescent ♥ Arctic Monkeys
About You ♥ The 1975
Electric Feel ♥ MGMT
The Scientist ♥ Coldplay
That Home ♥ The Cinematic Orchestra
Wings ♥ Birdy
Mind Over Matter ♥ Young the Giant
Fine Line ♥ Harry Styles

1

NOW

Elle

Bright rays of sunshine stream in through the windshield. Warm air flies in through the open window, whipping strands of brown hair across my face. They get caught in my sunglasses and stuck to my lips, but I don't roll the car window up or use the elastic on my wrist. I press the gas pedal down harder, watching the speed tick higher and enjoying the small burst of adrenaline that accompanies the thrill of going too fast.

It's a perfect spring day, the sort that makes hope blossom in your chest, no matter what mood you happen to be in. The sun shines down, blinding and relentless, not a single fluffy white cloud visible in the sky. The air tastes fresh, like it was in hibernation all winter and has returned rejuvenated.

I flick the right blinker and tap on the brakes, spinning the wheel slightly as I coast off the interstate's exit ramp. A pile of road salt sits on the corner next to the stop sign that marks the start of the intersection, the gray a few shades lighter than the asphalt. It was a long, harsh winter, today's temperature tropical by comparison.

Lana's distinctive voice is easier to hear now that I'm off the highway, the bittersweet lyrics and ethereal melody my favorite song on the playlist Juliet calls my "*sad girl* music." She asked me to send it to her once, in college, after a breakup.

I doubt she's listened to it since. Because that's what normal people do. They heal from heartbreak and move on.

Another left, then a right.

The wheel turns without me even having to think about it. This route is so familiar; I could drive it blindfolded.

I wish it were foreign.

I wish I'd been brave enough to turn my back on this town.

I wish I were normal.

Home is such a strange concept when you think about it. How we assign importance to one place based on familiarity or its proximity to certain people. How our perception of it shifts as we grow older. How it doesn't.

The trailer park isn't a prettier sight in the sunshine. It sits like that heap of salt—bland yet obvious. Unchanged by shifting surroundings. The brightness beaming from the sky casts a harsher spotlight on the general state of disrepair.

Five years ago, the dirt road was paved. Since then, there's been little, if any, maintenance to the asphalt. The suspension bounces with each pothole I hit. They're impossible to avoid, more crevices than smooth and flat surface.

I park alongside the second-to-last trailer, right next to the tiny porch that is barely big enough for two people to stand on. Grab the orange box off the passenger seat and climb out of my car.

"Must be the second Saturday."

My fingers comb the tangles away from my face until my eyesight is cleared. Mrs. Nelson is reclined in her beach chair. It's the first appearance the striped mesh seat has made this year. My last visit was in March, and a thick layer of snow covered the ground that was mostly grass worn down to its roots.

"Nice to see you, Mrs. Nelson," I tell the broad brim of her straw hat.

She's never shared her first name with me in the years I've been coming here. She's also never asked me why I continue to show up here each month, an unexpected kindness from the woman who appears unbothered by her *busybody* moniker.

"You're more reliable than my calendar, dear," she comments, tilting her head back so I can see more of her wrinkled face. Her eyes are shaded by huge sunglasses shaped like daisies.

My lips curve at the cheerful sight, the first upturn that hasn't felt forced all day. I dread these trips as much as I look forward to them. As much as I need them.

"Bella bought them for me," Mrs. Nelson explains, noticing my amusement. "I don't know where she gets her absurd fashion taste." She sighs, then sips from the glass in her hand. Judging from the strong smell emanating, I don't think it's water.

I have a good idea where Mrs. Nelson's granddaughter inherited her flair for flashy accessories, like flower sunglasses—today's outfit a prime example: neon-pink capris, paired with a flowing turquoise top—but I don't say so.

"I like them."

Mrs. Nelson sniffs. "I'll tell Bella." She glances at the trailer looming behind me, nearly identical to her own. "Nina's been waiting for you. Curtains keep twitching."

"There was some traffic."

There wasn't. The freeway was wide open. I'd tossed and turned most of the night, anxious about today, then overslept because I don't normally set an alarm on Saturdays.

"What's in the box?"

"A gift," I answer.

Mrs. Nelson shakes her head, the motion making her straw hat wobble. "You're a sweet girl."

I'm a *selfish* girl.

I come here to check on Nina because I care about her. But these visits are for me. Because *not* coming would be far more painful than showing up has ever felt.

This time, my smile is forced. "Enjoy the sunshine, Mrs. Nelson."

"Oh, I plan to." She takes another gulp from her glass.

I head for the steps, the two wooden stairs creaking under my weight as I approach the front door.

Nina appears a second after I knock, a few flecks of white paint falling as the door swings wide open.

We don't hug. She doesn't even smile.

"Nice day," Nina comments, stepping closer to the door so I can squeeze past her and enter the small kitchen.

"It is," I agree, walking straight toward the square table tucked along the wall and attempting to ignore the heaviness expanding in my chest as the first wave of bittersweet nostalgia hits.

Memories.

Mistakes.

Magic.

He's more than a ghost here, which is exactly why I drive all this way. It's the place I feel most sane, surrounded by proof he existed.

It hurts to remember.

Forgetting is even more painful. Pain is more manageable when you know the source.

My steps to the chair facing the fridge are automatic. Nina's memorized the same routine, taking her usual seat directly across from me. The scarred surface of the wooden table is empty, aside from a teapot and two cups. A glass jam jar, decorated with a couple of stubborn remnants of paper label, holds some yellow flowers. Goldenrods, just like the ones lining the road to town. Another squeeze in my chest as I picture Nina picking the blossoms to brighten up the small space. She cleaned recently, the distinctive scent of citrus cleaner mixing with the floral fragrance in the air.

Nina pours the steaming tea, pushing one of the cups toward me.

"Thank you." I lift the box from my lap, set it on the table, and slide it her way. "For you."

"There's nothing I need," Nina mutters.

She offers some form of protest each time I bring her something, which is every visit. No matter what she says, I know she appreciates the gifts. I gave her the tea set we're using right now, and she goes through the bags too quickly to only use it when I'm here. The candle I brought back in November is nearly gone. One of the juice glasses, painted with oranges—a present from a couple of years ago—sits, dripping, in the drain rack.

Nina's opening the box, smoothing a palm across the patterned silk scarf once the tissue paper parts.

"Just a fun pop of color to add to an outfit," I say. "Wear it to work maybe."

"They'll think I robbed the place." Nina is still stroking the silk. "Can't afford this on a cashier's salary."

Nina's cycled through many jobs over the years. Her current

position is working as a cashier at a grocery store one town over. She says she enjoys it, but I doubt she'd tell me if she didn't.

"It was on sale," I lie. "I got a great deal."

Nina glances up. The dark circles under her eyes are less noticeable, the sunshine beaming through the window casting her expression in a warm golden glow. "You do too much, Elle."

I shake my head. "I was out shopping already."

"I meant driving all this way."

"I don't mind the drive. It's nice to get out of the city sometimes, especially on such a beautiful day."

"Today must be a hard visit."

I take a long sip of tea—jasmine, my favorite flavor—before glancing up and meeting Nina's gray gaze.

Her eyes are the exact same shade as his.

Mysterious and moody.

They can shift from soft to stormy in a second. They act oblivious but see too much. They draw you in, even when you know you should keep your distance.

I nod instead of responding, knowing she won't press for more of a reply. We have good boundaries, Nina and I. We know what to share. What's best left unsaid.

"It gets easier," Nina says softly.

I rub a finger against the smooth china side of the teacup. "I know."

Different wounds heal in different ways. It depends on the type of loss. Death and distance aren't the same heartbreak.

And I would know.

I've experienced both.

I stop at Fernwood's only grocery store, Provisions, on the way to my parents'. It's busy, which I should have foreseen. Nearly noon on a sunny Saturday is prime time for all ages to be out and about. There are families shopping with young children, retired couples, teenagers hanging out with friends. I spent most of the walk toward the back of the store observing that last group, experiencing a strong mix of nostalgia and bitterness.

I remember that age. Remember thinking that adulthood would be easier. Exciting.

What a lie.

I manage to make it to the rear of the store—to the floral section, my destination—without running into anyone I know. Unfortunately, that's as far as I get.

"Oh, Elle! So nice to see you. How are you doing, dear?"

I swallow the sigh that wants to escape and turn to face a friend of my mother's. "Fine, thanks. Nice to see you, Mrs. Williamson."

"Marie, please, honey. Are you home visiting your parents?"

I nod, the motion stiff. She doesn't remember the date despite claiming to be a close confidant of my mom's. It's demoralizing to realize how well my fakeness fits in here. How easily it seems like no time has passed at all and nothing has changed.

Mrs. Williamson doesn't notice the tension humming through my stiff posture. "What a wonderful daughter you are. I hardly get to see Fleur these days. She works at the most charming little art gallery in New York. I must admit, I don't really understand most of what they display …"

The little attention I was paying Mrs. Williamson fades when I spot Archer Hathaway approaching the buckets of tulips. He hasn't seen me yet, so I don't avert my gaze right away. His dark blond hair is shorter than it was in high school, neatly trimmed and combed. He gave up on ever growing a beard, I guess, because his jaw is clean-shaven. Unsurprisingly, he's dressed in the preppiest outfit possible—pressed khaki pants, boat shoes, and a polo shirt. He's either headed to the country club to play golf or coming from there.

"Elle? Elle?"

I refocus on Mrs. Williamson. "Sorry. What were you saying?"

Archer has seen me.

My cheek tingles with uncomfortable awareness as Mrs. Williamson says, "I was asking you about law school. You're close to graduating, right?"

"Yes," I say. "Next month."

"How exciting! Your mother told me you were already hired at one of Boston's top firms. Hardly a surprise, of course, but still very impressive. Congratulations."

My cheek muscles are rigid as I shape my expression into something I hope looks modest and appreciative. "Yes, it is exciting. Thank you."

"Well, I should go find Edward. I'm sure he's still wandering around, looking for the cheese that I asked for. Give my best to your parents."

I keep my smile fixed in place. "I will."

Mrs. Williamson nods and spins. She glimpses Archer halfway to the aisle, her steps stuttering as she quickly glances between us. No doubt debating turning around so she can witness this encounter firsthand. There's nothing Fernwood loves more than a juicy piece of gossip. But basic decorum wins out, and she continues down the cereal aisle to find her husband.

"Hi, Elle." Archer takes one step closer, still leaving a gulf between us. A beautiful bunch of red tulips are clutched in his left hand, one of Provisions' wicker shopping baskets held in his right one.

"Hi." My tone is flat as I stare at his wedding ring. The gold band is impossible to miss against the backdrop of bright green stems.

I knew Archer got married last summer. My parents attended the wedding even though it wasn't a celebratory event for them. More of a wake—the death of their dream of me becoming a Hathaway. As if that outcome hadn't been determined a long time ago.

"How have you been?" he asks.

I'm still staring at his wedding ring, incredibly irritated by the shiny, obvious sight. Even Archer fucking Hathaway got his happy ending. I'm bitter enough to resent him for it.

"I'm great." I force yet another smile, certain he can tell that it's fake.

"I was eavesdropping. Big, fancy job all lined up. I'm not surprised."

"Me neither," I reply.

That's what happens when you follow all the rules—you end up exactly where everyone expected you would.

Archer nods, one corner of his mouth lifting an inch. "Wouldn't want my lawyer to go up against you."

"Then be careful who Daddy insures."

Archer glances down, any lightness in his expression bleeding away. "I'm sorry, Elle. Truly. If I could go back and—"

"You can't." I inject steel into the two words.

My life is already plagued by plenty of what-ifs. I don't need to pile Archer's regrets on top of my own.

"I know," he says. "I just wanted to make sure you … knew that."

"Yeah, got it. *Thanks.*" I look away purposefully, hoping he'll get the strong hint I'm finished with this conversation and keep walking.

"They don't have any roses."

I say nothing, running my tongue along the backs of my teeth as I continue to stare at the metal buckets filled with flowers and pretend he's not here.

"That's why you're in town, right?"

I don't like that Archer remembers anything about me. Even if his recollection of the anniversary of Rose's death is only because our mothers are best friends and not as my ex-boyfriend.

My mouth stays stubbornly shut. I'm done socializing, and I don't owe him any explanations about where I go or why.

Archer exhales, realizing the same. He rubs his jaw once, pulling the skin taut over his cheek and drawing my attention to the thin white line there. The sight of the scar stings. I don't like this serious, somber, *remorseful* version of him. I prefer him as a smug prick who's neither agreeable nor apologetic.

"I hope you're happy, Elle," he tells me quietly, then walks away.

I stare after his retreating back, my teeth clenching the inside of my cheek hard enough that I taste the metallic tang of blood.

I haven't been happy since I was seventeen.

That's not entirely Archer's fault. But I blame him.

Partly because he bears some responsibility.

And mostly because Ryder isn't here to blame instead.

A terse, "You're late," is my mother's heartfelt greeting when I arrive at my childhood home.

I slam my car door closed. Gravel crunches beneath my shoes as I walk toward my father's car. It's parked just past the front door, around the curve that surrounds the stone fountain. I can see his tall profile through the tinted window, waiting in the driver's seat. Impatiently, I'm sure. He usually spends Saturdays at the golf course with Mr. Hathaway and the rest of his friends. Once this unpleasant outing is over, I'm sure the country club will be his next stop.

My mom climbs into the passenger seat without waiting for a response.

I slide into the back seat. "Sorry. Bad traffic. Hi, Dad."

"Hello, Elodie."

My mom clicks her tongue as she buckles her seat belt. "You should have left earlier."

"Sorry," I repeat.

I don't defend my excuse. She'd be more understanding if I mentioned I ran into Mrs. Williamson and Archer at the market. She'd get more annoyed if I mentioned the cemetery is only ten minutes away and open until sunset, so there's not exactly a strict deadline regarding our departure time.

Instead of saying anything at all, I stare out the window at the passing houses of the neighborhood I grew up in. The stately homes look larger than I remember, like my perspective has shrunk—instead of grown—as I've gotten older. The thought is depressing, almost as crushing as the omnipresent silence sitting in the car like a fourth presence.

It's so quiet that I can hear the steady hum of the engine and the soft hiss of air-conditioning blowing out of the vents. It can't be more than sixty-five degrees out. But that's my parents—cold and impractical.

I rub my arms in an attempt to combat the bumps rising, the rasp of skin against skin audible in the silent car.

The cemetery where my sister is buried is small, the gravel road to reach the rows of graves narrow. A silver Jaguar partially blocks the thoroughfare; my father's annoyed huffs as he maneuvers around the sedan the only commentary, aside from the car's noises.

My palms dampen with sweat as we draw closer to the massive oak tree that marks the prime plot my parents paid an outrageous amount of money for. The wet stems of the tulips I'm holding don't provide any absorbance.

This annual visit—on the anniversary of her death—is the only time I visit Rose's grave.

I wish I wanted to come here more often. Wish I felt like there was something here, aside from stone and sorrow.

I was twelve when my older sister died. I'm twenty-five now. More than half my life, I've felt like an only child. My most vivid memories of Rose are these annual visits to the hunk of rock that marks her final resting place with my parents.

The walk to Rose's grave is short and as silent as the car ride. Between us at least. A few birds chirp overhead. It sounds like they're celebrating the weather, and I wish such a beautiful day hadn't dawned on this particular date. Today has always felt like an anniversary more fitting for heavy rain. It poured the day of her funeral.

We stand as a somber trio, me between my parents, all staring at Rose's grave. The gray surface is flawless, unmarred by time or the elements. Polished to a sheen resembling glass. Sunshine glints off the smooth stone, making me squint behind the shield of my sunglasses. I crouch down to set the bundled tulips on the grass that's growing green again, brushing my fingers against the carved letters that spell out Rose's full name. *Beloved Daughter and Sister* is written below the dates of her birth and death. I linger on the last word, then let my hand drop and stand.

"Pretty tulips," my mom says.

The pink flowers are a vibrant spot on the ground against the green and gray of grass and graves.

"They didn't have any roses," I reply softly.

Most days, my mom would take that as an opening for criticism. Ask me how many stores I stopped at. Mention that many flower shops allow you to place orders ahead of time, that it just requires minimal planning in advance. Frances Clarke has a gift for finding criticism in any situation.

Today, all she says is, "The thought is what counts."

We're very different, my mother and I. She and Rose were similar, both effortlessly poised and endlessly critical.

I'm not much like my dad either.

I'm some strange combination of my parents, which means neither understands me. I have my dad's drive, but not his detachment. My mom's charm, but not her composure.

The invisible barrier that often separates us is thinner here. There's no mystery behind my father's stoicism or my mother's lack of judgment.

They're grieving. They lost a child, suddenly and senselessly.

And if there's one thing I understand, it's sudden and senseless loss.

2
THEN

Elle

The eight becomes a nine, meaning I only have a minute left. I pull in a deep breath, then release a long exhale. I wait until my lungs are burning to inhale again. The slight discomfort isn't the shock to the system I was hoping for.

Today is the first day of senior year. The final first day of high school. The start of the last chapter.

I should be nostalgic or excited or nervous. Not ... numb. The day hasn't even started, and I already know how it'll go. How it'll end.

Reassuring, I guess. Also boring.

Twenty-nine turns to thirty. I hit the off button before the alarm can begin blaring—a stupid game I play every morning.

"Elodie?" There's a rapid, efficient knocking on my bedroom door. "Are you awake?"

"Yes," I respond, injecting plenty of false enthusiasm into my tone.

We're both happier when my mom isn't worrying about me.

"I didn't hear your alarm. Is it broken?"

"It went off," I lie.

Explaining I try to beat my alarm each morning isn't a concept my mother would understand. She'd probe and analyze and look at me like I was crazy until the silly ritual was ruined.

"Good. Breakfast is ready."

"I'll be right down!"

Retreating footsteps are the only response.

I hold one more breath before tossing the sheets away and climbing out of bed. I can hold it for a lot longer than I used to be able to. Maybe I should quit cheerleading and try out for the swim team instead. Do *something* different so that senior year doesn't look just like junior year did. To escape the endless déjà vu.

My bedroom has its own connected bathroom, so it's a short trip to start getting ready. I make my morning routine last as long as I can, wanting to shorten breakfast with my parents as much as possible before my boyfriend, Archer, picks me up.

I would prefer to drive myself to school, but people rarely take what I want into consideration. And fighting the tide gets more exhausting the longer you do it. Pathetic as it sounds, I've mostly given up on challenging any currents.

A yogurt parfait and hard-boiled egg are waiting when I enter the formal dining room—same as most mornings. I wonder if my mom remembers this was Rose's favorite breakfast, not mine.

"Good morning, Dad," I tell today's edition of the *Boston Globe* as I take a seat at the table.

The newsprint lowers to reveal my father. Combed hair. Trimmed beard. Shrewd eyes.

"Good morning, Elodie." He takes a bite of oatmeal, then a sip of coffee, careful not to let either spill on the navy suit he's wearing. He wears some variation of this outfit every weekday and most weekends, down to the pressed pocket square and monogrammed cuff links. "Ready for your first day?"

"Yes," I respond, knowing that's the only acceptable answer.

Clarkes are always ready.

"This is an important year," my father tells me.

"I know."

He nods. "Good."

I can tell his attention is already drifting back toward his paper. My father limits his paternal responsibilities to pleasantries, monitoring my report cards, and paying for a credit card with an unknown limit I've never managed to hit.

"I'm taking an Architecture class this semester," I tell him.

"Architecture?"

Twin lines appear between my father's eyes. Brown, like Rose's were. I inherited my mom's blue ones.

"For my elective. It's a new offering this year."

"What about Mock Trial?"

"They're not offering it as an elective any longer. It's an after-school activity now."

My father frowns. "Won't that conflict with cheerleading?"

"Yes."

He shakes his head. "I'll call Principal Walker on my way to the office."

I don't protest. If anyone can get the Fernwood High School schedule changed, it's Michael Clarke. My father controls every situation he's a part of, running his life with the same efficiency as a judge in a courtroom.

My mother breezes into the dining room a few seconds later, carrying a platter of freshly cut fruit. I quickly swallow the final clump of yogurt-coated granola and wash it down with some orange juice.

"Is that dress new?" she asks after taking the high-backed chair across from my dad.

"Yes. I got it with Keira and Juliet last weekend."

Her hum is disapproving.

I glance at the grandfather clock next to the fireplace, then drain the rest of my juice. "I'd better get going. Archer will be here any minute."

That announcement distracts my mom from my outfit, just like I knew it would. "Archer is driving you to school? How considerate. He's such a sweet boy."

I resist the strong urge to roll my eyes, knowing all it will earn me is a lecture.

Sweet isn't an adjective I'd use to describe Archer Hathaway. My sole interest in him is that he's hot and ... well, his appearance is his main selling point. And that dating him gets my mom off my back about dating him. She's best friends with Archer's mother. I'm pretty sure they've been planning our wedding since kindergarten. Resisting it became ... exhausting.

"Uh-huh," I say, standing and then pushing my chair in at the table. "See you tonight."

"Have a good day, honey," my dad says.

From my mom, "Love you."

"Love you too," I respond as I walk into the soaring entryway. I grab my backpack out of the front closet, where it's been sitting with the winter coats since June.

It still feels like summer when I step outside, no sign of fall's crisp chill in the late August air. I pass my car—a cherry-red convertible I'm still shocked my parents agreed to buy me. A convertible is one of the most impractical vehicles you could have in New England, which is my favorite thing about it. It's something different, something unexpected.

There's no sign of Archer. He'll probably be late.

I take a seat on the edge of the stone fountain that sits in the center of the circular driveway, tipping my head back so the sun warms my face. I sit like that, basking in the sun's rays like a lizard, until I hear gravel crunch and open my eyes.

Archer isn't alone in his Mercedes, which I'm not surprised by. We spend most of our time together as part of a larger group. We don't have much to say to each other when we're alone.

The SUV slows to a stop, and Archer rolls down the window to flash me a broad grin. He looks good, his tan skin and blond hair emphasized by the blue T-shirt he has on. "Hey, babe. We match."

I glance down at the dress I'm wearing. The one my mom raised her eyebrows at. It's shorter than the ones she buys for me, but that wasn't why I chose it. The color was what I loved, and Archer is right. It's very similar to the shade of his shirt. That makes me like it less, not more.

"Yeah, we kinda do," I say, glancing past Archer at his best friend, Perry Welch, who's sitting in the passenger seat, scrolling on his phone. "Hey, Perry."

He glances up, smirking as his gaze dips from my eyes to the low neckline of the dress. "Hey, Elle."

We fooled around a few times before Archer and I officially started dating in the spring. Mostly because I was hoping my showing interest in his best buddy might cause Archer to lose interest in me. No such luck. My feelings for Perry were no stronger than any I have for Archer, but at least he has a more entertaining personality to be around. Archer's attention has already shifted to the screen in the dashboard, four words all he could come up with to say to me.

"I'm not riding in the back," I tell Perry, crossing my arms.

No matter how many times Archer takes his car to get detailed, the faint odor of sweat lingers from his football equipment.

Perry rolls his eyes but opens the passenger door and climbs out of the car. He holds it open as I round the front fender, taking a mocking bow before shutting it. "Your Highness."

Archer snorts, then revs the engine.

Once Perry is slouched in the back, Archer takes off in a spray of gravel that will piss off both my father and the gardeners. Unlike my mother, my dad isn't part of the Archer Hathaway fan club. He'd rather I wait to date until I'm in law school—or even better, a first-year associate at one of Boston's top firms. He only agreed to let me go out with Archer because he's a Hathaway.

Loud rap music pours out of the car speakers, making conversation impossible, which I'm fine with. I tune out the racket as best as I can and focus on the streets of Fernwood flashing by instead.

Fernwood is a small town, about forty-five minutes outside of central Boston. It provides all the allure of small-town living—sprawling lots, fresh air, and plenty of square footage—while also allowing for a reasonable commute to the downtown offices, where most of its adult residents work.

The three-story colonial I grew up in is located in Fernwood's most exclusive cul-de-sac, obnoxious stone facades marking the entrance to almost every driveway. Several blocks later, we pass the small downtown section with a few restaurants, a movie theater, a general store, and a couple of gift shops. The post office and the library.

I look wistfully at Brewed Awakenings, the local coffee shop, as

Archer speeds by. If I'd driven myself, I could have stopped for a latte and a doughnut. My mom considers coffee a gateway drug and only serves tea at breakfast. I'm positive my dad cheats and gets his caffeine when he arrives at the office, but Fernwood High's cafeteria lacks a barista.

Five minutes later, Archer parks—crooked—in a spot in the front row. The silence is deafening when he turns the car off and the music stops. Perry pops his door open, allowing shouts and exclamations from the lot to enter the car. I climb out next, slinging my backpack over one shoulder.

A crowd is already forming around Archer's car. Mostly football players. A few girls, who offer me sweet, fake smiles as they gush over my dress.

I possess a popularity I didn't lobby for and don't really understand but is a combination of every cliché you could think of. I'm the captain of the cheerleading team, dating the varsity quarterback. Student council president. Head of the Honor Club. The college applications my parents insisted I spend the summer working on are all for the most prestigious universities in the country. Perfect is an objective, impossible standard. But I know it's how most people describe me. It's probably how I'd view my own life if I wasn't living it.

"See you later, babe." Archer presses a wet kiss against my mouth, prompting plenty of hooting and hollering from his football buddies.

I nod and manage a smile, no part of me surprised he's not walking in with me. Unless it's an opportunity to badger me about sex, Archer avoids spending alone time with me. It's like dating me is all he wanted, and now that we're officially together, his work is done. I should probably care, but I don't.

"Have a great day, *babe*," I reply, fighting the urge to wipe my mouth with the back of my hand.

I'm sure Archer has told anyone who will listen that we go at it like rabbits every chance we get. But honestly, if his kissing technique is any indication of his bedroom skills, I have no desire to change my mind about sleeping with him.

Archer doesn't catch the subtle sarcasm, but Perry does. He reaches up to tug the brim of his hat lower, half covering his smile.

I hate being called babe, and Archer acts like it's my legal name.

I turn and head toward Juliet's car, parked right next to the brick entrance of Fernwood High. There's no sign of Keira yet, predictably. She's as late as I'm punctual.

Juliet's leaning against the bumper of her sedan, eating a muffin. I eye the iced coffee beside her elbow enviously.

"Hey!" she says as soon as she spots me.

"Hey," I reply, stopping a couple of feet away.

Juliet scans my appearance, then nods approvingly. "I was totally right. That dress looks amazing on you."

I smile before stepping forward and taking the spot beside her, surveying the filling parking lot as I rest most of my weight against her car. "Bonus: Frances hated it."

"They're her genes. I would kill for boobs and legs like yours. She can't blame you for showing them off."

"I'm sure she'll manage to."

Juliet laughs and takes another bite of her muffin. "How was last night?" she asks after swallowing.

"As bad as I had expected."

"Did you and Archer … you know?"

I shake my head. "He got wasted during pool pong. Took him an hour to realize I'd left."

Juliet rolls her eyes. "Boys."

"Boys," I agree.

"I got you a coffee, by the way. It's in the center console."

"Bless you." I stand and walk over to the passenger door, salivating over the sight of the iced coffee in the cupholder. The plastic is damp with condensation, the cool water refreshing against my palm.

"Don't forget the straw," Juliet teases as I return to her side, pulling one out of the back pocket of her jean shorts and handing it to me.

I flick some water drops toward her bare arm. My mom's other fear of coffee, aside from the potential caffeine addiction, is that it stains teeth. Reluctantly, I peel the paper sleeve off the straw and stick it in the opening. *Sorry, turtles.*

"I forget, did you get Gibbons for History?"

"No. I have Anderson."

Juliet sighs. "Ugh. Like having it last period wasn't bad enough."

"I'd trade last period for taking regular over AP." If there's an advanced section of a class, I'm taking it this semester.

"Oh, you poor smarty-pants."

I roll my eyes before taking a long pull of coffee. I work hard for good grades. They've never fallen into my lap the way everyone assumes.

"Thanks for the coffee."

"What are best friends for if not smuggling illicit substances? I got one for Keira, too, if she ever shows—"

Loud music announces the arrival of my other closest friend. The decibel rivals Archer's rap, but it's a song I actually like.

Keira parks her Jeep four spots down, then practically skips over to us. "Happy senior year!"

"Gah!" Juliet says in response to Keira's loud exclamation. "Some of us still have our hearing."

Keira snorts, then focuses on me. A wide smile spreads across her face as she stares at what I'm wearing. "Yes! You're wearing the dress. Did Archer love it?"

"Sort of." If commenting on the color counts. Not exactly a compliment.

Keira nods. "Typical."

"I got you a coffee," Juliet tells Keira. "Not that you need it."

Keira beams, then bounces over to the door to grab her coffee. "Whatever did Mrs. Clarke say?"

"She wasn't a fan of the dress either," Juliet says.

"Told you that you should've gotten it in two colors," Keira comments.

"Maybe next time," I reply.

The car door slams shut, and then Keira reappears with her coffee in hand. "Guess what. Nicole and Alec broke up."

"She wasn't at Perry's last night, so I wondered," I respond.

"And you didn't text me?" Juliet exclaims. "Elle!"

I swallow more coffee, savoring the cold caffeine. "Alec? Seriously?"

"You're the one dating *Archer Hathaway*."

"Yeah. And you know why."

Keira scoffs. "When are you going to stop letting your mom run your life?"

"You've met her. When I'm fifty."

Juliet laughs.

The three of us have been best friends since kindergarten. They know most of the ugly truths about my relationship with my parents. They held my hands at Rose's funeral. They helped pick out my junior prom dress for my first official date with Archer. And they've spent enough time around the two of us as a couple to see past the pretty facade the rest of the school reveres.

"Oh, guess what else I heard," Keira says. She forges ahead without waiting for any predictions. "Ryder James is back."

I drop my coffee, my numb fingers going slack with shock.

"Elle!" Juliet screeches as she jumps away from the icy spray.

My shins are soaked, chilled coffee running down my bare legs in tiny streams. I can't feel it.

"Sorry. Wet cup—cold hands—slipped." I stumble through an explanation neither of my friends is listening to.

Juliet has already pulled out napkins, dabbing at her shorts before passing a few to me.

"Thanks." I bend down to wipe the coffee off my legs, my head spinning so fast that I feel dizzy.

There's a muffled roar in my ears that drowns out most of the commotion around us. Heat radiates off the blacktop, but my skin burns hotter.

Today was supposed to be predictable. He was supposed to stay gone.

"Nice, butterfingers," Keira teases as I stand. "Good thing you're becoming a lawyer, not a surgeon."

My nod is wooden as the first bell rings, signaling five minutes before homeroom. Streams of students start toward the front entrance.

"Let's go!" Keira says, striding ahead.

I trail behind her, and Juliet falls into step beside me.

"What were you saying?" I suck in a deep breath as we walk inside the air-conditioned lobby and continue down the locker-lined hallway, my eyes darting around the familiar sight. I've spent more of the past three years inside this building than my house. "About Ryder James?"

It's a thrill to say his name. It also sounds wrong, like a secret spoken aloud.

"Oh. Maddie said she saw him with Tucker and some of the other Twos at Robinson's last night. He left after freshman year, remember?"

Remember? I'd need a severe case of amnesia to forget.

"Maybe," I say instead. "Is she sure it was him?"

Fernwood is a very wealthy town. The Twos are the kids from the trailer park that sits on the far edge of the town limits. An invisible boundary line many residents—including my parents—have attempted to redraw in order to exclude anyone with that address from attending Fernwood's public schools, which are considered some of the best in the state. Attempted unsuccessfully. The best they could do was alter the zip code so that one section of town is 02612 instead of 02611. An invisible geographic line that extends inside the school. The Twos keep to themselves. That includes Ryder James, who moved to Fernwood at the start of high school and left at the end of freshman year. I doubt Maddie Peterson ever spoke to him, much less knows what he looks like after two years.

Keira shrugs, unconcerned and unbothered. Entirely oblivious to the way my heart is banging against my ribs. "She said it was him."

My lips press into a thin line as we continue down the hallway, chatter bouncing off the lockers. Juliet and Keira pull out their schedules to compare teachers. I walk in a daze, too stunned to reply to any of the voices calling out greetings to me.

I'd be lying if I said I don't still think about Ryder sometimes.

But it's the absolute truth that I *never* expected to see him again.

Juliet and Keira follow me into Mrs. Andrews's room. Neither of them is actually assigned to my homeroom, but no one cares. I'd say it's a perk of being seniors, but it's really just a perk of being *us*. Or me, rather. No one reprimands Elle Clarke. I'm deemed innocent before ever being found guilty.

The loudspeaker crackles to life to share the morning announcements, but the noise level in the classroom barely drops. Mrs. Andrews doesn't make any attempt to quiet students, just continues to write notes for her first class on the whiteboard.

I grab the restroom pass off the hook and head down the hallway that's now empty. The ladies' room is also still and silent, thankfully. The plastic pass hits the laminate counter with a quiet *thunk* when I reach the sinks. I wet a handful of paper towels, wipe my legs of coffee residue, and then toss the wad of wet paper into the trash.

I clutch the edge of the counter, focusing on deep inhales and long exhales as I stare at my reflection in the mirror. The loose curls in my hair have held, and there aren't any coffee stains on my new dress. But there's a stubborn wrinkle between my eyes that won't smooth, no matter how hard I try to relax my face. It remains, worried and willful.

Maddie's wrong. She must be. A guy from the trailer park probably had a friend visiting who tagged along to the local diner, and that's who she saw at Robinson's. Maybe his name is also Ryder, and that's why she thought it might be him.

Because why would *he* be back after *two years*? Someone said he moved to Florida.

And of course, there were the juvie rumors, which swirl around all of the Twos. Stereotyping at its finest. Living in a mobile home doesn't make you a criminal.

Wherever Ryder ended up, that's probably where he still is.

But the wrinkle remains. I blow out an exasperated sigh, then grab the pass off the counter and head back to homeroom. The bell signaling first period rings right as I walk into the classroom.

"See you at lunch," Juliet says, passing by as I grab my backpack from the spot on the floor where I left it.

I nod in response.

"What wing are you headed to?" Keira asks as I smooth my dress flat.

"G," I answer.

"Cool. Me too. Economics."

I nod again. I barely drank half of my coffee before painting the parking lot with it, but I feel wired and jittery. Unfocused and unsure.

I'm mostly convinced Maddie must be wrong. But what if she's *right*? That slim possibility has my every sense on high alert.

Keira is still ignorant to my distracted state as we head toward the social studies wing, talking about the party set to take place on Friday night. It's an annual back-to-school bash, but this year's will be special for the obvious reason that it's the last one. Next year, we'll be scattered at universities across the country. I mostly *mmhmm* along as she runs through outfit options until we reach the door of the AP European History class I have first period.

"Elle!"

I glance over one shoulder at an approaching Kinsley Henderson. She's the vice to my president on student council.

"See you at lunch," Keira tells me, then continues walking.

"See ya," I say, pausing for Kinsley to catch up.

I haven't seen her all summer. We're more school friends than close confidants.

"Hi! How was your summer?" Kinsley asks, pushing her tortoiseshell-rimmed glasses up closer to the bridge of her nose.

"It was great," I reply. "How was yours?"

"Busy. Lots of college visits."

"That's—"

"You're blocking the door," a male voice interrupts.

I freeze. My muscles lock, and my stomach drops with an unpleasant lurch.

Maddie Peterson was right.

Kinsley is staring, wide-eyed, over my shoulder. I spin around slowly, taking advantage of every possible second before I have to face him. But I can't postpone the inevitable forever. Part of me doesn't want to. Has waited—*hoped*—for this moment for two years.

Flinty gray eyes meet mine, higher than I expected.

At fourteen, Ryder James gave me butterflies.

At seventeen, I can only hope I'm not visibly drooling.

His eyes are the exact same. Everything else is different. His brown hair is darker and shaved short so none of his face is hidden. He's sporting a dark tan that makes me think maybe the rumor about Florida was true. But the biggest change is his height. He was the tallest freshman, but he must be over six feet now. Not only that, but he's also got muscles that make him look a lot older than seventeen. The tendons in his forearm and biceps contract as he grips the strap of the backpack slung over one shoulder.

He's still the hottest guy I've ever seen. And holding eye contact with him still feels like standing at the edge of a cliff on a windy day, anticipating a fall.

"You're back." I make sure the two words don't hold any indication of my feelings about his return.

Easy, since *I* have no idea how I feel about it. All I've ruled out so far is indifference. Apathy isn't staring at someone for a minute without choosing to.

"Yeah." Ryder smirks, but there's nothing carefree or amused about the shift in his expression. It's a challenge. An appraisal. His eyes harden to the consistency of metal, not just the color. There's no lust or worship in his expression, the way most guys look at me.

No warmth.

No apology.

He's acting like we're the strangers anyone would call us.

"For good?"

It's a stupid question. If this were a short visit, he wouldn't have shown up for school.

"You're still blocking the door," he says, apparently agreeing that didn't require a response.

Ryder takes a step closer. He's three feet away from me now, maybe less. Waves of heat wash over my body, my breathing turning too rapid.

I forgot how exasperating he is. How blunt. How captivating.

Electricity buzzes across the surface of my skin as I register his closer proximity. I have yet to process that he's really *here*, near enough to reach out and touch. My fingers curl into fists, nails digging into the soft flesh of my palms, and I hope he doesn't notice.

"Yeah, you should get to class. Your attendance record is pretty terrible."

Amusement appears, flashing across his perfectly symmetrical face, in response to my casual reference to his two-year disappearance. The sight of it feels like a victory. Satisfaction spreads as we continue to stare at each other while I battle against all the questions I want to ask.

Why did you leave?

Why did you come back?

Did you miss me?

Rather than voice them, I move out of the way. Ryder sidles past me without another word, so close that I can feel the heat emanating from his body.

Three deep breaths later, I follow him into the classroom. Kinsley's curious eyes remain on me the entire time.

Ryder's standing at the front of the room, talking to Mr. Anderson. I take a seat in one of the front rows like the teacher's pet that I am. Kinsley takes the desk next to mine as I reach down to pull a new notebook out of my backpack. I deliberate between a black or blue pen for a ridiculously long time, trying to appear busy.

"Hi, Elle," Brock Patterson greets as he walks by. He's on the football team with Archer.

"Hey, Brock," I respond, sitting up and flipping through blank pages.

Ryder chooses my row to enter the sea of desks. I don't know if it's intentional—I sat in the middle of the five, and at least six other students have also passed me by—but it *feels* intentional. I keep my eyes fixed straight ahead as he walks past, attempting to ignore the heat I can feel flooding my cheeks as my body reacts to his proximity.

Class begins a couple of minutes later.

Mr. Anderson launches right into a lecture, dropping a stack of papers at the front seat in each row to be passed back. The course syllabus. I dawdle as I scan the top page, trying to avoid turning around until I have to. When I do, I keep my eyes on Liza Jones, who sat behind me, passing her the stack with a small smile before spinning right back around.

Mr. Anderson continues outlining the first topic of the semester— World War I—as I flip through the pages of the syllabus. Normally,

I'd be taking careful notes by now. But calming myself down seems like a more pressing task at the moment.

As I page through bullet points on decades of world events, I mull over how ironic it is that this is the class I'm facing Ryder in.

But that's *all* we share now.

History.

He made damn sure of that.

3
NOW

Elle

My parents are waiting, beaming, beneath the broad branches of one of the many old trees that cover campus. They weren't this jubilant at my college graduation three years ago. Probably because we all knew that was simply a stop along the way, and this was the final destination. A relief to reach. But I have to fake the answering smile I know they're expecting.

My shoulders square under the suffocating blanket of my graduation gown and hood, the sticky humidity in the air seeping into the heavy fabric. The pride on their faces is almost enough to make the past three years worth it. Almost.

"Wait! Stop!" my mom calls out.

I pause, nearly stumbling over a gnarled root.

"This lighting is just perfect, and I've got the law library right behind … there."

"I can keep walking?" I ask dryly.

"Get over here, kiddo," my dad says.

The wide grin on his face is both a surprise and expected. I'm so used to his stoicism. My father doesn't share his feelings freely. He keeps most of his emotions locked away. A trait I've been told we share and a comparison I don't find flattering.

But today is his dream come true. For my dad, there's no greater achievement than me graduating from his alma mater and pursuing a career in law. That's success to him, confirmation I was raised right. If Rose were still alive, maybe he wouldn't have cared as much about what I did with my life. But she's not; she's gone. And ghosts can't struggle with choices or make mistakes or earn degrees. Rose was the daughter who went into the office with my dad during the summer, while I was the one who went to sleepaway camp in Maine.

My dad hugs me more tightly than I'm expecting. Hard enough I feel a little guilty for my thoughts. Maybe I'm not the spare daughter in his mind. Maybe it matters to him that *I* went to law school, not just that he guided one of his children to what he considers to be the best career path.

"Congratulations, Elodie," he tells me, dropping his arms and taking a step back. "We're so very proud of you."

"Walking across the stage wasn't all that difficult."

Another rare smile appears as he reaches out to straighten my crimson stole. "The work it took to get here didn't go unnoticed. And to celebrate …" He pulls a small box out from inside of his suit jacket. The wooden surface glows a soft honey color in the sunshine as he holds it out to me. "Don't smoke them all today. Or any of them ever. But that's what my father gave me when I graduated law school, so I thought …"

I flip open the lid, inhaling the scent of leather, wood, and tobacco. Rub my finger against the paper wrapping, remembering the one and only time I've smoked. Resenting how *he's* the place my brain always goes first.

My grandfather was a tough, harsh man who made it easy to see where my father learned his stolid demeanor. I'm not surprised to learn his graduation gift to my father wasn't a sentimental one.

"Thanks, Dad."

"And a more *appropriate* gift." Even without the heavy emphasis my mom places on *appropriate*, I'd know she disapproves of the cigars. She considers *coffee* an illicit substance after all.

I take the paper envelope she's holding out, knowing it contains a check without looking inside. "You guys paid for law school and my place. You don't need to—"

"We wanted to," my mom interrupts. "You're our only child. Let us spoil you."

The second reminder of Rose. The first being the bouquet of pink blossoms my mom is holding. Roses are the only type of flowers she'll buy. A sweet, sad tribute. But just like the breakfast I ate for years, I think it means she's forgotten peonies are my favorite. Or that Lily is my middle name.

We rarely discuss Rose directly, but she hovers as a phantom presence anyway.

I'm always surrounded by ghosts.

"Thank you," I say.

"Congratulations, sweetheart." My mom steps forward to kiss my cheek, pressing the bunch of blooms into my hand. An overlooked thorn snags my sleeve. "You earned it."

Earned a degree, she means. Earned their pride. Earned this money.

Because I wasn't brave enough to find out what I'd end up with if I didn't follow the expected path. I'm somehow resentful and relieved

I'll never know.

"Now, let's get a few more photos, and then you should really take that robe off, dear. Your face is awfully red."

I pose for photos—with my parents, with fellow graduates, by myself—until my facial muscles are quivering from the strain of holding smiles. My mom must have hundreds from today. She made me and Prescott stand for dozens in front of the law building before the ceremony.

Atlantic Oyster Bar was my request for lunch. The food is overpriced and the atmosphere overly formal, but the view overlooking the harbor that was once teeming with tea can't be beaten. Seaport has always felt like the least restrictive section of the city to me. All the towering buildings and crowded streets are invisible from this vantage point.

The restaurant's decor is classy and elegant, decorated in shades of white, pale blue, and navy with a clear nautical inspiration. We're led to an outdoor table, the breeze reviving my smothered skin as I inhale deeply.

"Warmer today than I was expecting," my mother comments, reluctantly shrugging her dress's matching jacket off.

"Feels like summer," my father agrees, busy perusing the menu.

My mom slips her sunglasses on. "Is Prescott on his way?"

My boyfriend also graduated today. He was visiting with some friends after the ceremony, then is supposed to be meeting us for lunch.

I pull my phone out and scan the recent messages.

Prescott: Leaving now.

Prescott: Twenty minutes.

The second message was sent fifteen minutes ago.

"He'll be here in five minutes," I say, then continue reading through the messages in my group chat with my best friends.

JULIET: CONGRATULATIONS!!!

JULIET: Our very own Elle Woods. I'm so proud.

KEIRA: Congrats, babe!!!

KEIRA: So sorry we couldn't make it to the ceremony. We're shitty friends.

JULIET: Speak for yourself.

KEIRA: I *was*.

JULIET: Oh.

JULIET: Forgot you're a *we* now.

KEIRA: I'm only marrying the guy.

KEIRA: We're celebrating next weekend, Elle!!!

KEIRA: No wedding or work talk.

KEIRA: You're coming, right? You didn't reply to the email.

JULIET: Of course she's coming. Right, Elle?

KEIRA: Elle?

JULIET: She's probably busy with Mr. Tall, Dark, and Serious.

JULIET: Bring him to the Vineyard. I want to meet him.

KEIRA: You'd better be there next weekend.

KEIRA: Love you!

JULIET: Drink lots of champagne!

"Is that Prescott?" my mom asks.

I set my phone on the table and shake my head. "Just some texts from Juliet and Keira."

My mother nods. "Your father and I ate at The Franklin the other night. It was excellent. I had my doubts about that space, but Keira worked miracles."

"I think Tucker Franklin deserves the credit there."

"Ah, right. I'd forgotten about her boyfriend's little construction business."

Last I heard, Tucker's crew was up to fifteen guys. Impressive, especially for a town of Fernwood's size. My mom's problem isn't with the scale of his operation, but rather what part of town Tucker grew up in. My parents are snobs, plain and simple. They judge people based on how successful they are, and they measure said success from how much money they have.

"They're engaged, Mom."

"Oh, that's right. When is the wedding?"

I smile at the waitress filling the water glasses on the table. "September."

"You'll be in the bridal party?" my mom questions.

I sip some ice water and nod. "She asked me to be her maid of honor."

Keira, Juliet, and I made a pact in middle school. I would be Keira's maid of honor. Keira will be Juliet's maid—matron—of honor, and Juliet will be mine. Not that Juliet or I are close to getting married. Juliet has self-diagnosed herself as allergic to commitment. And I can't picture myself getting engaged anytime soon, much to my mother's dismay.

"How lovely." There's a wistful note to her voice that I'm sure has a lot to do with the lack of a diamond ring on my left hand. At my age, my mom was married and expecting me.

My phone begins buzzing on the table. My father clears his throat, glancing at the buzzing device pointedly.

"Sorry. I'll just …" My voice trails off as I catch a glimpse of the name on the screen. "Sorry," I repeat. "I have to take this."

I stand and walk away from the table before either of my parents can say anything. There's a cluster of more casual seating set away from most of the tables, wicker couches and armchairs meant for sipping cocktails, which I head for.

Nina has only ever called me once before, when she picked up an extra Saturday shift and had to move our monthly get-together. Aside from that, we communicate when I show up at the trailer.

My heart pounds, and my head spins, considering the reasons why she might be calling me. I don't think I mentioned the exact date I was graduating. Even if I had, I can't imagine Nina calling to congratulate me.

"Hello?" I answer, sinking down onto one of the striped cushions.

"Hi, Elle."

I have a hard time reading Nina in person. Over the phone, it's practically impossible to tell what she's thinking.

"This is a surprise," I say. "I wasn't expecting to talk to you until next week."

"I hope I'm not interrupting anything. I thought this might be the best time to reach you."

"It's a good time," I tell her. "I just got back from walking Scout."

That's what I wish I were doing right now at least. The next couple of hours will be an uncomfortable balance of my dad discussing the bar exam and starting work at the firm while my mom drops hints about how soon I should be thinking about marriage. At least Prescott has met my parents before and has some idea what to expect.

"I'm glad you got that dog," Nina tells me.

I smile. "Me too. I'll bring him with me next week."

Nina coughs. It rattles in her lungs, the sound ominous instead of ordinary. "That's why I'm calling."

"O … kay." Nerves are crawling across my skin, confirming that something else is going on.

"I should have told you when you were here last month. But I …" She sighs. "It's meant a lot, you coming by all these years. I hope you know that. I know I'm not always … well, I'm not sure I've ever said it."

I shove, "I wanted to," out through wooden lips, bracing for the blow that's about to come. Certain that something is about to change irrevocably.

"I'm sick, Elle. Lung cancer. The doctors think I have a year left, if I'm lucky."

Nina delivers that news in the same matter-of-fact way she always speaks. The same brisk manner I used to find abrasive and now appreciate.

My palm presses against my mouth to keep any sound from escaping as I stare down at my pale knees. The hot prickle of tears stabs at my eyes like tiny swords. I look up, blinking rapidly, to watch a sailboat's slow progress across the water. Disbelief spreads, numbing my senses. The sun's warmth and the smell of seafood fade away, my awareness narrowing to nothing except the terrible news.

"I'm so sorry, Nina," I choke out. "Have you started treatment? Is there—"

"I lost most of my dignity chasing clueless boys in acid-wash jeans," she tells me. "I'd like to leave this world with what little I have left. Not the way I entered it—bald and unable to sit up on my own."

Despite—or maybe because of—the serious topic, a laugh bursts out. "You don't know that—"

Again, she interrupts. "I do know. The doctors know."

There's a clink of china in the background, and I'm certain she brewed a cup of tea before making this call. That she's sitting at the square kitchen table and sipping from a floral-patterned cup. I can picture it so clearly in my mind, like I'm sitting across from her right now.

Pain lances through my chest when I realize Nina called to tell me memories are all I'll have of her soon. A year sounds long by some metrics, but it's also so, so short.

"Please—if there's anything I can do, anything *at all*, please let me know. I'll be by next weekend, and I can bring whatever you need."

"Next weekend won't work, Elle."

"Oh. Well, I can do the weekend after, if that's better."

"I think it might be best if you don't come by here anymore." Nina's voice is gentle, but it does little to soften the hit. Her tone is purposeful, like she's weighing each word before she speaks it. Like there's some subtext I'm missing and need to search for.

"Facing this alone isn't going to make it any easier," I tell her gently. "I'm sure it's scary and overwhelming, but anything I can do to help … *please* let me help."

A long pause follows.

"I won't be alone," Nina finally says.

"But … Cormac isn't finished with the semester for a couple more weeks."

Nina's younger son is in his second year of college at Boston University. Another devastating wave of sadness hits as I look past my own sorrow and remember Nina is leaving a lot more than our monthly visits behind. But I don't let my thoughts drift any further than Cormac.

"I don't mean Cormac," she tells me.

"Oh. *Oh*," I realize. "I didn't know you were … seeing someone."

Nina barks a laugh. "Dating? I'm dying, dear."

She says nothing else. I glance toward the table where my parents are seated. Prescott has joined them, my spot the only one sitting empty. But I wait, everything in me insisting this conversation with Nina is more important than lunch.

"I'm … confused," I admit.

Her exhale is heavy. "Elle … I'm rarely wrong about people. I was wrong about you. You're stubborn and kind and extraordinary. Everything you've done, for me, for Cormac, it will never be forgotten. I-I don't want to make you uncomfortable."

I've never heard Nina sound so unsure. She's second-guessing each word she says, it sounds like.

"I'm still confused."

"Ryder made his own choices. I don't blame you for anything that happened. If it's ever seemed otherwise, I'm sorry."

I swallow hard. My throat is starting to close up, making talking difficult. "Why … what are you talking about?"

She's never brought Ryder up, not since that first day I showed up under false pretenses. And the one mention does nothing to prepare me for Nina's next words.

"Ryder is getting released next week, Elle."

4

THEN

Ryder

Fernwood High School hasn't changed much in two years. Hardly surprising. This whole town is like a time capsule. Everyone who lives here is content with their shiny, happy lives. They embrace—enjoy—the status quo.

It's annoying. But again, not surprising.

I toss the football I'm holding in the air and catch it, half listening to the two guys standing closest discuss how they're getting a keg to a party on Friday night. I'm tempted to tell them it's as simple as a good fake ID and some confidence, but I don't talk to the rich jerks who make up about half of Fernwood High's population unless it's absolutely necessary or I'm in the mood to stir up some shit.

Five girls are whispering to each other directly across from me. One of them, a blonde, looks me over pretty obviously and then flips her ponytail over one shoulder. I wink at her, then toss the ball again. The girls start tittering louder, like birds, and Mr. Medina, the gym teacher, gives up on his overview of the class rules. Or maybe he just finished running through them. I wasn't really listening.

The loose circle of students disbands.

"Don't forget a change of clothes tomorrow!" Mr. Medina calls after the disappearing backs.

I doubt I'll bother. None of the guys at the garage will care if I show up sweaty, and my standard summer uniform is athletic shorts and a T-shirt. The temperature has yet to dip below seventy since I've been back in Massachusetts, so I doubt that'll change anytime soon.

I tuck the football into the mesh bag by the long metal bench, then turn toward the sports building that houses the gymnasium and locker rooms.

"Hold up a minute, Ryder."

I blow out a long breath as I pause halfway across the running track that surrounds the football field. "I've got places to be, Mr. Medina."

"This won't take long," he says, walking toward me with a clipboard tucked under one arm.

In addition to teaching gym, Medina also coaches the football team. I only need one guess on what he wants to talk to me about.

"The answer is no," I tell him.

"Why?"

He doesn't take offense to my straightforward approach, which I appreciate. It almost makes me wish I could give him a different answer. Medina's one of the few teachers I have positive memories of from freshman year. He treats students based on their behavior, not their home address.

"I have a job after school," I answer. "I don't have a rich daddy bankrolling me."

Medina might act oblivious to the social hierarchy here, but there's no way he doesn't know I live in the trailer park.

"What about practicing before school?" he asks.

"I'd rather sleep."

Mr. Medina half smiles. "I'm offering you the starting spot, James."

Both my eyebrows rise, betraying my surprise. "Thought that was Hathaway's gig."

"We'd hold tryouts again, of course."

But I'd win. That's what he's saying. And it's nice to know.

Archer Hathaway is the exact sort of rich prick I can't stand, and based on his behavior in Calculus earlier, he's only gotten richer and prickier in the two years I was gone. I'd love to steal his roster spot and rub it in his face, but I wasn't lying about my job. I can't afford to get fired—literally—which is exactly how me not showing up at the garage would go. Tucker went out on a limb to get me the gig, and I can't do that to him either.

"I can't. Really."

Mr. Medina nods slowly. "I understand your situation is different from most students'. But I would really like to help you, Ryder. Colleges love to see extracurriculars like sports on applications—"

"I'm not going to college."

He sighs. "Keeping your options open is—"

My phone vibrates in my pocket. Probably Tuck, wondering where I am.

"I have to head out," I cut Medina off—again. "See you tomorrow."

He doesn't try to stop me this time, just nods.

I stop in the locker room to grab my backpack and then head straight toward the parking lot, which is still full. I appear to be the only one eager to get out of here. Countless groups of students are clustered around expensive cars, socializing. The largest cluster is right by the obnoxiously oversized entrance to the high school. Twin columns frame the double doors that keep opening as more students spill outside.

Elle Clarke stands in the center of the crowd, laughing at something the girl next to her said as she slips on a pair of sunglasses. I recognize the blonde beside her vaguely. Her name is Julia? Maybe? She and Elle have been friends for a while.

"So, you survived, huh?"

I glance over at Reese Porter, who's approaching me. She's a fellow Two, which is what the rich snobs we attend school with call us. Better than *trailer-park trash*, I guess.

"Yeah," I reply. "This town is all bark and no bite."

Aside from some whispers and stares, most people ignored my return.

Reese snorts. "Not much has changed." She follows my gaze to the large cluster of our peers by the main entrance. "Same pecking order. Same hero worship, starting with Queen Elle."

I say nothing. I've never told anyone what happened between me and Elle, knowing exactly what my friends thought—think—of her. But she's different than most people see. Or she used to be at least. People change. I have.

"Oh goody. Here comes the jock parade." Reese scoffs. Saying she harbors some resentment toward the wealthy section of town would be a massive understatement.

I watch several guys head toward the crowd congregated around Elle. Archer Hathaway is in front. He pushes his way right to Elle, then kisses her in full view of the entire parking lot.

My abs clench as the invisible hit registers. It feels like I was just kicked in the stomach.

"She's dating Hathaway?" I don't mean to ask the question; it just comes out.

"Oh, yeah." Reese rolls her eyes. "He asked her to prom in front of the whole school. They were crowned king and queen. It was a vomit-inducing spectacle. Be glad you missed it."

I am. And I'm not surprised Elle is dating someone or that he's rich. I didn't think it'd be Hathaway though. Freshman year, Elle agreed with me that Hathaway was a self-centered asshole.

"*You* went to *prom*?"

Reese's face appears pinker than it did a minute ago. "It was lame. Whatever."

I smirk. "Are there pictures?"

Reese is a tomboy through and through. I've never seen her wear a skirt, let alone a dress. Right now, she's wearing jean cutoffs and a faded David Bowie T-shirt.

"*Bye*, Ryder."

I chuckle as she walks off, resuming my surveillance of the parking lot. Finally, I spot Tucker's green truck parked on the far side of the lot. Before heading in that direction, I steal one last look at the commotion near the main entrance of the high school.

Elle is looking this way. Not just this way. She's looking at *me*.

There's an unexpected jolt, an electric paddle to the chest, as our eyes connect. The sunglasses Elle's wearing do nothing to diminish the impact of her stare. She's surrounded by her adoring subjects, standing next to her king, but her attention is all mine.

I break the connection first, turning and walking toward Tucker's truck. Surprised he hasn't left my ass here by now. I haven't been late once in the two weeks I've been working at the garage. Hopefully, that streak isn't about to end.

"Ryder."

I freeze, not because someone's saying my name. Because *she's* saying my name.

I spin around to watch Elle approach me with confident strides, her expression purposefully smooth. The blue dress she's wearing flutters around her thighs in the slight breeze created by the confident movement.

Fuck, she looks hot. My fourteen-year-old self would have told you Elodie Clarke was the most beautiful girl in the whole world, and that's an assessment I'm sticking by at seventeen.

Her dark hair is shorter, falling just past her shoulders in curls I know are manufactured. I prefer her hair wavy. Messy from my hands.

The careful curls make her look older. Maturer. More untouchable.

We never followed each other on social media, and I didn't look her up in the time I was gone because that would have made everything a whole lot harder. Now, seeing her in person, I sorta wish I had. I've been staring at her for too long, same as I did outside of the History classroom earlier.

"From Mr. Anderson." Elle takes one final step, leaving a couple of feet of space between us, holding a green folder out to me.

Rather than say *thanks*, I ask, "Why do you have it?"

I'm an asshole like that.

"He asked me to give it to you." She pushes her sunglasses up to the top of her head, pulling the hair away from her face and pinning me in place with a hard stare.

"Why you?"

Elle holds my gaze. "You know why."

Her taste in guys might have changed, but she's still every teacher's favorite student.

I flip the folder open to find it filled with study-guide materials and a flyer advertising the tutoring center's services. My jaw works. Yeah, same school. Everyone expects the best from her. The worst from me.

"I don't need extra help." There's an edge to my tone that has everything to do with my exasperation with this school after one day and nothing to do with her.

I'm embarrassed, though, that she's the one witnessing this. It's the first fucking day. Anderson couldn't even give me a chance to keep up?

I'm not expecting her to take the folder from me, so it slips through my fingers easily. Elle rifles through the papers. A wrinkle appears on her forehead as she scans the sheets. Then, she shuts the folder and rips it clean in two. Tosses the torn pieces back to me.

"You're welcome," she says.

I don't mean to smile. But I know I am. I can feel the stretch in my cheeks.

The words are right there, waiting on the tip of my tongue. *I missed you.* I *still* miss her, even while she's standing in front of me, knowing that I fucked up everything between us.

I never expected to have this opportunity. I thought any conversation we had would consist of her laughing in my face or looking right through me. Thought I'd be a blip so far in the past that she'd barely remember me.

Elle's looking at me like she remembers everything.

"I'm sorry." The apology is impulsive, but I mean the words. Mean them as much as everything else I ever told her. I hope she can hear it.

Elle says nothing in response. She's barely blinking. No reaction. I might as well have not spoken at all.

I try again. "Elle, I …"

She moves, her spin graceful and her posture perfect as she walks away from me. Back toward her large group of admirers, most of whom are staring this way. No doubt wondering why she was talking to me.

That went well.

Tucker is sitting in the driver's seat when I reach his truck, tapping his fingers against the door.

"Sorry for the delay," I say, climbing in the passenger side.

"Forget your way around?" Tuck asks. His gaze immediately focuses on the ripped papers I'm holding, one eyebrow rising.

"Nah. Medina stopped me after gym. He wants to draft me for the team."

"You going to play?"

"Of course not."

Although taking the starting quarterback spot from Hathaway is a lot more tempting after discovering he's dating Elle. I wouldn't hate watching her cheer for me either.

"Why not?" Tuck asks.

I lift an eyebrow. "You serious? The job you got me, for one."

"Uncle Hank is cool. He'd let you shift around hours. As long as the cars get fixed, doesn't matter what time it is."

"I don't *want* to play football," I tell him.

A partial lie. A partial truth. I resent most of the ridiculous pageantry of high school, but I do enjoy playing.

"You're good."

"I know I am. Doesn't mean I want to play with these dicks. One month, I'll be eighteen; I won't even have to show up to school at all."

Tucker groans as he turns the key in the ignition. The truck rumbles to life a few seconds later. "Don't be stupid, James. Get a diploma at least."

I tap the dashboard. "It's ten to three, man. Let's go."

"Pay up first."

My jaw works a couple of times as I glance over at him. "I don't know what you're talking about."

"Rearview mirror's got a great view of the parking lot."

I exhale.

"She looks good, right?"

I never told Tuck what happened with Elle, but he made a lot of assumptions. Most of which were correct.

I don't respond. I just tug a twenty out of my pocket and toss it toward my best friend. "Gas money. Not for the dumb bet I didn't agree to."

There's no way I'm telling Tuck not only did Elle talk to me, but that was technically our second conversation today.

The pack of cigarettes has been in my back pocket all day, so they're a bit crushed. They still light. Unlike my school in Jacksonville, Fernwood High follows the honor system. No random locker searches or metal detectors or drug dogs roaming campus. I pull my phone out too.

It wasn't Tuck who texted me ten minutes ago. It was my dad.

SPERM DONOR: *Talk soon, kiddo. Wish things had worked out differently.*

"I thought you quit?" Tuck asks.

I drop my phone in my lap. "Shut up and drive."

Tuck flips me off before shifting into drive. "I missed you, man."

I blow a stream of smoke out the window. "Yeah. Same here, Franklin."

I did miss Tuck. I missed my brother, Cormac, and my mom and Reese and the other friends I left behind here. I even missed having seasons. Florida was basically an endless stretch of humidity.

But the honest answer to what—who—I missed most?

The girl I made certain hates my guts.

5
NOW

Elle

Early morning sunshine dazzles off the smooth surface of the Charles as I sprint along the pavement path lining the riverbank. I'm soaked with sweat, breathing heavily, and setting a pace even Scout is struggling to keep up with. In his defense, he's stuck wearing a fluffy fur coat while I'm dressed in shorts and a tank top. The temperature feels like we skipped over the end of spring and jumped straight to summer.

I pause at a bench to gulp down half of my water bottle, watching a pair of pigeons fight over a crust of bread that fell out of the overflowing trash can.

Scout laps greedily from the collapsible rubber bowl I keep clipped to my running bag, the annoying bang against my hip for the past couple of miles worthwhile as I watch his pink tongue inhale liquid as quickly as possible. This is farther than we usually run, and today is rapidly turning into the warmest day in about eight months.

"That's a great invention."

I glance at the man approaching from the opposite direction. A golden retriever is tugging him straight toward me and Scout.

He's looking at the water bowl Scout is drinking from.

"It is," I reply. "A real lifesaver in the summer."

"I always try to pour some out of the bottle, but most of it just hydrates the pavement." The guy grins. He's cute. Tall with dark hair and lots of laugh lines creasing the corners of his eyes. "Do you remember where you got it?"

I shake my head. "No, sorry. My boyfriend bought it."

His smile dims, barely but noticeably, in response to the lie.

Prescott is not a pet person. He's allergic to cats, and he's never shown much interest in dogs either. He was more than a little taken aback when I adopted Scout, but he's been a good sport about the two times Scout chewed on his shoes. That tolerance hasn't extended to buying Scout anything, but it seemed like the easiest way to respond to this guy's interest shifting from the bowl to me.

"Well, I'll keep an eye out the next time I'm in a pet store," the guy says. "Enjoy the rest of your run."

"You too," I reply before he jogs off.

I toss the small amount of water Scout left in the bowl toward the grass and collapse it, then clip it back to my bag. A few stray droplets of water trickle down my thigh as we start running again.

Twenty minutes later, we reach the right street. A familiar car is parked halfway down.

Prescott stands when he sees me, smiling from his spot on the steps that lead up to the brownstone. "Morning."

I manage a, "Hey," between heavy breaths.

I'm going to be sore tomorrow. My legs feel stiff and heavy, the muscles tingling with lactic acid. The discomfort would be worthwhile if I felt any better. But all the thoughts I was trying to escape are rapidly catching up to me.

Prescott raises the bakery bag and tray of coffees he's holding. "Thought I'd surprise you *before* your run. You left early."

I nod as I fish my keys out. "Wanted to beat the heat."

Not even nine a.m., and I'm losing track of all the lies I've told today. Lying to my boyfriend feels worse than fibbing to a random runner.

"You're way too hot to do that," he tells me.

"*Lame.*" I'm smiling though when he presses me against the tall mirror that takes up one wall of the entryway and kisses me. "I'm all sweaty."

"Don't care," he murmurs.

I glance at the open door. "My neighbors might."

"If they're up this early, they deserve a show."

I laugh as I kick off my sneakers and peel off my sweaty socks, then unclip Scout's collar. "Surprised *you're* up this early."

"I wanted to see you," he tells me, following me into the kitchen. "Was kinda hoping you'd still be in bed."

"I have a breakfast meeting."

Twin lines form between Prescott's eyes as he watches me hobble toward one of the stools along the island. "At Gray & Ellington?"

"No." I rub my calf. "With a friend of my dad's. He's a partner at Pearson. We're just grabbing coffee so he can congratulate me on graduating and offer some advice on bar prep." I open the bag he brought and take a big bite of the muffin.

Prescott still looks concerned. "You okay?"

"Yeah." I hide the grimace that wants to appear as I shift on the stool. Why did I buy these? They're so uncomfortable. "Just pushed the pace a bit. Was feeling a little stressed."

"We still have two months to study," he tells me.

I nod before taking another bite, not bothering to correct his assumption about the bar exam being the source of my stress.

I've dated four guys since high school, and I've never so much as mentioned Ryder to a single one of them. He was always so removed from my life. But now … there's a chance Prescott could meet him. I'm planning to bring him as my date to Keira's wedding this fall, and she's marrying Ryder's best friend. Ryder will most likely show up for Tucker.

Another bite of muffin gets shoved into my mouth. I really need to stop thinking, and six miles didn't do it. I'm not sure what else to try. Downing a couple of tequila shots during breakfast won't reassure Prescott I'm fine, plus I have to drive in about twenty minutes.

"Well, I'll let you get ready for your breakfast." Prescott snags the second muffin out of the bag, then reaches for his coffee. "Got a big golf date to get ready for."

I swallow, then cough. "You do *not* need to do that."

My dad invited Prescott golfing at the country club during my graduation lunch. I thought Prescott was just being polite, accepting. Not that the outing would take place in less than a week.

I have this irrational fear my parents will ruin us. Their dreams for my life have never aligned with my own desires. Stupid as it sounds, their obvious approval of Prescott feels like a ticking clock to me. A bad omen. That's nothing I can mention to Prescott or my parents, and it's a problem I've pushed to the back of my mind. Easily, since every spare second has been spent thinking about Ryder James instead.

"I want to go," Prescott says. "I'll get to see where you grew up."

"Not much to see." My smile feels tight and forced, but I don't think he notices.

I lived in Fernwood for eighteen years. And eleven months defined my entire perception of my hometown. Everything I loved about that place, everything that haunts me there—all tied to Ryder.

"Yeah. A golf course is a golf course, I guess. Speaking of parents, I'm thinking of visiting mine in early July. I know it's close to the bar exam, but the firm is throwing my dad a retirement party. Anyway, think about it. They're dying to meet you."

I nod. "I will."

I was supposed to meet Prescott's parents at our graduation, but they had to miss the ceremony because of some health issues Prescott's grandfather was having.

He gives me a quick kiss. "I'll call you later!"

" 'Kay." I listen to the front door open and slam, methodically chewing my muffin and trying to muster some excitement about the rest of today.

Breakfast with Ian Kennedy, take my car for an oil change, get groceries. And of course, study for the bar exam. That's basically a given until I take the test mid-July. A few weeks later, I'll start working at Gray & Ellington LLP, and … that'll be my life.

I should feel grateful, I know. For having parents who support me financially and make the absence of a paycheck hardly noticeable. For having a position waiting at one of Boston's top law firms. But I feel like an actor playing a part. Like I'm comprehending emotions, but not experiencing them.

My laptop is open on the kitchen counter. I close it without waking the screen, glad Prescott didn't knock it accidentally. He would have had questions about why I'm researching lung cancer. Pretty pointlessly, considering I have no medical background or any knowledge specific to Nina's case.

I should have asked her more questions about her health when she called. I barely stumbled through a coherent goodbye after she told me about Ryder's early release. Reaching out for more details— ignoring her wishes to stay away—seems inconsiderate when she has so much going on.

And, selfishly, I'm terrified to. Scared of showing up at Nina's trailer and him being there. Frightened of calling and him answering.

I've had time to prepare to see him again. Lots of time.

Just not enough.

Because there's also a tiny part of me that wants to drive to Fernwood and demand answers. That wants to scream and yell and sob and rage. That wants a glimpse of the only guy I've ever loved.

But he's gone, even if Ryder is back.

It's a struggle to stand when I finish my muffin and coffee. Lying down and napping sound wonderful. Instead, I limp upstairs to shower and change into a navy shift dress. I have to search through my bedside table's top drawer for some ibuprofen, my hand stilling when I accidentally brush the paper flower. I should have ripped or burned it a long time ago. But I've never been able to.

I hastily shut the drawer and then head downstairs after swallowing a white pill.

Driving downtown takes twenty minutes, but I'm running early as I walk into the coffee shop where I'm supposed to meet Ian. The line is long but moves quickly. Three customers from the register, I pick up a newspaper to skim.

After paying for my latte and the paper, I head for an open table. I sip and scan, not looking for anything in particular.

And then I see his name.

Ryder's case garnered a decent amount of news coverage seven years ago. Crime is common in the city. Not so much in Fernwood, Massachusetts. The local police force is made up of two middle-aged officers who spend most of their time settling arguments over lawn decorations or parking ordinances. His arrest fanned a lot of flames of the ongoing outrage regarding the trailer park in town, which made for some flashy headlines.

I skim the article that restates a story I have memorized. I was grateful for the amount of media attention back then. Desperate for details no one would tell me.

Now, it's all reminders I don't want.

"I remember that case."

I startle, biting my tongue instead of the lower lip I was gnawing on. I quickly fold up the paper and stand. "Good morning, Mr. Kennedy."

"Ian, Elle," he corrects warmly as we shake hands.

Ian Kennedy is a longtime friend of my father's. They attended Harvard Law together and have kept in touch since. He's been a mentor to me since college, offering advice on studying for the LSATs, applying to law school, interviews, internships, and most recently, jobs. I've known Ian and his family my entire life. But his serious attitude, so similar to my father's, has always made me act more formal around him.

I match his smile. "Right. Sorry. Morning, Ian."

He takes the seat across from me and reaches for the newspaper I abandoned on the table. "I haven't read today's paper yet. Ryder James was the kid's name, right?"

Hearing his name burns, like salt poured in an open wound.

"Right." I tuck a wayward strand of hair behind one ear, hoping my tongue will stop throbbing soon. Praying that will be the end of the topic.

"I had some friends in the DA's office back then," Ian tells me. "They threw the book at that kid, and he landed Boyd as a public defender." He snorts. "Would have been better off representing himself."

I reach for my water and take a long sip, wishing I could cover my ears. Looking into Ryder's case as a licensed attorney was a thought in the back of my head ever since I started law school. Before then, honestly. I knew he couldn't afford to pay for representation. That he took a crappy deal.

My heartbroken seventeen-year-old self was in no position to do anything about it. Armed with a law degree, I could have. *If* he'd let me represent him, which I doubt he would have. The rejection might have been worth it, to see the look on his face.

"Surprised it's getting this much attention," I say.

One article in a major newspaper isn't wall-to-wall news coverage. But it's more than most cases get. And it would have been a hell of a way to find out Ryder is getting released early if Nina hadn't called me last week.

"Drug-related deaths have increased by twenty-eight percent in the past five years," Ian says. "It's a hot topic in the mayor's reelection campaign. Half the city wants to crucify him for not doing more; the rest want to criticize him for ruining the lives of kids who get in over their heads."

I nod.

Ian takes a sip of coffee. "He lived in Fernwood. Your paths ever cross?"

"The town is pretty segregated," I hedge.

"Mmhmm," Ian replies. He taps the paper with one finger. "Cases like this don't help."

"He's a fucking Two, Elle. What the hell were you thinking?"

I push the memories from the past away, where they belong. "No, they don't."

Ian relaxes back in his chair. "So, how is studying for the bar going?"

"I've barely started," I admit.

"That's all right. You just graduated. You've got plenty of time."

Ian and I talk for another hour, sipping coffee and discussing various legal topics.

And the entire time, I'm fighting not to look at the paper.

6
THEN

Elle

"**W**hat are the chances we'll win tonight?" Juliet asks as she plops down on the grass beside me to stretch her hamstrings.

The ground is damp and cool, the sun sinking behind the barrier of the full bleachers. It's starting to feel like fall.

I exhale, then lean over my left leg. "Does it make me a bad captain and a terrible girlfriend if I tell you we have no chance?"

"Probably."

I roll my eyes before glancing at the field where the two teams are warming up. Fernwood High's green jerseys stand at one end. Thompson High's blue ones at the other. Thompson finished last season, ranked third in the state. We finished … a lot lower than that.

"I mean, we *could* win. Miracles happen."

Juliet laughs. "You're a bad captain and a terrible girlfriend."

"I know."

Juliet hears the shift in my tone from sarcastic to serious. She raises one eyebrow as she lifts her arms over her head and rolls her neck from side to side. "Something happen with Archer?"

Ryder James came back.

I chew on the inside of my cheek as I pull one foot up against my thigh and lean forward. Ryder's not the only reason I've felt restless this week. But he's a ... reminder. Proof I once did what I *wanted*, not what was expected or easy.

"I just ... it kinda hit me that this is senior year. And I'm sick of so much staying the same. Of my life being so ... *predictable*."

"Is this about cheer?" she asks. "Or about Archer?"

"Both," I reply.

"The season is only a couple of months. You've gotten through three of them. Only one to go. And Archer ... you guys have only been dating since May. That's, like, four months, Elle. Not that long."

I nod. It feels like a lot longer than four months—and not in a good way.

Juliet is studying me closely, so I force a smile before switching legs. I lean farther forward this time, so my ponytail falls to cover most of my face.

I lie all the time, but rarely to Juliet or Keira.

Everything I told Juliet is technically true.

I've never liked cheerleading that much. Rose cheered, so everyone always assumed I would too. My older sister has been gone for five years, and sometimes, it feels like I'll never escape her shadow.

Ghosts set an impossible, memorialized standard, one I'm sick of striving toward. Rose was fifteen when she died. Each year I outlive her, it feels like the pressure increases. Like I'm responsible for living her life too. For making the choices she would have.

Archer isn't a bad guy. He's self-centered, but he can be sensitive too. I've known him my entire life. I assumed he'd grow up and my feelings would grow with him.

And then Ryder James had to return and blow that theory to smithereens. To prove what I'd suspected all along—I haven't developed feelings for any guy in the past two years because I'm in love with Ryder. Still.

It wasn't teenage hormones. It wasn't a childish crush. It wasn't the thrill of sneaking around. We were the real damn thing.

"Sorry I'm late." Keira drops her cheer bag down, then plops onto the grass beside me.

"No worries," I say.

Keira laughs once. "*No worries*? Are you feeling okay, girl?"

"She's having an identity crisis," Juliet supplies.

"Ooh. About what?" Keira asks, pulling her hair out of its bun and starting to braid it.

"Archer and cheerleading," Juliet replies.

"Oh. That's easy." Keira shrugs a shoulder carelessly. "Dump the guy and quit the team. I would *love* to have my afternoons and Friday nights back. No offense, Captain."

I roll my eyes. "I'm not quitting the team. The season just started, and I *am* the captain. I can't screw the squad over like that."

Keira sighs, then ties her braid off and starts stretching. "Yeah, I thought you'd say that."

"What about Archer?" Juliet asks.

"I'm going to end it." It feels good to say the words, like a powerful form of relief. A weight lifted. Salve on a stinging wound. A decision I've been dreading made.

Keira's head whips up, her eyes wide.

Juliet looks just as surprised. "Really?"

"Yeah. Why do you look so shocked?"

"I just … honestly? I kinda thought you two would end up married someday. Maybe break up during college, and then he'd show up at your graduation with a five-carat ring and beg for a second chance."

I snort. "You've obviously been spending way too much time at my house, around my mother."

"Hey, if you want to break up with him, break up with him. I'm just saying, he's hot and rich, and he obviously adores you. Don't end it on a random whim."

I stare at Juliet, totally taken aback. Archer *obviously adores* me? "I think you're confusing *adoration* with *he wants to sleep with me.*"

Juliet shrugs. "Maybe. But he cares. He's the one who planned your whole birthday party. Keira and I barely did anything."

I glance at Keira, who nods.

"It's true."

"He just wanted an excuse to keep partying after the Fourth," I say.

My birthday is July 5, so it usually gets lost in the inevitable, hungover letdown following the national holiday.

A whistle on the field signals the end of warm-ups. I climb to my feet, brushing a few errant blades of grass off my bare thighs before walking over to the bench.

Thompson wins the coin toss and takes the kickoff, starting the game. I move into formation on the sideline with the rest of the squad even though I doubt we'll have much to do until our halftime performance.

Sure enough, Thompson scores three touchdowns in the first half. Green jerseys trudge off the field with slumped shoulders.

"Rough start," Maddie Peterson mutters under her breath as we walk out onto the field.

"No kidding," I whisper back.

The Fernwood fans in the crowd perk up as we start our routine. That energy quickly fizzles as play resumes. Fernwood improves, only allowing one more touchdown during the remainder of the game. But the zero on the scoreboard for our side doesn't suggest much to celebrate.

As soon as the final whistle is blown, I gather up my gear, stuff it in my cheer bag, and then follow Keira toward the parking lot. She's driving me home to get ready for the party tonight—our stereotypical Friday nights.

"See you soon!" Maddie calls out, skipping by with Fleur Williamson.

Maddie is hosting tonight's party. She lives a couple of streets over from me, and her parents travel out of town a lot. Both make her place an ideal location.

I pull my phone out of my pocket as I cross the parking lot, gnawing on my bottom lip as I debate what to text Archer. *Good game* doesn't work. *Sorry you lost* isn't great either.

A few seconds later, my phone gets pushed back into my pocket. I'll decide on a message in the car.

The parking lot is crowded, everyone eager to leave. Not much socializing is happening. Mostly just headshakes or shoulder shrugs as people pass each other.

Fernwood is used to being the best at everything. It's the wealthiest town in the state. The football team's terrible record is an ongoing source of embarrassment. A reminder that talent is something you can't buy.

I glance around, looking for Keira's Jeep since I've lost sight of her. My steps slow as soon as I spot the sedan parked in one corner of the parking lot.

Ryder is sitting on the trunk, talking to a guy who has his back turned to me. Based on what I can see of the guy's profile, I don't recognize him. Ryder's left leg is blocking the insignia, but the car he's perched on appears to be brand-new. I've never seen Ryder hang out around Ones before, but maybe he's branched out and made some new friends in my zip code this week.

He's wearing shorts and a T-shirt, which is all I've seen him wear since his return to town. Plus a backward baseball cap. I watch as Ryder tugs it off and scrubs a palm across the top of his head before tugging the hat back down into place. He glances this way, like he's attuned to my attention, and our eyes connect.

My stomach flips when he holds my stare. Over and over and over again, like I'm bouncing on a trampoline.

Ryder's eyes drop to the striped skirt I'm wearing. I *feel* his gaze trail down my bare legs, all the way to the white sneakers that are part of the uniform. I'm too far away to tell for sure, but I think one corner of his mouth curves up. One of those devastating not-really-a-smiles that makes my blood swim with forbidden heat.

I'd pay the contents of my trust fund to know what he's thinking right now. The curiosity is so acute that it burns.

"Elle! Come on!"

My head jerks away from Ryder toward Keira. She's leaning out the window of her car, which is parked two rows up, waving.

I hurry in that direction, trying to escape the flush crawling steadily across my skin.

Juliet has already claimed shotgun, so I crawl in the cramped back with the bags, tossing my legs over the pile of canvas and tipping my head back to enjoy the breeze as Keira joins the line of cars waiting to exit the parking lot.

Finally, I text Archer.

ELLE: Headed home to change, then to Maddie's.

ELLE: See you there!

No response. I'm sure he's having a shitty Friday night. This was the first game of the season. Everyone was hoping it would go a lot better than it did. That things would finally turn around for the team.

Impulsively, I open a new message. The fact that I never deleted his number is not something I planned on letting Ryder know.

I'm mad at him. Hurt. Angry he strolled back into town with no explanation and a lackluster apology.

But beneath all that … I want to talk to him. I'm pissed off about that too. At myself and my lack of willpower.

ELLE: Enjoy the game?

He replies instantly, which doesn't really surprise me. Ryder was never the type of guy to play games, which made his disappearing act all the weirder.

RYDER: Nope.

RYDER: You?

I stare at his name on the screen. I was too proud—too heartbroken—to continue texting him after the messages started to go unanswered. But there's this warmth expanding in my chest, seeing the two new texts from him after all this time. I don't think normal crushes survive two years of not seeing or talking to someone, but that's the giddiness Ryder elicits in me. Then. Now.

ELLE: Not really.

I stare at the short exchange as Juliet and Keira sing along to a Taylor Swift song. His lack of a *who is this* makes me think Ryder never deleted my number, and I'm not sure what that means. It doesn't fit with taking off without warning and ceasing all contact. He's avoided me since our conversation in the parking lot. The only times I've seen him since were in our one shared class.

I shut my phone off and toss it on the piled bags, relaxing against the seat until Keira stops in front of my house.

"See you guys there," I say, gathering up all my cheer stuff and grabbing my phone.

"You're not going to do it tonight, are you?" Juliet asks I climb out of the car.

"Break up with Archer?"

She nods.

"No." My phone feels heavier all of a sudden, the texts I just sent—answered and unanswered—weighing it down.

I'm dreading the conversation, and it must be obvious on my face because Juliet and Keira both aim sympathetic smiles at me.

But I'm buoyed by the prospect of *fighting*, unfamiliar energy thrumming through me. I thought not challenging anything was easier, but it's draining in its own way. Debilitating.

Keira drives off, and I head inside. My parents are at a fundraiser in the city tonight, so I have the house to myself. I flip on lights as I walk through the silent, massive house, heading upstairs to my bedroom.

After debating for a few minutes, I slip on the blue dress I bought for the first day of school. I touch up my makeup, curl my hair, and stare at my reflection in the mirror.

I look poised and put together, no sign of the turmoil I'm experiencing obvious in my expression.

I blow out a long breath, then head downstairs.

7
NOW

Ryder

Nothing's changed.

I think that's the most depressing part out of the plenty to choose from.

Seven years.

Seven fucking years.

And nothing has changed.

I stare at the exterior of the trailer where my mom still lives, and it looks the same. I could have been gone for a week. Or a month.

I thought *something* would look different. So far, all I've noticed is the dirt road leading to the trailer park was paved. Based on the bumpiness driving here, it would have been better left alone.

"My shift ends at six," my mom tells me. "I'm low on groceries, but I'll bring something back for dinner. Cormac should be here in a few hours."

I nod, not coming up with anything to say.

My mom refuses to talk about her illness. Suggesting she cut back on her hours at the store will only devolve into another fight. And I can't offer to go get groceries because I have no car and no money. I'm helpless. Useless. Sitting around and waiting for my little brother to return from college is an unappealing prospect. And my only option.

I climb out of the sedan she's had forever. I tuned up the engine, back in high school when I was working at Hank's garage. My mom has never mentioned car trouble, so I guess it's held up all right. One thing that didn't go wrong.

My mom reverses as soon as I shut the car door, turning around and avoiding the worst of the potholes.

The asphalt I cross is more cracked than complete, evidence of harsh winters and minimal upkeep. I'm sure the town put up a fight about paving it in the first place. They like to pretend this place doesn't exist, not invest time or money in it.

"Ryder."

I pause, halfway across the small yard, to glance at the neighboring trailer. Mrs. Nelson is standing, holding an orange watering can, staring at me like I'm an apparition that fell straight out of the sky.

The polite smile appears automatically. She's a bit of a busybody, but Mrs. Nelson was always willing to help out with Cormac or to grab a package. Seeing her is surprisingly nostalgic. She still dresses like she's hoping to be seen from space.

"Hi, Mrs. Nelson."

None of the shock has dimmed from her expression. "I didn't know you were coming home."

My mom is the furthest thing from an oversharer. And your child getting released from prison, even if it's eight months early for good behavior, isn't exactly a proud parental moment to brag about.

"It was sudden," I say.

Not that seven years passed quickly.

"I know a lot of people will be happy to see you."

My brow furrows at the odd phrasing. My mom is relieved I'm out. She's also dying, preoccupied by more important matters than my criminal record. Cormac is consumed by his own life, finishing his sophomore year of college and excited about a summer internship that's set to start soon. The only other person I told about my release was Tucker. That's not a lot of people.

She's being polite, I guess. I know I look like shit, bedraggled and beaten down.

"Nice to see you," I say, then continue walking toward the front door.

When I reach the stairs, I realize why my hands feel so empty; I left the plastic bag of my belongings in the back seat of my mom's car.

Not that it really matters. My phone is useless—dead and disconnected from service—and my lack of a car makes my expired driver's license unnecessary as well. All I care about are the letters.

I've got *nothing*. It makes leaving so tempting.

Starting over sounds so much better anywhere else. Some town where I can walk around without being stared at or whispered about. Someplace without painful memories.

But I can't leave my mom. I'd never forgive myself, even if she would.

I fish the spare key out from under the ceramic turtle Cormac painted in art class the year we first moved here, then unlock the front door. A slight breeze stirs the air before I step inside, making the wind chimes someone hung up across the street tinkle. I glance over and glare at the cheerful sound before stepping inside and shutting the door behind me.

Staring at the interior of the trailer is incredibly nostalgic. The kitchen is neat and tidy, which wasn't always the case when I was younger and is a relief to see. My mom has been living alone for most of the past two years, ever since Cormac left for college. She easily could have backslid into bad habits.

I flip through a few magazines on the counter, then walk over to the fridge. My mom was right; it's mostly empty, but I'm not that hungry anyway.

I shut the fridge door. Take a seat at the kitchen table and drum my fingers against the worn wood. Pick up the landline and dial the phone number I still have memorized.

"Franklin Construction."

"How come you don't have a work phone?" I ask.

"Ryder?" Tuck laughs. "Holy shit, man. You're out?"

I rub at a scratch on the scuffed surface. "Yep, I'm out. Couple of hours ago."

"Wow. Congrats."

"Thanks." My tone is dry. I'm not sure if years of counting down days is an accomplishment to cheer completing.

"Not the right sentiment, huh?"

"Hell if I know."

Tucker chuckles. "Well, we're celebrating anyway. You doing dinner with your family?"

"Yeah," I reply.

" 'Kay. I'll pick you up at eight. We'll get beers at Malone's."

"Can we go to the house instead? I'd rather avoid the stares and finally see this place in person."

Three years ago, Tucker started his own construction business. He focused on smaller projects at first, then bought an old house in the One section of town with the intention of flipping it. Ever since the sale went through, he's been saying he wants me to manage the renovation. Business has grown to the point that he can't oversee everything on his own.

There aren't many places hiring in town, even fewer who would consider hiring *me*, so I agreed as soon as I found out about my mom's cancer. I could use a steady paycheck and something to keep my mind occupied.

"Yeah, sure," he responds. "Just … promise me you'll give it a chance."

I frown. "What are you talking about?"

"Well … it's been sitting empty for a while. It's in rough shape. Needs a lot of work."

"I've got a lot of time on my hands, Tuck."

He chortles. "Right. Yeah. I just … there's a reason the bank sold it dirt cheap. I don't want you to get discouraged."

I lean back in the chair. "I won't."

"Okay, I—oh, crap. Plumber is walking over with his bad-news face on. I'll see you later, okay?"

"Yep." I hang up, then go back to staring into space.

After a few minutes, I haul myself up and head down the hallway. The door to my bedroom is shut. When I open it, the air is musty.

Cormac should have taken this room instead of letting it sit empty. It's larger than his, and he's almost as tall as I am now.

I walk over to the window and stare outside. My favorite part of the view—the boxwood hedge—was torn out and replaced by an ugly plastic fence.

My high school textbooks sit in a dusty stack on the desk, next to a pile of papers. My mom didn't get rid of or move anything.

I crack the window, letting fresh air in. It's at least sixty degrees out, cloudy but not chilly.

Rifling through a few drawers confirms nothing got cleared out of my room, so I head back to the kitchen to grab a couple of trash bags.

They're not stored in the cabinet above the fridge anymore. I open the next cabinet over and stare at the row of colorful tin boxes lined up neatly. I pick up a yellow one and glance at the label. *Himalayan Ginger and Lemongrass*, it reads.

I've never seen my mom drink tea. Certainly not *expensive* tea, which this appears to be based on the pastel shades and fancy lettering of the packaging. These tin boxes are the nicest items in this entire kitchen. The nicest things in this whole trailer, probably.

I shake my head and keep searching, finding the trash bags two cabinets later.

The next hour is spent sorting through clothes that no longer fit and papers I no longer need. I shower, then sprawl out on the couch to wait for my mom and Cormac to get home. All I can find on television are reruns, which I half watch while absorbing how strange it feels to be entirely alone.

At five forty-five, I hear a car outside. I straighten on the couch, then stand right as Cormac walks in with a backpack over one shoulder and a duffel slung over the other. He barely fits through the doorway, carrying the two bags. As soon as the door shuts behind him, he drops them unceremoniously on the kitchen's linoleum floor.

"Hey!"

"Hey." My greeting is noticeably more subdued, not because I'm unhappy to see my little brother. Because it's setting in, slowly, how much time actually passed.

The trailer might not have changed, but Cormac sure has. I saw him about a month ago, during one of his regular visits. But it's different to see him here when the last memories I have of him in this kitchen are of a gangly thirteen-year-old.

"Man, is it good to see you."

I open my arms as he approaches, my throat thickening with emotion as he hugs me tight. Fuck, I missed so much. All of his high school years. Half of college. Teaching him how to drive. Telling him where to buy a fake. Buying him condoms. All that shit I had to figure out for myself, which I swore Cormac wouldn't have to go through alone.

"Good to see you too," I choke out as he claps me on the back. "You didn't have to come all this way though."

Classes are finished for the semester, but he still has a week left of finals.

"You kidding?" Cormac pulls back and grins. "Not every damn day your big brother escapes the slammer."

I roll my eyes. "Not much of an escape when they let you out."

"I know. But that sounds way less cool."

"Glad I could entertain you." I glance at the bags on the ground. "Not sure you brought enough back."

"Figured a few small loads were better than one big one. Speaking of, what's with the trash bags outside?"

"I went through my room. Don't think I'll be needing my Calc textbook anytime soon, and half the clothes don't fit anymore. You should have moved in there, by the way."

Cormac makes a face. "Why? It's your room."

"For now."

"You mean, until Mom dies or until you take off in a couple of weeks?"

I clear my throat and sit back down on the couch, hating his blasé tone. I know he had to grow up fast, but he shouldn't be so cavalier about any of this. "I'm not going anywhere."

Cormac leans against the kitchen counter. "I wouldn't blame you if you did. Gotta be weird, being back here."

"It is," I admit. "But I'll adjust. I'm going to work for Tuck. Help him flip that house he bought."

"The Warren place?"

"I guess so."

"Huh. Do you know how to renovate a house?"

I flip him off. "Tuck's got a whole crew. I'll just be pitching in with whatever needs to get done."

"That's what you want to be doing?" Cormac asks.

"I don't exactly have a ton of options," I reply quietly.

"You could apply to college. You got better grades than I did in high school, and I got into a decent school."

"I think that ship has sailed, Cor."

"Says who? There's a guy in my Econ class in his fifties. He hated his old job, so he's switching careers."

"Maybe one day," I say, mostly just to placate him. I wasn't planning to go to college, even before my life derailed. "I'll see how the construction gig goes."

"She doesn't want help, you know. Or treatment."

My jaw tightens. "She might change her mind."

"Maybe," Cormac says, but I get the feeling he's the one offering me false assurances now. "I'm going to stash this stuff in my room. Mom's shift ends at six?"

"Yeah," I reply. "She said she'd bring dinner."

"Great. I'm starving." Cormac disappears down the hallway with his bags, leaving me sitting on the couch.

My mom arrives home twenty minutes later with a few bags of groceries. I scrutinize her closely as I help unpack them, but she appears normal. Tired, with dark circles under her eyes, but no signs of sickness. As awful as it sounds, I wish there were signs. It's too easy to pretend like nothing is wrong without them.

"I stopped and picked you up some clothes," she tells me while dividing dinner between plates. "Figured you could use a few new things."

"Thanks, Mom. You didn't need to do that."

"Would have been a long walk to the store," she says in that blunt way she often speaks.

I snort before sitting down at the table. "Uh-huh."

Cormac returns from the bathroom a few minutes later, and we sit down to eat as a family for the first time in a long time.

No one mentions the reason I spent so many years missing meals here. Or cancer. We talk about Cormac's internship, and my mom tells a funny story about a customer, and I share what little I know about Tuck's renovation project. It's nice and normal and rare.

After we finish eating, my mom moves to stand.

"I'll grab it," Cormac says, rising quickly.

I sip my water as I watch him run through what's obviously a routine. Turning on the electric kettle, grabbing a flower-painted teacup out of a cabinet, then pulling out one of the fancy boxes I noticed earlier. He shakes some leaves into the teacup, soaks them with hot water, and then brings it over to our mom.

"Thanks," she tells Cormac, leaning forward to inhale the fragrant steam.

I still, suddenly realizing why the familiar jasmine scent is making me tense. "Since when do you drink tea?"

She shrugs, not meeting my eyes. "It's good for you."

"So, you just woke up one morning and decided to start drinking tea?"

Another shrug.

I'm not sure why I'm so focused on this. But something about the way my mom is avoiding my gaze makes me feel like I'm missing something. It's just ... strange. Something that's changed, amid a whole lot that hasn't.

"Where's the tea from, Mom?" I ask.

Those tin boxes in the cabinet looked too fancy to be from Wegman's, the supermarket chain where she works. They look like something that would come from a store that sells nothing *but* tea.

No response. No eye contact, which only increases my paranoia.

"She visits Mom," Cormac tells me.

"Cormac!" our mom snaps.

"He should know." Cormac shifts in his chair, the confident spread of his limbs another reminder of how much he grew up in my absence.

And I'm ... stunned. I don't need to clarify who *she* is. There's only one person Cormac could possibly be referring to.

It never ever occurred to me that Elle might keep in touch with my family.

"How often?" My tone is all overdone casualness, which they can probably hear. It's my best attempt to combat the furious pound of my racing heart.

It's been seven years. I'm over her, and I'm sure she's over me. So, what does Cormac mean that she *visits*?

Cormac's lips are pressed into a thin line. My mom's hand twitches toward the spot where her box of cigarettes used to sit, then falls into her lap.

More than once or twice then.

"*How often do you see her*, Mom?"

"Once a month." She pauses. Glances at Cormac. "For the past seven years."

Eighty-four visits. My brain does the math automatically, but is too surprised to manage anything else.

A light breeze could blow me out of this chair right now. I'm flabbergasted. I would have been shocked by once a *year*.

My mom is unfriendly. She doesn't try to get to know people or care what they think about her. She's brash and opinionated. I can't picture her and Elle sitting at this table a single time, let alone *eighty-four times*.

Shock ebbs into anger. My hands curl into fists under the table. But I can't act on it—can't expel—the hot rush of rage. Because my mom is sick and because I was gone and because I'm not supposed to care how Elle spends her time.

I hope it haunts you—how you ended things.

Elle must have already started these visits when she sent me that letter.

Thankfully, my voice is calm as I ask, "Why?"

I need more of an explanation. I need some part of it to make sense.

"She's a good person," my mom tells me. "You two were young, and she grew up differently. Don't hold how things ended against her."

I stare at my mom, a fresh wave of shock spreading through my system. I didn't think it was possible for me to feel any more surprised, and I was wrong.

She's *defending* Elle. She's defending Elle without knowing the whole story. Defending her, thinking that *Elle* was the one who abandoned *me*.

Meaning … Elle didn't tell her. Eighty-four fucking visits, and she didn't explain how we'd ended. It makes me wonder what they *did* talk about.

"You should have stayed away," I state.

My mom scowls at me, and Cormac appears equally annoyed.

"She came here, Ryder. Mom didn't hunt your ex-girlfriend down and ask for all the gifts."

"*Gifts*?" I question. "There was more than the tea?"

They exchange a look that tells me I won't like the answer.

There's a honk outside. I glance at the clock on the microwave. Eight p.m.

Immediately, I stand. "That's Tuck. I'll be back in a couple of hours."

"Ryder …" my mom starts.

I shake my head. "It's fine."

Then, I hurry out of the trailer like it's on fire, more eager to escape that kitchen than I was to leave prison, my head still spinning.

Cormac said I should know? I wish he'd kept his mouth shut tight. Wish I hadn't looked twice at that tea.

Rather than the beat-up green truck Tucker used to drive, a shiny black one is idling at the end of the short driveway. *FRANKLIN CONSTRUCTION* is printed on the door in neat block letters.

Tuck waves enthusiastically as I approach, but doesn't step out of the truck. I realize why when I open the door.

"… not sure that I should mix the two, you know?" a woman's voice is saying. "It was nice of her to offer, but what if I hate it all? How would I tell her?"

"Honey, we've eaten at her restaurant twice," Tuck replies. "Remember how good that duck was? You're not going to hate anything, and you said she has a long waiting list. What's the point of having connections if you don't use them?"

Tuck leans over to hug me once I've settled in the passenger seat, punching my shoulder twice before he relaxes back in his seat and mouths, *Keira*.

I nod.

"So, you think I should accept?"

"I do," Tuck confirms. "But it's your call. If you want to find a different caterer, let's do that. I gotta go, okay? I just picked Ryder up."

There's a noticeable pause. The smile Tuck aims my way is amused and a little apologetic. The air in the cab turns tangible, thickened by history and nostalgia and mistakes.

"Hi, Ryder."

"Hi, Keira," I respond.

"It's nice to, um, hear your voice."

I give Keira credit for effort at least. We barely know each other, our closest connection being Tucker. She also has plenty of reasons to hate me, by proxy.

"You too," I say. "Congratulations on the engagement."

"Thanks. I'll, uh, talk to you later, Tuck."

"Sounds good," Tucker replies cheerfully. "Love you."

"Love you too."

There's a soft click as the call disconnects.

Tuck immediately leans over for a second hug. "*Man*, it is good to see you."

"Yeah, you too." I grin at my best friend, the heaviness in my chest lightening some.

Tucker Franklin is just one of those people it's difficult to be depressed around.

"Won't miss that drive to Leavenworth."

"Won't miss a lot about that place."

Tuck snorts. "I bet. You sure you don't want to hit Malone's? Won't be any women at the jobsite."

"I'm sure," I tell his smirk.

Sex isn't worth enduring the stares and speculation at the local watering hole.

"Reese is excited to see you. She called a few days ago to check in, and I shared the good news. Hope that's okay."

"Of course," I say absently, staring at Hank's garage as we pass it by. It's deserted now. Tuck's uncle closed up shop a few years ago.

"Her folks are trying to get her to move down south with Knox, but she's holding firm as far as I know."

"Knox?"

"Her kid."

"Oh. Right. Dad still isn't around?"

"Nope." There's some anger in Tuck's voice that tells me there's more to the story. "He—he looks a lot like Phoenix."

"Ah."

"I've never asked. I don't know for sure. And I can't believe Reese would do that to you."

"It wasn't Phoenix's fault, Tuck."

Tucker scoffs. "You weren't dealing, Ryder. You took the fall for that piece of shit and his brother, and they didn't do a damn thing to help you."

"I took the deal. If they'd come forward, they would have just ended up in there with me."

He shakes his head. "You're too forgiving, man."

I swallow. "It's finally behind me. I want it all to stay there."

"Okay. Message received."

"So, how's wedding planning going?" I don't manage to get the whole question out without laughing.

Tuck groans. "We don't have to talk about it."

"Nah, I'm really asking. How is it?"

I was shocked when Tucker told me he was engaged. He and Keira dated on and off for part of senior year, then broke up in college. After graduating, Keira moved back to Fernwood to start her own restaurant. Tuck was still living here, working for Hank and getting his construction business going. They had reconciled and didn't waste much time deciding it was permanent.

I'm trying to be supportive, same as Tuck has always been toward me. To get over the surprise of my best friend getting *married* to a woman I barely know. To not resent who her best friend happens to be.

"It's good," he tells me. "Venue is booked. Band is booked. Invitations go out next week. Keira's still deciding on her dress. And the food. We're going cake tasting this weekend."

"That all sounds great, man."

"Yeah, it is. Keira's amazing. You'll have to come over for dinner soon, get to know her better."

"I'd like that." My fingers tap a nervous rhythm against the door. *Fuck it.* "They're still friends?"

Tuck clears his throat. "Yeah. She's, uh, she's Keira's maid of honor."

Not married then, is my first, idiotic thought.

"I was going to ask you to be my best man," Tuck continues. "But if it's too weird …"

It won't just be weird. It will be strange and uncomfortable and awkward.

Elle and I were volatile under perfect circumstances. There's just too much of … everything between us. And after everything I learned during dinner, I have so many more questions than I thought I would.

But for Tuck, I will get through it. If he wants me up there with him on the happiest day of his life, then that's exactly where I'll be.

"I'd be honored, Tuck."

"Cool." His nonchalance doesn't fool me. I can hear the emotion in his voice. "Okay, here's the place."

I glance out the window at the house, whistling under my breath as he stops along the curb.

Tuck sighs. "I told you."

I climb out of the cab and lean back against the door, crossing my arms as I survey the property.

This is one of Fernwood's oldest and nicest neighborhoods. The only reason Tucker could afford this place was the elderly woman who lived here died in debt with no living family. The house itself is in a total state of disrepair, the land that's covered with overgrown weeds the most valuable part of the property.

"Come on," Tuck says, walking toward the brick path with a six-pack in hand. "The inside is worse, but it'll look better after a beer. Or two."

I chuckle under my breath, then push away from the door and follow him toward the house.

8

THEN

Ryder

I glance between Phoenix and the mansion we're stalled in front of. "This isn't Malone's."

"Pit stop," Cruz, Phoenix's older brother, says from his spot in the front seat. He glances back at me. "Know who's a better customer than rich kids?"

"*Drunk* rich kids?"

Cruz grins. "Exactly. Sure you don't want in, man? You've got great business sense."

I rub a hand along my jaw, studying the exterior of the huge house. "I'm sure."

As tempting as easy cash sounds, I've heard too much. Cruz isn't small-time, selling weed he grew in his basement. He's part of a huge operation based out of Boston. Dangerous shit that has huge payoffs—if the brand-new car we're in is any indication—and lots of risk. Something I should stay far away from.

Phoenix and Cruz live a few trailers down with a rotating door of family members. Our paths didn't cross much when I lived here last, but Phoenix is working at the garage with me. When he suggested we grab a burger tonight, I thought that meant we were actually going to get a burger. Instead, we ended up at the football field, another "pit stop" that lasted twenty minutes.

Cruz shrugs, then turns back around. "Suit yourself."

Zane, who's driving, blocks a BMW in. Then, all the doors, except mine, are opening.

I look at Phoenix, who's halfway out of the car. "Thought this was a pit stop?"

"Yeah, yeah. We'll get burgers in a bit."

This was all planned, I realize. Part of a familiar pattern.

"You seriously party with *them*?" I ask.

Phoenix spent most of our shift earlier complaining about how snobby and stuck-up most people in this town are.

He shrugs. "They want what Cruz is selling. And the girls might be bitchy at school, but here?" He smirks. "They're up for anything. Seriously."

"Not interested."

This is the big postgame party. I'm sure Elle is here, and I really don't need a front-row seat to Hathaway slobbering all over her.

"If you say so."

Everyone else is out of the car. I exhale, bang my skull against the headrest twice, and then climb out as well. I leave my Rays cap on the seat even though I wouldn't mind the camouflage of a brim. The car alarm chirps obnoxiously as the rest of the guys head inside.

The front walk is lined with trimmed hedges. Tall columns flank the front porch. Everything about this place suggests its owners are loaded.

Inside is an atmosphere I'm more familiar with. In Jacksonville, we'd mostly party on the beach around bonfires and by lifeguard huts. But aside from the lack of smoke and salt air, being surrounded by drunk teenagers is nothing new to me.

The crew I came with has already disappeared. I scan the living room, avoiding eye contact with any of the girls checking me out. Phoenix was right, I guess. Although it's the same scrutiny I get at school, just more blatant.

"What are you doing here?"

I spin to face Tuck, raising an eyebrow. "What am *I* doing here? What are *you* doing here?"

He half smiles, rubbing the back of his neck. "I hang out in this scene sometimes."

"*Really?*"

"Yeah. A few of the guys are cool."

I snort. "If you say so. Is Reese here too?"

Tuck scoffs. "Of course not. Figured you two were *hanging out* tonight."

"I told you, it's not like that."

"It's like that for her, man."

Tucker is convinced Reese has a thing for me, but I don't see it. We were tight freshman year, and she's the one person I kept in touch with from here, aside from Tuck. But she's never acted any differently around me than she does him, as far as I've noticed.

I go to run my fingers through my hair and end up basically just rubbing my scalp instead. I'm not used to the shorter length yet.

"I thought Phoenix and I were grabbing burgers. He forgot to mention a couple of stops."

"You're here with those guys?" Tucker frowns.

"I'm not selling. Just along for the ride."

"That doesn't—"

"Tucker! Here you are!"

Two girls are approaching. I lift an eyebrow at Tuck, and he smirks back. *Cool guys*, my ass. He's here for the chicks.

There are only about a dozen Twos at Fernwood High. The hookup pool is pretty small, so it's not entirely surprising that lines have blurred the past couple of years. And I'm hardly one to judge. I stepped right over the line freshman year.

We end up in the crowded kitchen. Still no sign of the group I came with. I'm sure Phoenix is off with some girl, and Zane and Cruz must be busy conducting "business." Archer Hathaway is leaning against the kitchen island, talking to a couple of guys, but there's no sign of Elle. I relax a little.

"You drinking?" Tuck asks me.

I shake my head. "Nah, I'm good."

"Watson! Beer me!" Hathaway hops up onto the counter, sending several red plastic cups skittering to the floor.

I don't know whose house this is, but I'm guessing they have a cleaning service. Some maid is going to be on her hands and knees tomorrow, scrubbing at the sticky residue that just spilled.

A blond guy tosses a can of beer at Archer.

Hathaway's still a shitty quarterback. I figured, based on Medina's request. I didn't pay any attention to the game earlier, but the somber faces in the parking lot told me Fernwood lost.

He misses the catch by a lot, and I doubt it has much to do with how much he's had to drink. Pure reflex has me reaching out to snag the can before it can hit the floor and make even more of a mess.

Archer's lip curls as he turns to me and holds a hand out for the can. "Buy your own beer." He tilts his head. "Oh, wait. Can you not afford to?"

I toss the can in the air and catch it one-handed. Whenever it gets opened, it'll probably explode. "Might want to slow down, man." I raise an eyebrow. "Oh, wait. You can't catch sober either."

There are a few muffled laughs around the kitchen. Watson, who threw the beer, lifts a cup to cover his grin.

Archer is popular, but not the way Elle is. Not because people actually like him. He's popular because he's supposed to be. Because he's got the rich family and the right zip code, and that translates to certain privileges.

His eyes narrow. "Who invited you, Two?"

"It's a *party*, Archer. Lighten up." A girl I don't recognize steps forward, rolling her eyes. She's pretty. Long light-brown hair. Perky tits that Archer blatantly checks out. *Pig.*

I'm looking, too, but only one of us has a girlfriend.

"Let me show you around, Ryder."

She grabs my hand and pulls me toward the doorway. I let her, mostly out of surprise, glancing back at Tuck.

He grins at me, lifting his beer, then mouths, *Go for it.*

I'm not really in the mood for this shit, but I suppose it's a smarter plan than getting into it with Hathaway.

Rather than enter the crowded living room like I'm expecting, the girl steers us into a bookshelf-lined office. It reminds me of a library, all dark, old-looking wood and brass fixtures.

She closes the door behind us, muffling the blaring music. Drops my hand and then sashays over toward the fireplace, picking up a crystal glass and nearly filling it with amber liquid. "Want some? Way better than warm beer."

"No thanks."

"That's refreshing." She smirks, then sips, appraising me carefully over the rim of the glass. "Do you know how to build a fire?"

"It's August."

"Just for ambiance. The AC is on."

I shake my head and make for one of the leather armchairs, still not sure if being in here is a good idea or not. I won't be able to talk Phoenix into leaving before Cruz is ready, but I could probably convince Tuck to drive me home soon.

"Everyone's wondering if you're going to join the team. That's why Archer was so peeved."

Hathaway hated me long before he found out I had a decent arm, so I don't think that's the real—or only—reason.

But I just shrug. "I'm not playing."

"Why not? I hear you're good. And it would be nice to cheer for the winning team for once. Even Elle gets sick of being supportive, and she's practically a saint."

At that, I snort. Elle's a good person, one of the best I've ever met. But she's no saint.

The girl—I should've asked for her name, probably—raises both eyebrows. "You don't like Elle?"

She's masking her interest pretty well, but I can sense it bubbling beneath the surface. Elle is the last topic I feel like discussing.

"I don't know her." It's not a lie exactly, but it tastes a lot like one. "But I don't like any Ones really. No offense."

She sips more straight alcohol. "I don't buy into that whole *we're better than them because we have more money* thing, you know."

"How progressive of you."

She giggles. "I mean it. Archer doesn't let you guys come to his parties, but me? Everyone is welcome."

I glance around the room again. "This is your place?"

"Uh-huh."

"It's nice."

She smiles, then walks toward me. "Thanks."

I tip my head back to hold eye contact as she approaches. "What's your name?"

She rolls her eyes, silently agreeing I should have asked a while ago. Or maybe annoyed I didn't already know.

"I'm Maddie. We had English together, freshman year. You sulked in the back the whole time."

I remember sitting in the back of the classroom. I don't remember Maddie, which must be obvious on my face.

"Ouch," she says, shaking her head. One knee lands next to my left thigh, then the other by my right so she's straddling me. "Well, you'll remember me after tonight, right?"

Her hips are rocking against mine, her boobs right in my face. And rather than enjoy the experience, I'm busy cataloging all the ways her face is different from Elle's.

It's not Maddie's fault her hair isn't darker, and her eyes aren't blue, and her smile doesn't make me feel like all the air in the world has disappeared.

She wasn't supposed to still matter. I don't *want* her to still matter, but my brain—not to mention my dick—doesn't seem to care.

My feelings for Fernwood's golden girl were supposed to dissipate as soon as I left. Not linger like a hollow echo for the twenty-six months I was gone and then flare back to life with shocking strength after seeing her again. Every glimpse I got of her at school this week is burned into my memory like a brand. I spent the whole drive here obsessing over what her texting me earlier meant.

"I gotta go," I say.

Maddie frowns, then stills. "What?"

"I gotta go," I repeat.

Maddie straightens and climbs off. "Seriously?"

I'm being a dick, I know. But I'm not going to fuck her. Not tonight. Not ever. I could make up some bullshit excuse to soften the blow, but that's never been my style.

As soon as she's off my lap, I stand. Sitting was obviously a mistake.

"I can't stay. I've got somewhere to be. I will remember you though, Maddie. Promise."

I hustle out of the room before she can say anything else.

My phone buzzes in my pocket as I walk down the hallway. I pull it out, hoping it'll be Phoenix, ready to head out. It's not. It's an unknown local number.

I answer. "Hello?"

No response. Although it's almost impossible to hear as I walk closer to the living room, which is where the music is blaring from. I swerve left and head upstairs, ignoring the glances from a couple of girls stumbling down them.

The hallway is empty, most of the doors shut. I rub the back of my neck and exhale, then try to call the number back. It rings with no answer.

Halfway down the hallway, there's a landing for a second set of stairs. Maddie's home is huge. I've driven past the houses in this exclusive part of town, but never been inside one before. There's a reading nook with more bookcases across from the landing, then doors that lead outside. I open one and step out onto the balcony that overlooks the backyard, tugging the box of cigarettes out of my pocket. I exhale as soon as the cool, fresh air hits my face, relaxing for the first time since we arrived.

"Thought you quit."

I glance over one shoulder, my heart doing a silly skip when I confirm it's really her. Elle's leaning against the side of the roof, her expression inscrutable as she stares at me.

My eyes fall to the red cup she's holding. "Thought you didn't drink."

"Water's a precious resource. I'm doing my part to help save the planet."

I snort as I fish a lighter out of my pocket and ignite the end of the cigarette. "What are you doing here?"

"Maddie and I have been friends since first grade. What are *you* doing here?"

"I meant, hiding on a balcony. Your adoring subjects must be missing you."

She straightens, walking over toward me. I tense, tracking the shrinking distance between us.

My resentment toward Phoenix grows with each of her steps. This night has gone totally off the rails. I didn't want to talk to Elle like this, us alone. Nothing good can come from closer proximity. I'm having a hard enough time getting her out of my head already.

"Only the ones who weren't busy welcoming you back to town in the study."

I raise both eyebrows as Elle rests an elbow on the railing and glances down.

"Do you think I could make it into the pool from here?" she asks.

I follow her gaze. It's thirty feet, maybe more. "You still like to consider dumb shit, huh?"

"I do more than *consider*, Ry."

She's not touching me. She's not even looking at me. Yet I'm flooded with everything I should have felt when Maddie was grinding on my lap, instantly hard the second she calls me *Ry*.

"I'm dumb shit?" I ask.

Elle says nothing. She just stares down with a calculating expression, like she's actually considering jumping. The thought terrifies me. Elle in danger affects me like nothing else. I know she's smart and strong and capable of taking care of herself. Somehow, that scares me even more. Because I know she doesn't damage easily.

I hurt her. She let me in, let me hurt her, and I hate myself for that.

"I know the timing sucked. I *am* sorry."

"Did you hook up with Maddie?"

She's still looking down, not at me, so I can't read her face. Can't tell if she cares about the answer.

"How did you even—"

Elle tugs her phone out of her back pocket and hands it to me. I try to keep my eyes off her ass, but I do a shitty job of it. The screen is covered with dozens of message notifications. Some names I recognize. Others I don't. A play-by-play of everything happening downstairs.

A new text from Maddie pops up as I'm staring at Elle's phone, but I'm more focused on something else. "Nice background."

She takes the phone back from me without looking this way. But the small section of her cheek I can see in the dim light appears pinker. "I'll hear about it whether you tell me or not. I'm just—"

"Nothing happened."

"Right. Rich girls aren't your type."

Her grip on the cup is loose enough for me to lift it out of her hand. I sip, making a face at the sour burn.

"Jesus. Want any cranberry juice with your vodka?"

"I like it."

"Sure. I'd need to get that drunk to date Hathaway too."

Elle reaches out to grab her cup back. She fists it from the bottom, making sure our fingers don't brush. "You've been gossiping about me, huh?"

"Got stuck listening to gossip about you, yeah. What are you doing with that dick, Elle?"

Instead of answering, she asks, "Why did you come back, Ryder?"

"Wasn't my call."

She takes a drink, and I experience a stupid thrill knowing we're swapping spit.

"Was leaving?"

My jaw works a couple of times. I should lie. Instead, I admit, "No."

My phone buzzes in my pocket again. I pull it out to see another unknown number.

"Hello?"

"Ryder?"

I recognize my little brother's voice. "Cormac?"

"Yeah, it's me. Can you come pick me up?"

I close my eyes. "Pick you up from *where*?"

He's supposed to be home. Asleep.

A pause.

Then, "The playground."

"What the fu—hell are you doing there? It's after eleven."

"Don't get mad, okay? Owen wanted to bike around, but I got a flat."

I exhale. "Whose phone are you using?"

"Some kids were already hanging around here. Mav and them. He said he'll stay until you get here. And he'll take my bike in his truck."

"Damnit, Cormac. I don't … I'll be there as soon as I can."

" 'Kay. Thanks."

I hang up and blow out another long breath. I thought my mom was exaggerating about Cormac's behavior. Bailing him out isn't much of a lesson, but I can't just leave him there overnight to sleep in the mulch. I'm sure he left a lot out of his story. No way he just ended up there.

"Everything okay?" Elle asks quietly.

"I think so. Just Cormac making stupid choices." I glance at her. "You can say it."

"I didn't know you in middle school. Maybe you were a perfect angel."

I huff a laugh. "Right. I gotta go find a ride so I can pick him up."

"You can take my car." She reaches into her pocket again and tosses me a set of keys. "It's the red convertible."

"Perfect for New England winters."

Elle rolls her eyes. "It's not snowing right now. You'll be fine, Florida boy."

"You've been gossiping about me, huh?"

"Got stuck listening to gossip about you, yeah." She parrots my line right back.

"I was in Jacksonville. With my dad. He taught me how to surf."

Her gaze roves over my face like she's trying to find more than I just shared, which was already a lot more than I'd intended to tell her.

"You miss it?"

"No."

She nods. "Right. You don't get attached."

"I get attached." I hold her keys out to her. "I can't take your car."

"Why not?"

"Because I'm not leaving you stranded at a party with no car. Not that you should be driving anyway … but still. You should have it. Where's your friend? Julia?"

"*Juliet* is in the pool house with Alec Hamilton." Elle sips more of her lightly flavored vodka. "I'm fine. I can crash here if I have to, or I'll get a ride with someone. My house isn't far. I could walk."

"He's wasted, you know."

Elle's eyes narrow. "I didn't mention Archer."

"I appreciate the offer. But I'll figure it out."

I hold the keys out, but Elle doesn't take them. I sigh, then step closer and slip them back into her shorts. We're closer now, way too close, her familiar scent—jasmine and lemon—washing over me. My dick twitches as her head tilts back and her teeth sink into her full bottom lip.

"You used to kiss me before touching my ass," she says.

I pluck the cup out of her hand and toss it over the balcony railing. "Switch to water, Clarke."

"I have enough people telling me what to do. I don't need it from you too."

"You make your own choices, Elle."

Her eyes narrow. "Fine."

Then, her hand is wrapped around mine, and I'm getting pulled along by a girl half my weight for the second time tonight. Elle tugs me down the hallway to the left, lifting a ceramic figurine off a table, grabbing a key, unlocking a door, and then returning the key to its hiding spot.

"What the hell are you doing?" I hiss as we walk into a pink bedroom.

"Well, you won't leave me here without a car, so I'm coming with the car. You can pick up your brother and then bring me back here like the gentleman we both know you're not."

"Doesn't explain why we're in Maddie's bedroom."

Framed photos cover one wall, Maddie front and center in most of them. I wonder if Elle's bedroom has a similar display.

"I don't feel like dealing with downstairs."

I snort. "So, you're jumping out a window?"

"No. I'm climbing down the trellis. I've done it before." She opens the window, then sticks her head out.

For fuck's sake, this is insane. But I don't really want to pick up Cormac with Phoenix, Cruz, and Zane in tow. Cormac's making enough bad decisions without their influence. And Tuck has done plenty for me. I don't want to ruin his night.

I sigh, then stride over to the window. "Wait. Let me go first."

"If I fall, are you going to catch me?"

"I'll at least *consider* it."

Elle rolls her eyes, but steps to the side so I can climb out of the window first.

It's an easy climb, one I manage in less than a minute. Elle does it quickly as well, requiring no assistance from me. I'm more disappointed about that than I should be.

"I'm down the street," she says once we're on solid ground. "It's best to avoid the gridlock."

"Smart," I compliment. I can't even spot Zane's car in the mess of vehicles at odd angles.

"I have my moments."

We weave through haphazardly parked cars until we reach the sidewalk. It's perfectly paved, not a crack in sight.

Every house we pass is as big and expensive-looking as Maddie's.

"Your place like these?" I ask, staring at one of them.

It's the only distraction I have from Elle walking right next to me. We're alone out here, the sounds from the party fading more with each step.

"There's no pool."

One corner of my mouth turns up. The side opposite Elle, so she can't see.

Most people are predictable. She always surprises me.

"Aside from the pool?"

"Yeah. It's big. Too big. My mom doesn't know what to do with Rose's room because there's already so much extra space."

"Put a pool in there."

When I glance over, she's smiling. My chest squeezes.

"Yeah. I'll suggest it."

"They'll have another empty room next year."

Unlike me, Elle's headed to college. One of the best schools in the country, I'm sure. That difference in our futures didn't seem as relevant freshman year. Adulthood looked far away. Now, it seems glaring. Imminent.

"I'm planning on coming back though."

"Yeah?"

From what she's told me, Elle's relationship with her parents has always been strained. And it got worse when her older sister died five years ago. They expect perfection from Elle, like it's her responsibility to make up for their loss. If I were her, I'd leave this town and never look back.

"Yeah," she replies. "There are a few things I like about Fernwood."

"Like what?" I ask, genuinely curious.

We reach her car, the color and model standing out among the other cars parked on the street.

Rather than unlock it, Elle climbs over the side of the convertible and stays standing in the passenger seat. Her alarm is useless because it doesn't go off.

"Like driving a convertible in the snow," she tells me, leaning against the top of the windshield. She fishes her car keys out of her pocket and spins them around on one finger. "You?"

"Me what?"

"Is there anything you like about this town?" Elle holds my gaze, appearing far less drunk than I thought she was. Her head tilts in the same direction as the rest of her body, studying me closely as she waits for a response.

I didn't see this choice coming. I was enjoying talking to her without looking ahead at the approaching split.

This answer will matter. The longer I hesitate, the more it'll mean. I apologized twice, and that was supposed to be it. Closure.

I swallow. "Yeah."

If the answer didn't include her, I would have said it aloud. I'm pretty sure Elle knows that, based on how she breaks eye contact so I can't read her expression.

She tosses her keys at me, sitting once I catch them.

We've never left a party together before. Never been in a car together before. Tonight is the most we've talked in over two years.

This should be awkward.

But it's not.

9
NOW

Ryder

More light creeps across the horizon, illuminating the patchy yard. I sip some coffee from the cup in my hand, shifting in place so that the railing I'm leaning against hits a different spot of my spine. It looks sturdy, but it also creaks ominously each time I move, like it could collapse at any second.

A bird swoops down from the old oak that's the stateliest part of the property. It pecks at the overgrown grass for a few minutes, then flies off when a shiny Mercedes drives down the street.

The neighbors must hate this place. It's an obvious eyesore amid the immaculately maintained houses that surround it. Tuck said the previous owner lived here for sixty years. At one point, it was undoubtedly the nicest house on the block. The surrounding homes lack the big lot and charm of this property.

I stretch my legs out and close my eyes. I didn't sleep well last night, which has been a consistent pattern since I moved back into the trailer. My twin bed had been too small when I was in high school. I haven't gotten any smaller since. Bed hasn't gotten any bigger either.

But I'm not even sure if you could fit a double in the space.

A distant slam sounds as a car door shuts nearby. I reach up and tug the brim of my ball cap down lower, trying to block more of the rising sun. Based on how warm it is already, it's going to be a scorcher.

I must doze off at some point because Tuck's voice startles me. "How long have you been here?"

"A while," I answer without opening my eyes.

"You must love your job to show up so early. Awesome boss?"

I snort. "That's exactly it. Plus, it's nice to be outside whenever I feel like it."

"Shit." Tuck takes a seat next to me.

Reluctantly, I open my eyes.

"One of those things you don't really think about, huh?"

I nod, then yawn and rub a palm across my eyes. They feel dry and gritty. Worse than they did before my nap.

"Seriously, everything okay?"

"Yeah. Just adjusting."

"Must be tight in the trailer. Cormac's back for the summer, right?"

"Yeah, he finished finals a few days ago."

"If you need a place to crash …"

"I'm good, Tuck. You've done plenty. But thank you."

"I can still ask around. I'm sure you could find your own place. They put up those apartments by—"

"I can't."

I feel his eyes on me.

"You can't?"

He's expecting me to take off, same as Cormac. They both know how I feel about this town. About everything that went down here.

I exhale. "My mom's sick. Lung cancer. I need to stay in the trailer so I can help her out. Cormac's there, too, but he'll be in the city most of the summer and then back at school in the fall."

"*Fuck*. Ry, I'm so sorry."

I rub my eyes again, trying to wake my face up. I can hear the pity in Tucker's voice, and I don't want to have to see it too. I get why my mom's avoided having this conversation; it's awful. Far as I know, she hasn't told anyone, except me and Cormac.

"How … how bad is it?" Tuck asks.

"She's terminal. Doctors are estimating a year."

"Jesus. Man, I'm …"

I swallow. "I know."

"Anything I can help with, let me know. Repairs around the trailer, time away from here, hot meals. Just let me know."

I stiffen when he mentions food, sure that he means from Keira's restaurant. Will he tell her about my mom? Will Keira tell Elle? I'm no longer sure what the hierarchy is. How Tuck divides his loyalties between me and his fiancée. How Keira divides her loyalties between Tuck and Elle.

Not worth worrying about, I decide. They'll all find out at some point anyway.

"Thank you," I tell Tuck. "I appreciate … everything you've done. I really appreciate it."

As far as best friends go, I'm well aware I won the goddamn lottery. If I were Tuck, I would have given up on me a long time ago.

"Don't mention it." He reaches down and yanks a weed up from the path. "How's it going with the guys?"

"Great. The whole crew is awesome."

"Yeah. They're a good group." He glances over one shoulder at the house. "I've got a plumber and an electrician coming by later. Once they assess, should be a clearer picture on priorities."

I nod. "Plenty of cleanup to do in the meantime."

That's how the last few days have gone—ripping out old kitchen cabinets, removing peeling wallpaper in the dining room, and getting rid of the massive pile of rotting firewood in the backyard.

Tuck grins. "No kidding. I got a floor sander in the back of my truck. Mind giving me a hand with it?"

"Of course not." I stand and drain the rest of my coffee.

"How'd you get here, by the way?" Tuck asks as we head down the walk.

"Jogged."

He glances down at my leather work boots, eyebrows raised.

I chuckle. "My mom has the day off work. Got my license renewed, so I drove her car."

"Where the hell did you park?"

"Around the corner," I reply. "Didn't want to clog up the street."

"I own this place, man. Park wherever the hell you want."

"Wow," I comment, grinning. "Dating a One has really changed you. You the king of this town now?"

Tuck flips me off. "Says the guy who pulled Elle Clarke—twice."

My smile instantly disappears.

He notices. "Talking about her is still off-limits, huh?"

"She visited my mom," I blurt.

"What a bitch."

When I don't react, Tuck sighs.

"We talking about it? Or are you just telling me?"

"I just … I don't get it. Why would she do that?"

"You wouldn't let her visit you. Your mom is the closest she could get."

I raise an eyebrow. "She told you I wouldn't let her visit?"

"No. You just did. I've never talked about you with Elle. But I know you, Ryder. You shut down when things get hard. And things got really hard for a while there. No way you were going to let Elle see you like that."

He knows me better than I realized. "I just—"

"Hey. I thought that was you, Tucker."

I freeze at the sound of the familiar voice. Turn around slowly, watching Archer's eyes widen when he spots me.

"Ryder. Hey."

I nod once, acknowledging the greeting. "Hi, Hathaway."

Tucker clears his throat. He knows most of the history between me and Archer Hathaway, but not the most important parts. I'm sure there were rumors about the role he played in my arrest. But Hathaway has only done one thing I consider unforgivable, and I've never talked about it with anyone, except Elle.

"I, uh, heard—I mean, I saw that you were getting out. Getting released, I mean."

"Saw?" I question.

"Local paper ran an article." Tuck is the one who answers, watching me carefully from his spot, leaning against the bumper of his truck.

I can't tell if he's worried I'm going to take a swing at Hathaway or if he's trying to intimidate the guy.

"Of course they did."

Hathaway shifts his weight between his feet. He's dressed for running in matching black shorts and a tight black top I guess is meant to show off his muscles. He's about as built as he was in high school—not much.

"You live around here?" Tuck asks.

Archer nods. "Few blocks over." He glances at the old Warren house. "That's a big project."

"Someone's gotta tackle it," Tuck replies.

"True. Town council is going to love you. Neighbors have been complaining about this place for years."

"Yes, they really should have evicted the elderly woman sooner," I drawl.

Tuck gives me a *cut that shit out* look.

I was teasing him earlier about changing, but all of a sudden, it feels like there's a little more truth to it. Like he's a part of this town, no longer separated by an *us* and a *them*.

Archer's smile is highly uncomfortable. "Well, I should keep moving. Don't want to be late for work. Good to see you, Tucker. Ryder."

"See you, Archer," Tuck responds.

I manage a nod before Archer continues jogging, then glance at Tuck. "You and Hathaway are buddies now?"

Tuck blows out a breath. "I did some work on his folks' place. Put in a patio, did some reno work on the downstairs. Archer was over there a lot. He got married last summer. Some girl he'd met in college at Michigan. She's sweet. I know he was a dick in high school, but people change, Ry."

"Keira know you're friendly with him?" I ask.

"Yeah. Why?"

"No reason," I reply. "Let's lift this."

Moving the sander is an easy job with two people. I carry the base while Tuck guides the handles. We deposit it in the dining room, up first for floor refinishing, then head back outside. A couple of guys from the crew have arrived.

We're standing in the front yard, shooting the shit, when my phone buzzes in my pocket. I got a new one two days ago, miraculously managing to keep my old number. At least, it felt like a miracle at the time. One thing that went right.

Staring at the Colorado number flashing across the screen, I'm less sure.

"I'll be right back," I tell the guys before walking toward the backyard. I really don't want an audience for this call.

I answer, but say nothing. He can talk first.

"Hello, son."

"Dad."

I've never called him Sperm Donor or Dax to his face, but I've been tempted too many times to keep track of.

"How's it going?"

Jesus. I crack the fingers of my left hand, staring at the dirt patch where the firewood was piled. "Great. Just got back from an Antarctica cruise. Saw a ton of penguins."

His sigh is heavy. "I don't appreciate the sarcasm, Ryder."

"Then why are you calling, Dad?"

"I haven't talked to you in seven years. I need a reason to call?"

"Yeah, you do. Because not talking to me for seven years was your decision."

"I wasn't the one who got himself incarcerated."

I tip my head back to track a cloud's progress across the sky. It's silent, so quiet that I think maybe he gave up and hung up.

"Look, your mom called and told me you'd been released, and I just thought—"

"She mention she's dying?"

More silence.

"No. That didn't come up."

I snort. "And let me guess … you're too busy to come see her. Or me."

"I have some very important—"

"Save the speech, Dad. I've heard it before."

"Do you need money? I can send some."

Part of me is tempted to take it. He owes my mom about fifteen years of child support. But it'll alleviate his guilt—make him feel better about himself—and that's the last thing I want.

"No. I got a job."

"That's great." His tone is too chipper, awkwardness bleeding beneath. "Doing what?"

"Construction."

"Hard work," he comments.

I kick a piece of firewood that got overlooked yesterday. "Yep."

"I'm happy you're out, Ryder. And so sorry to hear about your mom."

"That makes two of us."

"I'll give Nina a call soon; check in with her."

"She'll love that." This time, there's no sarcasm.

She will. If Dax cared about her half as much as my mom loved him, they'd still be together.

Something my dad knows, based on the uncomfortable pause that follows.

"I gotta get to work," I say, letting him off the hook.

I've got plenty of my own regrets. I don't need to carry his too.

"Okay. Talk soon, son."

"Bye." I hang up, reach down, and fling the piece of firewood as far as I can. It hits the wooden fence that marks the edge of the property line with a dull *thunk*.

"Stick had it coming, I'm assuming?"

I turn to watch Keira Parker pick her way across the overgrown yard toward me. "Hi, Keira."

"Hey, Ryder." She pauses about a foot away, holding the coffee cup she's clutching out. "Brought Tuck some coffee and thought you could use one too."

"Thank you," I say, totally taken aback. "I appreciate it."

"I just …" She shrugs. "Little *welcome back* gift."

"Thank you," I repeat, not sure what else to say. This is probably the longest conversation we've ever had.

Keira's not looking at me with any anger or resentment, which makes me think Elle kept the details about our breakup from more than just my mom.

"Well, I should get going," Keira says. "I've got a shipment coming into the restaurant."

I nod. "Thanks again."

She smiles. "It's just a coffee, Ryder."

I watch her turn and sidestep a clump of weeds. "Keira?"

She glances back. "Yeah?"

"How are … people?"

There's a brief pause, during which I have no clue what Keira is thinking. Her poker face is impressive.

"People are good," she finally answers. "People just graduated law school."

"Law school, huh?"

"First in her class at Harvard."

I nod. "Thanks for … thanks."

"See you around." Keira continues walking.

I take a long sip of the coffee she brought. It's good—a hell of a lot better than the sludge I brewed this morning.

Then, I head for the back door to find out what Tuck has deemed top priority for today.

10
THEN

Elle

I'm making him uncomfortable.

Ryder's shoulders are tense as he drives my convertible, his fingers curled tightly around the steering wheel. I should feel bad about his unease. Stop my blatant staring. But too much of me is thrilled by his reaction. By the knowledge that I still affect him in any way. Ryder is a hard person to rattle. He's confident and controlled and assured.

A couple of blocks from the elementary school, we hit a red at one of Fernwood's few stoplights.

Ryder glances over, meeting my gaze straight on. "What?"

"What?" I repeat.

"You're staring."

"I know."

"Why?"

I lift one shoulder, then let it drop. "I like looking at you."

I've said a lot tonight that I shouldn't have. Most I'll likely regret when I wake up sober tomorrow. But I like being honest with Ryder. I like the way he stares at me after the truth spills out, like my honesty is something precious to him.

He says nothing in response, just continues scanning my face like he's looking for a different answer. Searching for a lie.

Then, the light turns green, and we're moving again, the playground where his brother is waiting appearing on the right a few seconds later.

Ryder pulls off into the space reserved for school buses during daylight hours and turns off my car. "I'll be right back."

I slouch down in the passenger seat and rest my bare feet on the dashboard. I kicked my shoes off a few minutes into the drive. "Take your time."

Ryder shakes his head a little before climbing out of the driver's side. I watch as he strides across the sidewalk toward the mulch. The group of kids loitering by the swings look too young to be *awake* this late, let alone out here by themselves.

I wonder if Cormac has done this before. If Ryder ever did this.

Sometimes, it feels like our lives aren't that different. Other moments, it seems like we're from different worlds. This is an example of the latter, where I feel sheltered and naive for being surprised about this scene.

My phone won't stop buzzing, so I pull it out, scanning the most recent messages.

JULIET: You were right.

JULIET: Alec was a mistake.

KEIRA: What happened?

MADDIE: Are you guys outside?

KEIRA: What do we think of Tucker Franklin?

KEIRA: He's kinda cute?

JULIET: I'm with Fleur by the fireplace.

ARCHER: Whare r u?

I skip over the rest of the unread messages, only responding to Juliet, Keira, and Archer.

ELLE: Felt sick. Left early.

I power my phone off before any responses can come through, sick of the nonstop buzzing. Drop it in the cupholder and glance toward the playground.

Ryder is standing by the swings, talking to the group of kids. He towers over the tallest by a couple of feet.

I've never met Ryder's little brother before. He's five years younger than us, so he's still in middle school.

I tilt my head back to stare up at the night sky, tracing patterns in the stars above and enjoying the lingering buzz of vodka. Rather than regret leaving Maddie's party early, I feel relieved.

A couple of minutes later, I catch motion out of the corner of my eye. My head turns to track the two figures headed this way.

Cormac stops walking when he spots the car. Or sees me. Glimpses something. He glances at Ryder, who has a resigned look on his face as he continues toward the driver's seat.

"Well, *hello* there," Cormac drawls.

Ryder's confidence seems to be hereditary. The brothers look alike, too, even though Ryder told me they have different fathers. I can't tell what color Cormac's eyes are, but his hair is the same shade as Ryder's. Several inches longer, the style similar to the way Ryder used to wear his freshman year. I doubt that's a coincidence.

I smile. "Hi, Cormac. It's nice to meet you."

Cormac starts walking again as I climb out of the passenger seat and pull it forward to access the back. I forgot about my bare feet until they kiss cold concrete, too buzzed to care about the chilly temperature or the hard texture.

"*Very* nice to meet you." His grin grows.

"Cormac," Ryder snaps, "get in the back."

"This your ride?" Cormac ignores Ryder and stays focused on me. "Sure is."

"*Wicked* car." Cormac shoves some of his shaggy hair out of his face to get a better look at my red convertible.

"Thanks," I respond, smiling at his blatant admiration.

"Are you hooking up with Ryder?"

"Cormac, shut up and get in the fucking car."

Cormac groans, but he listens to Ryder this time. "You should watch your mouth, dude. It's rude to swear in front of pretty girls."

I don't quite manage to smother the snort that wants to come out as I climb back into the passenger seat. I wasn't expecting Ryder's little brother to be this entertaining. Bossy big brother is a side of Ryder I've never seen before.

"You're grounded," Ryder says.

"Yeah. Sure." Cormac sounds unbothered by the prospect.

Ryder pinches the bridge of his nose before turning the car on.

I glance at the kids still on the playground. "What about them?"

"They're good," Ryder says. There's a note to his voice that tells me not to ask any more questions.

"So, you're a One, huh?" Cormac asks me from the back seat.

I glance over my shoulder. "I'm Elle."

"Holy shit. *You're* Elle Clarke?"

"*Language*, Cormac," Ryder chastises.

There's a clear note of warning in his voice, but I'm not sure it's about the swearing. More like it has to do with opinions the Twos have about me. We might judge the kids who live in the trailer park, but they judge our mansions too.

Cormac sighs heavily. "Yeah, yeah."

"I've gotta drop him at home, and then I'll get you back," Ryder tells me.

"No rush," I reply, masking the excitement I'm experiencing.

Up until tonight, we hadn't spoken since I handed him the History papers in the parking lot on the first day of school. He slouches in the back of our one shared class each morning, appearing not to pay attention, but answering every question correctly when Mr. Anderson calls on him.

I thought that meant he was over me. That any interest faded a long time ago and his avoidance was proof of that.

Now, I'm not as certain.

I didn't give him much of a choice in taking my car tonight. But if there's one thing I know about Ryder, it's that he doesn't do things he doesn't want to. Him bringing me to his house—even if it's just to drop off his delinquent little brother—feels like it means something. Just like him texting me back meant something. Just like him standing on that balcony with me meant something.

Or maybe I'm just looking for the signs I want to see. Inflating the bare minimum so it adds up to something significant.

"You ever been here before, Elle?" Cormac asks as Ryder takes another turn. His voice is teasing, sure of the negative answer. He's still at the age where the segregation in town seems amusing, not plain prejudice.

"Once," I reply.

Ryder glances over at me, but I keep my eyes straight ahead.

"Huh," Cormac comments. "That's a surprise."

I say nothing in response, relieved when he doesn't ask any more questions. Ryder's also silent as he drives along the dirt road that's bumpier than when I was here last. My car handles the potholes better than my bicycle did.

Ryder brakes about three-quarters down the road, beside a trailer that blends in with the mobile homes on either side. Marks on the grass serve as a parking spot that Ryder pulls into. There are a couple of overgrown bushes by the stairs that lead up to a small porch.

"Thanks for the ride." Cormac vaults out of the back seat without waiting for me to climb out. "You know where I live, Elle, when you get sick of Ryder's shit."

Once Cormac disappears inside, I expect Ryder to reverse right out of the spot. He doesn't. He taps his fingers against the steering wheel, staring straight ahead at the thick hedge that separates the lot behind this one.

"Confident kid," I say.

"Yeah." Ryder exhales, then rubs a hand across his face. "He's a handful."

I'm in no hurry to leave, so I tuck my feet under me and continue studying the outside of Ryder's home as we sit in silence.

"When?" he asks suddenly.

I swallow. "A few days later. I got … worried."

"I'm sorry."

"Yeah. You already said that."

"I mean it."

"Uh-huh."

His exhale is exasperated. Ryder reaches for the gearshift, and I reach for him. He freezes as soon as my fingers close around his wrist, so I do too.

We both stare at the spot where we're touching.

I loosen my grip slowly. "Can we stay? Just for a few more minutes?"

He looks at me, and I look back, and it feels like one of the most intense moments we've ever shared. And we've shared a lot of intense moments, so it's a high bar.

It's disarmingly intimate, holding someone's gaze purposefully. Especially when you've already memorized their features. He still has a freckle above his right eyebrow. The curved scar in the left corner of his mouth—a middle school football injury from an opponent's elbow—has faded some but not entirely. His gray eyes, more soft than stormy right now.

"Yeah." Ryder clears his throat. "Yeah. Sure." He kills the engine, the headlights shutting off a minute later.

I recline my seat a little so I can see the sky better. Ryder rubs his thumb along the side of the steering wheel.

Neither of us talk. We just sit.

Even around Keira and Juliet, my closest friends, I feel some compulsion to act a certain way. To play a part.

I'm honest with Ryder. Around him, it's easier to be myself.

I wish that had changed in the past two years. Wish I didn't know this feeling of safety and serenity still existed.

"I like your dress."

The smile comes automatically before I glance over and catch him looking at me. "Yeah?"

"Yeah. Matches your eyes."

"It's new," is the only thing I can think to say in response.

"Figured you had some special *first day of school* outfit."

The warmth in my chest glows brighter, realizing Ryder remembers what I wore on Monday.

"So, you surf now?" I ask.

"I can, yeah. Going to be tough to get to the Cape without a car." He drums his fingers against the steering wheel. "Tuck got me a job at his uncle's garage. There's an old beater he said I could fix up for some wheels."

"You're working at a garage?" There's one on the periphery of town, near the trailer park, which must be the place Ryder is talking about.

"Yeah. After school."

"So, you're not the new quarterback?"

He huffs, his hand dropping from the wheel as he relaxes against the seat. His knee knocks against the door. It's strange, seeing him in my car. Good strange. A sight I want to get used to.

"No. I ... I need the money."

"Is he a good guy? Tucker Franklin?"

Ryder's eyes snap to mine. He hesitates before answering, an unspoken *why* hovering in the silence. "The best," he answers.

"Keira's interested in him." I offer the explanation he didn't ask for.

"She's a friend of yours?"

"Her family has money, if that's what you mean."

"No, it's not. Tuck doesn't care about that shit."

"That would be weird, huh?" I ask.

"If your friend dated mine?"

"Yeah."

He looks away again.

I trace his profile with my eyes, the outline of his face and then down to the broad stretch of his shoulders. "It's a small town."

"Tucker know about us?"

"Not really," Ryder replies, which isn't the *no* I was expecting.

"What does that mean?"

"Means he noticed some things and made some assumptions."

"Things ..."

Ryder clears his throat. "I like looking at you too," he says softly. "And I do it enough that Tuck noticed."

"Oh."

He used present tense, just like I did. Didn't say he stared at me freshman year and imply he's stopped paying attention since.

"You ready to go?" Ryder asks.

"You should stay here. I'll drive myself home."

"No."

"I only had the one drink. Most of which you tossed in the yard. I'm fine, I promise."

"Not happening." The same steel as when he was bossing Cormac around reappears in Ryder's voice.

Not wanting me to get into a car accident is a terrible litmus test for judging a guy's feelings. But I like how the certainty in his tone sounds like caring.

Still, I can't resist saying, "You said I should make my own choices."

There's a sound of amusement in the back of Ryder's throat as he turns the car back on. "Not about this."

"How are you going to get back here?"

"I'll figure it out. Put your seat belt on."

"You're bossy."

His cheek creases, revealing the dimple that rarely appears. "You like it."

My stomach flips, a flash of heat dousing me like a downpour. He's right. And this is bad. So, *so* bad.

"Why'd you text me earlier?" Ryder asks.

I'm honest. "I wanted to know if you'd respond. Since you'd stopped."

"You can always text me, Elle. Or call. I saw your messages. I just … needed a clean break."

"Did you know you were leaving? That night?"

Ryder's smile instantly disappears. His jaw works a couple of times before he shakes his head. "Doesn't matter. I'm not asking you to forgive me."

"Too bad." I click my seat belt into place. "I already did."

11
NOW

Elle

A salty breeze blows straight into my face, lifting my hair off my neck. I smile, staring out at the dazzling spread of blue in front of me.

Blue water. Blue sky. Both stretching as far as the horizon goes.

I haven't been to the Parkers' beach house on Martha's Vineyard since college. The past two summers were spent at stressful internships. Taking any break felt like losing momentum. And I was scared if I stopped ... I might not start again.

I forgot how much I missed this. The sea-brine scent in the air. The clumps of seaweed scattered in the sand. The sight of the lighthouse silhouetted against the sky.

I feel freer here. Wilder. Younger.

My phone rings, so I abandon my spot leaning against the balcony rail and walk back into the guest room where I'm staying.

I pick up my vibrating phone off the pine dresser, my enthusiasm dimming slightly when I see who's calling.

It's Prescott.

I suck in a deep breath, take a seat on the edge of the bed, then answer. "Hey."

"Hey." There's a muffled thud, like binders being stacked. I'm sure he's studying for the bar, and it makes me feel guilty I'm not doing the same. "Are you going?"

"Going where?" I ask.

"Founding Fathers. For Jenny's birthday. Krista texted a couple of hours ago. I was studying, so I just saw it."

"Oh. Uh, no, I'm not going."

A pause.

"Everything okay?"

I tug at a loose thread on the quilt. It's pink and embroidered with yellow flowers. "Yeah, everything's good. It's just …"

"Just …" Pres prompts.

I blow out a long sigh, then lie back to stare up at the ceiling. Weathered wood beams interrupt the white plaster.

I don't know how to describe the claustrophobia I've been experiencing recently. All my law school friends—including Prescott—are stressed about the bar exam and excited about starting their careers. And I'm … numb to it. Or I was, until I stepped on the ferry earlier. The farther it churned into the Atlantic, the more weight fell off my shoulders.

"I'm visiting Martha's Vineyard for the weekend."

A long pause follows.

When we first started dating, I think Prescott liked that I was so independent. I *know* he's annoyed by it now, even though he tries to hide it.

I'm more concerned why I don't rely on him. I like Prescott. He's thoughtful and intelligent and considerate. I enjoy spending time with him. But I don't crave his company. I don't miss him when we're apart. Admitting that feels like a failure, especially when there's nothing wrong with our relationship. When it should work.

"Martha's Vineyard? You're on *Martha's Vineyard?*" His voice is mostly surprised, but I think he's just hiding the annoyance beneath.

"Uh-huh."

"You're joking."

"What's funny?" I say to lighten the mood, but I doubt Pres is smiling.

"I—you didn't even mention it, Elle."

"Keira's parents have a place out here. It was just a last-minute girls' trip. I needed a break from stuffing my brain with UCC rules."

"I'm not mad. Just … surprised. Why wouldn't you tell me?"

"We didn't have plans this weekend."

Prescott scoffs. "I haven't seen you all week. You didn't think I might want to spend time with you this weekend?"

"I'm not a mind reader."

He blows out a breath. "Wow."

I rub my forehead. "I'm sorry, okay? I just needed a …"

"Break. Yeah, you said. Except we haven't seen each other since last weekend, so I'm not sure what you need a break from."

"Pres …" I wait for him to fill the silence with something, but he doesn't. So my voice just trails awkwardly, highlighting how one-sided our relationship has become.

I noticed Prescott was the more invested one of us a long time ago. I think he's just starting to.

"Take your break, Elle. We'll talk when you get back."

"Okay. Tell Jenny happy birth—"

He hangs up on me mid-word.

I toss my phone away, still staring up at the ceiling. My boyfriend of six months basically just broke up with me. I should be sad or angry or hurt. Instead, I'm an empty shell. A hollow husk.

Scout whines, so I slide off the edge of the bed to sit on the floor with him. I have a partial view of the ocean as I stroke his soft fur.

Streaks of pastel color are spreading across the horizon, orange and pink and purple. It's stunning. I stare, transfixed, trying to remember the last time I sat and watched a sunset. I can't come up with an answer.

"Elle?" There's a soft tap on the door.

Scout leaps to his feet, barking once. I'm slower to rise.

"It's okay," I tell Scout, tossing a treat toward his crate before hobbling toward the door. My feet fell asleep a while ago.

"Hey." Keira studies me closely once I open the door. The light is on in the hallway, emphasizing how dark my room has become. "Everything okay?"

"Yeah. I was just … resting."

"Time to perk up, girl. I haven't seen you in weeks, you just kicked Harvard Law's ass, and Juliet already raided the fully stocked liquor cabinet. Do you have a drink request?"

I shake my head, smiling. "I'm good with whatever. Just let me feed Scout, and then I'll be down."

"Okay. Sushi should be here any minute."

"I thought we were grilling?"

"Yeah … it turns out, I don't really know how to work the grill. And I also didn't feel like cooking."

I laugh. "Okay."

After feeding Scout, I decide to change. Keira was wearing sweats and a tank top, so the evening's vibe seems casual.

I pull a pink pajama set out of my suitcase, twist my hair up into a bun, and head downstairs.

"Finally!" Juliet cheers when I reach the bottom of the stairs.

The first floor has an open concept, the kitchen, living room, and dining room all sharing most of the main space.

"Martini or gin and tonic?" Juliet asks as I approach the counter, covered with crackers, cheese, and a bunch of bottles.

"Martini," I answer.

"Here." Juliet hands me a glass a minute later. "Made it extra dirty for you." She winks.

"Thank you." I stick my tongue out at her before walking over toward the long table, where Keira's sitting with Avery and Ophelia around a huge spread of sushi.

Avery was Keira's freshman-year roommate, and Ophelia works in the kitchen of Keira's restaurant. I'm not as close to them as I am with Juliet and Keira, but they're both kind, accomplished women.

Juliet joins us a few seconds later, a drink in hand.

The sushi is delicious, maybe the best I've ever had. No shortage of fresh seafood when you're surrounded by the ocean.

I don't talk much during dinner, soaking in the relaxed atmosphere and sipping on my martini as I listen to Ophelia joke about her worst experiences with dating apps.

Once we finish eating, the empty sushi containers get tossed in the recycling. Glasses get drained.

Ophelia heads up to bed first, followed by Avery soon after. Juliet takes a call from Gavin—her on-again, off-again boyfriend—and wanders toward the sunporch.

I go upstairs to let Scout out of his crate, then bring him down and out onto the deck. While he sniffs around the beach grass, I settle in one of the Adirondack chairs. The animal rescue didn't know much about Scout's backstory, but I'm guessing this is his first visit to the ocean. So far, his highlights seem to be digging in the sand and chasing seagulls.

There's a soft swish, and Keira steps out onto the deck, closing the sliding door behind her. She tightens the white sweater wrapped around her shoulders as she takes the seat next to mine.

The sun's disappearance has dropped the outside temperature by at least ten degrees. Paired with the breeze wafting off the water, it's chilly out.

I run my finger around the rim of the martini glass that has an inch of liquid left, smearing the prints from my lip gloss. My feet are falling asleep, propped up on the railing, but I don't move them. I just stare out at the moon-drenched sea.

"I never want to leave," I confess. "I forgot how perfect this place is."

"I'd get bored," Keira says. "I'm jealous you ended up in Boston."

"Open up a second location of The Franklin," I suggest.

She groans. "I'm still exhausted from getting the first one off the ground."

"That's what I'm saying. Just relax here. Look out at the ocean and listen to the waves."

"Maybe *you* should move out here."

I laugh once. "I can't."

"You can do whatever you want, Elle."

"There's not a lot of legal work on most islands."

Keira fishes the olive out of her martini glass and pops it into her mouth. "And no fancy brownstone or fancy job or fancy boyfriend."

I exhale. "We're taking a break."

"You and Prescott?"

"No. Me and my fancy townhouse."

She snorts. "What happened?"

I swallow more salty gin. "I don't know. It just … happened." My finger rubs the rim again, until it squeaks. "He was annoyed I hadn't told him about this trip."

"You didn't tell him about this trip?"

"Nope." I pop the *P*.

"I put *plus-ones allowed* in the email mostly for you, you know. I wanted to meet him."

"It's a girls' weekend."

"Only because Gavin pissed Juliet off, and Ophelia has terrible luck with dating apps, and Tuck is obsessed with the new renovation."

"What's the new renovation?"

"The old Warren house. He's planning to flip it."

"Oh. Cool."

Scout bounds up the stairs, plopping down on the wood planks next to my feet. I lean down to brush sand off his fur.

"Tuck texted earlier. Some materials he needs got delayed … so he might come tomorrow."

"That's great," I say.

"He might bring Ryder."

I freeze, glad I'm bent over so Keira can't see my face. I assumed Tucker knew about Ryder's release. Figured that meant Keira did too. I even considered it might come up at some point this weekend.

I was absolutely not expecting to *see* Ryder this weekend.

My stomach lurches, the gin and sushi threatening to make a reappearance.

"Elle?"

I force my spine to straighten. Paste a smile on my face. "I heard you. I was just ... surprised."

"I'm not sure if he's coming. I just wanted to ... I thought you should know."

"Yeah. Thanks."

"Are you okay with Ryder coming? Because I can tell Tuck—"

"Of course I'm okay with Ryder coming." The lie tugs at the stitches in my chest. "It was forever ago. And it's nice that he and Tuck still get together. That they're still friends."

My mind is racing as fast as my heart. I'm not even aware of half the crap spilling out of my mouth.

"He's working for Tuck. On the Warren project."

A weak "Oh" is all I can think to say.

I drain the rest of my martini. The soundtrack of the waves is no longer calming. It sounds like they're pounding the shore, raging and riled.

I last less than a minute before the curiosity is too much to contain. "Have you seen him?"

"Yeah. He was at the jobsite when I stopped by a few days ago."

"How-how did he look?"

"*Hot*. Like all he did in prison was work out."

I huff. "That's not—I meant like ... happy. Did he seem ... okay at least?"

"He seemed a little pissed off. When I got there, he was throwing stuff around the backyard. But he was nice. Thanked me for the coffee, like, three times. Seemed normal. But I'd never really talked to him before. That was always ... you."

"Right." I start stroking Scout's fur again, hoping it'll help calm my sprinting heart. "Well, I should get to bed. This guy loves to wake up early."

"He asked about you."

I freeze halfway out of the chair. "He did?"

"Uh-huh."

Keira is watching me closely, and I'm too stunned to act indifferent.

"What-what did he say?"

"Just asked how you were. I told him you were good, that you'd just graduated law school. That was it."

"Oh."

"Kinda interesting, how your relationships run into trouble whenever Ryder James returns to town. First Archer, now Prescott."

I unfreeze long enough to send Keira a sharp look for that insinuation. "This is different. Pres and I … it's just a transition period after law school. It has nothing to do with Ryder."

"You knew he was out though."

"Yeah. Nin—I saw the article in the paper."

I've never told Keira or Juliet about my visits to Ryder's mom, and this feels like the exact wrong moment to bring them up.

I fake a yawn, then stand. "Thanks for dinner. Sushi was delicious."

Keira waves my appreciation away. "Of course. Tomorrow night, there's this new bar I want to go to. So, rest up."

"Sounds good," I reply. "Night."

"Night, Elle."

I head inside and upstairs, not relaxing until I'm lying under the covers, replaying my conversation with Keira.

So much for being a restful weekend away from my law books. If Ryder shows up … I have no clue how I'll handle that. I figured I'd see him at Keira and Tuck's wedding—months from now. As two people out of hundreds. Not in a small group—tomorrow.

What bothers me most about my conversation with Keira is, she's right—my relationships always run into problems around Ryder. Mostly because he always makes other guys seem like consolation prizes. By comparison, they were less. Less excitement. Less passion. Less … love.

And I resent Ryder for it.

Just not as much as I resent him for never picking me back.

12
THEN

Elle

Loud laughter filters in from the backyard as I heap more roasted potatoes onto my plate. They're the tiny, perfectly round kind, almost impossible to cut. It'll give me something to do for the rest of dinner.

Archer glances at me as I walk out onto the patio, his smile small and a little tentative. It's just the two of us tonight—well, the two of us and our parents. But no loud friends. No rap music. No distraction from the few words we've exchanged since his family arrived two hours ago.

It's Mrs. Hathaway's birthday. My mom went all out with the food, spending most of the day cooking in the kitchen.

"How's senior year going for you, Elle?" Mr. Hathaway asks after swallowing a bite of steak.

"Good, thanks," I respond.

Why is *school* always the topic adults ask about?

Mr. Hathaway nods. "Still getting those straight A's?"

"She sure is," my dad says proudly.

My lips curve into the expected smile before I reach out for my water glass.

"And balancing student council with cheerleading," my dad continues. "Only reason she's not doing Mock Trial this year is that it conflicts with everything else she already has going on. She's taking an Architecture elective instead."

"Architecture, really?" Mrs. Hathaway says. "How interesting."

"Tell her about the class, Elle," my mom encourages.

I'm too busy staring at my dad. We haven't discussed school since the first day of classes. And yet he managed to make it sound like he's the most involved parent to ever exist. It's a special, annoying talent of his.

"It's, uh … we've mostly observed buildings and conveyed our observations into sketches. Next week, we're translating on-site measurements of a building into scaled drawings and adding design elements based on style and symmetry."

A beat of silence follows my explanation.

"Well, it sounds very interesting," Mrs. Hathaway tells me. "Maybe you'll pursue architecture instead of ending up in law school."

I glance at my dad. He's sipping wine, appearing unconcerned by the suggestion. Confident I'll follow through on the plan that's been in place for as long as I can remember.

"Maybe," I say.

"Archer, what elective are you taking this semester?" my mom asks.

Archer straightens from his slouch at the opposite end of the table. "Uh, Pottery."

"How fun. Is your mom going to get a mug as a birthday gift?" my mom asks.

"We'll see," Archer replies. "It's still in the shaping stage."

"I'm trying to get Walker to relax his policy a bit," Mr. Hathaway tells my dad, loud enough for us all to hear. "Rather than playing with clay, Archer could use the extra football practice. Any college recruiter is going to laugh in my face with the stats he's put up so far this season."

Archer's expression resembles a marble statue as he glowers at his plate.

"These potatoes are delicious, Mom," I say, attempting to cut into one. It slides away into the pile of dressing left behind by my salad.

"Yes, everything was incredible, Frances," Mrs. Hathaway says.

Murmured agreement sounds around the table, and my mom beams.

We finish eating and sing "Happy Birthday" to Mrs. Hathaway. My dad disappears into his study with Mr. Hathaway. My mom stands to clear the dishes, and I rise too.

She waves my hands away. "You keep Archer company."

My mom and Mrs. Hathaway head inside, chattering the whole time.

I slump back in my seat, watching the leaves dangling from the wooden terrace dance in the slight breeze.

"Fun dinner," Archer comments dryly.

"Yep."

"I've barely seen you all week."

"I know. I've been busy."

And actively avoiding him. He showed up here the day after Maddie's party with soup, saying he hoped I was feeling better. We watched a movie, and I spent the entire time trying to come up with the right words to end things. Before I could, one of his buddies called, and he left. Since then, all we've done is exchange a few words at school.

Archer exhales. "Yeah. Me too. My dad has me running extra drills when I get home from practice each night."

"That sucks."

"Caught Watson talking to that Two kid a few days ago," he tells me. "Guy caught a *can of beer* at a party, and they act like he's Tom Brady. Be nice if the guys had a little faith in me."

I stiffen, certain *that Two kid* is Ryder. Literally bite my tongue to avoid mentioning *the guys* have watched Archer fail for three seasons. Faith runs out eventually. It doesn't help that this year seems to be following the same pattern as years past—rusty start, followed by extra drills and a burst of determination, then deflating into blaming receivers, and skipping practices. It seems like we're rapidly approaching phase three.

Archer looks around the backyard. "Too bad your folks never put in a pool. Warm enough for a swim." He glances at me and grins. "Miss seeing you in a bikini."

My answering smile is forced.

Archer is attractive. Classically handsome. But I can't say I'm dying to see him shirtless.

I thought that apathy was because I'd known him since we were toddlers in diapers. Because we'd been dating for months and so the thrill of newness had worn off.

But I think those are excuses. That chemistry is this mystical force that can't be created or duplicated. It's there, or it's not, and you don't get to choose which. Or with who you experience it.

Archer shoves away from the table and stands. "Come on. Let's play some H-O-R-S-E."

Reluctantly, I stand too. Basketball is better than just sitting here, I guess.

Archer heads into the garage to grab a ball while I pull my hair back into a braid.

"Ladies first," he says, bouncing the ball to me.

I catch it, which bodes well for my chances of winning. When I was little, I'd wait in the driveway for my dad to get home from work, and we'd shoot around some. I'm decent, and last time we played, Archer wasn't any better at basketball than football.

"Who said I'm a lady?" I ask, smirking.

Archer snorts. "You're a virgin who always makes high honor roll."

A vein in my temple pulses. He's insecure because I won't have sex with him, but that doesn't make the belittlement okay.

"How do you know I didn't have sex with Perry?" I ask.

Archer laughs like the idea is ludicrous. "He would have told me. *Any* guy would have told me, rubbed my face in it."

Not any guy.

I smile, suddenly so grateful to my younger self for choosing Ryder as my first. He wasn't the obvious choice. Keira and Juliet would have tried to talk me out of it, which is why I never told them. But he was the right choice.

I take the first shot, my grin spreading wider when it swishes through the basket.

Archer grabs the ball and strolls over, stopping about a foot away.

"Not from there. From *here*, behind the line."

He rolls his eyes. "Jesus, Elle. You always have to be such a rule follower?"

"You're the one trying to cheat," I snap.

Another eye roll before he takes the shot.

He misses, and a petty part of me wants to smile.

We alternate taking shots in silence, the bounce of the basketball against the asphalt the only sound aside from the occasional street noise.

I make a three-pointer, then pass the ball to Archer. He has four letters. If he misses this shot, he loses.

So, part of me isn't surprised when he drops the ball and reaches for my hand instead, tugging me over to the side of the garage.

"I'm sorry," he says, resting one hand against the shingles as he leans toward me. "I shouldn't have brought up you being a virgin. That was a dick move."

I don't disagree. And I'm so tempted to tell him the truth—that I'm not one—but it's none of his business. Not to mention, it'll prompt a whole bunch of questions I don't want to answer. Archer already has a vendetta against Ryder because of football. Finding out I had sex with him will make that a thousand times worse.

He leans closer. I let him kiss me for a few seconds, then turn my head to the left.

Archer huffs. "Come on, Elle. I'll stop mentioning sex. If you want to wait, that's fine. But now, you won't even kiss me?"

"I'm not in the mood."

"Let me change that." His hand lands on my hip.

"No." I push his chest, and he doesn't budge. "Archer, I mean it." I shove his chest harder, adrenaline spiking through my system. I'm breathing heavier now than I was when we were playing. "I-I need some space."

Archer scoffs as he steps away, turning and retrieving the basketball from the spot it rolled to in the grass. "I don't fucking get you, Elle. I gave you space all week, hoping you'd reach out, and you just take it. I try to spend time around you; you ask for space. What the hell do you want from me?"

Nothing.

There's never going to be a good time to do this.

"I want to break up."

He stares at me, his expression absolutely incredulous. "Unbelievable."

"I'm sorry if—"

"Nah." Archer shakes his head. "Don't do that. Don't *apologize* for dating me."

"I-I just think we're better off as friends."

"Friends," Archer states flatly.

I nod.

He flings the basketball toward the garage door. I flinch when the rubber slams into aluminum.

"No thanks. Have fun telling our moms."

I stare after him as he stalks around the side of the house toward the front drive. That's the best he can come up with?

Although I am dreading it.

I blow out a long breath, then head for the French doors that connect the patio to the kitchen. My mom and Mrs. Hathaway are standing in the kitchen, sipping from full glasses of wine and giggling. The dinner dishes sit in a dirty pile in the sink.

"Hey, honey," my mom says, spotting me. She glances behind me. "Where's Archer?"

"Dunno. We broke up. I'm going to Keira's."

I breeze past their shocked expressions, snagging my car keys from the hook by the front door and heading outside. My convertible is the only car in the roundabout, which makes me think Archer had keys on him and took off. Great. Him stranding his parents at my parents' house will inevitably be considered my fault for breaking up with him.

Keira only lives three blocks away. I could easily walk, but blaring music on the short drive here is somewhat therapeutic.

Mrs. Parker answers the front door. "Elle! How lovely to see you."

"Hi, Mrs. Parker. Is Keira home?"

"She's upstairs. Come in." She steps to the side for me to enter, then turns toward the staircase. "Keira! Elle's here!"

My phone vibrates in my pocket. I pull it out and smile at the new message.

KEIRA: *Come up.*

"She said to come up," I tell Mrs. Parker.

Keira's mom shakes her head. "You kids and your gadgets. Let me know if you girls need anything."

"I will. Thanks."

I head upstairs and down the hallway, tapping lightly on Keira's closed door.

It opens a few seconds later.

One sec, Keira mouths at me, gesturing for me to enter.

I walk into her bedroom and take a cross-legged seat on the mattress, watching as she shuts the door and smiles.

"Yeah, that sounds good," she says. "I'll, uh, talk to you then. Okay." She smiles. "Bye."

"Who was that?" I ask as she drops her phone on her desk and then joins me on the bed.

"Tucker."

"Tucker? Tucker *Franklin*?"

"Uh-huh. He gave me his number at Maddie's party, and we've

been talking. He's nice."

"You're blushing," I tease.

"Fine. Nice *and* cute."

"Do your parents know?"

The Parkers aren't as obviously snobby as my parents are, but I'm guessing they'd have a lot to say about their only daughter dating a guy from the trailer park.

"No. We're just flirting. It's no big deal." She sips from a can of seltzer, then glances at me. "What are you doing here? I thought you had that dinner with Archer and his parents tonight."

"I did it."

Keira gasps, her eyes wide. "You had sex with him?"

"What? No. I *broke up* with him."

"Oh my God. How did it go?"

"*Great.*"

She winces. "That bad?"

"He threw a basketball at the garage door, then took off and left his parents at my house."

"Well, he's always been a sore loser. Remember the game against Alleghany last year?"

"Yeah, I sure do."

"I've got some vodka hidden in my closet," Keira tells me.

I lie back on her bed, relaxing against the same pink comforter she's had forever. "I drove here."

"You can spend the night," she offers.

"Thanks, but I should get back soon. My parents will want to … discuss tonight's events."

"Your dad won't care."

"My mom will though."

Keira's silent for a moment, knowing I'm right. "She'll get over it. She wants you to be happy."

I grab one of the pillows on her bed, playing with the tassel in the corner. "Why didn't you tell me you and Tucker have been *flirting*?"

"You've had a lot going on. And I don't know what it is really. We don't talk at school, but we text during lunch and stuff. It's been kind of fun, keeping it a secret, you know?"

I do know. I know exactly what she means.

"Have you guys kissed?"

"Yeah. At Maddie's party."

"Have you met his friends?"

"Other Twos, you mean?"

"I guess." I keep fiddling with the tassel.

"No. He was alone at the party, and we haven't hung out in person since. We just text and talk on the phone."

"What do you guys talk about?"

"Random stuff. He's not one of those guys who just talks about himself and expects you to listen, you know? He's a big baseball fan. His mom is gone, so he just lives with his dad. He works at his uncle's garage. He's building a coffee table out of scrap stuff he found. He mentions Ryder James a lot." Keira reaches for her seltzer again.

"I had a thing with him." I didn't plan the words; they just came out.

A few drops of water land on my arm as Keira sputters.

"Keira! Gross!"

"With *Tucker*?" Her voice flies through a couple of octaves, and I know she's underplaying how much she likes him.

"*No*. With Ryder."

"*You* had a thing with *Ryder James*?"

"Uh-huh."

"*When?*"

"Freshman year. And, like, a little since he's been back. There have been a few moments."

"I ... what do *you guys* talk about?"

"Everything."

"Wow. I—wow. I get the physical thing—he's hot. But he's so scowly and serious all the time."

"Not when you get to know him."

"How come you never mentioned it?" she asks.

I shrug the best I can while lying down. "Same reason as you. It was fun, keeping it a secret. And then he left, so ..."

There's a knock on the door.

"Keira?" Mrs. Parker says.

"Yeah?" Keira calls out.

"Mrs. Clarke just called. She needs Elle home for a family matter."

Keira and I exchange a glance, both knowing exactly what that is.

I sigh and roll off her bed. "I'll talk to you later, okay?"

"Yeah. Good luck."

I nod, then leave to face my mom's disappointment.

13
NOW

Ryder

lamshells crunch as Tuck's truck rolls toward a three-story house. The wooden shingles covering the exterior are weathered gray from the sea air, which is blowing in from the open window. We must be really close to the water.

"You call this a *cottage*?" I ask.

Tucker grins as he turns off the truck and hops out of the cab. "Nice place, right? Keira's folks hardly ever come here. You still surf?"

"It's been a long time. Not since I lived in Jacksonville."

"We should go. I'll kick your ass, but that'll be good for my ego."

I shake my head, smiling as we grab our bags out of the truck bed. We'll only be here for one night, so I barely brought anything.

"Don't let me forget to take you to the clam shack," Tuck tells me as we walk along the stone pavers. Each slab of the path lies perfectly straight, the lush grass surrounding them neatly trimmed. The landscaping at this place is immaculate.

Everywhere I look is pristine, and it's not just the contrast from spending a lot of time at a construction site lately.

"I don't like clams," I inform Tuck.

"You'll like the fritters," he replies confidently. "They're crispy and fried and, *fuck*, just so good."

"I'll try *one*."

"There's also this new brewery I've been wanting to go to."

I grin. "That sounds more like it."

The smile slides right off my face as we round the trimmed hedges and I'm blinded by red paint. A shiny convertible is parked next to a vintage Range Rover in the two spots to the left of the front porch.

"There are some old surfboards in the garage that we can—" Tuck stops talking when he realizes that I'm no longer walking. He glances between me and the convertible, rubbing the back of his neck nervously. "I wasn't sure if you'd still come. That's why I didn't tell you."

I'm not sure I would have either. An unpleasant prickling sensation creeps along my skin as I stare at the unmistakable car.

I knew I'd see Elle eventually. But I was expecting some warning. And I thought the reunion would be at Tuck's wedding. Not … here, under very different circumstances.

"You should have told me."

I'm apprehensive about seeing Elle. I'm certain she doesn't want to see me. Not after the way we left things. The way she told no one about, shielding me from the crimination I deserve.

"Sorry," Tuck says, shame-faced. "I just … seemed like you might need this."

He's referring to how I've acted like a hermit since returning to Fernwood. I go to work, and that's pretty much it. Tuck isn't the only one who's noticed. My mom and Cormac were thrilled when I mentioned going away for the weekend. Worried about me, or relieved to have more space in the cramped trailer, or both.

"It's fine," I tell Tuck, because what else can I say?

He drove us from the ferry, so I can't take off alone. He's my boss, so I can't make up some work excuse. I'm literally stranded on an island.

I've spent seven years telling everyone—including Elle—that I'm over her. I convinced a part of myself it was true. But my palms are sweating, and my breathing is too fast, and I'm nervous, and none of that feels like indifference.

The front door is unlocked.

I follow Tuck into a soaring entryway. The floor is wide planks of honey-hued wood. The walls are painted a cream color, decorated with watercolor paintings of sailboats.

This place had to have cost several million, easily.

Voices drift from the left, the direction Tuck heads in.

My heart beats faster as we pass through a living room with a huge fireplace and a full wall of bookshelves, filled with leather-bound spines. Then a long dining room table before turning a corner and entering the kitchen.

I spot Keira's beaming face first, though the smile is mostly meant for Tuck. She's standing at the stove, flipping pancakes, a dazzling view of the ocean visible through the wall of windows behind her. This place is right on the beach. Make that ten million.

Two women I don't recognize are seated at the breakfast nook in the corner of the kitchen.

"Hey! You made it!" Keira abandons the pancakes to kiss Tuck, then shoots me a smile. "You guys made good time."

"No traffic and smooth water," Tuck tells her, ambling over to a cabinet. "Coffee, Ry?"

"Yeah. Thanks." I drop my duffel on the floor next to the spot where Tuck left his.

"Ryder, these are two of my best friends. Avery, Ophelia, this is Ryder, Tuck's best friend."

"Hi! I'm Avery." The woman with curly blonde hair stands and walks over. Her smile is wide and bright. "Nice to finally meet you. Tucker talks about you all the time."

"True," Tuck says, setting a steaming mug down on the counter in front of me.

I mouth, *Thanks*, and he nods.

"And I'm Ophelia." A woman with auburn hair pulled back in a long ponytail walks over as well, so we're all clustered around the kitchen island.

"Nice to meet you both," I say.

"Avery and I went to college together," Keira tells me. "And Ophelia is my pastry chef."

I glance at Ophelia again. If she works in Fernwood, she's probably heard a lot about me. But there's nothing but open friendliness visible on her face.

"Best job ever," Ophelia states. "I mean, look at this place. It's—"

A high-pitched bark is the only warning before a blur of fur shoots into the kitchen. The dog—I'm assuming it's a dog because of the bark, not because I can get a good look at it—races around the kitchen twice, yapping excitedly.

For some reason, it stops next to my feet, whining until I bend down to pet it. A wet tongue darts out, coating my cheek with saliva.

I lift my shirt to wipe it away, more amused than annoyed, then glance at Tuck. "You guys got a dog?"

"He's mine."

I stiffen, swallow, then stand.

Elle's standing at the bottom of the staircase, wearing a pink silk pajama set. Her dark hair is loose around her shoulders, a little messy and a little wavy.

She looks different. More reserved and more composed than the last time I saw her. There's no trust or warmth on her face—the way she used to look at me—just cool indifference.

She looks different, but she's so *Elle.* So achingly familiar. So perfectly unique. Exactly what I've looked for in so many faces that have never been quite right.

Technically, I've been home for two weeks.

This moment—standing in the kitchen of a house I've never visited before—is the first time I've felt it.

I jam my hands into my pockets, feeling like an awkward teenager. "Hi, Elle."

"Hello, Ryder. Nice to see you." Her tone is polite and inscrutable. Detached, like talking to me is an obligation. Like this conversation is simply an item on her daily to-do list. *Greet Ryder—check.*

"Nice to see you too."

She stares at me for a second longer, and then her gaze drops to the dog at my feet. A flash of annoyance breaks through the mask. If I had to guess, I'd say she's not thrilled her dog seems to like me.

Elle taps her thigh. "Scout. Come."

The dog—Scout—bounds over to her, and she clips the leash she's holding onto its collar. They walk toward the French doors that open out onto a large deck. Stairs lead down from the deck to the sand.

"Don't take too long. Pancakes are almost ready," Keira says.

Elle glances at her, and they hold a silent conversation I'm pretty sure involves me. I'm positive Keira gave her some warning I was coming. Elle's a good actress when she wants to be, but not *that* good.

Keira starts offloading pancakes from the griddle, and Tuck passes out plates. Avery and Ophelia load up theirs, then return to the nook in the corner.

"I thought vacation was supposed to include sleeping in." Juliet Mason strolls into the kitchen, wearing a pajama set very similar to Elle's. Hers is an icy shade of blue.

"No one woke you up," Keira tells her.

"Elle's loud dog did." Juliet glances at Tuck, then me. Her eyebrows fly upward. Apparently, my arrival wasn't a group conversation. "What happened to girls' weekend?"

"I never said it was a girls' weekend."

"Elle did. That's why she didn't bring Prescott."

I take a sip of coffee. It's no surprise Elle is dating someone. Hearing she is wasn't supposed to feel like a swift kick to the stomach though.

"I told you Gavin was welcome," Keira tells Juliet.

"I know." Juliet looks at me. "Hi, Ryder."

"Hi, Juliet."

"Long time."

I nod. "Yeah."

Juliet studies me for a few more seconds, then grabs a plate.

I wander over to the doors that lead out onto the deck, staring out at the view. It's stunning, sand and blue water stretching as far into the distance as you can see. Dancing blades of beach grass frame the bottom of the scene.

Elle's standing close to the edge of the water, staring toward the horizon, while Scout runs circles around her. Her hair flies wildly in the wind. It's shorter now than it was in high school, just brushing past the bottom of her shoulders.

"You forgot this on the counter." Tuck approaches and presses the mug into my hand. He glances outside, noticing where I'm looking. "That went well."

I nod.

But I actually feel like it couldn't have gone worse.

"What's the point of this again?" Tuck asks me.

"It'll keep you from slipping off the board when you're paddling toward waves," I reply. "And help your feet keep traction on your board."

Not that it'll be necessary today. The surf is practically nonexistent. We'll be paddling out simply to bob in the ocean, I'm betting.

But Tuck is excited about surfing, so I haven't burst his bubble about the lack of decent waves. Maybe we'll luck out.

I finish waxing my board and sit back on my heels, glancing around. I don't know if this is a private beach or if it's just early enough in the summer season, but there's no one else around.

"Pretty sure Ophelia has a thing for you," Tuck comments.

I huff a laugh as I tug my wetsuit over my shoulders and yank the zipper up. "Yep."

Ophelia's flirting wasn't much of a distraction from Elle's silence, unfortunately.

I'd forgotten what it was like to be in a room with Elle, to have my attention pulled to one spot like a magnet's force. She's a distraction like no other.

But I'm trying to follow her lead and make this weekend as not awkward as possible. Elle's ignoring me, so I spent breakfast fighting the urge to look at her.

"You gonna go for it?"

"No," I reply.

"Why not? Ophelia is great. Her lemon meringue pie is one of the best things I've ever tasted. She lives in Fernwood, right by Keira's place. And you know what they say about redheads ..."

"What do they say about redheads?" I ask.

"They're ... fun?"

I shake my head.

"It's been seven years, Ry. She's dating some lawyer. She won't care."

I know it's been seven years. I know she won't care. And that'll hurt.

Not that I'm admitting that to Tuck. He's worried enough about me already.

"I didn't come here to hook up, man."

"You should've," he tells me. "You can't be getting laid in that trailer much."

I snort. He wouldn't even believe me if I told him how long it's been since I had sex.

"I'm a mess, Tuck. You don't want me getting involved with Keira's friend and employee, trust me."

He tilts his head, considering. "Yeah, you're probably right. Maybe you'll meet a local at the bar tonight."

I stand. "We doing this or what?"

"Yeah." He stands too, glancing toward the house. "Hey, we got a cheering section."

I follow his gaze to the deck, where the five women are sitting. Only one isn't looking this way, and I know without squinting that it's Elle.

God, she's stubborn.

I turn toward the water. "Great. They can watch us imitate ducks."

"What the hell does that mean?" Tuck asks, zipping up his suit and then following me.

I flinch when the water hits my feet. Damn, it's cold. "It means there's no surf, man."

"What do you mean? There are waves."

I don't bother replying, just duck under as soon as it's deep enough to.

He'll figure out what I mean soon enough.

14
THEN

Ryder

lack grease clings stubbornly to my skin, no matter how harshly I scrub at my palms. I give up on the stains, tossing the rag away, and climb into the driver's seat to turn the key. The engine roars to life on the first try, and I smile, satisfied, as I clear the sweat from my forehead with the back of my arm.

Before Hank hired me, I knew next to nothing about fixing cars. I've picked up more than the basics pretty damn quick.

"Yo, James! Come on!"

I shut the car off and glance toward the doorway. Tuck is standing there, slouched and impatient.

"Come where?"

"We're headed to the pond."

I laugh once, relaxing against the seat. "You've gotta be kidding."

"Nope." Tuck pops the *P* obnoxiously. "Don't tell me cold water doesn't sound amazing right now."

It does.

Three weeks into September, and summer feels closer than ever.

It must be at least eighty-five out today, and the garage doesn't have air-conditioning, aside from the office where Hank sits and customers pay.

I've been sweaty since I showed up for work this morning, and replacing the shift solenoids on this SUV has taken me most of the day. But I'd like my cold water to come with salt and waves. It's been over a month since I last surfed, and I never expected to miss it as much as I do. Everything else was easy to leave behind.

The pond is on the One side of town. Going there will likely involve lots of territory pissing and muttered insults I'm not really in the mood for.

"I'm good. Still got stuff to finish up here."

"Like I didn't just hear it start. Hurry up. Everyone's waiting."

Tuck disappears from the doorway without giving me a chance to respond. To refuse.

Dick. Dick who's my ride home. It's not that far to walk, but it'll feel like a marathon in this heat.

I swear under my breath, then climb out of the car.

Tuck is waiting in his green truck when I walk out of the bay. Phoenix is in the car behind with a few other guys from the garage.

I give Tuck a *one sec* gesture, then head into the office.

Hank has his glasses on, peering at a computer screen.

I toss the Toyota's keys on the counter. "All set."

Hank leans back in his swivel chair. Some piece of it creaks. "Impressive, son."

I nod, hiding the visceral reaction I have to the endearment. It just reminds me of my dad. "You're a good teacher."

"More than that. I've had guys here for years who would have taken longer to make that repair."

I smile. "I'll see you tomorrow."

"Sounds good. Have a good night."

"Thanks." I glance at the clock. It's already four p.m., later than I thought.

Tuck sighs dramatically when I climb into the cab of his truck. "*Finally.*"

"What are the chances I can talk you out of this?" I ask, clicking my seat belt into place.

"Zero," he replies, pulling onto the street.

I sigh, settling back against the seat. "I'm not wearing a suit."

"Relax, princess. I'm not either. We're stopping to change."

"Okay."

"You're coming, Ry." Tuck says it like he knows exactly what I'm thinking—a ride home means I won't have to go after all.

I groan. "*Why?*"

"You could use some fun."

"At the *pond*? You know Ones will be there. Wait." I look over. "Is that what this is about? That girl you've been texting?"

"I have no idea if Keira will be there," Tuck tells me.

"Mmhmm." I glance back out the window, not sure if I believe him.

We reach my trailer a few minutes later.

"I'll be back in five," Tuck tells me.

I nod, then climb out of the truck. The trailer is empty when I enter it, no sign of my mom or Cormac. I have no clue where either of them is. They each have their own routine established. It's been just the two of them for the past year, since Cormac's dad packed up and left—again.

My mom has always done her own thing, but my little brother's schedule is more of a mystery. And concerning. He hasn't called me to pick him up again, but that doesn't mean he's been staying out of trouble.

I change into board shorts, scrub at my hands again, then head outside to wait for Tuck. He's right; I haven't done much besides work and school lately. I've avoided hanging out with Phoenix after the failed burger trip. Tuck and I spent last night watching movies with Reese, but I haven't hung out much with anyone, except the two of them.

Tuck smiles when he sees me waiting, cranking up some country song on the radio.

The drive to the pond takes about ten minutes. Tuck parks his truck behind a long line of other cars. We definitely aren't the only ones here.

The "path" to the pond is basically just trampled grass and bent branches that leads to the clearing surrounding the water. There are a few benches and a couple of picnic tables, but not much else around.

I spot Phoenix and a few other familiar faces underneath a tree and point them out to Tuck. We head in that direction. Reese is part of the group, which is a surprise.

I sink down in the grass next to her, leaning back on my elbows. "Hey."

"Hey yourself." Reese is busy eating grapes out of a plastic bag.

I squint over. "Wasn't expecting to see you here."

"Ditto."

"Tuck," I explain.

"He's a real dictator."

I snort, glancing around. I don't recognize anyone in the other groups camped around the water.

Tall maples shade the edge of the water, casting skinny reflections on the pond's surface. A tire swing hangs from the tallest one. The water looks clear, but I've never actually swum here. Dapples of sunshine filter down through the trees' leaves.

I've only been here once before, and it was freshman year. Elle has a photo from that trip as her phone background, and it's one of many parts of our conversation on Friday night that's haunted me.

Something hits me in the cheek.

"Oy!" I swat the air and glance at Reese, who's doubled over with silent laughter.

I pick up the grape from the grass and throw it back toward her. My aim is as good as hers, bouncing off her shoulder.

"Bet you can't do this," she tells me, tossing a grape in the air and catching it in her mouth.

"Try me," I say.

"Fine. Ready?"

"Ready."

She pitches another grape my way. I catch it neatly in my mouth, flashing Reese a satisfied grin before chewing and swallowing.

"Beginner's luck," she grumbles.

"He's weirdly coordinated," Tuck says, plopping down in the grass beside me. He went over to greet Phoenix and the other guys, which seemed unnecessary to me. We spent most of the day together. "You knew that."

"There's nothing *weird* about it," I tell him.

"Yo! Incoming."

I roll my head to look at Phoenix. He's focused on the opposite side of the pond, so of course the rest of us do too.

The group coming down the path is large, at least fifteen people.

My gaze goes straight to Elle, who's walking with several other girls. Archer Hathaway and a bunch of his football buddies are trailing a few feet behind, all of them headed toward a picnic table near the tire swing.

"This should be interesting," Reese comments, lying back on her elbows.

I glance at Tuck, who's keeping busy plucking blades of grass. I think that means Keira's part of the group, but I don't know what she looks like to confirm.

"Hathaway's looking rough," Roman comments. He's a fellow senior and Two. A cool guy, as far as I can tell, but I don't really know him that well.

"That's what going oh and five and getting dumped will do to you," Phoenix responds, chuckling. He's pulled out a joint, the sweet smoke replacing the scent of grass and sunshine.

My chin jerks in his direction, betraying my interest. "What are you talking about?"

"Football team hasn't won a single game this season." Nix shakes his head and blows more smoke. "You should really reconsider playing, James. It's past pathetic at this point."

I ignore the advice and ask, "Hathaway got dumped?"

Roman shrugs. "Supposedly. Hard to know with the Ones. They like to keep it all in the family, you know."

"He definitely got dumped," Zane says, taking the joint from Nix. "Hathaway is in my Spanish class, and all he does is bitch in English. Lately, it's been about Perry Welch moving in on his girl."

"Nah, she's fair game if they broke up," Roman replies. "Good for Welch. Didn't know he had those balls on him."

"Have you *seen* Elle Clarke?" Nix asks. "Every guy on the team must be taking a pass at that." He glances at Zane. "We should hit the postgame party this week, man. I bet I can talk Cruz into bringing some favors."

I glance at Tuck, who's watching me more closely than I'd like. He'd obviously already heard about Elle breaking up with her boyfriend, and I'm surprised he didn't tell me. I guess he believed me when I said I was over her, or he's been too wrapped up with Keira to mention it.

My feelings for Elle have always felt like a weakness. Like something to hide. Fleeting and temporary and never worth announcing.

If the guys keep discussing her, I'm liable to do something stupid. Like stake a claim on her.

I stand and shuck off my shirt. "I'm going in."

"Bottom is slimy," Reese warns me.

"Well, we came here to swim. Right, Tuck?"

He doesn't move from his spot in the grass. "Yeah, yeah. I'll be right there."

I snort, then head for the tire swing. There are a couple of guys treading water at the opposite end of the pond, but everyone else seems to be here to sunbathe.

I reach the edge of the pond, gripping the rope and staring at the flat surface of the water. It's impossible to tell how deep it is from here.

"You're blocking the swing."

I glance behind me, my hold on the rope tightening as I fight to keep my eyes above Elle's shoulders. "Hey."

"Hey." She pauses about a foot away. Her eyes are on me, not the swing or the pond. "What the hell happened to your hands?"

I release the rope. "Grease. From the garage. I was there all day."

"You should wear gloves."

"Probably. Makes it harder to handle tools though."

Elle makes a sound in the back of her throat, then glances at the tire. "So … you going or just thinking about it?"

"I heard some more gossip about you," I say instead of answering.

"Oh, yeah?" She crosses her arms, seriously testing my willpower as I fight to keep my gaze on her face. "About what exactly?"

"About you and Hathaway."

"Hmm." Elle tugs the hair tie out of her ponytail, snapping the elastic against her wrist. Her hair falls free, and all I can think about is sliding a hand into it.

"You broke up with him?" I ask, not managing to play it cool at all.

A breeze picks up, blowing some pieces of hair across her face and partially covering her expression. My fingers twitch with the urge to brush them away.

"Maybe he dumped me."

"Nah. Even Hathaway isn't that much of an idiot."

A smile plays with the corners of her lips. "Then what does that make you?"

I swallow. "An asshole."

Elle smirks, and the urge to kiss her is so strong that it burns.

I'm not an impulsive person. I've done plenty of things I shouldn't have. Said lots I shouldn't. But those were all choices. It was never about the desire being so strong that I couldn't resist.

Elle Clarke makes me reckless. Around her, I'm incapable of making careful choices.

I rub my jaw, trying to act like I'm still in control. Glance at the tire swing swaying slightly in the warm wind. "You jumping?"

"Yeah. Just wish it were higher."

"Higher?" I lift an eyebrow. "You an adrenaline junkie now or something?"

"Or something."

I lose the battle not to drop my attention, my focus falling farther south than I was supposed to look.

Elle's blue eyes are amused when I meet her gaze again. She tilts her head, dark strands spilling over her shoulder and slipping between the curves of her breasts.

And … fuck. I'm checking her out again.

I can feel the eyes on us. We're drawing attention from both our respective groups, standing here together and talking.

I shove my hands into the pockets of my board shorts, rocking back onto my heels and deliberating if the eyes on us should bother me. I thought they'd bother Elle. But she seems oblivious to the interest aimed this direction, her posture poised and relaxed as we stare at each other.

I nod toward the tire. "Go ahead."

"Were you asking or overhearing?" she says.

It takes me a second to realize what Elle is referring to. The blue bikini she's wearing is partly to blame. The rest is just … her, infiltrating and overwhelming all my senses. Muddling my thoughts.

"Does it matter? I asked *you*."

I care, is what I'm admitting. She broke up with her boyfriend, and I care. I'm hoping I'm not foolish for thinking it had something to do with me.

"You've also been avoiding me," she says.

Avoiding is a strong verb. I haven't made any effort to approach Elle since the Friday night I borrowed her car because I was certain she'd wake up on Saturday and regret every word we exchanged. Because I was sure any forgiveness was proof she no longer cared. Because she had a boyfriend.

"Something wrong with the swing?"

Elle breaks eye contact and glances behind me. Her posture stiffens, barely, but enough that I notice, shoulders tensing and chin lifting an inch.

Reese stops right beside me, propping a hand on her hip.

"Seems fine," I answer.

"What's the delay then?" Reese asks. "You usually move pretty fast, Ry."

I glance at her, but Reese isn't looking at me. She's focused on Elle, who's staring right back. I have this weird urge to step between them while also feeling like I'm stuck in the middle already.

I clear my throat, wishing it were a louder sound that might cut through the tension that's appeared out of nowhere. "You know Elle?"

"Not really." Reese's tone is cool. "And I didn't know *you* knew her."

She's expecting me to deny it. An awkward silence lingers when I don't.

"You jumping?" I ask Reese.

"If you jump, Jack."

I smile. Reese has a thing for classic films and has roped me and Tucker into watching plenty. Last night was a Hitchcock marathon, but *Titanic* is her all-time favorite.

She smiles back, proud I caught the reference.

"You chicken out, James? It's gotta be, what? A five-foot drop into calm water?"

I snort as Tuck completes our usual trio, his curious gaze landing on Elle the same way Reese's did. Minus a lot of antagonism. Like I told Elle, he's always taken the *us versus them* mentality a lot less seriously than the rest of our neighborhood. Unless they give him a reason not to, he gets along with everyone.

"Hey. I'm Tuck."

I watch as my best friend holds a hand out to Elle, reading her reaction closely. I've never seen her talk to a Two before.

"Hey." She smiles back at him. "I'm Elle."

Tuck chuckles. "I know who you are, Clarke."

"Right. Small towns."

"That's not what I meant," Tuck replies, his grin growing.

Elle glances at me, a move Tuck doesn't miss. I'm guessing Reese doesn't either, but I don't check to confirm. She's going to have questions later.

I look at Elle instead. "You can go first."

She rolls her eyes. "Ladies first?"

"Sure." I pause. "If there was a lady present."

Reese and Tuck both look at me like I'm crazy, but Elle laughs. The sound hits me square in the center of my chest.

Elle steps toward the swing. I spot the divot in the grass a split second before her foot lands on it, grabbing her hand and tugging her toward the left. Straight into my body. She collides with my bare chest. We stand like that, her pulse thundering against my thumb as my fingers encircle her delicate wrist. Probably from surprise. But I flatter myself and think of how many times she blushed that Friday night. Maybe it has something to do with me touching her too.

She's not the only one affected.

All I can think about is the last time we were this close to each other wearing this little clothing.

"Typical," she says.

I glance down at Elle, who's looking up at me. "You're welcome."

"You can't resist catching. Doesn't matter what it is."

"It matters. You're heavier than a football."

Elle bites her bottom lip to keep the smile from forming. But she can't do anything about the creases of amusement that appear in the corners of her eyes. "*Much* heavier than a can of beer."

"You heard about that, huh?"

"Came up during my breakup actually."

"I'd say I'm sorry, but …"

"Yeah, I know. You're not." She steps back.

My hand drops reluctantly.

"You're a real hero, Ry," Reese says. "That hole had to be three inches deep at least."

I glance over and raise an eyebrow at her. She raises one right back, and I'm not sure what to make of it.

Elle grabs the rope and pulls it back, way farther than I expected.

"Elle …"

It feels like there's a rubber band squeezing my chest. The same panic as when she was staring down at that pool appears.

There could be rocks on the bottom. Sharp sticks. Who the hell knows what, aside from slime?

She glances over at me and winks. "Relax, Ry. You won't have to catch me."

Before I can respond, she's flying through the air. The band around my chest tightens as she lets go of the rope and spins. She flips twice, then drops cleanly into the water. I finally exhale when she breaks through the surface and starts swimming toward the edge.

Tuck reaches out to grab the swing as it returns to shore. "I should have made that bet a hundred."

I flip him off, but I'm pretty sure he's too busy climbing on the tire to notice.

15
NOW

Elle

A loud knock interrupts my deep breathing exercises.

"Elle! You said five minutes."

"I know; I know," I call back, scrambling to find my lip gloss in the bag of toiletries. "Almost ready."

"Okay. We'll be waiting outside," Keira says.

I hear her footsteps fade away.

Crap. I didn't realize I was actually holding things up.

I'd forgotten about the bar Keira had mentioned last night until it came up this afternoon. Everyone else was enthused about checking it out, so saying no didn't seem like much of an option. Juliet came upstairs to get ready an hour ago, whereas I put it off until the last minute. Juliet is the type of extrovert meant to live in a big city like Boston. She loves going places and doing things, whereas I'm more of a homebody.

My level of enthusiasm about this weekend has also plummeted in Ryder's presence.

I got through greeting him. Got through breakfast. He and

Tucker headed down to the beach to surf as soon as the pancakes got finished. I hung out on the deck with the rest of the girls, painting nails and drinking tea, before heading into town to do some shopping. I bought a new top that I'm wearing tonight. When we got back here, there was no sign of the guys. According to Keira, they went to a brewery.

And now, we're all headed to a bar.

A prospect I'm ridiculously nervous about. I don't even know why. With the exception of Ryder, these are all people I'm comfortable around. And Ryder might have broken my heart—more than once—but he's not a bad guy. Seven years seems like too long to hold a grudge for.

Then again, I'm not normal.

I find my lip gloss, slick a layer across my lips, and then release a long exhale as I appraise my appearance in the bathroom mirror.

I left my hair natural—if using product and my expensive hair dryer counts—and changed my jeans three times. Somehow, I feel both overdressed and underprepared.

Why has no one written a book about spending time around your ex, following an excruciating breakup and a seven-year absence? I'm flying blind here. Do I ignore him? Make polite chitchat? I have no idea what small talk with Ryder *is*. How do you discuss the mundane with someone you considered your soulmate?

I'm out of time to figure it out.

I slip Scout a treat in his crate, make sure I have my phone, and head downstairs. It's empty, suggesting I *am* the last one ready.

Embarrassment joins the anxiety I'm already experiencing. I hate being the high-maintenance girl who takes forever to get ready and makes everyone else wait.

"We have to take two cars," Keira tells me as I step out onto the front porch, where everyone is standing. "Do you mind driving?"

"No, of course not," I say, pulling my keys out of my clutch.

"She does mind," Juliet contradicts. "She needs to get *drunk*. Girl just graduated Harvard Law with a perfect GPA. She hasn't had fun in three years."

I roll my eyes.

"I don't mind driving home," Avery says.

"Elle hates it when other people drive her car," Juliet replies.

I choose this unfortunate moment to look at Ryder. He's leaning against the railing, looking devastatingly gorgeous in dark jeans and a blue button-down with the sleeves rolled up. Ophelia is standing right next to him, beaming at Ryder like he's the best sight she's ever seen.

Something cold and slimy and unfamiliar slithers in my stomach.

It's been a long time since I was jealous.

Seven years, to be exact.

"I don't hate it," I say. "Let's go." I stride toward my convertible without waiting for any more discussion. All of a sudden, I *really* want a drink.

Resentment bubbles beneath my skin. It's so fucking unfair that he *still* affects me this much. Time is supposed to heal wounds.

Juliet and Avery follow me. Keira, Tucker, Ryder, and Ophelia all climb into the Parkers' SUV that stays on the island year-round.

I catch Juliet glancing at me a few times as I drive toward the small downtown section, but she doesn't bring up Ryder. If *Juliet's* noticed I'm acting strangely around him, it's a bad sign. I adore her, but she has a tendency to be more focused on her own drama than anyone else's.

Downtown is just as scenic as it was a few hours ago. The brick sidewalks are lined with benches and buildings covered with white clapboard, decorated with American flags and boxes of colorful flowers. The bar we're headed to is down by the pier the ferry runs from, next to a popular seafood restaurant with a line that's spilling outside.

I find a spot on the street and park, rubbing my arms once I step outside my car. The temperature is dropping rapidly now that the sun is starting to set.

Juliet slings an arm over my shoulders as we crunch across the gravel parking lot that leads to the bar. It's already full of cars.

"You good?" she asks low enough for only me to hear.

"Of course!" My voice sounds good. Cheerful and unbothered.

There's something so miserable about acting happy when you're secretly struggling. So lonely and isolating. But I don't know what else to say. If time didn't work, I'm going to have to fake indifference toward Ryder until I actually feel it.

"Good." Juliet squeezes me, then drops her arm and slaps my left butt cheek. "Let's show the locals what they're missing, living on an island."

I shake my head as she skips ahead.

"She's a handful, huh?" Avery asks, catching up to me.

"She sure is," I say affectionately.

"Oh, there's everyone else."

I follow Avery's attention to the approaching group. Tucker and Keira are in front, holding hands. Ryder and Ophelia are a few steps behind, deep in conversation.

"I think Ophelia has a crush," Avery whispers conspiratorially. "I mean, good for her. He's *hot*." She giggles.

I force my frozen facial muscles to smile in case she looks over.

"Where's Juliet?" Keira asks, reaching us.

"Probably a few shots deep by now," I reply.

Keira rolls her eyes. "Right. Well, let's head in."

I stick to the front of the group, passing the tables in the roped-off section outside the bar and then heading inside. The bar is casual yet upscale, most of the interior reclaimed wood weathered to light gray. Starfish prints decorate the walls. A long bar top stretches the full length of the space, endless rows of glasses and expensive liquor behind it. It's packed inside, just like the full lot suggested.

"There's Juliet," I say, spotting her talking with two guys by one of the tall tables spread throughout the space. She waves. "I'm going to grab a drink," I tell Keira.

"Okay," she replies. "I'll go check in with Juliet. Maybe she's trying to get that table. We can take shifts, hanging on to it."

"Sounds good," I respond, then push my way toward the bar.

I just need … a minute. And a strong drink.

I barely adjusted to Ryder being here, and now, he's flirting with a girl he met less than twelve hours ago.

He has every right to. He was in prison for seven years, for fuck's sake. Getting drunk and getting laid are probably his two main priorities right now.

But I'm going to lie in bed tonight, possibly crying, imagining him in Ophelia's room down the hall from me.

Wondering if I'll have some sixth sense of what's happening in the same house as me.

Mourning the loss of everything that's lived and died between me and Ryder James for the thousandth time.

If my bloodstream is mostly tequila, it'll be a lot more bearable.

"Hey. What can I get for you?"

I stare at the bartender, his smile fading more with each second I stay silent, stuck in my own head.

"Uh, margarita," I answer. "Please."

"You got it." He moves on quickly, toward more talkative customers.

My drink appears a couple of minutes later. I opt to keep the tab open.

Juliet's right. I could use some fun. It's been a long time since I had a night out that wasn't a glass of wine at a networking event or a pint of beer after a study group. My life has turned into everything I once told myself it wouldn't be—predictable and bland.

A warm arm presses against mine. I don't jerk away the way I should from a stranger's touch, not realizing why until I glance over at the body beside mine.

I know him by heart.

I swallow, then take a hasty sip of my drink. It's delicious, the salt rim balancing the sour lime and smoky liquor.

"Cool spot," Ryder comments, glancing down the bar.

"Yep." I take another lengthy pull from my margarita, just to occupy my mouth.

When I set the glass down, he's still standing next to me. I glance over, surveying the strong lines of his profile. I'm pretty sure I could pick it out of thousands—the slight bump on the bridge of his nose and the line of his jaw that's as straight as a razor's edge. Warmth spirals through me, and I'm worried it has little to do with the amount of tequila I just sucked down.

"What are you doing?" I ask.

Ryder looks at me. There's an answering thud in my chest, right where my hollow heart beats. "I was planning on ordering a drink."

"Oh."

There's about thirty other feet of bar top he could have chosen to order a drink from instead. I can't come up with a polite way to point that out.

We've barely spent any time together today. I smiled through it all—the pancakes and the watching him surf and the shopping. But my smile has grown more and more strained because I knew this moment was coming. Knew we'd talk again at some point.

And I'm worried this—Ryder standing close enough I can smell the salt and sun and soap on his skin—might make me crack.

He's still looking at me. And I'm staring back.

One corner of his mouth lifts.

"What?"

"You, uh …" He swipes a hand across his jaw, not quite managing to hide his growing smile. "You have some salt on your nose."

Heat creeps into my cheeks as I vigorously rub my nose with the palm of my right hand. "Gone?"

"Nope."

I rub again. "Now?"

"No. Still there. Little higher."

I finally find the tiny, gritty bits and brush them off.

Ryder's still smiling at me.

My stomach flips, and my skin tingles. I can feel my heartbeat in my fingertips. He makes me feel like the same teenager with a crush. But it's deceptive because it's not a crush. It's this huge force, my feelings for him. Nothing light or easy.

"Stop that," I say.

His grin fades, and the intensity left behind is almost worse. "Stop what?"

"Being nice to me."

"Fine." He swipes a finger along the rim of my glass, brushing off some more of the salt crystals, then lifts his hand and sprinkles them on my nose.

I bite the inside of my cheek to stop from smiling. There's a giddy flicker in my stomach, a bubbly flash of brightness. A reminder that I loved this boy. That a large part of me still does. His harsh rejection, followed by seven years of silence, ended our relationship. But it didn't damage all the feelings that had already been there, just took away their outlet.

Ryder's pinkie brushes my chin before pulling away. My teeth clench until the coppery tang of blood fills my mouth.

I look away. "Don't touch me."

"Sorry."

I sip more margarita. The sour alcohol stings the cut on the inside of my cheek. I'd rather focus on that pain than on fighting the urge to look at him again. I couldn't for so long. The sight is like offering an addict a favorite drug. Ryder is a substance I should no longer crave.

You're supposed to avoid what will hurt you.

I should know better. He's broken my heart twice before.

"I'm sorry about a lot, Elle," he says softly.

My eyes sting. A lump grows in my throat as my fingers tighten around the cool glass. Could I shatter it? It feels like I could. So fragile, just like me. Falling apart from a two-minute conversation.

"It was a long time ago. Don't dredge up the past, Ryder." My tone is perfect. Casual and cool and unbothered.

But there are more cracks appearing, webbing across my chest. I have no idea how I'll make it through the rest of tonight, let alone tomorrow, if this is how much damage he's done in one day of barely speaking to me.

"Okay." His tone is gentle and sincere.

And I hate it. I need him to be harsh and aloof, like he was that day at the prison. I *need* to hate *him*.

Because if I don't hate him … I'm terrified of what I'll be left with.

I turn and walk away.

Just like he did.

X ♥ X

"I *love* summer," Avery announces, sprawling back against the wooden booth. Some of her hair brushes against my arm.

"Technically, it's not summer for a few more weeks," Juliet replies.

"Well, it feels like summer," Avery says. Her cheeks are pink, and her curls are a wild tangle.

My hair probably looks worse. It tends to frizz in humidity, not to mention the salty air gusting in every time the door gets opened.

I arch my toes under the table, relieved to be sitting down. We've spent the past hour dancing, and my feet are already feeling it. The three margaritas I've had dull some of the soreness, but I'm sure I'll feel it tomorrow.

Avery giggles, leaning forward. "Wow. I've never seen Ophelia like this over a guy."

Juliet and Keira both glance at me instead of the spot by the bar where Ophelia and Ryder are standing, talking.

I pretend not to notice.

Avery does. "Ah. So, that's what the weird vibe was at breakfast."

"There was no weird vibe," I say, then finish off my drink.

Silence follows.

I glance at Keira, who's playing with the edge of her napkin.

"I mean, *we* knew there was a weird vibe. I didn't think others would … notice," Juliet says.

"It was a long time ago," I tell Avery. "High school."

"Aww." She presses a hand to her chest. "Was he your first love?"

"Yeah."

Juliet's eyebrows are halfway to her hairline. I told Keira about freshman year, but Juliet thought Ryder was just a rebound from Archer. A rebellion from the confines of my life. A fun fling with the town bad boy.

And they both think I accepted the seven years of separation. They don't know about the letters I sent. The secret trips to the state prison. The humiliating way I begged him not to break up with me.

Because it was raw and painful and embarrassing, and talking about it would've changed nothing. It still won't.

"Do you still have feelings for him?" Avery's face is alight with interest as she leans forward.

Love stories are fun to discuss—when you don't have to live with the heartbreak.

"Of course not." I sip some melting ice, savoring the sour saltiness stuck to the rim.

The flavor washes away the bitterness of lying—again. But I'm sure bits of this conversation will make it to Ophelia and Tucker and possibly even to Ryder himself. Honesty isn't an option.

Seven years of practice, and my voice is exactly right. Detached and slightly incredulous.

I'm an excellent liar. It's a survival skill I've perfected. The only person who's ever found the fiction is talking to a pretty redhead who might make him happy.

I should want that for Ryder—happiness.

I stand. "I'm grabbing another drink. Anyone want anything?"

Avery and Keira shake their heads, both being responsible. There's no way I'll be able to drive my convertible home.

"I'll take another G and T," Juliet says.

"Coming right up."

I head for the bar, hoping they'll take my quick exit to mean that I'm bored by the conversation about Ryder, not bothered by it.

The bartender is busy at the other end of the bar when I reach an empty stool. I take the seat, my feet still bothering me, and rest my elbows on the rounded edge of the worn wood. A gritty rub against my elbow distracts me from trying to catch the bartender's eye. My stomach flips when I realize it's spilled salt.

I brush the crystals off my skin, then pull out my phone. I have a new message from Prescott.

PRESCOTT: Hey. I made a dinner reservation for Monday night. 7 PM at Canteen. Does that work for you?

PRESCOTT: Hope your trip is going well.

My stomach roils. He's being forgiving and sweet and the bigger person, and I hate it. I want him to yell. I want a storm, not for him to smooth the waves. I want it to be *hard*, just for a little bit. Even in my head, it sounds crazy.

ELLE: *Sounds great. See you then!*

"Hey there."

I glance up at the two guys who have appeared beside me. They're locals, I think. Surfers, judging by their shaggy hair and board shorts.

"Hey," I answer.

"You waiting for a drink?" the blond one asks.

I nod. "Slow service tonight."

"They're understaffed from the winter," he tells me. He steps closer, then leans down to talk right into my ear. "What do you want? Tate's a friend. I can put in a rush order."

Suddenly, this guy—this stranger—is all I can see. All I can smell or hear or feel. And all I can think about is the last time I was overwhelmed this way.

The air around me is suffocating. My mind spins, and my stomach churns. Panic claws at my skin, like a beast fighting for its way out.

"Excuse me," I choke out, then push past the two guys and basically sprint toward the nearest door.

It exits onto the porch that wraps around the building and leads to the side lot. No one else is around, which is a relief.

The earlier chill in the air has dipped to plain cold, the breeze coming off the water raising goose bumps on my skin. I gulp in greedy lungfuls of air, taking a seat on the top step and pressing my palms against my eyes until dots dance in my vision. The buoys attached to the railing tap against each other, the sound barely audible over the racing thud of my heartbeat.

You're fine. It's fine.

The silent reassurances don't help. My stomach heaves, and there's an excellent chance I'm going to throw up. God, why did I drink so much?

The door behind me opens and slams shut.

"Elle. Elle, are you okay?"

Keira's voice, I think. It's hard to hear over the roaring in my ears. I want to answer her, but it's taking all my effort just to breathe. To force the in and out that should be natural.

It feels like I'm adrift. And not in the peaceful, relaxing way that's free from worry or obligation. In the terrifying way of being dropped in the middle of an ocean without a boat or a raft in sight. Like I'm all alone in a sea of *nothing*.

My palms press tighter to my face, trying to block out more of the world. Thirty seconds to myself. That's all I need.

"What happened?" someone else asks.

"I don't know. She just ran out."

"Is she okay?"

More voices mix and mingle. This is humiliating. I try to pretend they're a movie around me, removing myself from reality until I'm equipped to deal with it.

"Where's Ryder?" someone asks. Avery maybe.

His name breaks through the fog.

"I'm fine." I lift my head, telling my lungs to take slower breaths. "I just needed some fresh air." The giggle sounds fake, but I force it out anyway. "Too much tequila. I'll meet you guys back inside."

I glance around and see they're all standing on the porch, everyone except for Ryder and Ophelia. I'm relieved he's not out here—and a little annoyed. Mad about being annoyed. I don't want him here, but that doesn't mean I want him distracted by another woman. I miss knowing he was in prison, alone, as horrible as that sounds. I don't want him to be happy and whole while I'm still falling apart.

Pretty soon, there will be no pieces of me left to fracture. I'm surprised it hasn't happened already.

Keira's face is pale and concerned. She's never seen me like this before. I've always hidden these vulnerable moments, had enough control to slip away quietly and break down without anyone noticing.

Another thing to blame Ryder for.

Fuck.

He's here now with Ophelia's wide, worried eyes following closely behind him. Guess they finally noticed our entire group left.

I stiffen, then slump, breaking eye contact first. God, he makes me so weak. I refocus on inhales and exhales because they're still uneven and because it's something to do.

Ryder doesn't ask what's wrong or what happened. He takes a seat on the step right beside me, so close that his bare arm brushes mine. I feel the spark, a jolt of electricity breaking through the crush of emotions. A point of heat to focus on as I stare down at his strong thigh pressed against mine. Keira was right—he must have worked out a lot in prison. He's more muscular than he was in high school. And he's so *close*.

"Breathe, Lo."

A choked gasp leaves my mouth when he uses the forgotten nickname. His palm lands on the center of my back, the warmth of it searing through the new shirt I'm wearing, and I'm suddenly suffused with heat.

"Just breathe. Deep inhales and long exhales."

His hand moves up my spine to the back of my neck, lifting the short, sweaty strands. His palm glides down my back, then back up. It feels like each place where he touches me is unfreezing, sensation replacing numbness.

"Someone get her some water." It's a command, not a suggestion. There's a flintiness to Ryder's voice that I should flinch away from. Instead, it's another shot of warmth.

He cares. He still cares—at least a little. There's worry in his tone, not pity.

I'm not *normal*, but I'm not totally alone either.

"I'll get it," Juliet volunteers.

I nod, not surprised when Ryder stays by my side. Not sure what it means when the rest of the group edges away and he still doesn't shift. Not sure what to make of how it's just silently understood Ryder will be the one who takes care of me. How even Juliet, who's never encountered a situation she didn't feel comfortable involving herself in, simply hands me a plastic cup of icy water and then continues toward the section of the parking lot where everyone else has migrated.

I gulp hasty sips of the cold liquid. I'm feeling better, but it has little to do with the water and everything to do with the circles Ryder is still rubbing on my back. I'm feeling *too much* now, my body betraying me once again.

"What happened, Elle?"

I deflate a little. I wanted him to call me Lo again.

"Elle?" he prompts when I don't answer.

"Nothing happened. I just got … claustrophobic in there. Too many margaritas." I stand, his hand falling away, relieved my legs feel somewhat steady.

Ryder stands, too, trying as hard to meet my gaze as I am to avoid his.

I'm cold again.

I clear my throat. "Thanks."

Look at me, thanking the boy who broke my heart. I'm not sure if it's mature or pathetic.

"Sorry to ruin your night," I add.

Pathetic. Definitely.

Ryder tilts his head. "You didn't ruin my night."

Right. Of course. Ophelia is staying under the same roof tonight. If he wants to fuck her, my mini meltdown won't stop him.

I start toward our friends without saying anything else, the crunch of gravel beneath my sneakers oddly soothing.

"Has that happened before?" Ryder catches up to me easily.

"Please drop it. I've humiliated myself in front of you enough."

Too late, I realize *in front of you* was unnecessary. Even if it's accurate.

"You've never humiliated yourself, Elle."

I scoff. Pretty sure the prison guard who witnessed our breakup would disagree.

"I'm … worried about you."

"I'm not yours to worry about, Ryder."

When I glance over, his jaw is taut.

"I didn't see your boyfriend when you were having a panic attack on the porch."

I wonder who mentioned Prescott to him. Tuck, probably, although I'm not sure how that would have come up. Did Ryder ask if I was single? I stop that dangerous thought from going any further.

"I'm fine," I say coolly.

"No, you're not."

He's right. I'm not. I'm a mess. But he isn't supposed to be able to tell that.

Thankfully, we reach the group before he can say anything else.

16
THEN

Elle

Rather than turn left, in the direction of my house, I take a right, heading toward the outskirts of town. I've never been to the local garage, but I've driven past it a few times before. Fernwood is one of those towns tiny enough that it's easy to have a general sense of where everything is, even the places you don't visit often.

My speed slows as soon as I spot the illuminated sign ahead. Streetlights are few and far between, so *Hank's Garage* shines like a beacon through the darkness around me.

I flick on my blinker and pull into the small parking area.

One end of the structure looks like a storefront with glass windows and a door that reads *OFFICE*. The rest of the building is separated by massive metal sliding doors, each bay with a number painted on it, stretching upward several feet. The lights are on in one.

I head for the normal-sized door next to the large garage one, which is propped open with a paint can. Peek inside.

Ryder is bent over the front end of a car that appears several decades old, tinkering with something beneath the open hood. He's wearing a white undershirt that's stretched tight across his back. It does nothing to conceal the flexing of his muscles as they shift and bunch while he works.

If I was a little more secure about where we stand, I'd wolf whistle.

He's alone. The whole space is open, two other cars inside the garage. One of them is up on a lift.

Shelves cover the back wall, every inch of them filled. There are orange plastic bottles, metal spray cans, stacks of rags, disposable gloves, clear containers, drills, and a lot of twisted metal I'd guess are car parts, but I couldn't even attempt to name them. A radio croons in the background, spilling out lyrics to a leisurely country song that seems out of place under the harsh fluorescent lights.

"Hi," I say.

Ryder's shoulders tense a split second before he straightens and turns around to face me.

I ogle the roped muscle lining his forearms unashamedly as he wipes his hands on a rag and then tosses it away, leaning back against a headlight. "Hey."

"This your car?" I ask, taking a few steps forward to look more closely at it.

I don't know much about any vehicle, including my own. But I'd rather focus on the car than try to get a read on how Ryder feels about me showing up here.

"Right now, it's a hunk of metal on wheels. But, yeah, eventually. If I can get it to run."

"It's cool. Vintage." I walk forward to run my fingers along the fender, focusing on the scratched paint job because I could really use a distraction from the dangerous flips my stomach keeps doing. "I like the roof."

When I turn around, Ryder's staring at me. "What are you doing here, Elle?"

"I was in the neighborhood."

Ryder makes a disbelieving sound in the back of his throat, which is a little offensive. We're not *that* far from my house. Ten minutes at most.

I rub at a smudge of dirt above the door handle, attempting to ignore the prickle of awareness that tells me he's still looking this way. I round the back, continuing to study the car, like this side looks any different from the one I just appraised.

"Can I drive it?"

"It doesn't run, Lo."

My insides start a new acrobatic routine as soon as the syllable leaves his mouth. "No one's called me that in a while."

"Good."

The dark possessiveness in his voice sends shivers down my spine.

I swallow, my throat so dry that it makes no difference, then pop the driver's door open. It smells like tobacco and old leather inside—a scent I associate with my grandfather's study. The seat is cracked, worn, and surprisingly comfortable. I relax into it, running my index finger in circles around the steering wheel.

A creak is followed by a slam as Ryder climbs in next to me.

"Did you have fun at the pond?" I ask.

"Uh-huh." He's fiddling with the chair controls, a high-pitched squeak as it slides back and allows his long legs to stretch out.

"Surf sucked."

Ryder barks a laugh as he shifts in his seat. "Yeah, it sure did."

I glance down at my lap, rubbing my palms against my pink

cotton dress. It tugs the fabric higher up my thighs. "So, Reese is a …"

There's a pause, during which I'm too cowardly to look over. I focus on fixing my bunched dress instead.

"Friend."

"Oh." I find a stray thread on the hem of my dress's skirt and tug at it.

She likes Ryder. That much was pretty obvious when she glared at me at the pond. But Ryder's much harder to read.

"You jealous?"

Ryder doesn't ask it like a taunt. It's a genuine question, like he's really wondering. Like he's as uncertain of what we are as I am. And I don't know why. *I* didn't abandon *him* freshman year with no warning and no explanation. He broke *my* heart, not the other way around.

The thread snaps, and I watch the pink string fall into the footwell. "Why would I be? We were nothing."

"We were nothing," Ryder repeats, his tone flat. "Is that really what you think?"

"It's what *you* think."

"No, I don't."

My teeth dig into my lower lip. "Don't lie to me."

"I've never lied to you, Lo."

The air around me feels like it's contracting. Turning tangible. I can feel this moment taking place like it's a memory I'm already in possession of. Solidifying around me. I'll lie awake later, replaying each word.

"I *couldn't* tell you I was leaving," Ryder continues. "And I know that's really shitty. If I could go back and …" He exhales. "Toward the end of freshman year, Cormac's dad came back. He and I … we didn't really get along. So, my mom decided to ship me south for the summer. A few months turned into a couple of years. And then it just ...” His head tilts back, his hand lifting to rub across his face.

“You didn’t think you’d come back.”

“Yeah. I didn’t think I’d come back.”

He doesn’t elaborate on what changed, and I don’t ask.

“But you are back.”

One corner of Ryder’s mouth lifts. “Nice of you to notice.”

“Yeah.” I tap my finger against the steering wheel. “Yeah, I’m having trouble *not* noticing actually.”

My entire body is buzzing with electricity as I stare straight ahead at the huge closed door, way too aware of the fact that we’re alone and inches apart.

This overwhelming feeling is only familiar because I’ve experienced it around him before. And I wrote it off as my age mostly. The giddiness of first love that wasn’t unique to Ryder. But I think it *is* unique to Ryder—and not only because he claimed all my firsts.

I shouldn’t have shown up here. I should have left a long time ago. But I don’t climb out of the car. And neither does Ryder.

“Come here,” he says softly, shattering the silence between us.

I roll my head to look at him. The feelings in my chest expand as soon as I get a glimpse of his face.

It aches in a beautiful, devastating way, seeing him look at me so tenderly. Like this moment matters to him too. Like *I* matter to him.

I abandon my shoes in the footwell and pull my feet up. There’s no center console, making the maneuver out of my seat a little easier. The bucket seats are larger than the ones in my car, but it’s still a tight fit. The top of my head bumps the roof of the car, my hair falling forward to curtain both of our faces. I grab Ryder’s shoulders automatically for better balance, my knees landing on either side of his hips. His hands skim up the sides of my rib cage. My nipples pebble, anticipating his touch, but he passes by my breasts to tangle his fingers in my hair and move the strands out of my face.

And we just ... stare at each other. Same as we did in my car, before he drove me home.

There's nowhere to hide, this close. The garage lights are bright, but his eyes still manage to look shadowed and mysterious. Mine are probably broadcasting exactly how I feel about being on his lap. Ryder's solid, and so is the seat under him, but I'm experiencing the dizzying sensation of vertigo. I'm holding my breath, each movement feeling precarious.

I lift my hand to touch his hair. "It's so short now."

Ryder's eyes hood as I stroke the prickly strands. His Adam's apple bobs before he says, "It got pretty long in Florida. I wanted a change."

"Are there pictures of the *long hair* era?" I ask.

One corner of his mouth lifts, creasing his cheek like a comma. "Might be some of me surfing."

He sweeps my hair out of my face again, and then his hands fall to my hips. I shift an inch, seeking, biting my bottom lip when I find what I'm looking for.

Ryder inhales sharply, his hands falling away as I rock our pelvises together. Fever creeps across the surface of my skin, a heady mixture of desire and excitement humming urgently.

"I want to see the photos."

His eyebrows are pinched together, the tendons of his neck corded and taut. If I glanced down at his hands, I think they'd be curled into fists.

It's a rush, watching him react to me. I caught him checking me out at the pond, but I wasn't sure how much that had to do with *me*.

He's a guy and I was a girl in a bikini. This—the tortured, aroused expression on Ryder's face—doesn't look like simply biology.

"You're sitting on my phone."

"Should I move?" I ask, switching to swiveling my hips.

Ryder lets out a low, husky groan that has me clenching around nothing. I'm drunk on him. The clean, soapy scent of his skin. The unmistakable bulge pressed against my thigh. My stomach swoops as I imagine it filling me, the hesitation I started to associate with sex glaringly absent.

"Elle …"

"Lo," I correct. "I love it when you call me Lo."

His eyes darken to graphite. His hands find my hips again, his grip tight enough that I can feel it this time. "You're playing with fire, Lo."

I lean closer, well aware the change in position means I'm grinding directly on top of his erection. "No. I'm begging you to burn me."

Another groan that vibrates against my body and ignites my insides.

I feel *alive* for the first time in so long. Like I'm participating in life instead of observing it as a bystander.

My breathing is rapid and ragged, my lungs struggling to keep up with the powerful flames scorching my skin.

Our lips are only a couple of inches apart. A gap that would only take a second to close. But I don't lean forward. I wait for Ryder to make the next move, ignoring the voice in the back of my head whispering caution. Last time was a lot of thrilling moments and secret kisses. And it ended with me charred and alone.

His fingers find my chin, tilting it up as he scans my face. "I missed you," he murmurs. "I missed our *some*thing."

My lips curve up automatically, right as he kisses me. I've been anticipating it ever since I climbed into his lap, and yet Ryder still manages to catch me off guard.

I freeze as soon as I feel the soft press of his mouth against mine, the light touch somehow a shocking jolt. My heart takes off at a sprint, a speed so fast that it seems impossible he can't hear it. He kisses me once, twice, three times, then pulls a couple of centimeters away. I suck in a greedy breath of oxygen, less embarrassed when I hear Ryder's inhale sounds unsteady too.

Ryder glances down at my heaving chest, a satisfied smile curving up the corners of his mouth. "That feel good?"

All I can do is nod, too overwhelmed by the sensations swirling inside of me. We were kids, pretending to be adults, the last time we fooled around. We're still kids, I guess. But this feels more intense. I'm more aware of its fragility maybe. I've learned, over the past two years, that this feeling is rare. That it matters who is touching you, not just that someone is.

I squirm, trying to force more friction.

Ryder's chuckle is dark and dangerous and hungry as he tugs my underwear to the side and sinks a finger inside of me.

My back arches as I adjust to the invasion. He pumps in and out of me a couple of times, then spreads the wetness around my opening. My knees threaten to buckle when he circles my clit.

I breathe his name, all my senses a slave to the surge of pleasure rushing through me that's stronger than anything I've ever experienced before.

"Fuck, you're wet," he tells me, sounding very smug about that fact.

"You're hard," I remind him, dragging my hand down his chest and cupping the outline of his erection.

Ryder huffs a laugh that sounds more pained than amused. "Trust me, I'm aware."

My fingers creep under the hem of his T-shirt. I trace the elastic waistband of his shorts, back and forth. His hand is still busy between my legs, making it very hard to think straight, much less talk.

But I manage to say, "I want to have sex."

His eyes, which were focused on the spot where he's touching me, snap up to mine. "Now?"

I'm too impatient to tease him or finesse a more subtle seduction. I just nod. "Now."

Ryder's head tilts back, his gaze flicking from my face to the roof of the car as he weighs a response. "I'm not going anywhere."

"That's not what this is about. And … it doesn't have to mean anything. I just want to."

His eyebrows bunch together as our eyes meet again. "You just want to."

I nod, holding his stare. It feels like there's a spotlight beaming down on me, making me sweat.

Ryder sees too much. He always has.

I want him, and I can't stay away from him. I'm also scared he'll break my heart—again. Right now, those two urges—pursuit and caution—are superseded by lust.

Ryder believing all I want from him is a physical release is my best attempt at getting what I want while preserving a little dignity. Yeah, he apologized. And I don't need him to chase me. But I'm not brave enough to venture out on a limb alone. He's never said he regrets ending things. Never sought me out. Never told me he wants more.

My fingers slide under his waistband, the elastic stretching easily.

Coarse hair brushes my fingertips, and a swell of anticipation washes over me.

This—us—feels like an inevitability. At least, I *hope* it's an inevitability. Ryder still looks conflicted, and I can't figure out what the root of his hesitation is. I'm sitting on the evidence that he wants this too. We've done it before. And I'm sure he's more experienced than me. Certain he left behind some Florida flings who loved his long hair. I didn't think he'd have any reservations about no-strings sex.

"Please." I reach the hard length of his cock inside his shorts, too dazed to feel embarrassed by the naked need in my voice.

I'm drunk and dizzy and so turned on that it's difficult to focus on anything, except the throbbing between my thighs. He's not touching my clit anymore, his hand pressed against the curve of my hip instead.

"Please fuck me."

I feel the burn of embarrassment this time. I don't swear very often, so I usually feel like a fraud when I do. I'm not the sexy, mysterious bad girl I always assumed was Ryder's type. The most rebellious thing I've ever done was having sex with him at the end of our freshman year. Not *that* rebellious since I never told anyone it happened.

And I'm used to rejecting advances from guys, not begging for them.

Ryder still looks uncertain, even as his erection thickens in my tight grip.

I don't regret not sleeping with Archer. But his fixation on sex makes Ryder's behavior more confusing. Am I acting *too* eager? Why can't Ryder act like a normal teenage guy when it comes to sex? When it comes to anything?

This moment, which started out feeling so soft and special, is slipping away. Shifting into something cheap and empty. Making me feel vain.

Not every guy wants you, Elle.

Not enough at least.

"All right then," I say, withdrawing my hand from his shorts and sitting up as much as the small space will allow. Somehow, I forgot we were in a car in a garage. That's how much power Ryder has over me. Yeah, it's thrilling. It's also terrifying. "Not like I can't get it somewhere else."

Ryder's expression hardens and darkens. "If you wanted it somewhere else, you wouldn't be in my lap, rubbing your pussy all over my dick."

I swallow hard, the filthy words and flinty tone captivating me the same way his tenderness does.

Yeah, we're older.

His hand moves to cup the place where I'm empty and aching. "Seems like you're here because those rich assholes can't satisfy you."

"What makes you think I wasn't hooking up with Twos while you were gone?" I snap.

Ryder rolls his eyes. "Because I would have heard about it."

"How do you know?" I ask. "*You* didn't say anything."

A muscle jumps in his jaw. "Neither did you."

"Because you *left*, Ryder. What was I supposed to tell people? *No, I don't know why Ryder James mysteriously disappeared. But before he did, we used to kiss a lot.* Yeah, that's exactly what I want everyone knowing. You took off and moved on like I was just a toy you got sick of playing with."

Ryder looks away. "I thought you wanted us to be a secret."

He made me forget we were sitting in a car again.

My molars grind when I recall our exact position. I'm still worked up and turned on. Combined with the confusion and sting of rejection, I'm so frustrated, I could scream.

I blow out a breath, then fumble with the door handle, almost falling flat on my ass when it gives way. I right myself quickly, forgetting I'm barefoot until I feel the cool concrete.

I round the front of the car as quickly as I can without actually running, grabbing my shoes out of the footwell and then slamming the door shut. Ryder has emerged from the car, his arms spread across the car's roof and open door in a deceptively casual position. Or maybe he really is that unbothered. We fought plenty when we were fourteen and fifteen.

"You're leaving?" he asks.

I avoid looking toward the low rumble of his voice as I slip my shoes back on, trying not to think about what the large, dark stain on the concrete is. I'll shower and scrub my feet when I get home.

Ryder sighs. "Lo ..."

"Don't call me that."

"You just told me *to* call you that."

My cheeks burn with the reminder. "I changed my mind."

"Just about that?"

"If you think I'm having sex with you now, you're crazy. That was a limited-time offer."

Ryder scrubs a palm across his face. "Look, I was just trying to—"

"Stop, okay? Whatever you were *trying* to do, just stop. I shouldn't have come here. You've done nothing but avoid me since you got back. Message fucking received. Bye, Ryder."

As soon as I'm out of the doorway, I start running.

Worried he'll chase me.

Hating he won't.

17
NOW

Ryder

I suck in a deep breath, then lift my hand and knock. The rap of my knuckles against the wooden door echoes down the empty hallway, then fades into silence.

This is stupid. But I've partially committed at this point.

So, I knock again.

A few seconds later, there's a muffled thud inside the room. Ten seconds later, the door swings open.

I have to lift my hand and pretend to scratch my cheek in order to hide the wide smile that wants to appear.

Elle's hair is a chaotic tangle that resembles a bird's nest, creased impressions from her pillow webbing across the left side of her face. Her eyes are bleary as she squints at me.

My gaze dips lower, and any amusement fades. She's wearing a thin tank top that's molded to her chest and a pair of lace boy shorts. Nothing else.

Fuck me. Seriously. I did *not* need this mental image.

I clear my throat. "Good morning."

Elle's knuckles go white where they're gripping the door. "Morning."

"I'm going for a run," I tell her.

"Have fun."

I smile. I don't mean to, but I do. There's an answering tug in one corner of Elle's mouth.

"I was wondering about Scout," I say, getting the conversation back on track.

"My dog?" She sounds surprised.

"Unless you know of another Scout staying here." I rub the back of my neck. That was a stupid comment. "So …"

"You're here to exercise my dog?"

"What did you think I was here for?" I make the mistake of glancing down again as I ask the question, the words coming out more suggestive than I meant to.

She has a boyfriend. She hates you.

She's also the woman my body associates sex with.

"You don't have to do that," Elle says.

Her cheeks are pink when I meet her eyes again.

"I know," I reply.

She stares at me for a few seconds, then nods. "Okay. Uh, just give me one minute."

The door shuts, and I'm back to staring at white wood.

I want to bring up last night, but I'm positive Elle won't want to talk about it. She shut down after we left the bar last night, not even glancing in my direction for the remainder of the evening. I'm the last person she wants to discuss anything with, I know.

"I'm not yours to worry about, Ryder."

Problem is, she still fucking feels like it.

A couple of minutes later, Elle reappears. She's wearing the same pink pajama set as yesterday, all the bare skin that was just on display covered. Her hair has been pulled back into a bun too.

Scout is wagging his tail so hard that his entire body is wriggling. I smile and crouch down. "Hey, buddy. Feel like running?"

He whines like he understands what I'm asking, butting his snout against my stomach before licking my neck.

"Here's his leash."

"Thanks." I straighten, taking it from Elle.

"I already put his collar on. And here are some treats. And bags—to clean up. He'll probably go."

"You should've gotten one of those dogs that doesn't shit."

She rolls her eyes, but she's smiling. And still blushing.

"I'll take good care of him," I tell her.

"I know you will."

I nod, bending down to clip the leash on Scout. He's taken a seat right next to my foot, waiting expectantly.

"Okay. See you later."

"See you."

I don't glance back as I lead Scout down the hallway, stuffing the treats and poop bags Elle gave me into my pocket. I forgot my phone in the guest room, but I don't turn back for it. Disconnecting from the world for a little while sounds nice. And it's a lot easier to do here, on the edge of the sea, than back in Fernwood.

Downstairs is just as empty and silent as the upstairs hallway was. It's not even seven yet, and it was a late night.

It's foggy out, watery sunshine barely peeking between the clouds. I suck in deep lungfuls of the salty, damp air.

I love the ocean. The freedom, the power, the majesty.

No one tries to control the sea. It's this indomitable force that does what it wants.

If I could swing it, if my mom wasn't sick, I'd move to some small town right on the coast and wake up to this view every day.

Scout has his nose straight in the air, sniffing the sea air with the same enthusiasm.

"You like the beach?" I ask him.

He barks in response, and I smile.

I wouldn't have guessed Elle had a dog. She didn't grow up with pets, just rules. She never mentioned animals or wanting one. But Scout fits her, somehow.

Once we're past the first dune, I start jogging. Scout picks up the quicker pace joyfully, tugging the leash taut as he surges ahead. Fuck, this dog is fast.

Running on the beach is exhausting and irritating. My calves burn with each step in the sand, tiny grains working their way into my sneakers and abrading my skin. I miss pavement more with each stride. And I'm more grateful for the chillier temperature with each sweaty step.

I run until I feel like I can't go any farther. I have no idea what time it is or how much distance I've covered. For the first time in so long, I'm somewhere unfamiliar. Free of any restrictions or expectations. It feels damn good. Cleansing.

The sun has burned away the haze by now. The sky is a brilliant blue above, unblemished by so much as a single cloud.

I'm still alone on the beach, none of the houses along the sand ones I recognize. I let Scout off his leash to sniff around the dunes. Pull off my socks and sneakers and walk down to the water's edge, letting the bubbly foam wash over the tops of my feet. The water is as chilly as it was yesterday. Colder, without the rubber barrier of a wetsuit.

Scout whines. He's followed me as far as he can while keeping his paws in the sand.

"It's okay, buddy," I tell him. "I'll be right out to—*crap*."

Scout interpreted my words as an invitation, dashing straight into the next oncoming wave.

I panic and rush after him, getting completely soaked in the process. Through a combination of pushing and calling his name, I get him to paddle back to shore. I could carry him if I had to, but he appears to be a pretty good swimmer.

As soon as we're back on the sand, he shakes. Makes no difference since I'm already drenched. Now that I'm out in the water, under the relentless beam of the sun, it actually feels good.

I go to clip his leash back on—lesson learned about taking it off—but Scout takes off after a seagull. I call his name, and he races back, dropping into a down position and then rolling onto his back. He wiggles around in the sand until he's totally coated in it, then stands and shakes once again. Most of the sand sticks to his wet fur. You can barely see his fur under the thick layer of beige.

Fuck.

I pull the bag of treats out of my pocket, relieved they stayed dry in the plastic during my unplanned swim, and lure Scout over with one. He munches happily as I clip his leash back on, then looks up at me with his pink tongue lolling.

"You're in trouble," I tell him.

No reaction. He looks as unbothered as Cormac did anytime I tried to discipline him.

The walk back takes a while. I decide to carry my shoes rather than try to jog in wet, sandy socks. Scout trots along happily, appearing as energetic as when we left. I wish I could say the same.

Finally, I spot the Parkers' house up ahead. Scout and I climb the deck steps, leaving a trail of wet sand behind us.

I slide open the deck door a couple of inches, careful to make sure we're both staying outside.

"Hey, Tuck?"

"Yeah?" He turns around from the island, a wide grin stretching his face when he gets a good look at me. "What the hell happened to you?"

"Does this place have an outside faucet somewhere? And a hose?"

"Yeah, around front. Left side of the garage."

"Great. Thanks."

"You need help?" Tucker calls after me.

"Nah, I'm good," I reply before closing the door.

More clumps of sand fall as I lead Scout around the side of the house and along the stone pavers.

The spigot and hose are easy to spot. Not only is the hose a neon green, but Tucker and Keira are also standing right by it.

"How did *both* of you get like this?" Keira asks, glancing between me and the dog. She looks like she's trying very hard not to laugh.

"Scout wanted to go swimming. Then he decided to roll around on the beach."

"That doesn't explain why *you* look like a drowned sandcastle," Tuck tells me.

I roll my eyes. "I said I didn't need help."

"Oh, we're not here to help," he says, taking a sip from the mug of coffee he's holding. "Just to enjoy this."

I shake my head as I turn on the faucet, tempted to flip him off.

Scout pulls at the leash and whimpers. Apparently, he hates water again.

"It's okay. Good boy." I turn the pressure down slightly, aiming the end of the hose at the driveway.

"Oh. My. God."

My head whips up so fast that I hear a crack. Elle is standing at the end of the path that leads from the porch to the garage, wearing jean shorts and a white T-shirt, her blue eyes wide as she stares at her dog. Tucker and Keira exchange a nervous look.

"What *happened*?" she asks.

"He, uh … we went swimming," I reply.

"Scout *hates* water," Elle informs me. "Baths are his worst nightmare."

The dog pressed tightly against my leg, as far from the water's spray as possible, seems to agree.

"Well, he doesn't hate the ocean. He ran right in. Scared the shit out of me, but he's a good swimmer."

Elle raises an eyebrow. "You're going to need help rinsing him. He'll fight you hard on it."

"I'll be fine—"

Elle is already walking closer, and Scout makes a desperate lunge for his owner. The yank pulls me off-balance, and my arm flies up to steady me. I watch, horrified, as the hose I'm holding arcs water across the flower beds and then aims straight at Elle.

I drop the hose like it's on fire, but it's too late. She's already as soaked as me, her dripping T-shirt revealing a pink bikini underneath.

Tucker and Keira gasp dramatically. And unnecessarily. This situation is terrible enough without sound effects.

"Shit, Elle. I'm so sorry—"

An icy blast to the chest cuts me off.

My arms fall to my sides as I accept my punishment. The spray starts to move, down one arm and then the other. Elle avoids my crotch, which makes me smirk, but my legs get the same treatment as the rest of my body. My clothes are dripping again, so saturated that the fabric can't absorb any more water.

And Elle is laughing. So hard that she's having trouble standing up and aiming straight.

"Really?" I call out. "This is the thanks I get for exercising your dog?"

But I'm smiling as I say it.

Because I'm relieved. I'm so, so relieved.

This is Elle. Not the woman who silently picked at her pancakes yesterday morning. Or who looked lost on the bar steps last night.

She's a fighter. She bends the world to her will, just like the ocean does.

Staring at her, grinning with flushed cheeks and dancing eyes, I realize … I'm not over her.

I don't think I ever will be.

X 🖤 X

I'm sitting down by the water, staring out at the waves, when I catch a flash of movement out of the corner of my eye.

Elle walks straight past me and into the surf, not stopping until the water is up to her knees. She stands like that for a good minute, then runs back onshore. Drops down beside me, a few stray droplets splashing my legs. "It's cold."

"Not as cold as the well water."

She laughs under her breath. Amusement I'm not supposed to

hear.

After rinsing Scout, we both had to shower and change. Elle was right about him hating baths.

My morning run was the main topic of conversation at breakfast. But no one mentioned the hose incident. That felt like a private moment, somehow, between me and Elle. The first happy one we've shared in a long time.

"Where's Scout?" I ask.

"Asleep in his crate. You really wore him out."

"He's a good running buddy."

Elle nods. "We run along the Charles most mornings."

"That sounds nice."

"You should get a dog," she tells me.

"Maybe one day. Trailer is pretty tight with the three of us."

I study it carefully, but Elle's expression remains completely smooth. If my mom and Cormac had played it this cool, I'd have had no clue about her visits.

"I'm sure they're happy to have you home."

I nod, then draw the four tic-tac-toe lines in the sand between us.

Elle's inhale is sharp and immediate. "What are we playing for?"

"An honest answer. Winner gets one question."

"And if it's a cat's game?"

I guess we're a cat's game after all.

Does she remember the letters she sent me? Did she memorize them the way I did with the response I never sent?

"No winner."

"Deal." She takes the center spot, same as always.

My X goes in the top right corner. I'm playing fast, planning three steps ahead, hoping Elle will react impulsively and provide me an opening.

Two moves later, I see it. The spot I can mark that sets up two opportunities for three X's in a row. She can only block one.

Elle realizes the same, her hand falling to her side and then wrapping around her knees. "Congratulations."

Her face is aimed toward the ocean, so all I can read is her profile. She's nervous, if I had to guess. Unsure what I'm going to ask.

"Why'd you go to law school?"

"What?" She glances over, forehead wrinkled with confusion.

"That's my question. Why'd you go to law school?"

"*That's* your one question?"

"Yep." I lean back on my palms, waiting.

"Um, I … well …"

I hide the smirk that wants to appear, not wanting to make her feel more self-conscious. I know Elle must have a prepared response to this question. One she's used in job interviews and carefully phrased in essays on applications. But I figured she didn't have an honest one ready, and I was right.

"I couldn't think of something I'd rather do," she finally answers. "There was no secret dream of being an astronaut or a ballerina or a surgeon. And if there was nothing else I wanted instead—nothing else I wanted *more*—I figured, why not? There's a lot you can do with a law degree. It's a smart career move."

A seagull swoops down in front of us, then lands a dozen feet down the beach.

"Say something."

"Say what?" I ask.

"*Something.* Anything."

"Thanks for answering."

Elle huffs an unamused laugh. "You think I sold out. Gave in. Just rolled over and played the part."

"I didn't say any of that."

"But you're thinking it."

"I'm not thinking it." I shift forward on the sand, resting my elbows on my knees instead of leaning back. "And you shouldn't take career advice from a high school dropout."

Elle's silent for a minute. "You like working for Tuck?" she eventually asks.

I wonder how she found that out, but I don't ask.

"Yeah. It's … Don't know what I'd do without that guy, honestly."

"Keira said you're restoring the old Warren house?"

Mystery solved.

"Uh-huh. Well, I'm part of the crew that is."

"That's a beautiful house. I'll have to drive by the next time I'm in Fernwood."

I'm swamped with an immediate rush of uncertainty, thinking of the exterior paint color I just picked out. Would she recognize it? Remember?

"Give it a couple of years," I suggest. "It still needs *a lot* of work."

"You'll be around that long?" Elle asks.

I rub a hole in the sand with my foot. "Not sure yet."

I doubt I'll stick around after my mom passes. But Elle doesn't know my mom is dying. Doesn't know I would be long gone if not for that sick twist of fate.

"Ryder!" I turn to see Tuck standing out on the deck, waving his arms. "We gotta go!"

" 'Kay!" I call back. Then glance at Elle beside me. "Reason not to vacation with your boss, I guess."

I catch a glimpse of her smile before it disappears.

"Say bye to Scout for me?"

Elle nods.

I clear my throat, then stand. She stays sitting. "Take care of yourself, Elle."

"You too, Ryder."

I turn and walk toward the house, fighting the urge to look back the whole time.

And it's not the ocean I want one last glimpse of.

18
THEN

Ryder

Tuck casts me a concerned look as I climb into the cab of his truck. Reese is slouched between us, fiddling with the radio between bites of a Pop-Tart.

I'm well aware I look like shit. My concentration at the garage was shot after Elle left last night. I basically just sat there for another hour before biking home to stare at my bedroom ceiling all night.

I fucked up with Elle. Again. Left her with the laughable impression she's not the one girl I want because I'm scared to admit that to her.

Getting what I want is a foreign concept to me. It's fucking ironic, me telling Elle to make her own decisions when I don't do the same. My entire life has been determined by other people's choices. My mom, shipping me to Florida. My dad, shipping me back to Fernwood. My brother, creating messes he knows I'll clean up. Even Tuck, getting me the gig at his uncle's garage. Playing football would have been an irresponsible decision. But I wouldn't have hated it being an option.

Elle wasn't supposed to be an option. I assumed I'd come back to her hating me and dating someone else. I didn't even let myself consider an alternative, and it's scary to now.

I know my leaving hurt her. But it hurt *me* to leave her. And we might be in the same place again right now, but that'll change again soon. She'll leave for college, and I won't.

Staying away seems like the smart move.

But then I think about the look on her face last night when she left. The raw pain she tried so hard to hide.

I've already hurt her again, without meaning to.

"You wanna talk about it?" Tuck asks me.

Reese's head whips in his direction, then mine. "Talk about what?"

"Pretty sure James is having girl trouble."

"Really? Don't take advice from Tuck then."

I glance at Reese in time to catch the teasing look she tosses Tuck's way. He rolls his eyes as he turns off the trailer park's dirt road onto the paved street.

"It's nothing," I say.

"No, tell me," Reese replies. "I give great advice."

I was wrong about the pond, I guess. There's no trace of jealousy or annoyance on Reese's face. Her coldness toward Elle must have been about Elle alone. Reese has always taken a harsher stance when it comes to Fernwood's wealthier residents. To be fair, girls tend to be more vicious. Aside from Hathaway, who likes to antagonize me, most of the guys just ignore me unless we're in gym class and they want me on their team. The high school I went to in Jacksonville had a hierarchy too. It was just less obviously centered around money.

"It's nothing," I repeat. "I just ... I messed up."

"Then, apologize," Reese says simply.

I exhale, tapping my fingers against the door. "It's not that easy."

"It's a start. And better than doing nothing, which I'm betting was your plan."

I don't answer because she's right about that being my plan and right that it's a shitty one.

I have apologized to Elle. I keep apologizing to Elle.

We're past the point where that's enough. I'm not sure it ever was.

Reese sighs, then looks to Tuck. "Back me up here."

Tuck brakes at one of Fernwood's few stoplights, then glances at me. "We're talking about Elle, right?"

I nod, keeping my eyes straight ahead.

"*Ryder.*" Reese groans my name. "Seriously? Every guy at school has a crush on her. She doesn't care about you. She's just sick of dates at the country club and cars that cost more than your trailer."

"You don't know her, remember?"

"Neither do you," she tells me.

My fingers tap faster. I do, I think. This would be a hell of a lot easier if I didn't. If our connection was just a fascination with something different. Reese is right; I can't offer her anything like she's used to. I don't dress like I'm headed to a golf tournament, and I'll never be able to buy her a steak dinner.

"Thanks for the advice."

Reese sighs again. "I'm just trying to look out for you. I don't want you to get hurt."

I force another nod. Reese leans forward and turns up the radio.

Five minutes later, Tuck parks on the east side of the lot. I glance toward the main entrance reflexively, Elle's red convertible easy to spot in its usual place a few spots to the left of the columns. She's leaning against the bumper, talking with a few other girls.

"See you guys later," I say, pretending not to notice the look Tucker and Reese exchange before I walk away. Wondering what I'm about to do, same as me. I've only got a couple hundred feet to figure it out.

Elle's not going to approach me, not after how we ended last night. And I don't know much about relationships, but I do know the longer we go without talking, the bigger a deal last night will become.

She's laughing at something one of her friends said, raising a hand to tuck her hair behind one ear, when she sees me. The stutter in her movements and droop in her smile are subtle. But if you're watching closely, like I am, they're noticeable.

Fuck it.

I swerve to the right, my heart rate picking up speed with each step I take.

Elle goes completely still when she realizes I'm headed straight toward her. One by one, her friends notice and glance this way. Two of them share a surprised look.

"Good morning, ladies." I flash a polite smile around, wincing internally when I recognize Maddie is part of the group. After the awkward encounter at her party, I was kinda hoping to avoid her.

Maddie tilts her head, watching me closely.

I shove my hands in my pockets and focus on Elle. "Can I talk to you?"

She clears her throat, tucking more hair behind one ear while holding a textbook to her chest like a shield. "I'm busy."

I hold her gaze. "I'll wait."

Tangible tension hums in the air between us. It's cooler today, the first traces of fall's crispiness cutting through the heat that's lingered ever since I returned to New England.

Elle sucks her lower lip into her mouth, studying me. All it accomplishes is making me recall kissing her last night. Wanting to do it again.

The group of girls surrounding us is all silent, waiting to see what happens next. We're probably drawing attention from all over the parking lot.

As ridiculous as it sounds, me talking to a One is a rare event. There's already speculation about my departure and return. And Elle is *the* One. Unattainable and unapproachable.

"I don't think we have anything to talk about," she tells me.

"I disagree."

I've never paid much attention to the spaces between seconds before. But I'm painfully aware of each tiny stretch of time now, waiting for Elle's response.

"Fine," she finally says, flipping some hair over her shoulder with a bored expression I can tell is fake.

They all appear blatantly curious, but her friends start to move around us, grabbing backpacks and turning their attention to phones. I recall all the messages Elle showed me at Maddie's party, certain a text flurry about us is taking place right now.

"See you in homeroom," one girl tells Elle before walking off with the rest of them.

Elle doesn't move once her friends leave. "You just told everyone."

"I know."

She glances down, running a finger along the spine of her textbook. "So … talk."

I step forward. We're only a couple of feet apart now, but it's still not close enough. So, I step again, until I'm close enough to see the flutter of her pulse just below her jawline.

"Last night, I wasn't expecting for you to show up. Or for things to, uh, evolve the way they did."

Elle snorts, still not looking at me. "Sorry to disappoint."

"I wasn't disappointed."

"Just forget about it, Ryder. Whatever you think you need to say … you don't." She scoffs. "I should have seen it coming from miles away after last time."

I reach out, gripping her chin between my fingers and forcing her to look up at me. Her exhale is surprised, her blue eyes wide as they meet mine. They're the same shade as the clear sky above.

"I want you, Elodie Lily Clarke. I've wanted you since the first time I saw you. If you think that's changed … it hasn't. It won't. I know I've hurt you, and I swear I never meant to."

"You didn't want me last night," she whispers.

"Of course I did. I just … you said it would mean nothing. And it would've meant something … to me."

Elle rolls her eyes. "I said that because, in my experience, you're the *love 'em and leave 'em* type. Or the *have sex and then disappear for two years* type, if you want to get specific. I thought *nothing* was what you wanted to hear."

"I didn't have a choice about leaving," I tell her softly.

"You had a choice about telling me you were leaving."

I nod. "You're right. I did. But if I'd told you I was leaving, if I'd said goodbye, I wouldn't have been able to get into that car. And I thought you hating me would help you move on faster. It had nothing to do with me not caring. I swear, Elle. Believe that, if nothing else."

She reaches for the hem of my T-shirt, twisting the gray cotton around one finger. "You can call me Lo again," she says, her tone soft and almost shy.

"I'm getting whiplash from the nickname privileges."

Elle's nose wrinkles as she drops my shirt and shoves my chest.

"Never mind."

I grin. "See what I'm talking about?"

Her inhale is hasty as I take another step closer, near enough that our clothes brush together, but far enough that we're not actually touching.

"Another thing? I didn't think you wanted anyone to know about us. I thought you were embarrassed of me. That you liked having a dirty secret. That's why I've avoided you since I've been back. I figured I'd done enough. Me staying away was for you, not because it was what I wanted."

"Oh." Elle reaches toward the yellow travel mug that's sitting on the bumper of her car, fiddling with the handle. The steam rising from it smells like jasmine. "Oh," she repeats, then sips some tea.

I smile at her sudden uncertainty. "We can talk more later, if you want. I just—"

"No." Elle sets the tea down, then links her hands behind the back of my neck. "Stop leaving me, okay?" She whispers the words like a secret.

I brush some hair out of her face, tucking it behind one ear carefully. "I'm right here, Lo."

Then, she's kissing me. I'm aware of the noise level rising around us for a few seconds before it all fades into the background. All that matters is the sensation of her lips moving against mine, the tease of her tongue against mine.

We make out until the first warning bell rings.

Elle smiles at me before reaching for her mug again.

"You're a tea drinker?" I ask.

She rolls her eyes. "Sometimes. My mom hates coffee."

"Why?"

"Long story. And it'll make more sense once you meet her. I mean—" Her cheeks flush. "Not that you'll meet her. I just—"

"I'd like to," I tell her.

"Yeah?" Her eyes are wide and hopeful, and I think she understands what I mean. That this isn't small or temporary for me.

I nod. "Yeah."

My phone buzzes in my pocket. I pull it out, worried it's my mom or a problem with Cormac. It's my dad, so I shove my phone back in my pocket without answering. Glance at Elle, certain she saw *Sperm Donor* on the screen.

"We don't have to talk about it," she tells me.

"He never wanted kids. And he tries to be a dad sometimes, but we're both worse off for it." I half smile. "That would make more sense if you meet him, but I kinda hope you won't. Because he's a guy you need to *not* know to like."

"I'm sorry, Ry."

I nod. "I'm used to it by now."

The second warning bell rings, meaning there's only a few minutes before homeroom teachers start taking attendance.

"Come on," I tell her. "I'll walk you to homeroom."

"Oh, yeah?" Elle stuffs her textbook into her backpack, then grabs her mug. "Are you going to kiss me in the hallway too?"

I shrug. "Depends how the walk goes."

"Dick."

We're both smiling as we walk inside Fernwood High, holding hands.

I was pretty sure I never fell out of love with Elle Clarke before.

I'm completely certain of it now.

Elle

Rows of handwritten notes swim in front of my vision. I reach for the cup of coffee that turned cold a few hours ago, wincing as a sip of the forgotten liquid settles in my empty stomach.

My phone buzzes, and I reach for it, thrilled about the interruption. I've been studying nonstop since this morning.

"You free for a drink?" Keira asks, skipping a usual greeting. " 'Cause I could really use one."

I laugh. "Sure. You're in the city?"

"Yep. Had to meet with a couple of suppliers and do some wedding stuff. Juliet suggested meeting at The Adams Club?"

"Yeah, I know where that is. I can be there in twenty minutes."

"Perfect," Keira replies. "She's bringing Gavin, by the way."

The *nudge, nudge* in her voice comes through loud and clear. I roll my eyes, but don't respond to it. "Okay. I'll see you soon."

I hang up and head upstairs to get changed.

Prescott and I are … good. We've worked through most of the awkwardness following my trip to Martha's Vineyard that I neglected to tell him about. He apologized for overreacting. I apologized for not mentioning the trip to him. On the surface, our relationship is back to no ripples. We've gone out to dinner together twice this week. Wednesday afternoon, we met up with a group of law school friends to study-slash-commiserate about bar prep and talk about our approaching jobs. Most of them are set to start as first-year associates in late August, same as me. A couple are doing clerkships.

But beneath the surface, I'm treading water. I'm working to keep my head up. It's not effortless or easy.

All relationships require work.

This silent struggle feels like something else. And it would be an easier battle to fight if I stopped falling asleep with a paper flower in my hand, dreaming about playing tic-tac-toe in the sand.

I finish getting ready, then call Prescott.

"Hey, babe."

I grit my teeth, irrationally irritated by the endearment. Haven't I told him I hate being called babe? I must have. But I can't think of a concrete example, all of our conversations, recent and otherwise, one big blur in my head with no details standing out.

"Hey. You busy?"

Prescott sighs. There's rustling in the background, like flipping papers. "Just studying. Couldn't be happier about the interruption."

I smile as he echoes my sentiments. "Feel like grabbing a drink with a couple of friends of mine? Keira is in town, and Juliet is bringing her boyfriend."

"Yeah, that sounds great." Pres's response is genuine and immediate. I'm not as excited by his willingness as I should be, but I push my reservations away. Keira was right; it's weird they haven't met him yet. "Want me to pick you up?"

"Sure. We're meeting at The Adams Club though. It's out of your way."

"I don't mind. See you soon."

"See you soon," I echo, then walk toward the back door to let Scout out.

He sniffs around his favorite bush in the backyard for a few minutes, then finally lifts his leg. I feed him an early dinner, change out of the leggings I've worn all day, then load dirty dishes into the dishwasher until the doorbell rings.

"You look amazing," Prescott says, pressing an enthusiastic kiss to my mouth before we head outside.

It's the perfect temperature tonight, the June air warm but not hot. I doubt July and August will be this pleasant.

"Thank you," I reply, pushing aside the awkwardness he appears oblivious to. He's sunny and warm, and I feel like the dark cloud hovering. "You clean up pretty well too."

He smiles. "I was in sweatpants twenty minutes ago."

"Same."

"You still on contracts?" he asks as we walk toward his car.

"Yeah. You?"

"Civ pro today."

I groan, and Pres's grin grows.

The drive to the bar is filled with easy conversation, no lags or lurches.

That's the thing with Prescott—sometimes, it is easy. We *are* easy—for him. Prior to our argument about Martha's Vineyard, I can't remember the last time we fought. We were platonic friends for over two years before he asked me out on a date.

It makes me feel foolish—for craving challenge, for creating problems in my own head simply because uncomplicated seems wrong and boring. Wrong can be unfamiliar. Boring can be reassuring.

We're last to arrive at The Adams Club. Keira, Juliet, and Gavin are all gathered at one end of the bar, right by the hostess stand. I give Keira and Juliet hugs, then reintroduce myself to Gavin. I've only met him once before.

Keira flashes me a subtle thumbs-up as she talks to Prescott. I'm pretty sure he sees, his shoulders shaking with silent laughter for a few seconds before he regains his composure.

We place drink orders, eyeing tables that look like they might open up soon, when Keira suddenly calls, "Tuck!"

We all turn to watch Tucker look this way. His face lights up with a smile as soon as he spots Keira. My stomach sinks as soon as I see who he's with.

"I guess they travel everywhere as a couple now," Juliet whispers to me. "Keira's third-wheeling in her own relationship."

I manage a smile, feeling faintly nauseous.

I'm positive Tucker dragged Ryder here. He appears highly uncomfortable, looking around at all the mahogany and brass this place is decorated with. At the elegant woman playing piano while wearing an evening gown. This is everything he hates—ritzy and overpriced and pretentious.

And when Ryder's eyes land on me, I'm certain Tuck didn't mention I'd be here. He looks startled and unsure to see me, the ice I thought we'd broken through reappearing, even more so when he spots Prescott's hand resting casually on my lower back.

Thankfully, the bartender chooses this moment to return with the drinks, providing a distraction from all of us watching Tucker and Ryder approach.

I down half my martini in one gulp, but it does nothing to settle my stomach.

I knew I'd see Ryder again, obviously.

He'll be at Keira and Tucker's wedding. He's the best man. But that's not until September. The rest of my summer was supposed to be Ryder-free.

I'm uneasy about how we left things, about how quickly he broke through walls of resentment that had taken years to build.

Suddenly, I'm self-conscious of everything I wasn't a second ago—my hair, my outfit, my lipstick, my choice of drink even. Wondering what Ryder sees when he looks at me.

Because … I *care.*

I care what Ryder thinks of me. His opinion is the one that matters *most* to me.

That should have changed, but it hasn't. I please my parents because I love them and want to make them happy. Our relationship was irrevocably changed after Rose passed away. It simplifies my life to go along with what they want for me. To let the current sweep me where it thinks I should go rather than fight to swim in the opposite direction.

But I meant what I told Ryder on the beach. If I'd had a different dream, I would have chosen it, no matter what my parents thought of that choice.

If he'd let me choose him, I would have.

"Hey, man. I'm Tucker."

The guys have reached us.

"Prescott," Prescott replies, smiling at Tucker. "Nice to meet you."

"You too. Congrats on graduating."

"Thank you."

"Are you working at the same firm as Elle?" Tucker asks him.

"Nope," I answer, smiling. Standing silent isn't an option, not with Ryder a few feet away. I desperately need a distraction.

Prescott shakes his head. "I'm working at one of Gray's main competitors. We might have to go up against each other at some point."

"My money's on Elle," Keira says from her spot tucked under Tuck's arm. "No offense, Prescott."

"None taken," he replies, glancing at me. "My money's on Elle too."

"This is my best friend, Ryder," Tucker says.

I hold my breath, for some reason, when Ryder and Prescott shake hands.

"Nice to meet you, man," Prescott says.

Ryder nods, not saying anything.

I think Pres interprets his silence as shyness because he asks, "You live in Boston?" like he's trying to coax Ryder out of his shell.

"No. Fernwood."

"James is my best main contractor," Tucker boasts.

"I'm your *only* main contractor," Ryder replies. "It's a stupid title you made up to annoy me."

Tucker grins widely. "Bingo, buddy."

I experience a swell of affection toward Tucker Franklin. As far as I can tell, he's the one person who's always been there for Ryder. Who Ryder has always *allowed* to be there for him.

"Ryder James. Why does your name sound so familiar?" Prescott muses.

The vodka in my stomach hardens to ice. "I think I see a table opening up," I blurt. "We should go—"

"I just got released from Leavenworth," Ryder says quietly. "It was in the papers."

Prescott snaps his fingers, nodding enthusiastically. "Right! That's it. It must have been in the *Globe*." The satisfaction of solving his little mystery fades slowly, somberness replacing triumph. "How, uh, how long were you in for?"

"Seven years."

"Wow. I—wow. Must be nice to be out."

I'm certain Prescott has never met anyone who's served time in prison before. His childhood was as sheltered and privileged as mine. The closest he's gotten to criminal law is taking classes on it. It's obvious he has no idea what to say to Ryder.

Maybe I'm being too harsh. Most people would have a difficult time navigating this conversation.

"At least friends can't spring happy hours on you in the inside," I say, attempting to lighten the uncomfortable moment.

"Oh, Ry picked this place," Tucker says quickly, nudging Ryder with his elbow. "Soon as we packed up for the day, he was begging to go somewhere fancy."

Ryder rolls his eyes. "I need a beer."

"Wait till he sees the prices here." Tucker grins, then follows Ryder toward an opening halfway down the bar top.

"I didn't think Tuck would want to drive into the city after work," Keira tells me quietly. "He finished early, wanted to surprise me."

I hear the subtext loud and clear. She didn't know Ryder would be here.

"You got a good one," I reply, smiling so she knows I'm not upset with her.

I'm so happy for Keira. But, God, my life would be a lot simpler if she were marrying anyone else.

Keira's gaze follows Tucker, her expression softening. Her smile turns dreamy. "I know."

"How did you and Tucker meet?" Prescott asks.

Keira glances at me before answering. "We, uh, went to school together. We both grew up in Fernwood. Just … found each other, I guess."

"Table, guys! Table!"

We all look at Juliet, who's pointing toward an open booth in the back.

I grab my drink and follow Prescott over to the table. Keira pauses to tell Tuck where we're headed.

None of my dread dissipates as I slide across the cool leather of the booth, next to Juliet. Gavin's arm is draped casually over her shoulders as he types something on his phone. I find his lack of attention annoying, but Juliet doesn't seem to care. And I'm just as senselessly irritated by Prescott's polite conversation with one of the waiters as he orders another cognac.

"Want anything, babe?" he asks me.

My nails dig into my palm before I answer, "Sure. Another martini, please."

Our second round of drinks arrives at the same time as Keira, Tucker, and Ryder.

Keira ends up sitting on the other side of Prescott, their polite conversation easily audible as I sip on my martini. She's asking if he's from Boston originally.

"No, I'm a West Coast guy," Pres replies. "My dad works in tech. I grew up in San Francisco."

"Oh, cool," Keira says. "I went to Stanford for college."

"I loved Stanford. And I was playing tennis, so I was very tempted to go there. But I wanted to get a little farther from home."

"Where did you end up?"

"Michigan."

"My brother went there! He loved it."

"Yeah, it's a great school."

"Do you have any siblings?" Keira asks.

"Nope." Pres picks up his beer. "I'm an only child, like Elle."

A *very* awkward silence falls, making it obvious I wasn't the only one eavesdropping on Keira and Prescott.

Everyone here—with the exception of Gavin and, I guess, Prescott—knows I'm not technically one.

Prescott's brow wrinkles as he tries to figure out what the sudden undercurrent of tension is.

Ryder's expression is stony as he takes another sip of beer. I have no idea what he's thinking. Is he judging me for not telling Prescott about Rose? I never told Pres I was an only child. He just assumed, logically, from the lack of siblings in my life. Rose's death isn't a topic that comes up naturally. I'm used to the important people in my life already knowing about my late sister.

Since I can't come up with any natural way to redirect the conversation, I blurt, "Could I get out? I need to grab a water."

"We can flag a waiter," Prescott says.

"No, it's fine. I've been sitting all day. Standing sounds good."

He nods but frowns slightly at the flimsy explanation. I hastily slide out of the booth and hurry toward the bar.

It takes a minute for the bartender to work his way down to me.

"An ice water, please," I request.

"Make that two."

I stiffen at the sound of his voice, but Ryder says nothing else. When I gather the courage to glance over, his eyes are on the television behind the bar, focused on the baseball game. The Sox are losing.

"I didn't know you'd be here," I tell him.

"That makes two of us." His gaze falls to the varnished wood of the bar top. "Cormac's mentioned wanting me to see his campus, so when Tuck said he was headed into the city, I thought …" He shrugs. "I should get going soon. Cormac thought he'd be done at his internship at six."

I'm taken aback—stunned really—by the strong urge that slams into me.

I want to see it. I want to be there to witness when Cormac proudly shows off his accomplishments to his big brother.

But Ryder has no idea that I've kept in touch with Nina or Cormac. And he doesn't *care*, not the way I do. He never did.

"You're a good brother," I tell him.

"You're a good sister," he replies softly.

Cutting to the chase, like always. Not letting me hide. He knows exactly why I left the table.

I scoff. "Not really. I never talk about her. I only go to her grave once a year, on the anniversary of her death."

"So?"

"So, shouldn't I go more?"

"Why should you go more?"

I shake my head. "Stop asking questions. You only got the one."

"We could play again," he suggests.

"That's a bad idea."

"Why?"

"Another question. And you know why."

The bartender appears with two glasses. "Here are the waters."

I thank him, then take a long sip of one.

Ryder doesn't touch his. He's staring at me, and I feel like I'm standing at the edge of a diving board, having to decide whether to walk back or jump. I'm so, so close to admitting what I'm afraid Ryder has already realized—I'm not over him. I don't trust myself around him. Not even here, in a busy bar with my boyfriend nearby. I've never had to be alone with Ryder to feel like I am.

"That guy, Elle? Really?"

I freeze, my mouth full of icy water as my veins surge with heat.

I've been careful. To keep *us* in the past. To coexist. To support Keira and Tuck without causing any conflict.

With four words, Ryder blew it all up.

How dare *he?*

I'm furious, but I'm even more stunned. Smacked straight in the face with a foul ball.

Ryder walks away before I can manage a single word.

I watch him until the door shuts behind him and he's out of sight.

X ♥ X

Keira's drunk. Giggling as she leans heavily against a grinning Tucker. Juliet's spinning on the sidewalk, Gavin's full attention on her.

Prescott and I are the awkward, squeaky wheels tagging along with two happy couples. Standing with a foot of space between us.

Any buzz from the two martinis I drank has long since faded. I'm somber and sober.

Keira stumbles toward me with open arms. "*So* glad you came."

"Me too," I lie, hugging her back. Glance toward Tucker. "Get her home safe."

He grins. "Always. Ry took my truck, so I'll drive her car home."

Juliet gives me a hug too. "See you in two weeks. Maybe sooner."

"Two weeks?" I try to do some quick mental math on dates. Now that school has finished, all my days look the same. I barely know what day of the week it is.

"The Fourth of July!" Keira exclaims. "You said you'd come to the beach house."

"And to celebrate your birthday," Juliet adds.

Crap. I remember committing to that, back before graduation. It feels like a lifetime ago.

"Hopefully you can join us, Prescott," Keira says, glancing at him.

"I can't, unfortunately," he replies. "I'm going home to visit my parents."

Immediate guilt. He never mentioned the trip again, so I assumed he decided against it.

"Oh. That's nice," Keira comments.

"Come on, Parker," Tuck says, tugging on her hand. "We gotta get home."

"Past your bedtime?" she teases.

"Yes," he replies. "Crew's showing up at six tomorrow."

"Okay, okay."

We all exchange goodbyes, and then Prescott hands his ticket to the valet. Neither Prescott nor I say anything until we're in the car, driving toward my neighborhood.

"Your birthday is in two weeks?"

"Um …" I run my tongue along the backs of my teeth. Out of everything that happened tonight, that's not what I was expecting him to bring up. "Yeah. July 5."

A pause.

"Do you know when my birthday is?"

"Also July 5?" I joke.

"Nope."

"Sorry," I mutter. I'm not just apologizing for not knowing his birthday.

"Don't apologize. Makes me feel better about not knowing yours."

"Well, we're both past twenty-one," I say. "Birthdays don't matter as much. All downhill once drinking is legal."

My attempt to lighten the mood falls flat.

Prescott brakes at a red light, then looks over at me, his expression very serious. "When is Ryder's birthday?"

I flinch, and there's no way Prescott misses it.

"Answer isn't *I don't know*, right?"

"It was high school," I tell him. "Another life."

"Were you dating when he went to prison?" Prescott asks.

I swallow. "Yes."

"That must have been hard."

"It was hard to … watch it happen. He's a good person. People make mistakes."

Prescott snorts. "A *mistake*? He served seven years. That's a hell of a lot more than a parking ticket."

I sigh. "Can we not talk about Ryder?"

The light changes to green, and Prescott turns left. "Yeah. Sure. What *do* you want to talk to me about, Elle? Because lately, it's not anything except the fucking bar exam. It's not visiting my parents. It's not your ex. You sure don't want to have sex with me. So, it's getting real hard not to read into all that."

"Pres …"

"I'm trying to be understanding. I am. I'm just … do you even *want* to be in a relationship with me?"

"Of course."

He shakes his head. "There's no *of course*, Elle. Not after the way you've been acting lately."

"I'm sorry. I didn't mean to—"

Prescott exhales heavily. "I don't want you to apologize. I want you to … care, I guess. I want to feel like I'm not the only one invested in us."

"I do care, Pres. You're important to me."

"Important …" He muses on the word like he's never heard it before. "I'm important to you, but you've never looked at me the way you were looking at Ryder tonight."

"We have some history, is all."

"And what was the *only child* thing? What did I step into there?"

I close my eyes. "I don't want to talk about it right now."

This isn't how I want to tell him about Rose, as part of an argument.

"Has anything happened between you and Ryder?"

"I'm not a *cheater*." And two martinis were enough to punctuate that statement with plenty of righteous indignation.

"Felt like I was getting cheated on most of tonight."

I suck in a sharp breath. "*Wow.*"

"Not just … Ryder. All of your friends. You've kept us totally separate from your world. All the inside jokes and the awkward silences when they figured out how fucking clueless I was …"

"You're making it sound way worse than it was."

"Am I?"

Is he? I don't know. I was distracted by Ryder the entire time, his parting words bouncing around my head the rest of the night.

Prescott stops the car in front of my brownstone a couple of minutes later. "I think we're done, Elle," he tells me quietly. "Just … done."

The words hurt, but not the way they should. Not the searing agony I've experienced twice before.

It stings like salt in a wound. Unpleasant, but not life-threatening. Temporary. I know the pain will be gone soon.

I feel guilty for hurting Prescott.

And I'm angry with myself for my inability to be normal. To move on.

But I'm not heartbroken.

"That guy, Elle? Really?"

The *gall* of him to judge my relationship. To take one look at a nice, reliable guy and decide he's wrong for me. And worse, for that snap judgment to be right.

"I'm so sorry, Pres," I say softly. "Truly. I-I *never* meant to hurt you."

Prescott heaves a sigh. "I know."

I hope he does. Hope he's not just saying so.

I offer him a final weak smile, then step out of the car and carefully close the door behind me. Watch his taillights disappear down the street.

As soon as I'm inside, I flop down on the couch and pull my phone out. Scout jumps up to snuggle against my side. Stroking his soft fur usually calms me. Not right now. I hold the phone against my ear so tightly that it hurts, listening to it ring. His number might have changed. But, for some reason, I don't think it has.

He answers after two rings, yet says nothing.

We sit in silence, me glaring at the empty fireplace and petting Scout, until I can't take it anymore.

" *'That guy, Elle? Really?'* What the *fuck* was that, Ryder?"

My imitation of his voice is awful, but neither of us laughs at the bad impression.

Yelling at him feels good. Right, as wrong as that sounds. I've tried so hard to be polite. To rise above. And that civility has done nothing to release the simmering resentment and rage I've held on to for years.

"It was a question."

He's not being glib, just literal. Still manages to just piss me off more.

"You don't get to ask me that sort of question. Who I date is *none of your damn business.*"

His exhale is heavy. "I'm sorry I overstepped. I just want you to be—"

"I don't give a *shit* what you *want* me to be. I stopped giving a shit when you *broke up with me.*"

"Elle ..."

"Actually, you didn't just break up with me. You *abandoned* me. Twice! So, you don't get to have any say in how I move on or who I move on with."

A long silence, followed by a soft, "Okay."

And I hate him for being agreeable. For not doubling down. For not yelling back.

For not fighting. In the moments I really need him to, he sets down his sword.

It makes me feel even worse about my conversation with Prescott in the car. Because I know exactly how he feels. Because praying someone else will care more is draining and exhausting and, in the end, pointless.

"You thought I'd stay single for *seven years?*"

There's a pause as Ryder absorbs the poison in my words.

My thoughts and feelings are too snarled to sort out if the acid is unfairly aimed at him or not. If he deserves it or if I'm simply searching for an outlet for my own demons and shortcomings. Ryder's always been the one person who seems equipped to handle my darkness. Who has never expected anything and only accepted.

"No. I didn't think you'd wait," he finally answers.

The change of phrase pummels me. Because in so many ways, I *did* wait. I still am.

"What the hell was there to wait for?" I snap.

"We're over, Elle. We were never going to work. I've accepted that. You should too."

"A guy who cares more about you than his golf score or his college frat."

"You don't know him."

"Okay, fine. I don't know him. Why are you calling, Elle?"

Anger is draining away, leaving pure exhaustion behind.

"Because you said I always could," I whisper.

"Ryder?" a woman's voice says.

There's a muffled scuffle on his end, like a hand placed hastily over a speaker. Followed by a muted, "I'll be right there."

His hand doesn't manage to block the woman's answer, "Okay."

I hang up.

Ten seconds later, he calls. I watch it ring, then roll over and stuff my face inside the crease of the couch, deep enough that I can't hear or see and can barely breathe. Scream until my throat hurts.

Then, it dawns on me that he'll probably be part of the Fourth of July celebrations, and I'll have to start all over again.

20
THEN

Elle

Fat raindrops start falling from the sky as I take the turn that leads to the trailer park. I smile with a sort of grim satisfaction as one hits my cheek and rolls off my jaw. Dark clouds have threatened rain all day, and I should have put up the convertible's cover before leaving for school this morning. Ryder will roll his eyes that I didn't, and that will create this giddy bubble in my chest.

Happiness, I think.

I'm happy. And it's not just Ryder, although he's a large part of it. It's making my own choices, of feeling like I'm the driving force in my own life again.

Damp dust swirls in the afternoon air as I navigate the bumpy road the best that I can. The rain hasn't saturated the ground yet.

Ryder's already outside when I park beside his trailer, talking to a guy with shaggy black hair who I vaguely recognize from seeing around school. I grab my backpack off the passenger seat and climb out of my car, masking my uncertainty with a friendly smile.

"This must be your *plans*." The guy beside Ryder is talking to him but focused on me.

When our eyes connect, he smirks. There's a predatory gleam to his expression that makes my skin crawl. That screams untrustworthy.

I fiddle with the zipper of my jacket as a small distraction. I came straight from cheer practice, only making one quick stop in town, and I wish I'd taken the time to change as interested eyes rove over my bare legs.

"Yeah. I'll see you at work, Phoenix."

They're not good friends, based on the coolness in Ryder's tone. Or maybe he's noticed how Phoenix's attention has stalled on me, which I'm uncomfortably aware of.

"All good. I'll see you around. Nice to meet you, Elle." He flashes another wolfish smile.

I force a nod. "Yeah. You too."

Phoenix turns and continues walking down the road, his hands tucked into his pockets.

"You're early."

I drop the zipper and look at Ryder. It's raining harder now, darkening the sleeves of my jacket. "Sorry."

He lifts one eyebrow. "Not looking for an apology."

"Friend of yours?"

"Nix doesn't really have friends," Ryder replies. "He has people he likes to hang around with and people who owe him favors."

"Which one are you?" I ask.

"I don't owe him a favor."

I hike my slipping backpack up my shoulder. "You gonna invite me in?"

He glances at my car. "You gonna put your cover up?"

"Car could use a cleaning."

Ryder rolls his eyes.

I smile, then hit the button on the key. "Done."

The rain picks up even more as we walk toward the stairs that lead to the front door, saturating my scalp and spreading through my hair. The water feels refreshing on my face, although it's probably making a mess of the makeup I'm wearing.

Ryder tries the door, then swears under his breath.

"You lock yourself out?" I ask, pausing a few inches behind him.

The tiny porch is barely big enough for both of our bodies.

"Not exactly. The shitty paint on the door sticks when it gets wet. Last time I broke the lock to get in … my mom wasn't happy."

"That's … inconvenient."

Are we stuck out here then?

"Surprised your place doesn't have the same problem." Ryder grins, then heads down the stairs.

"Ha-ha," I respond, following him. "So, what are—"

Ryder rounds the corner, so I quicken the pace. By the time I catch up to him, he's reaching up to pull off a window screen. Rain is still falling steadily. Fast enough that it's altering visibility, adding a haziness to the air. The shoulders of Ryder's gray T-shirt look black.

He makes quick work of the screen, leaning it against the foundation, then starts jimmying the window frame.

"You've done this when the door worked fine, haven't you?"

Ryder doesn't turn so I can see his entire expression, but I catch the crease in his cheek that suggests he's smiling. "Yeah."

A few seconds later, he's got the sash wide open. He tilts his head toward the window, indicating I should go first.

I eye the distance from the ground to the opening. I'd estimate it's about five feet. Not an impossible distance. Not an easy one either.

"I'll wait for the door to unstick."

Ryder chuckles. "Come on, Clarke."

"I'm wearing a skirt."

"I noticed." His gaze sweeps down deliberately, his smirk suggesting he knows what effect it has on me. "Looks good on you."

"Flattery will get you nowhere, James."

He leans back against the side of the trailer, flashing that grin that should come with a neon-colored warning label. "Wanna bet?"

Not particularly.

Ryder's smile grows in my answering silence. "C'mere, Lo."

I never should have admitted how much I like him calling me that.

His hand lands on my lower thigh as soon as I'm close enough to touch. My breath hitches, and he hears it.

"Drop the bag and turn around."

I heave a sigh and listen. A few seconds later, I'm being boosted, the window's opening right in front of my face. Drops of water hit the backs of my legs as I wriggle through, landing on the floor in an uncoordinated heap. I sit up and survey my surroundings, experiencing a surprised jolt when I realize this is Ryder's bedroom.

"Elle."

I stand and reach for my backpack, pulling it through the window and then dropping it on the floor by the bed. It's only a twin, and I'm having a hard time picturing Ryder fitting on it.

With impressive dexterity, Ryder vaults through the window as well. He leaves it open, the percussive tapping of rain against the metal side of the trailer the only sound in the room.

I pull off my wet jacket, then take a seat on the bed and reach for my backpack, simply for something to do that's not staring at him or studying his bedroom.

"Whoa. Nerd alert."

"Shut up," I say. "You told me to bring homework."

Ryder grabs a towel off the back of the door and rubs his damp hair. It's starting to grow out a little. "And this is the one time you decide to listen to me?"

I roll my eyes as I pull out my sketch pad. "Whatever. This is due tomorrow, so …"

He approaches the bed. My entire body tenses in response, his proximity hijacking all of my senses so all I'm aware of is him.

"A house?" he asks, staring at the sketch.

"It's a project for my Architecture class. We're supposed to design our dream home."

"This is your dream home?"

"I mean, I like it," I reply. "It doesn't actually exist, so it's a pretty low commitment."

I'm fighting the urge to close the notebook, noticing how closely Ryder is scrutinizing the drawing.

"You wouldn't be able to use the screened porch most of the year," he tells me. "It's impractical."

I smile. "Like owning a convertible?"

"Yeah. *Exactly* like that."

My cheeks start to hurt. Anticipation is expanding in my chest, making my pulse race with recklessness. I slip off my shoes and tuck my feet on the bed, lying on my side and relaxing onto the mattress.

It's erotically intimate, lying in the same spot Ryder sleeps in every night, surrounded by his scent.

He stares down at me. "Elle …"

"I'm tired. Long cheer practice."

"Too much pom-pom waving?"

I reach for the pillow behind my head and toss it toward him. Ryder catches it easily.

"We work harder than the football team, which you'd know if you ever came and watched."

"I went once."

"And I sure hope the field didn't block your view of the parking lot."

Ryder snorts, then tosses the pillow back to me.

We stare at each other, neither of us saying anything, as the amusement slowly fades from the moment. Until I'm reacting to the intensity of it, my chest tightening like it's being squeezed by a massive fist.

He breaks eye contact first, clearing his throat and then glancing down at the floor. Everything about his pose is deceptively casual, his relaxed lean humming with invisible tension, like a live wire. If we were still out in the rain, it seems impossible he wouldn't crackle and spark, same as exposed electricity.

I sit up, reaching toward my backpack. "So … I have this vague memory of September 25 being your birthday."

There's a pause, which I fill by pretending I have to search for the carefully nestled box.

"A vague memory, huh?" His tone is inscrutable. Impossible to read, especially when I'm not looking at him.

I pull the white bakery box out and place it on the mattress, then glance up to meet Ryder's gaze. "It's a s'mores cupcake. It was that or lemon raspberry."

"No plain vanilla or chocolate?"

"Of course not. Butter & Batter doesn't do single flavors."

"Today's the twenty-fourth."

"You can eat it tomorrow, if you want."

His exhale sounds amused. And then he's kicking off his sneakers and climbing on the bed with me, careful not to jostle the box before lying down next to the wall. I scooch until I'm lying flat too. My left side is pressed against his, the bed not really wide enough for both of us. Heat radiates from every spot he's touching me, blazing through my body like the sun's warmth.

Ryder is looking at the box. "Thank you, Elle."

"Mmhmm." I grab my sketchbook and flip to a fresh page. Draw two horizontal lines, then cross them with two vertical ones. Leave the book lying on my stomach.

"What are we playing for?" he asks, reaching for the pencil and making a neat X in the top-right corner.

Rookie error. He should have taken the center spot, like I always do. And then I realize … that's why he didn't.

"What do you want, birthday boy?" I add an O to the center of the board.

He still hasn't confirmed I got the date right, but I don't think I'm wrong. My brain can't seem to forget anything about this boy.

"Nothing," Ryder answers.

"Nothing? How altruistic of you."

He smiles. "Nothing that's not right here."

I swallow, momentarily stunned speechless.

"All I've ever wanted out of life was a s'mores cupcake," Ryder continues.

My scoff sounds forced, my mind still reeling from the softness on his face.

His second X gets drawn in the bottom-right corner, forcing me to block him. He blocks me next, so I go for the top center. He blocks me again, lining up two X's and forcing me to block him again. I drop the pencil, the possibilities already played out in my head and all leading toward the same outcome.

"Cat's game."

"You're rusty."

"Haven't played in a while."

Ryder hums. "So … you still got a lot of homework to do?"

I roll my eyes as I toss the sketchbook onto the floor. "You told me to—"

"I know; I know." Ryder shifts so he's propped up on one elbow, leaning over me. I inhale sharply, registering how close he is all over again. "I wasn't sure where we stood on … stupid stuff."

His head lowers until his lips brush my collarbone, the gentle press of his mouth against my bare skin pushing a surprised, "Oh," out of my mouth. The flash of heat is silent at least, but he can probably feel the fever radiating from my skin.

My breathing becomes rapid and greedy. I know he can hear it when I feel the vibration of his chuckle against my skin. His lips move lower, tracing the raised line until he reaches the center of my chest. I moan as he brushes the curves of my breasts. Trying to regulate my breathing and failing miserably.

Ryder shifts again, so he's hovering over me, his gray eyes blazing like liquid smoke.

I lift my head off the pillow and kiss him, wrapping my arms around his neck and tugging him down. He's careful to keep his full weight off me, but doesn't resist my attempt to fuse our mouths together.

His tongue slides inside my mouth to touch mine, and I'm very glad I'm already lying down.

Ryder's a really good kisser. He's the one who taught me *how* to kiss, and maybe that's why our lips touching feels like reunited puzzle pieces.

We fall into a rhythm like choreographed dance partners. There's no awkwardness. No teeth clashing or tongue biting.

I'm nervous and euphoric and overwhelmed, my heartbeat speeding to a wild flutter in my chest. I'm rapidly reaching a point where *more* is my only thought.

My hands coast over Ryder's shoulders and down his back. The lines of bunched muscle are easy to feel through the damp cotton of his T-shirt.

He breaks out of my hold when I reach his waist, grabbing the white box that's miraculously remained upright on the mattress.

My entire body reacts, watching him swipe a finger through the brown icing. The sugar and butter concoction feels cool and smooth against my skin as he spreads a straight line up the inside of my thigh.

A surprised, strangled sound chokes my throat as his warm tongue follows the path of his finger. Ryder stops south of my skirt, his nose barely brushing the hem.

I roll my head for the best possible view.

Ryder glances up, his intense gaze colliding with mine. A mixture of desire and relief courses through me when I see there's no hesitation on his face this time. "You trust me?"

I nod.

He reaches under my skirt and tugs my compression shorts down, a small smile appearing as he tosses the navy fabric away. My lace thong hits the floor next.

Nerves pinball through my body as I fist the comforter. We've never done this before. I've never done this before.

My knees part slowly, excruciatingly aware I'm on full display. It's vulnerable. But I also feel powerful, not missing the way Ryder's forearm flexes or how his eyes hood.

The longer he looks, the more impatience erases embarrassment. I spread my thighs as wide as they'll go, tugging my skirt up so it's a belt around my waist.

He gets the hint.

Ryder's head lowers. A shiver quivers through me when I feel his breath hit the spot he just uncovered. He's blowing on the wetness there, and it's like the intolerable sensation of being tickled. I exhale harshly and lock my muscles in place, so tempted to squirm.

"Stop teasing." My voice sounds foreign to my own ears, breathy and high.

"Stop telling me what to do. You're not in control here, Lo." His lips land on my hip bone, the tip of his tongue drawing a circle on my skin.

I gasp, the throbbing between my thighs growing more insistent.

Juliet said Alec went down on her in the pool house at Maddie's party a few weeks ago. Her description of the act was a kid eating a melting ice cream cone. Everything about Ryder's position, including his confident grip on my leg, suggests skill. I try not to focus on what that means because it'll puncture the heady anticipation I'm experiencing. I want to pretend I'm the only girl he's ever touched.

My entire body jolts when I feel his tongue *there*. It's foreign and thrilling, an immediate rush of heat pooling low in my pelvis. He licks the sensitive flesh, and my hips rock into his mouth involuntarily. The flush of arousal is joined by a flash of embarrassment.

Ryder notices. Smirks. "You want more?"

God, I can't handle having a conversation with him while his face is between my thighs. Any brash confidence has been stripped away.

The next time we hooked up, I was planning to be mature. I was supposed to blow his mind. Not be this … puddle of hormones and emotions.

"Elle. Talk to me."

I clear my throat. "Yeah, I want more. It feels good. Just … weird too."

He studies my face, and I know he's reading the truth about my inexperience with this.

This time, he fills me with a finger. I inhale in response to the invasion, my body slowly adjusting to the sensation as his mouth moves to the bundle of nerves above his hand and sucks lightly. Ryder groans, like this is possibly as good for him as it is for me, a vibration that makes my toes curl. It's too much. So much. Exactly what I need.

A strangled exclamation leaves my mouth as I'm hit with a dizzying rush of pleasure. I can't recall ever experiencing anything this potent or powerful.

It doesn't let up. Doesn't wane. It ignites and spreads and overpowers, the heat burning away any thoughts at all. I can't focus on anything except how *good* it feels.

And then it's crashing over me, my muscles trembling and shaking and twitching. A complete slave to the consuming sensations. I can feel each chaotic beat of my heart, the pounding gradually slowing as I sink into the mattress. The craze has settled into a steady, satisfied hum, my limbs loose and pliant.

He's a really, really good kisser.

Ryder's smile is deservedly smug. There still a few stars twinkling behind my eyelids. His lips are shiny, and I try to memorize what that looks like. I want to remember what it feels like.

Mine.

"Wow." My voice sounds normal again, but the tone is definitely awed.

"Yeah?" Ryder reaches for his cupcake again, this time breaking off a piece and popping it into his mouth. The only way the sight would be sexier is if his shirt was off.

"Yeah."

He nods, then swallows. "Good."

I sit up, too, but don't reach for my underwear. I want him to know I'm still bare beneath my cheer skirt.

"Want a bite?" Ryder holds a piece of cupcake out.

"You didn't even wash your hands."

He smirks. "Didn't need to. You were already so … wet."

Cheeks burning, I take the bite. Chocolaty richness explodes in my mouth, followed by the faint aftertaste of marshmallow and graham cracker.

I swallow, then climb onto his lap. I'm still so sensitive that the brush of his mesh shorts between my legs feels incendiary.

"I want more. I want … you."

Ryder closes the cupcake box, his expression turning serious. I'm sure he's thinking about how our last conversation on this subject went.

"If you want to wait, that's okay," I say. "But … *I* don't want to wait."

I'm greedy for another orgasm. Eager to experience sex again. And he's the only one my body wants.

His Adam's apple bobs as he swallows. "Let me grab a condom. They're under the bed."

I don't allow myself to think about that convenience. I nod and swing my leg back off his lap, fiddling with the hem of my shirt. I should take it off. Or will he want to? My memory of the details from last time is fuzzy, faded by nerves and embarrassment and eventually anger.

Ryder reaches under the bed and returns with a box I'm ridiculously relieved to see is still sealed.

I use the tiny boost to confidently tug my shirt off, unclasping my bra and adding it to the growing pile of clothes on the floor. I glance toward the window. All that's visible is a green stretch of hedge. I can see the water clinging to the branches. It's still raining out.

He's pulling his shirt off, too, a foil packet visible in one hand as the rest of the box goes back under the bed.

I slip out of my skirt, then lie back down.

"*Fuck*," Ryder comments, his eyes on my body.

"You've seen it all before," I remind him.

He's focused on me so closely that I'm torn between self-consciousness and satisfaction about the intense attention.

"Not for two years. Your boobs are bigger. And you've started shaving more." He cups my hip bone, his thumb sweeping across the small section of hair no one else has seen.

Heat blazes in my cheeks. "I didn't know I was supposed to …"

"You're fucking gorgeous, Elle. Always have been. Always will be."

Then, he drops his shorts and boxer briefs, and it's my turn to gawk. Ryder tears the foil packet open with his teeth. He rolls the condom on, and then he's hovering above me again, this time skin to skin. He kisses me first, sucking lightly on my tongue. I bite gently on his bottom lip, running my hands into his hair. He groans as my nails scrape his scalp, his erection hot and hard against my thigh.

"Fuck. That feels good." His voice is low and husky and my own personal brand of arousal.

"I like your hair longer," I admit.

"Yeah?"

"Yeah. More to grab on to."

His hand travels down my rib cage until it reaches my hip. "I'll keep that in mind." Two fingers brush the inside of my thigh as he adjusts our position, fisting his cock and rubbing it between my legs. "Still good?"

"I'm good."

This is going to hurt, based on some hasty calculations. My body isn't the only one that's changed since we last did this. Ryder's dick looks twice the size. And I haven't had sex in two years. I'm basically a virgin. But I want this. Want it so bad that I can taste it.

The head of his cock hits my opening, and there's an immediate stretch. He starts to ease inside me, and I arch my back. We were fumbling around before. The purposeful way Ryder is thrusting inside of me feels very adult. Possessive and primal and intimate.

My inhale is swift and surprised.

"You've done this before?" He says it as a question, even though we both know the answer.

I swallow, forcing myself to hold his gaze as the pinching flares to true pain. "Once."

Ryder is excellent at hiding his emotions when he wants to. His expression doesn't change at all. The only noticeable reaction is the quick heave of his shoulders as he exhales and stills.

"You should have told me."

We're as closely connected as two people can be. But it's the way he said that—*You should have told me*—that makes butterflies flap in my stomach.

His expression isn't the only indifferent thing about him. As far as I can tell, what he cares about is a very short list. But I catch a fleeting glimpse of … something that makes me hope he might care about me.

"I just did."

He huffs what sounds suspiciously close to a laugh. "Little late."

"You're just … bigger."

This time, Ryder grins. The sight inflates my chest the same way my own happiness does. Like his emotions are my emotions.

"Sorry."

I roll my eyes. "No, you're not."

He's still grinning at me, a relaxed one that's boyish and a little mischievous. Then, he's moving—and not in the way I want. Away instead of closer. I grip his shoulders and clench.

Ryder grunts, "Relax, Lo."

"I don't want you to stop."

"I'm not stopping. Just adjusting. Move against me. Like that, there, yeah."

My hips lift, my breaths coming faster and harder as I feel that distinctive swell of pleasure start to build again. The flicker quickly strengthens, the feeling rising from some deep, secret place Ryder has exclusive access to. My hands explore his back, feeling the powerful shift of muscles as he pumps his hips into mine.

My orgasm takes me off guard this time. I'm so focused on Ryder, how he feels and how he looks and this entire moment, that the pleasure is almost muffled. I'm aware of it, but it's also secondary.

Ryder rolls away to take care of the condom, then pulls his shorts back on. I watch him walk over to the open window, red scratches visible on his back.

Mine, I think again.

I sit up, grabbing his T-shirt from the end of the bed and slipping it over my head.

He's lighting a cigarette, the scent of smoke mixing with the perfume of fresh rain and the smell of sex wrapped around me.

I raise an eyebrow. "So, you didn't quit."

Ryder rests one shoulder against the window frame, blowing a stream of smoke outside. "It's my last day of rebellion."

"Meaning you *are* turning eighteen tomorrow?"

He nods. "You have a good memory."

"Sometimes." I walk over to the window, mirroring his posture and leaning one shoulder against the opposite side of the window so I'm facing him. "Can I try?"

He holds out the cigarette. I pinch it carefully and lift it to my mouth gingerly, imitating the action I've seen others do before. Imagining the horrified look on my mom's face if she saw this makes me smile as I suck on the unlit end and then blow out a smoky breath. Immediately, I start coughing.

"Ugh." I cough again, trying to expel the ashy taste. "That's terrible."

"Takes some getting used to," Ryder tells me.

Eyes watering, I hand the cigarette back to him. "Why would you want to?"

Ryder is silent, staring out the window at the rain. He flicks the glowing tip, a few black flecks falling onto the sill. "My mom smokes. Whenever I got up in the middle of the night as a kid, she'd be sitting at the kitchen table with a cigarette. Just … sitting there. Not watching TV or reading or cleaning. She called it her thinking time. And so, whenever I was feeling stressed or overwhelmed, I'd do the same thing. Probably got ahold of these younger than I should've, but …" He shrugs a shoulder. "It'll be legal tomorrow."

"It looks sexy," I say. "Not that I want you to keep smoking. But it looks sexy … when you do it."

Ryder grins, his abs clenching as he rests more of his weight on the wall. "Why didn't you … with Hathaway?"

"I just didn't."

It's a cop-out of an answer, but Ryder nods, accepting it.

"Have you heard from your dad lately?"

"He's texted a few times, yeah."

"Have you answered?" I ask.

"No." He extinguishes the cigarette in a puddle on the sill.

"Why not?"

"Because he feels guilty about kicking me out. He's not reaching out because he actually cares."

"Do he and your mom keep in touch?"

"Depends on the year," he replies. "When she was back with Rory—Cormac's dad—not really. That's part of why Dax split. She started calling him again, asking about me. He didn't want her to have that excuse anymore."

"How-how long were they together?"

I keep waiting for Ryder to stop answering. To shut this topic down. He shared a few snippets of his childhood with me before— enough to illustrate how different our upbringings were—but not this much.

"Four years. I don't remember much of it. They had me pretty early on." He shrugs, shoving his hands in his pockets, then refocuses on me. "What are your parents like?"

"My parents?"

He nods.

We've talked about our families before. But that was more as kids, swapping complaints that felt monumental at the time.

"They're, uh …" I play with the hem of his T-shirt. "They're kind of snobs. Not cruel or unkind, just self-absorbed. They have this … *vision*, I guess. For their life. For mine. My dad's a partner at a big law firm in Boston. All he cares about are my grades. He expects me to go to law school and work at the same sort of place he does. And my mom … she's obsessed with my clothes and my activities and … the guys I date. She's best friends with Mrs. Hathaway—Archer's mom. She pushed for me to date him because it was perfect in her mind.

"They were more relaxed when Rose was alive. My dad would play basketball with me when he got home from work, and my mom would take me on these shopping trips in the city to redecorate my room each year on my birthday. And now … they don't really care what I think. What I want. They make all the big decisions and expect me to go along with it. Whenever I feel unhappy, I figure at least they're happy."

"The Elle I know tells the world how it's going to be. Not the other way around."

"Yeah, well …" I shrug. "I think I'm braver around you."

He smiles. So, I decide to prove it.

"And also … I think I did something stupid."

Ryder lifts one eyebrow, still appearing amused. "What? Did you miss one question on the History quiz earlier? Because a ninety-eight isn't that—"

"I fell in love with you again."

No response. No reaction. He's frozen, so still that I can't even detect the rise of his chest.

"Ryder!" a loud male voice shouts. "The damn door is stuck again. You home?"

"That's, uh, Cormac," Ryder says unnecessarily.

"RYDER!"

I avoid eye contact as I strip his shirt off and toss it to him, then get dressed faster than I ever have in my life. I sling my backpack over one shoulder, following Ryder down the hallway. He glances back at me twice, but says nothing as we enter the other end of the trailer. There's a small kitchen tucked to the left, a square table opposite from it, and then a couch with a television at the far end. It's tidy, plain, with very limited furnishings.

Ryder's focused on the door, jiggling the lock and inspecting the frame.

"Ryder!" Cormac calls again.

"Hang on," Ryder replies. "I'm working on it."

An exasperated huff is the only response.

Despite the lingering embarrassment burning through me, I smile. Something about Ryder's dynamic with his brother reminds me of Rose. And not in a tragic, depressing way. More of a fondness as I recall silly spats about dolls and clothes.

A minute later, Ryder has the door open.

"*Finally.*" Cormac strolls into the kitchen. "We have seriously got to—" He spots me and stops talking.

"Hi, Cormac." I offer an awkward little wave.

"Hi, Elle."

He inspects me closer than I'd like, considering how quickly I put my clothes back on. I'm worried *I just had sex with your brother* might be stamped across my forehead.

"Nice to see you again." I start toward the open doorway. I'm definitely not waiting around for Ryder to get it open again—or going out the window.

"Lo." Ryder grabs my arm as I go to pass him.

Cormac has the fridge door open, dividing his attention between the contents and glancing over here.

"It's fine," I say.

"No, it's not." He looks at his eavesdropping brother, then back to me. "Me too, okay? Me too."

"Yeah?" I whisper.

He nods. "Yeah. I love … dumb shit."

I love how he *gets* me. How this conversation would make no sense to anyone else.

"I should go."

Ryder squeezes my arm. "Drive safe."

I nod, then dart out into the rain.

21
NOW

Ryder

The basketball's steady staccato is oddly soothing. I relax into the folding chair Reese brought out from her kitchen, taking a sip from the bottle of beer in my hand.

She still lives eight trailers down from mine, in the same place she grew up. I wonder if it bothers her the way it bothers me. There's nothing wrong with living here, but *staying* here seems like a failure. There's no sense of accomplishment earned from moving nowhere.

Reese's son, Knox, takes another shot. He makes it. In the half hour I've been here, I've only seen the kid miss a couple, which is a pretty insane shooting percentage.

I glance at Reese sitting beside me. "You might have a future NBA star here."

She smiles and shakes her head, her expression proud as she watches her six-year-old play. "He prefers football actually."

"Really?"

"Uh-huh. He just prefers playing basketball solo. I have a weak arm, according to him."

I laugh before taking another sip. "I don't."

"I remember, Mr. Modest."

"Next time, I'll bring a ball. We can toss it around some."

"He would love that," Reese replies.

We haven't touched on the topic of Knox's father, and I don't bring it up now. If she wants to tell me, she will.

But Tuck was right; her kid does resemble Phoenix.

It's dusk, the final streaks of sunset fading from the sky. Mosquitoes will be out soon.

"So, South Carolina was good?" I ask.

"Yeah. It was great to see my folks. My dad's hip has been bothering him, so it's hard for them to get up here to visit. Knox got to go to the beach, and my mom and I did some shopping in Charleston."

"Shopping? You sure have changed," I tease.

"Shut up. I still prefer shorts and sweatpants, but the occasional dress hasn't killed me."

I smile. "Glad you had a good trip."

"I'm glad the timing didn't mean I missed you. I-I wasn't expecting you to stick around town. Don't get me wrong; I'm happy you have. Just …"

I pick at the wet label on the beer. "I wasn't expecting to stick around either. Things … changed."

She waits, letting me decide what else to share. Saying this hasn't gotten any easier.

"My mom's sick. Doctors are giving her about a year. I can't take off now, not after missing the past seven years. I want to help her out however I can. Need to … say goodbye."

Arguably the one thing I'm worst at. Just ask Elle Clarke.

It takes Reese a minute to speak. She knows my mom better than most people. "*Shit*, Ry. I'm *so* sorry. That's just—*damn*."

"Yeah." I tear more paper. "What the fuck can you do, you know? It's just … it is what it is."

"Cormac knows?"

I nod. "And Tuck."

Knox jogs over to us.

"Nice hoops, buddy," I say.

He nods. "Thanks. Can I have a Popsicle, Mom?"

"That's fine," Reese replies.

Knox races toward the trailer.

"Only one!" she calls after him.

"You did way worse shit than taking two desserts," I remind her.

"Don't you dare give Knox any ideas," she tells me. "He needs positive male role models, not troublemakers."

"Well, I might be fresh out of prison, but according to my parole officer I'm a model ex-con. Had a meeting with him earlier."

"Must feel strange to be out," Reese comments.

I nod. "Yeah, it is."

I haven't really discussed my time in prison with anyone since my release. Everyone—including me—wants to pretend it never happened. But I hear it in my sleep, the buzz of doors and the clang of metal bars. Wake up drenched in sweat, the claustrophobia of being contained in one space stifling.

Tucker's too cheerful to share that shit with. My mom has plenty to worry about. Cormac is a kid who should be busy enjoying his summer.

"Were you anyone's bitch?"

I glance over at Reese. I shouldn't be surprised. She's never encountered a boundary she couldn't bulldoze.

"Seriously?"

Her lips curve around the bottle of beer. "I won't tell anyone."

I shake my head. "*No.* I lucked out, honestly. My cellmate was one of the nicest guys I'd ever met. Loyal too. He kind of reminded me of Tuck."

"What was he in for?"

"Armed robbery. His mom had lost her job, couldn't afford rent. He had five younger siblings who were about to lose the roof over their heads."

Reese sucks in a sharp breath. "Shit. Is he out now?"

I shake my head. "He has two more years. Maybe a little less, if he gets released early like I did."

"You going to visit him?"

"Yeah. I just … it's going to be hard to go back. To be on the other side of it. To be in that building again."

"I still can't believe you got seven years. I mean, you weren't even dealing?"

There's a question lingering after the words.

Very few people didn't nod and think *of course* when they heard I'd been arrested holding two duffel bags of coke. They heard my address, and they made assumptions.

"Talking about it won't change anything," I tell her.

Just like I can't go back in time and tell my mom to stop smoking. Who knows if that's what caused her cancer, but it sure didn't help.

Reese gets the hint, shifting into a cross-legged position. "So, you dating anyone?"

I cough on the sip of beer I was swallowing. "What?"

"You've got some time to make up for," she reminds me.

"No. I'm not dating anyone. I think the criminal record is kinda a turnoff."

"Not as repellant as the *single mom* story. Girls love a bad boy. Worked on Elle Clarke."

My grip on the bottle tightens. "You ever see her?" I ask casually. At least, I hope it's casual.

Elle still hasn't mentioned the visits to my mom, and it's bothered me more each time we've talked. She didn't even bring it up when she called and yelled at me last weekend. And until she mentions it, I can't ask her *why*. It's the mystery that I mull over when I lie in bed after waking up from the nightmare of being in prison.

"*Elle Clarke?*" Reese's eyebrows fly upward with surprise.

I nod. "Yeah."

She must come back to Fernwood for more than her visits to my mom. Her parents still live here. Keira's restaurant is downtown. Rose's grave is in the local cemetery.

"Uh, no," Reese answers. "Not since that fall you left."

My forehead furrows. "That *fall?*"

"Yeah. She transferred to some private boarding school in Connecticut."

"She *did?*"

I'm totally taken aback. I had no idea Elle didn't graduate from Fernwood High.

"Yeah." Reese is looking at me strangely.

I'm failing at casual, but I don't really care.

"Why?"

She shrugs. "I wasn't friends with her. But if I had to guess, I'd say it had to do with the suspension."

I sit up straight. "What suspension?"

Reese laughs once. "You seriously don't know?"

"I was arrested and shipped off to prison, remember?"

"Yeah, fair point. But I figured Tuck would have told you."

Tuck wouldn't have told me. I made it damn clear to him that Elle was a subject I wasn't willing to discuss.

Reese sighs. "What does it matter now anyway? This was all years ago."

Another sigh as I continue to stare at her expectantly.

"She went ballistic on Archer Hathaway in the hallway the day you got arrested. Most of the school saw it. She was screaming. Shouting. Swearing. She even slapped him. Honestly, I'd had no idea Little Miss Perfect had it in her. Rumor was, she got a three-day suspension, but she never came back to school. Not sure what she thought Archer had to do with your arrest, but she was pissed at him about something. Guess I was wrong back then. You did mean something to her."

I force a smile, then wash the bitter taste in my mouth away with some beer. My mind is still spinning with questions, but the answers aren't ones that Reese can give me.

"How's working for Tuck going?"

"Don't tell him, but he's a decent boss."

Reese smiles.

"I like it. I get to work with my hands, see what I accomplished at the end of the day. Never thought I'd work in construction, but … never thought a lot of things would happen. It's been good."

"You going to stick with it past a year?"

I hear what Reese is really asking. Am I going to stay in Fernwood after my mom is gone?

"Probably not. This town … there's too much history. Cormac has this whole life in Boston. He showed me around his campus last week. I've never seen him so … He figured it out. He's going to get a degree and a good job and … I'm so proud of him. But it's not the life you want your older brother hanging around for. I'll come back and visit, but this isn't home for me."

Elle will always haunt me here.

I don't say it, but I'm thinking it. Anywhere I look, I'll be imagining how life might have worked out differently for us. Anywhere I go, I'll be waiting to run into her. One day, she'll have a ring on her finger or a baby on her hip, and it will break my heart.

"I get it," Reese says.

I nod, knowing she doesn't. But then I glance at the basketball Knox left by the hoop, and I reconsider.

Maybe happy endings are fairy tales. When my dad left, I learned that love isn't enough.

Tuck's black truck pulls up in front of Reese's trailer. He hops out a few seconds later, his usual smile stretching his face wide.

"Hey, guys."

He grabs the basketball, shoots, misses, and walks toward us to the soundtrack of uproarious laughter. For a few seconds, we're all kids again.

"Awesome aim," I manage between chuckles.

Tuck flips me off.

Reese is wiping tears from her eyes. "Oh my God. You—that—so bad."

"You should get Knox to give you some pointers," I suggest.

"Yeah, yeah. Let's go, James. I need you to help me with some measurements at the house so I can get them to the appliance guy."

"*Now?*"

"No. Next week, when the fridges are all out of stock again."

I glance at Reese. "What did I tell you?"

She nods. "Terrible boss. You're paying him overtime, right, Tuck?"

Tucker rolls his eyes. "Are you guys drunk?"

"Aw, he's mad we're drinking without him," I say.

"Just like high school," Reese adds. "When you'd go to the One parties for ... what did he call it, Ry?"

"Hanging out with the *cool guys*," I state.

"Ri-ght," Reese drawls. "That would be a charming anecdote to share at his wedding."

"I was not going to those parties for Keira!" Tuck exclaims.

"Oh. That's worse," Reese says. "Definitely don't mention it at your wedding then."

Tuck groans. "Ryder?"

"Yeah, yeah." I stand and stretch, then give Reese a hug. "Thanks for the beer. And the talk. Let's do it again soon."

"Absolutely." Reese ruffles my hair, then points at Tuck. "My shower is still leaking."

"I'll send a guy," he tells her. "Promise."

"Last guy you sent made it worse."

"It was free plumbing, Reese. But—" He obviously catches a glimpse of the look on Reese's face. "I will send my best guy to work on it this week. Promise."

She nods. "Thank you. Knox is worried the kids at camp will make fun of him for smelling."

My heart sinks. I remember those days as a kid. Waiting for the comments about the holes in my sneakers or the empty space in my lunch box. Kids are cruel.

Tuck's expression is serious as he surveys Reese. I didn't know him until high school, but he probably had some of those same experiences. "I swear I'll take care of it."

"Lighten up, guys," Reese says, noticing our faces. "I was just kidding."

She wasn't though, and we all know it.

Tucker is marrying into one of the wealthiest families in Fernwood. His kids will never be the outsiders.

Reese's son wasn't as lucky. If Knox *is* Phoenix's kid, I hate him for abandoning his kid a hell of a lot more than I resent him for hanging me out to dry with the cops. Growing up without a dad sucks.

"You guys will be there next weekend? Right?"

Reese sucks her bottom lip into her mouth, toeing a weed in the grass. "I'm not sure …"

"It will be fun, I swear. Knox will love the ferry."

"They're *Ones*, Tuck."

"We're too old for that shit, Reese. She's my fiancée. Everyone will be welcoming."

I glance between the two of them. "What are we talking about?"

Tuck's exhale sounds exasperated. "The Fourth of July. Keira and I are hosting at her parents' place on Martha's Vineyard." He looks at Reese. "It won't all be Ones. Ryder will be there."

"Maybe I have plans," I say.

Tuck's snort is offensive. He could at least pretend to believe I have a life.

"Maybe my boss is making me work."

He rolls his eyes. "You have the day off."

I don't ask what I really want to know. *Will Elle be there? Will her boyfriend?* I didn't make it twenty minutes around them without making a comment I should have kept to myself. A whole day—a whole weekend—sounds like a terrible idea.

"If Ryder's going, I'm in," Reese decides.

Damn it.

"Okay, yeah. I'll be there," I say.

Tuck grins like a little kid, then punches my shoulder. "Let's go."

I drain the rest of my beer, then follow him to his truck.

22
THEN

Elle

"We should only show up for halftime," Juliet grouses as she stuffs her pom-poms into her cheer bag.

"Better yet, we should switch to cheering for another team," Keira suggests. "Maybe soccer?"

I shake my head, grab my bag, and head for the parking lot. Juliet drove tonight, so I look for her car. The spaces are half empty, just like the stands were. Seven losses into the season, everyone—including the cheer team—has given up hope of things turning around. We could win all the remaining games on the schedule and still not make it to the playoffs. In all the ways that count, the season is over. Rooting for a lost cause is a hard ask.

I haven't spoken to Archer since we broke up. I haven't forgiven him for how he acted that night, and he's made an obvious effort to avoid me. There are most definitely hard feelings, especially since there's no way he hasn't seen—or heard about—me and Ryder.

But I have *some* sympathy for him, knowing he's getting most of the blame for the football team's terrible record.

"Wow, you're in a rush," Juliet says, skipping until she catches up to me. "Does that mean *Ryder* will be there tonight?"

"No. He has to work."

If he didn't, I'd be skipping this party to hang out with him.

"Tucker too," Keira says, falling into step next to me. "I thought garages had, like, normal hours?"

I shrug. Far as I can tell, Ryder spends most of his time at the garage. If not for a paycheck, to work on the car he's fixing up for himself.

"So, neither of you is single?" Juliet's nose wrinkles on the last word.

She has a tendency to lose interest in guys pretty fast. My guess is, some of her relationships have only lasted as long as they have because Fernwood has very limited options.

I glance at Keira, hoping she'll answer first.

Ryder and I haven't had *the talk*. We've had sex a few more times, and we text multiple times a day. But neither of us has brought up the words we exchanged before I left the trailer that rainy afternoon. We've never eaten a meal together or done anything that resembles a traditional date. He's never referred to me as his girlfriend or introduced me to his mom.

Based on the uncertainty on Keira's face, Tucker hasn't been any clearer with her.

For all his faults, at least Archer was very clear about his intentions. He asked me to prom in front of the whole school. Called me his girlfriend at dinner before the dance.

Juliet gets distracted, digging through her bag for her keys, saving us from answering. Once she finds them, we drive to my house. Juliet and Keira planned ahead, packing outfits for the party so we only have to make one stop.

My mom is sitting in the living room, flipping through a magazine. Her eyebrows creep up her forehead as we traipse into the entryway. I toss my cheer bag into the hall closet, not wanting to bother carrying it upstairs.

"Elle?"

"Hi, Mom."

She strolls into the entryway, smiling politely at Keira and Juliet. "Hello, girls."

"Hi, Mrs. Clarke," they chorus.

My mom glances at her watch, then at me. "I wasn't expecting you home this early."

"We're just getting changed, then going to Maddie's."

"Oh. You didn't mention it."

"Mention what?" I ask.

She lifts one eyebrow. "Could I speak to you for a minute, honey?"

"I'll meet you guys up there," I say, then pass the stairwell and follow my mom into the kitchen.

"I would have had some refreshments ready had I known you were bringing company over," she tells me, pausing by the kitchen island and resting a palm on the granite. Her bracelets clink against the stone.

"Like I said, we're just getting changed quickly. You didn't need to do anything, Mom."

She hums, clearly disagreeing.

"Where's Dad?" I ask.

"Work."

My dad works late a lot. I don't think it's because he's cheating or because he's avoiding being home—he just genuinely loves his job.

But it makes me sad, imagining my mom sitting alone in this big, empty house next fall.

"How did the game go?" she questions.

"We lost."

"Did you talk to Archer?"

I clench my jaw. Shake my head.

She backed off some after we first broke up. My mom thinks she knows better than me, but she's not on a mission to make me miserable. I told her I wasn't happy with Archer, and she's accepted that as much as she's capable of. Meaning she's waiting for me to grow up and realize he's actually perfect for me.

"If the team's doing that poorly, I'm sure he's having a hard time."

"Not my problem."

"That's not very becoming behavior, Elodie."

I exhale. "Juliet and Keira are waiting …"

"Fine. Make sure you're home by midnight. The Historical Society brunch is tomorrow."

"Yeah, I remember."

The Honor Forum requires a certain number of volunteer hours for membership. My mom arranged for me to do mine through one of the organizations she's on the board of.

"Have fun with your friends."

"Yeah. Thanks." I turn and head upstairs.

Keira and Juliet have already changed. I pull on a skirt and a cute top, touch up my makeup, and then follow my best friends back downstairs. I grab my keys to drive myself so that I'll save Juliet a stop on the way home later.

Music is blaring when we meet up again outside of Maddie's mansion. After three-plus years of these parties, I know exactly what to expect inside.

We head into the kitchen first. I opt for a seltzer since I drove.

Maddie approaches me as I'm pouring the fizzy water into a cup. I hate drinking out of cans.

"Hey, Elle."

"Hi, Mads," I reply. "Cute dress."

"Thanks. It's new. Figured it's my last chance before it's snowing out."

"Uh-huh," I say.

It hasn't dipped below fifty yet. I think blizzards are a long ways off.

Maddie leans closer. Her breath smells like sniffing straight tequila. "So, are you, like, *dating* Ryder James?"

My "Yes" is immediate.

I haven't forgotten about the study.

Maddie's not asking because she wants a wingwoman, like Juliet was. She's asking because she wants Ryder.

"Wow." Maddie twirls her hair around one finger. "Did not see that one coming. Is he, like, friendly with you? Because he was kind of a dick when I was on his lap."

"I hate it when strangers sit on my lap too," I say, then walk off toward the living room.

Was that uncalled for? Probably.

Satisfying? Also yes.

I feel possessive toward Ryder in a way I've never experienced with another guy. Claiming him is a thrill, not just because other girls want him. Because *I* want him. My whole life, most things have come easily. I haven't had to struggle or fight for much.

I'd fight for Ryder. Fight hard.

Once I'm in the living room, I chat with Kinsley and a few other cheerleaders. Juliet appears and insists we perform the choreography to a pop song we made up a dance to sophomore year. I drain the rest of my seltzer after the exertion, then decide to use the bathroom. Knowing the lines downstairs will be ridiculous, I walk into the hallway.

"Hey. Ryder's girl."

I turn. The dark-haired guy from Ryder's trailer—Phoenix—is leaning against the wall, next to a door I know leads into a closet, his foot propped up against the plaster like he owns the place.

"Hi," I reply cautiously.

"She speaks." He grins, that same unpleasant one as before. "Does that mean you are his girl?"

I chew on the inside of my cheek. This feels like a test—one I don't know the correct answer to. This is a very different dynamic than a drunk friend. This is Ryder's world. Roughness I've never had any exposure to.

"Ask him."

Phoenix is still smiling. "Tried that. James is hard to crack, like Fort Knox. You seem ... friendlier."

"I'm not."

He raises an eyebrow at my flat tone, then nods and reaches into his pocket. I stiffen as soon as the little packet of white is waved in front of me. "You one of those pretty rich girls who likes to forget how pretty and rich she is?"

Drugs. A little of Ryder's evasiveness—his vague mention of favors—makes more sense. Phoenix is into drugs—and not weed or nicotine. Hard-core stuff.

"No, I'm not."

"Suit yourself." He stuffs the cocaine back into his pocket and straightens. "See you around, Elle." He heads down the hallway.

I continue upstairs. The bathroom connected to Maddie's locked bedroom is guaranteed to be empty.

I grab the key from under the vase, unlock the door, then replace the key before walking into Maddie's bedroom.

Close the door behind me, not noticing the figure sitting on the edge of her mattress until it's clicked shut.

"Hey."

Archer doesn't bother to look up from the cup he's holding. "Hey."

"Sorry to … interrupt," I say. "I was looking for a bathroom. Knew the one in here would be empty."

"Yeah, it is," he tells me, nodding toward the door I know leads to the en suite.

Rather than head that way, I walk over and take a seat next to him on the mattress. "Sorry about the game."

He grunts.

"You … okay?"

"Not really."

"You wanna talk about it?"

"Not with you." Archer drains his cup, then tosses it away. The plastic hits the wooden floorboards with a light tap.

I frown at it. "If that changes, I'm here."

He snorts. "Don't pretend to give a shit now."

"I *do* care, Archer. We were together for months. We've known each other our whole lives. Just because we didn't work out as a couple doesn't mean that—"

"Why didn't we work out as a couple, Elle? Because, as far as I can tell, one day, we were good, and the next, we weren't." He reaches down and grabs a can of beer I didn't notice before, cracking it open and taking a large gulp.

"You don't want me. Not really. You're mad about how things ended. But when we were together? You never even noticed when I was around."

"That's bullshit. Don't rewrite history just to make yourself feel better."

"I-I didn't think you cared, Archer. Honestly."

He scoffs, drains the rest of the beer, and tosses that away too. I flinch, the clang of aluminum louder against the wood.

"I fucked Maddie on this bed last weekend, you know. How's it going with your Two? Has he figured out you won't give it up yet?"

"You're an asshole."

"I'm honest, Elle. We're going to end up together. You'll see."

I shake my head. "You're wrong—"

His mouth covers mine, cutting me off. My entire body goes rigid, the press of his lips against mine somehow both familiar and foreign. My brain has no time to catch up to current events before he's rolling on top of me.

The cushion of the mattress pressing against my back feels strange and unexpected, not soft. Lying down wasn't part of the plan.

The malty taste of beer fills my mouth as Archer's tongue takes advantage of my shock. His hands roam down my sides to cup my ass, pulling me into his growing erection before sliding lower to hoist the material of my dress higher.

A hot flash of alarm unfreezes me. I start to struggle, the heavy weight of him above me crushing and claustrophobic.

My nails find the bare flesh of his biceps and dig deep. Archer groans into my mouth, his hips humping greedily. Either he can't tell

I'm an unwilling participant or he doesn't care. I hope it's the former, that he's deluded himself into thinking I still have feelings for him— that I ever had feelings for him—but I can't tell. He's drunk and angry. And any pity or guilt I was experiencing a minute ago is long gone.

His fingers are creeping higher and higher up the inside of my bare thigh.

I don't want this.

Annoyance flares into true fear as I panic about how far he intends to take this. I've known Archer Hathaway my entire life. He can be selfish, but I never thought he'd disregard me so entirely and just take what he wanted.

A buzzing sound starts in my ears. My stomach rolls with nausea. I'm still struggling, but it's hard to move. He's all I can see and smell and feel. Each second, it seems like he's growing heavier. And my movements are muffled by shock. A large part of me can't comprehend that this is truly happening. That searching for a bathroom evolved into this situation.

I fight through the numbing disbelief, a sharp stab of terror fracturing the senselessness. I bite down on his tongue as hard as I can, rewarded and repulsed by the taste of blood filling my mouth. Archer swears, shifting so there's enough space for me to lift my knee straight into his crotch.

"What the fuck, Elle?" He's curled on his side, his features twisted with pain.

I don't stick around to explain it to him. I flee the bedroom as fast as I can, my heartbeat a chaotic pounding in my ears as I rush downstairs. The sudden commotion is overwhelming, the laughing and joking and loud music no longer muted by the floorboards.

Juliet is standing over by the fireplace. She spots me and heads this way. I run a hand through my hair hastily. I have no idea what I look like. I feel disgusted. Violated.

"Hey. You okay?"

"Yeah, I'm fine. Just have to go to the bathroom."

Juliet's forehead wrinkles with confusion. "You just left to go to the bathroom."

"Couldn't find an empty one," I lie. "Going to try the basement."

"Okay. Be quick. Keira wants to do another dance routine."

I force a nod before turning around. Nothing sounds worse right now. The girl who laughed and shimmied earlier feels like a foreigner. And at some point, Archer is going to come downstairs. Facing him fills me with dread.

I pass the kitchen, turn left, and head out onto the back deck. It's still warm enough that plenty of people are outside. I smile at everyone who calls out to me, but I don't stop walking until I'm around the house and on the street.

I climb into my car and start driving. The wind whips through my hair as I speed along, my tight grip on the wheel relaxing some once I'm a few blocks away from Maddie's house.

There's no specific destination in my mind, but I'm unsurprised when I see the garage sign ahead.

I reach into the glove compartment and pull out a pack of gum once I've parked, popping a piece into my mouth and crushing the silver wrapper in my palm. The taste of mint explodes on my tongue, overpowering the less pleasant flavors lingering. I grab a jacket out of my trunk, then head for the one open door.

Male voices become audible as I walk closer. I can't decide if I'm relieved or disappointed that Tucker is still here.

Both guys glance at me as I reach the doorway. They're standing, staring at a bunch of metal car parts laid out on a green tarp.

"Hey." I manage a smile. "How's progress?"

Tucker grins back. "Great. It's—"

"What's wrong?" Ryder interrupts, frowning.

I shake my head as my smile collapses. Damn, he's perceptive. "Nothing. I just—"

He's in front of me in a few strides, his eyes stormy as they search my face. "Tell me."

"I'll, uh, I just remembered I need to do something, with, uh, something." Tucker hustles toward the opposite end of the garage and away from the tension rolling off Ryder in waves. The intensity is overwhelming.

"Just a weird night. I thought I'd say hi before heading home."

"Weird how?" Ryder questions.

"Um …" I wet my lips nervously.

Do I tell him? I wasn't planning to. Wasn't expecting him to instantly know something was wrong either. I want to forget it happened. I'm not sure if talking about it will help with that or make it harder.

The longer I hesitate, the more pronounced the crease between Ryder's eyes becomes. "What happened?" he asks softly.

My eyes prickle with the telltale warning of tears.

I'm not emotional because of what happened with Archer. I'm devastated by the tenderness in Ryder's expression, the concern on his face so blatant. I'm not used to sharing my struggles.

"Promise me you won't do anything," I say.

"Do anything about *what*, Elle?"

"Promise me. Please."

A muscle jumps in his jaw. "You don't trust me?"

"Of course I trust you. I wouldn't be telling you this if I didn't trust you."

Ryder's exhale is all frustration. "Can we stop talking in circles? Tell me *what?*"

"Promise?"

He studies me for a second, more gravity appearing in his expression as he considers why I'm insisting. Finally, he nods. "I promise."

I play with one of my bracelets, too nervous to meet his gaze. "I was, um, looking for an empty bathroom at the party earlier. I ran into … Archer upstairs. We were talking and he was upset and he started, uh, kissing me. It lasted a few minutes, until I could push him, um, off."

When I gather enough courage to glance up, Ryder's expression resembles a thundercloud. "That motherfucker did *what?*"

"You promised," I remind him quickly.

Ryder's nostrils flare with anger. "He *assaulted* you, Elle. You should tell your parents and the police and—"

I shake my head wildly. "No! No. I don't want anyone to know. He was drunk and mad, and I'm fine. Really."

"Don't make excuses for him. There *is* no excuse."

I nod. "I know. But I just want to forget it happened. He did a bad thing. He's not a bad person."

"You're too forgiving," Ryder tells me.

"I forgave you," I say.

His eyes harden. "That's my point. Someone should protect you from yourself. Actions have fucking consequences."

I close my eyes briefly. I'm too drained to argue with him about this. "I'll, uh, I'll let you get back to work."

I turn to leave, but Ryder reaches for my hand. As soon as I feel his warm fingers weave with mine, I pause.

One gentle tug, and I'm pressed against his chest, inhaling the scent of laundry detergent and sandalwood soap.

"I love you," he whispers into my hair. "I'm mad because I love you so fucking much, Lo."

My arms lift to wrap around his waist. I exhale, a sense of peace washing over me for the first time since I stepped into that bedroom. "I love you too."

We stand like that, him rubbing soothing circles on my back that make the rest of the tension melt away.

"I saw Phoenix at the party."

Ryder stiffens slightly. "Yeah?"

"You know he's a drug dealer?"

"Yeah. How'd you find that out?"

"He offered me some."

Ryder swears under his breath. "I'll take care of it. Make sure he stays away from you."

He says it like it's that simple. Like he has more power than Phoenix.

"Have you ever done ... favors?" I ask.

He pulls back far enough to see my face. "*No*. No, Elle. I know those guys from ... they live right by me. But I'm not involved in any of that shit."

"Okay."

"It would be really easy to make sure Hathaway stays away from you too."

There's steel in Ryder's voice. As much confidence as when he said the same thing about Phoenix.

I'm seeing a lot of Ryder's world tonight. And maybe it should scare me a little. But I trust Ryder, trust him implicitly.

"You promised," I remind him again.

"Promised if you didn't want me to do anything. I'm asking if you're going to change your mind."

"He's not worth it," I say. "He didn't … you know."

"It's not okay because it didn't go that far, Elle."

"I know. But it's not okay for you to do whatever *making sure he stays away* means either. You're better than him."

His jaw flexes a couple of times. "You're sure you're okay?"

"Positive."

"Promise?"

I smile. "Promise." I glance at the tarp. "Can I help?"

He lifts an eyebrow. "Help?"

"Watch."

He smiles. "Yeah, you can watch. C'mon. I'll find you a chair."

I never thought I'd feel so at home in an auto garage.

But I know it's not the garage.

It's Ryder.

23
NOW

Elle

The front door slams.

"Honey, I'm home!" echoes through the first floor.

Keira rolls her eyes. "Kitchen!" she calls back.

Tucker appears a few seconds later. He's dressed casually in a sweatshirt with *Franklin Construction* printed across the front and a backward baseball cap. "Oh, hey. Am I interrupting ladies' night?" he asks, scanning the table that's covered with drinks and food.

"I guess you could call it that," Keira says. "We're drinking wine and wedding planning."

"I thought the wedding was already planned," Tucker says, grabbing a sports drink out of the fridge. He drains most of it in one gulp.

"It is. Mostly. There are still details to decide."

"Do you need, uh, help?"

Keira's expression is wry as she glances at her fiancé. "No. You're off the hook. You'll be using whatever napkin color I decide on."

"Never had strong opinions on napkins anyway." Tucker kisses the top of Keira's head, then reaches out for one of the slices of pizza on the table. "I'll be back in a bit, okay?"

"You just got here."

"I know. But you're busy, and Ryder asked to borrow some tools for a project at Reese's. Figured I'd drive them over myself, help out a bit."

"Okay," Keira replies. "I'll see you later."

"Bye. Later, ladies!"

"Who's Reese?" Ophelia asks once Tucker walks out of the kitchen.

"She's a friend of Tucker's," Keira responds.

"And Ryder's?"

I glance at Ophelia. I thought her interest in Ryder had waned following the weekend on Martha's Vineyard. Now, I'm not as sure. I'm not close enough to Ophelia to ask, and I'm too close to Keira to avoid her reading into it. Which she will, even though I haven't shared the news that I'm single yet.

"Mmhmm. They all grew up together." Keira's attention is on her laptop screen. "What do we think about 'Dancing Queen'?"

"A classic," Ophelia says. "Definitely put it on the list."

After taking a first pass at the seating chart and choosing pale pink for the napkins, we're working on the reception playlist.

I glance out the window at the cute house next door. Keira lived in an apartment downtown when she first moved back to Fernwood, only buying this place six months ago. It's a bungalow, one of the few more modest homes in the residential section of town. On the far fringes of the One zip code.

This is the first time I've been back in Fernwood since Ryder's return. Part of me thought it would feel different. That the air would have changed. That I'd be able to sense his presence somehow.

It felt strange, not heading to the trailer park first. I've respected Nina's wishes and stayed away since she called me.

I miss her. I mailed her more tea a couple of weeks ago. But I can't call or visit without risking Ryder finding out about my trips to see his mom. And if we were in a friendly, cordial place, that might not be so bad. Instead, we're in a place that has me hanging on for dear life.

Two hours later, we've finalized the playlist and migrated into the living room.

I head into the kitchen to use the bathroom that juts off it and top off my wine. A male voice sounds as I'm washing my hands. Tucker must be back, which is probably my cue to leave. I only stopped at my parents' house briefly to drop off Scout, and I have been delaying heading back there ever since. I haven't told them about the breakup with Prescott either. My mom will be disappointed because she wants to plan my wedding as soon as possible. My dad will be bummed about losing his golf buddy.

Footsteps sound as I'm adding another inch of rosé to my glass.

When I turn around, Ryder is standing in the doorway. My entire body reacts. My palms start sweating, and my heart starts sprinting, and my stomach starts flipping.

Will I ever be able to look at him and just feel … normal? All signs point to no.

We haven't spoken since I called him the night Prescott broke up with me. And that conversation did *not* end on a civil note.

"I was at Reese's," he says before I can speak a word.

"Yeah. Tucker mentioned."

"No. I mean—yes, I was there tonight. I also went over there last Friday. That's where I was when you called."

"Cool. Thanks for the update."

I've sipped one glass of wine all night, knowing I'll have to drive home. But with Ryder staring at me—offering explanations I didn't ask for—I swallow most of what I just poured.

"Yeah. *You're welcome.*" He says it sarcastically, and I'm relieved. Civility is gone between us, and it's like a whiff of fresh air after straight smog.

Being around Ryder has always made me feel safe. But it's never been easy or comfortable. It's always the edge of a cliff. Pure anticipation of what will happen between us next. What he'll say. What he'll do. What I'll say. What I'll do. It's never predictable.

I hold up the empty wine bottle. "Doubt you wanted any, but it's gone."

I've never seen Ryder drink wine. Or hard liquor. He's a beer guy.

He leans against the doorway, arms crossed, not even glancing at the wine. His attention is all on me, and it's thrilling and terrifying and ... temporary. "You didn't graduate from Fernwood High?"

My eyes dart around the kitchen. Looking for an escape route. Making sure there are no witnesses.

"And you got suspended senior year?"

My grip tightens on the glass stem and the wine bottle. *Fucking Reese.* I'm positive she told him.

The longer I stay silent, the more irritated Ryder appears. I don't know how he thinks *he* has any right to be the vexed person standing in this kitchen.

"What the hell happened, Elle?"

"None of your business," I snap.

"Yeah, I've heard that one before."

My molars grind. "I'm sure Reese already—"

"I want to hear it from you."

"Too bad we don't always get what we want, isn't it?" I taunt.

He shakes his head. Annoyance has departed, leaving anger behind. "Why the fuck would you—"

"No." I slam the wine bottle down and step closer. "No *fucking way* are we doing this, Ryder. I *begged* you to talk to me. I *begged* you for answers. *No fucking way* are you demanding any from me. You. Shut. Me. Out. My life—my decisions—is none of your damn business. You've heard that before? I'll tell you a thousand more times. That's all you're getting from me."

"Are the gifts you brought my mom none of my business too, Elle? The *seven years* of visits? You think Cormac didn't tell me about the way you edited his college essays and helped him get the internship he's so proud of?"

Crap, crap, *crap.*

Everything he wasn't supposed to know is laid out right in front of me. And if he found out, he wasn't supposed to care enough to ask me about any of it. To demand explanations like he has any right to them.

My shoulders square. "Yeah. That's all none of your business too. I'm not going to apologize—for any of it."

"I'm not asking you to apologize. I'm trying to figure out what the fuck happened after I left."

"If you wanted updates, you should've let me visit," I snap. "I would have explained it to you."

"I was in *prison*, Elle! It wasn't rehab or juvie or—"

"I saw it, Ryder. I know what it looked like. Or are we pretending that never happened either?"

"I'm not pretending anything." He rakes a hand through his hair angrily. "I just don't get it."

"Don't get *what?*"

Our voices are rising, echoing off the marble counters and high ceiling.

"*Any* of it! Why you switched schools for the rest of senior year. Why you visited my mom. Why you—"

"You don't want answers to those questions," I tell him.

He shoves away from the doorway, stepping closer. Both of his hands go up, locking behind his head. "What are you talking about? I'm literally asking you—"

"You don't want to know that my parents shipped me off to boarding school so there was no record of my suspension. You don't want to know I got grounded for a month after they found out I'd driven to a prison—a prison I had to lie my way into because it was the only way I could see you. You don't want to know that the monthly visits with your mom started because I felt bad about stealing her ID so I could pretend to be someone you'd approved for visits. You don't want to know that I started spending time with Cormac because he had shown up at my house over the holidays and asked that I give you another chance. That he'd go with me to visit you, if I was scared to show up at a prison alone. So, *fuck you*, Ryder James. Fuck you for not caring and fuck you for acting like I shouldn't have either."

Ryder's arms drop, his hands forming fists at his sides. "*Of course* I fucking *cared*, Elle. Are you kidding me? I was in love with you!"

The past tense stings. Yet another reminder that I've held on to my feelings all these years like a fool and he let go a long time ago.

"Maybe you thought you were. But you weren't. You don't treat someone you love like you treated me."

Some of his indignation disappears, sadness bleeding across his face. "I'm sorry, Elle. So sorry about all of it."

"Stop fucking apologizing!" I shout. "All you do is apologize, and I don't want it. Okay, Ryder? I don't want it! And if you could stop judging the guys I date, that would be great too."

"I wasn't judging—"

"Yeah, you were. Prescott broke up with me on the drive home from that bar, you know. Twenty fucking minutes around you, and he gave up. Decided I wasn't worth fighting for because I never gave him any reason to. I hate you for that. I hate you for so much."

Ryder clears his throat, then glances down at the floor. "I know. I know you do."

I drain the rest of my wineglass and set it down on the counter. "I'm going to visit Nina on Thursday night before I leave for Martha's Vineyard. She told me to stop coming because of you, but I want to see her. There's only so much time left …" I swallow. "Don't be home. Please."

Ryder looks stricken. He might have known about my visits to his mom. He didn't know I knew about her cancer. "She told you?"

I pass him without answering, heading down the hallway. It's not until my blurry vision registers the photo of me, Keira, and Juliet framed on the wall that I remember where I am. Recall the size of Keira's house and the volume of our voices. Realize … everyone inside heard all of that.

Like the terrible friend that I am, I don't stop in the living room. Forcing a smile or pretending like everything is okay isn't something I'm capable of right now.

I grab my purse off the coatrack by the door and step out onto Keira's front porch.

Halfway down the stairs, I hear, "Elle!"

It's not Ryder's voice, so I slow. Swipe at my cheeks and blink rapidly before spinning around to focus on Keira's sympathetic expression.

"You ... okay?" Her voice is soft.

One look at her face, and I know I was right about sound carrying inside.

"Not really," I admit.

"I didn't know ... most of that."

"I know."

"If I had, I never would have ... the weekend on Martha's Vineyard. The bar. I thought you were okay with seeing him. Thought maybe it'd be good closure. You should have told me."

I shake my head. "You're getting married. You're entering this whole new exciting chapter. I wasn't going to ... and selfishly, I didn't want to talk about it."

"Getting married to his best friend."

"It's not your fault. Not Tucker's either."

"I wish you'd told me about Prescott."

"Yeah, well ..." I lift a shoulder, then let it drop. "I'm a mess, if that wasn't obvious by now. I'll be fine."

I'm always *fine*. Nothing better, nothing less.

The door opens again. My heart tumbles, only settling when the features register.

It's Tucker, not Ryder. He looks different without his usual smile.

"I should go," I say. "I'm sure Scout has worn out his welcome at my parents'."

Keira manages a smile. "Okay. I'll talk to you soon?"

I nod.

Tucker steps forward. "I'll walk you to your car."

I glance at it, parked fifteen feet away along the curb. "Uh, okay."

Keira heads back inside. Tucker falls into step beside me. We head down the front walk silently.

"Phew. We made it." I exhale a dramatic sigh of relief when we reach my convertible, digging my keys out of my purse.

Tucker doesn't crack a smile, still uncharacteristically serious. He presses a hand against the driver's door, preventing me from opening it.

"When I was fourteen, this guy moved into the trailer five down from mine. I was always aware of where I lived. Not embarrassed exactly, but I couldn't forget about it. Most of the kids who lived around me were into stuff I wasn't. They snuck beer, and they got into fights. And I felt like I didn't fit in with them. Definitely didn't fit in with the rich kids either. Then, this new kid arrived. He was just ... cool. He didn't smoke—often." Tucker grins briefly. "Didn't get into fights or care about any of the stuff the other kids did. But everyone just ... paid attention when he was around. Never messed with him, like the way they made fun of me. They cared what he thought and what he did. And I felt like I'd won the lottery when he wanted to hang out with me." Another smile, one lost in memories as he stares into space. Then, Tucker glances at me. "Ryder didn't care about anything ... except I kept catching him looking at this one girl. Every damn chance he got. Whenever I teased him about it, he'd act like he had no idea what I was talking about. But then I'd look over a minute later, and he'd be staring at her again."

I swallow, my throat too thick.

"I don't know the full story. Ryder keeps most shit to himself, and maybe I'm overstepping and making everything worse. Tell me if I am. But, Elle ... I know Ryder. He's like a brother to me. He's a good man. And he loves you. He's loved you for a long, long time.

Whatever he's done or said, however he's hurt you, he thought he was doing the right thing. I promise you that."

I'm an overflowing glass. Tucker's pouring more in, and I have no place to hold it.

The rough edge of a key digs into my palm as I blink rapidly. "He didn't let me visit him. For seven years, he shut me out."

Tucker nods. "I know."

"He told you?"

"I assumed."

"Assumed?"

"You really thought he'd let you see him like that? Locked away with no life? Wearing a jumpsuit and getting an hour of sun a day?"

The key digs deeper. I've done a good job of avoiding thinking about what Ryder's life in prison was like, and Tucker is painting too vivid of a picture.

"I thought he'd want to see me, yes."

Tucker shakes his head. "Ryder would have rather never seen you again than have you step a foot in that place, Elle. He put your interests above his happiness. *That's* love." His hand falls away from my door. "Drive safe, okay?"

He walks away without saying anything else, which is good. I'm not sure my heart could have handled another word.

X ♥ X

"So, this is where the dog disappeared to."

I glance over my left shoulder at the house. My dad is walking toward the table on the patio where I'm sitting. It's Saturday, and he's wearing slacks and a button-down that lacks a single wrinkle. Some things never change, I guess.

"You were obviously keeping a close eye on him," I reply.

There was no sign of my parents when I got home from Keira's, so I headed out into the backyard with Scout.

"Dogs need to roam," he tells me, taking his usual seat at the head of the table.

"Which you know from all your years of pet ownership?"

My dad has always been too busy with work. And my mom holds too much affection for her white couch. She closes the drawing room off entirely every time I bring Scout over here.

"I did some research," he tells me.

"Really?"

He hums, glancing at Scout sniffing around the hydrangea bushes. "There are only so many law articles one can read, as I'm sure you've realized."

I blink at him. My dad jokes so rarely that I'm never sure if he is. "Yeah."

I wait for him to ask how studying for the bar is going. Whether I've recently spoken to anyone at Gray & Ellington, the firm that hired me.

But he doesn't.

"Did you have a nice time at Keira's?"

"Yeah." It's not entirely a lie. Until Ryder showed up, the evening was pretty pleasant.

"How is Prescott doing?"

I close my eyes for a few seconds. I could lie, but I'm too drained to. "We broke up, Dad."

A pause.

"Oh. That's too bad. What happened?"

I put my feet up on the arm of the chair next to mine. Wait for my dad to raise an eyebrow or make a comment about table manners. He doesn't, surprising me once again.

"Ryder James was released from prison."

A much longer pause follows.

Ryder is a touchy subject, one we haven't discussed since my senior year of high school. I got suspended and switched schools, and my parents acted like private school had been the plan all along.

"Yes, I believe I saw something about that in the paper," he finally says.

"People love to gossip," I comment, watching Scout continue to explore my parents' yard.

And judge.

"You didn't answer my question," my father says. "About Prescott."

I look over, meeting his gaze straight on. "Yeah, I did."

I watch that register on his face. My dad doesn't miss much. Any bluntness I have, I inherited from him. He knows what I mean, what I'm really saying.

"He's a criminal, Elodie."

"He didn't *murder* anyone. Good people make mistakes. There's a lot more to Ryder than just … that."

My father huffs what sounds suspiciously like a laugh. "He has moxie—I'll give him that."

I sit up straight. "What are you talking about?"

As far as I knew, my dad's never met Ryder.

"He came here. The day before he got arrested. You were off at a brunch with your mother."

"*Ryder* came *here*?"

"Yes."

"To … why?"

"To see you, I believe he said. I was more focused on a stranger trespassing on my property."

I roll my eyes. My dad can be so dramatic.

And intimidating. I can only imagine what he said to Ryder.

Yet, somehow, my dad left the encounter thinking Ryder had *moxie*.

"Why didn't you tell me?" I ask.

"I just did."

I huff a sigh. "You know what I mean. Then. Why didn't you tell me then, Dad?"

"He was arrested the following day, Elodie. Hardly appropriate company for—"

"You didn't know he was going to get arrested the next day," I interrupt.

My father studies me for longer than I'm used to. Really looks, like he's not certain what he's appraising.

"I'm sorry," he says, shocking me. I've never heard my father say those two words before. "I should have."

All I can manage in response is a jerky nod.

"Are you two … together?" He asks it so simply. As if reconciling with Ryder would be easy.

"No," I answer.

My father hums in response, a sound that's impossible to decipher. "Feel like shooting some hoops?"

I stare at him, totally taken aback. We haven't played basketball together since I was in middle school. Since before Rose died.

"Um, sure."

My dad nods, then stands, acting like this is a normal occurrence. I do, too, following him over toward the garage. The last time I played here was when I broke up with Archer, which is not a pleasant memory. But before that, all the times I played with my dad, those are.

That was back when it felt like he saw me as a daughter, not a legacy.

Scout comes over and sniffs at my leg as my dad disappears into the garage to get a ball out.

When he reappears, my dad's expression is serious.

"I liked Prescott," he tells me, giving the ball a few experimental bounces. "But I don't think he was right for you."

I lift both eyebrows. I thought Prescott was exactly who my dad—not to mention my mom—expected me to end up with. Right down to the Harvard Law degree and rich parents.

"Why's that? He a bad golfer or something?"

"No. Because he had no idea you like to play basketball."

He takes a layup.

And I stand there, slowly absorbing what he means.

This moment with my dad—the honesty, the hoop towering over me?

I have Ryder to thank for all of it.

24
THEN

Ryder

Elle's house is even bigger than I remembered. I've only been here once before, the night I dropped her off after she let me borrow her car to pick up Cormac.

In the daylight, the place is huge. And intimidating. Covered by shingles painted an unblemished, blinding white, a stone chimney and an ivy trellis the only spots of color.

Gravel crunches as I walk toward the front door, skirting the enormous granite fountain that looks like it belongs to a European castle.

"Can I help you?"

A man has appeared around the left side of the house. He's tall, over six feet. Almost as tall as me. Dressed in a golf outfit with a full head of gray hair that's neatly combed.

"I'm looking for Elle," I tell him.

His forehead wrinkles slightly before it smooths. "You're trespassing on private property."

"I'm just here to talk to your daughter for a few minutes."

He crosses his arms. "Elodie isn't home."

"Do you know when she will be?"

"Yes." No elaboration.

I wasn't expecting Elle's parents to like me. But it still kinda sucks, staring at her dad and realizing he's already decided how he feels about me. That he'll warn Elle away from me and tell her how much better she can do.

"Can you let her know I stopped by, please?"

"I don't even know your name."

I step forward and hold out a hand. "Ryder James, sir."

Mr. Clarke studies me for a good minute before finally shaking my offered hand. "I don't recognize the name."

I don't miss his double meaning.

He's trying to make me second-guess Elle's feelings. I must not matter, he's saying, because she's never bothered to mention me.

It's also a dig at my address. Everyone who matters, he knows. He's correctly assuming I didn't walk here from one of the mansions down the street.

"I just moved to town."

"From where?"

"Jacksonville."

"Well, welcome to Fernwood." Some of the sternness has left his expression. It's more like he doesn't know what to make of me now, not that he's debating chasing me off with a shotgun.

"Welcome *back*. I lived here once before."

"Did you trespass on my property then too?"

I almost smile, catching myself just in time. "No, I didn't, Mr. Clarke."

"You're interested in my daughter, Ryder?"

"I'm in love with her, sir."

He digests that information silently, looking me up and down. "And how does Elodie feel about you?"

Talk about a loaded question.

"She wouldn't call me being here trespassing."

Maybe I'm imagining it, but Mr. Clarke looks a little more amused than he did when I first showed up.

"I'll let her know you stopped by," he tells me.

It's a clear dismissal, one I should heed. Elle isn't here. I'm worried about her after what happened with Archer last night. She insisted she was fine. That doesn't make me any less worried. But since she isn't answering her phone and isn't here, I'm out of options to reach her.

Before I turn to leave, I glance at the basketball hoop by the garage that's twice the size of the trailer I live in. "You play?"

Elle's father follows my gaze. "Not often."

"My dad played football with me a few times when I was a kid. Those are some of my favorite childhood memories."

Mr. Clarke's eyebrows bunch together as he stares at me.

He's a smart man. He's figured out that Elle told me her dad used to play basketball with her, and he's trying to decide why I'm mentioning it.

"She's a lot more than a report card, sir."

Then, I turn and walk away.

I'm about to leave the garage when my phone vibrates in my pocket. I grab it out, hoping it's Elle. She finally texted me back a few hours ago, letting me know she was fine and at a brunch with her mom earlier. She didn't mention me stopping by her house, and I'm not sure if that's a good or bad sign. What her dad told her. *If* he told her anything.

It's not Elle calling. It's an unknown number, but a 617 area code.

"Hello?" I answer.

"Ryder, it's me."

I exhale. "Why are you calling me from some random phone, Cormac?" *Again*, I tack on silently.

"I, uh, I'm at a party. Can you come pick me up?"

I pinch the bridge of my nose, squeezing my eyes shut. "You're at a party? That'd better be code for playing video games at Mav's house."

"I'm sorry, okay? They all wanted to go. What was I supposed to say?"

"No! You say *no*, Cormac."

He's silent for a minute. There are muffled sounds in the background. Nothing distinguishable, but enough to tell me the party isn't a small one.

Finally, "Mom's at work."

I know she's at work. She's a night owl who always takes late shifts when they're an option. And I know Cormac would probably call her over me if it was a choice because she'd simply tell him to make smarter decisions and that would be the end of it.

"Where are you?" I ask. "What's the address?"

"Thirty-two Maple Avenue."

"You're at a *One* party?"

Maple Avenue is on the opposite side of town. A couple of blocks from where Elle lives.

"I just—we wanted to see what it was like."

I blow out a long breath. "I'm at work, and I rode my bike here. I'm going to have to call Tuck, see if I can borrow his truck to come get you. I'll be there as soon as I can."

"Okay." Cormac's voice is calm and contrite.

I hang up, then immediately call Tucker. He doesn't answer. I kick the tire of the car I was working on. "Fuck!"

"What's wrong?"

I turn. Phoenix is walking toward me, wiping his hands on a rag.

"My little brother ... he's at a party on Maple. I have to go get him, and I don't have a car."

A *One* party. A *high school* party.

I'm going to kill him. He just turned thirteen. What the hell was he thinking?

"That's where I'm headed," Phoenix tells me. "Want a ride?"

My head snaps in his direction. "Really?"

"Yeah, Cruz and Zane just got here. We're about to leave."

They're going to sell at this party, I realize. My anger at Cormac mounts.

"A ride would be great," I say.

I'll try Tuck again once I have Cormac to see if he can drive us home. Worst-case scenario: I could call Elle for a ride. But I really don't want to bother her with this. In her texts earlier, she mentioned she isn't going out tonight because of an early morning. She's going to tour Dartmouth.

"Come on." Phoenix heads for the door.

I close the hood of the car I was working on, then follow him.

Cruz is in the driver's seat of the same car I rode in before, smoking.

"Picked up a stray," Nix says, sliding in the back seat.

"Hey, guys," I say, shutting the door.

"James," Cruz greets.

Zane just nods. He never says much.

I drum my fingers against the door impatiently as Cruz zips through town ten miles over the speed limit.

Phoenix makes a disgusted grunt in the back of his throat as we roll into the richest part of town. The difference is immediate and obvious. The houses get bigger. The lawns greener. The sidewalks wider. The cars, parked in driveways lined with trimmed hedges, are sleek and shiny.

I feel the same resentment shown in Zane's curled fists and Cruz's sneer. These houses are fifteen minutes from where we all live, yet their lives are totally different from ours. It's hard not to take that personally.

I spot the crowd of cars before the 32 that marks our destination. Cruz parks on the street since the driveway is about five vehicles too full.

"If I lived in this place, I'd bitch a lot less than Hathaway does," Phoenix comments as we cross the street.

"This is Hathaway's house?" I ask.

"Yep." He pops the *P*. "Ridiculous, right?"

I'm busy mulling over my shitty luck. Hathaway is the last person I feel like seeing right now. I promised Elle I wouldn't do anything. That promise is going to be a lot harder to keep if I run into the guy.

So, of course, he's in the front yard with a few of his football buddies. They're crushing empty beer cans with a baseball bat.

Hathaway is the first one to spot us. His eyes slide over the rest of the guys, then land on me.

"Whoa, whoa, whoa." Archer walks toward us, swaying a little. He's wasted. "You three can go in." He points to Zane, Cruz, and Phoenix. "*He* isn't allowed inside." Archer's refocused on me.

"I'm not here to sell," I tell him. "Just to get my brother."

"I don't give a *shit* what you're here for, James. You're not getting it. You shouldn't have crossed me."

"Crossed you?" I repeat incredulously. "What the hell are you talking about? I've done *nothing* to you, Hathaway."

"You think the team decided you were a great option for quarterback by themselves?"

"I think they took one look at your stats and decided."

Archer glares at me, the hatred rolling off of him in palpable waves. "You're a fucking game to her, you know. This is what Elle does. She gets bored. She teases. She's just using you to make me jealous."

I take a few steps closer until I'm right up in his face. "Don't you dare say her name, you piece of shit."

"Hit a sore spot, huh? Did she already dump you?"

"She told me what happened last night."

There's a flicker on Archer's face. Just a flash of guilt, but enough to tell me he knows exactly what I'm talking about. He might be wasted, but not drunk enough to forget.

"And the only reason your face isn't a bloody, bruised mess right now is because she asked me not to hurt you. The girl you fucking *assaulted* last night saved your ass. Does that make you feel like a man, Hathaway?"

"You're wasting your time dating her," he spits. "Elle won't put out."

I swing without consciously deciding to, the crunch of my knuckles connecting with his cheekbone one of the most satisfying sounds I've ever heard. Hathaway doubles over like I socked him in the stomach instead of punching him in the face.

"I told you not to say her name."

When Archer manages to straighten, blood is already dripping down his cheek from a split that will probably scar. He'll likely have a black eye too.

My stomach twists. *Fuck.* I don't regret punching Hathaway, but it was definitely a dumb thing to do.

"Get the fuck off my property," he snarls. "I'm five seconds from calling the cops."

Hathaway is no longer the only guy glaring at me. Zane, Cruz, and Phoenix all look pissed. They *are* here to sell. If Archer calls the cops to his own house—a stupid thing to do, considering it's filled with drunk teenagers, but he's obviously not in a logical mood—they won't be able to. Not to mention, Cormac could get in trouble for being here.

Cruz steps forward. "Look, man, I don't have any beef with you. Your guests are expecting us. We'll be in and out in twenty minutes."

Blood is dripping off Archer's jaw, landing on his shirt. It's a grisly sight. He looks at me, then glances at Cruz. Drains the contents of the cup he's holding. "Just you."

"I can sell more if—"

"You can never sell at one of my parties again, asshole. I can make sure you never sell at *any* party in this town again."

Phoenix looks nervously at his brother.

"Fine." Cruz tosses the keys to Zane. "Wait in the car."

Archer scoffs, casts one last murderous glower my way, then heads inside. His friends follow.

"Cruz—" I start.

"You do *not* want to talk to me right now, James. You have no fucking clue the mess you just made."

"He's a senior," I remind him. "He'll be off at some fancy university next year."

"He has connections. If he wants to make it hard for me, he can.

He will."

I swallow. "I'm sorry."

"And over some One?" Cruz shakes his head. "He's right; she'll dump you soon."

I'm in no position to argue, so I don't. "Cormac is in there. He's *thirteen*, man. Too young for all this."

Cruz is silent for a few seconds. "I'll grab him, okay?"

Relief spreads through me. "Thank you."

Cruz continues into the huge house. Phoenix, Zane, and I head back to the car.

Phoenix says nothing. He's either mad or resigned to the direction this night has taken. Zane sticks with silence too.

I stare into space, glancing toward the house every few minutes and hoping Cormac will appear. If Cruz doesn't come out with him, I'll have no choice but to go inside myself.

Twenty-five minutes later, Cruz walks outside. I exhale, relieved, when I see Cormac is right behind him.

"Thanks," I tell Cruz.

He nods once before opening the car door.

I squeeze Cormac's shoulder before he climbs into the middle. His eyes are wide—from excitement or apprehension or maybe both.

Loud rap music shakes the car the whole drive back to our part of town. No one talks. Phoenix fiddles with his phone.

When Cruz stops in front of my trailer, Phoenix climbs out with me and Cormac. Cruz takes off without waiting for his brother.

"Head in," I tell Cormac. "I'll be right inside."

He's remorseful enough to do it without arguing—for once.

As soon as the trailer door bangs shut behind him, I glance at Nix. "What is it?"

"You caused a lot of problems tonight. We did you a favor, giving you a ride, and all you did was fuck shit up."

"And?"

"We're square, Ryder. Hathaway had it coming."

I relax.

"You and I are square, I mean. Cruz … he holds grudges."

"He sold," I say.

"Not as much as he would have if all three of us had gone in. And if Hathaway decides to follow through on any threats …"

"He can sell elsewhere."

"This is the richest town in the state," Nix tells me. "It's why we moved here. How Cruz keeps the guys he works for happy."

"So …"

"So, you owe him a favor. Cruz has a shipment coming on Monday. He has other places to be, and I'm risking a suspension if I have any more absences at school. I just texted them your address."

"You did *what?*"

"Relax. They'll drop off around ten. All you have to do is hold on to it until Cruz grabs it around lunchtime. Just stay home sick and watch TV."

My jaw works. I'm pissed—at Hathaway, for obvious reasons. At Cruz and Phoenix, for getting me involved in their shady shit. At myself, for making this mess.

"Fine."

Nix claps my shoulder. "Awesome. Talk soon." He starts walking toward his trailer. "Nice right hook, by the way," he calls over one shoulder.

I stare after him, still pissed.

25
NOW

Ryder

As soon as I see my mom walking down the hallway, I stop bouncing my knee and stand. I'm jittery and anxious after spending forty-five minutes slouched in a hospital chair that felt like it had no cushion at all.

She heads to the nurses' station first, exchanging a few words that are wrapped up by the time I reach her side. Purposeful, I'm sure.

Today's doctor's appointment is the closest I've gotten to concrete answers about my mom's health. The only reason I even found out about this appointment was that I answered the landline when the hospital called to confirm it.

"Everything go okay?" I ask my mom. Scrutinize the nurse's reaction.

"Fine," my mom answers. "Thanks, Nora."

"Have a great rest of your day, Ms. James," the nurse—Nora—says cheerily.

I follow my mom outside, inhaling the fresh breeze deeply. The hospital smelled like prison—chemical cleaner and stagnant air. I'd experienced enough of that when I went to visit my former cellmate, Duke, yesterday.

"So, it went well?" I ask as we cross the parking lot.

"It went fine."

I exhale, exasperated. "What does that *mean*, Mom?"

"It means nothing's changed. I told you coming would be a waste of time."

"Is it really that unbelievable I wanted to? I'm trying to—"

"It's a shit hand, Ryder. I'm stuck playing it out. You're not."

"So, I just … what? Leave? Let you deal with it all alone? Is that what you want, Mom?"

She stops alongside her car, shading her eyes as she looks up at me. "Have you seen Elle?"

"Fuck you, Ryder James. Fuck you for not caring and fuck you for acting like I shouldn't have either."

Those two sentences have been on an endless loop in my head since she shouted them at me.

I can't get the look on her face out of my head either. The anger and the pain and also the *conviction*. She wasn't just saying it. She *believed* it. Elle really thinks I stopped caring. That my feelings for her were a switch I flipped off.

I swallow, the span of time since my mom asked the question already stretching too long. "We've spoken."

"And?"

I'm tempted to parrot Elle's *none of your business* line.

Instead, I say, "She's … she's planning to visit you on Thursday."

My mom smiles. The first one I've seen since I showed up at the trailer earlier to accompany her here. One of the few I've seen at all since I've been back.

I figured there was affection there after so many visits. But I'm taken aback by how apparent it is on her face.

We haven't discussed Elle since my first night home.

"Why aren't you getting treatment, Mom?" I blurt.

Her smile instantly disappears. "I already told you."

"Yeah, you told me you weren't getting treatment. Not *why*."

"It's my decision, Ryder."

"Is it the money? Because I can—"

"It's not the money," she tells me. "It's—that's not how I want to spend my last days. Doctors don't think it'll make much difference anyway."

"They don't know that for sure. It'll make *some* difference at the very least," I argue.

Her chin lifts. "I've made my decision. If you want to fuss over something, plenty to keep you occupied in your own life."

No need to guess what she's referring to.

"Elle and I are over," I tell her.

Removing myself from Elle's life was the best thing I could have done for her. I didn't know she would be on Martha's Vineyard. I didn't know she'd be at that fancy bar in Boston. Tuck neglected to mention she'd be there when we returned the tools to his garage last week.

I've *tried* to stay away.

My mom sniffs. "I don't think that lawyer is right for her. They sound too similar."

"They broke up," I confess like an idiot. I'm trying to put a fire out, not add kindling.

I don't mention the twenty minutes, but I think it. It's probably fucked up that I'm a little proud of that. I barely even spoke to Elle during that window.

It would be different if the guy made her happy. She looked uncomfortable for most of the twenty minutes I was there, although that might have been because of me and not her boyfriend.

"Really?" My mom looks thrilled about my impulsive confession. *Damn kindling.*

"It doesn't change anything, Mom. We're over—for good."

"You're too young to decide anything is *for good*, Ryder."

I exhale. "Elle didn't decide not to visit me in prison, okay? She tried—tried hard. I … I refused to see her."

A pause.

"Why?"

"Because I didn't want her to see me like that. I didn't want her coming to that place. I had nothing to offer her. I never really did. But there, I truly had *nothing*."

"Did you tell her that? Explain?"

"No. I needed her to let go. She would have argued, pushed back. Elle's stubborn."

"She's also entitled to her own feelings," my mom says sagely.

"Fuck you, Ryder James. Fuck you for not caring and fuck you for acting like I shouldn't have either," runs through my head again.

I recall Elle sitting on steps with hunched shoulders. Staring at the ocean with a lost expression on her face. Standing in Tuck and Keira's kitchen last week with a suspicious sheen covering her blue eyes.

All scenes so, so different from how I thought she'd look seven years later.

Reese wasn't the only one wrong about Elle's feelings for me.

"She hates me."

Rather than agree, my mom laughs. "Bullshit."

"She does. She should."

"She showed up for seven years. Those visits weren't for me. Or for Cormac."

"I—too much has happened. Too much has changed. I wouldn't even be asking for a second chance. We're so far past that … it's pointless."

"Maybe," my mom says. "Or maybe not giving it a chance, after everything, would be pointless."

She lets me sit with that the whole drive back to the trailer. The nearest hospital is twenty minutes from Fernwood.

If the topic was less serious—less tragic—I'd be impressed by her success at totally turning our conversation around on me. I wasn't supposed to be the one second-guessing.

My mom parks alongside the trailer, then glances over at me. "If I did treatment … that's not how I want you boys to see me. To remember me."

"That's not how we would remember you, Mom."

"It's not what I want, Ryder."

I literally bite my tongue, trying to keep more protests from coming out. "Okay."

"Your father called a few days ago."

When I say nothing, she sighs.

"You shouldn't have told him."

"Why?" I ask. "Because he'd come running to see you?"

Another sigh. This is an ancient argument between us. She's always been quick to forgive my dad for his recurring disappearing act. So, I've held on to the resentment she let go of. Piled it on top of my own.

She climbs out of the car, so I do too.

"Do you need the car the rest of the day?"

My mom shakes her head, then tosses me the keys. "All yours."

Tuck told me to take the rest of the day off, but I'm in the mood for manual labor. The screened porch is only halfway done, meaning there are still a lot of nails to pound.

"Thanks."

She glances back, surprised, when I follow her toward the stairs. "You aren't headed out?"

"In a minute. I need to grab something."

She nods, heading straight into the kitchen when we walk inside. Without looking that way, I know she's making a cup of her tea. It's what she does now instead of smoking a cigarette.

I walk down the hallway to my bedroom. It's so bare now, none of the stuff I threw out when I got home replaced. Blank walls. Bare furniture.

Digging through the closet takes me at least five minutes. I buried this box, trying to avoid temptation.

Not that it matters. I memorized every line of the letters Elle had sent me years ago.

I have to search once I find the box, too, in order to find the one letter I wrote to her in response. It's at the very bottom, resting against the cardboard.

I stare at it, deliberating. Just like I've done ever since Elle told me I never cared last week.

There's a lot I can handle. *Easy* isn't an adjective I'd use to describe my life. There's always been a lack of *something*.

A father.

Money.

Freedom.

Elle thinking she never mattered to me isn't one of the things I can handle. Maybe she needs to read this—the explanation I never sent her—to move on. To shut that chapter—my chapter—of her life. Solve the mystery of our past.

I stand, the letter in my hand, and head back to the kitchen. My mom is sitting at the kitchen table, flipping through the mail delivered earlier.

I toss the envelope down next to the stack of bills and flyers.

"What's that?" my mom asks.

I don't buy her nonchalance. *Elle* is all that's written on the outside. I didn't know where to send it—what college she ended up at. I'm sure her parents would have burned it if I sent it to her house.

"Can you give that to her on Thursday?" I walk toward the door. "Thanks. I'll be home for dinner."

If my mom says anything else, it's lost in the close of the hinges behind me.

26
THEN

Ryder

My mom frowns when I walk into the kitchen on Monday morning. I'm not even having to fake the uncomfortable look on my face. "What's wrong?"

"I don't feel well," I tell her.

It's not a lie. I barely slept last night, stressed about today. Ever since Phoenix walked away on Saturday night, I've tried to come up with some way to get out of this. Mostly because I resent the hell out of him and Cruz for using me like some sort of lackey because of something that had nothing to do with them. I showed up for Cormac. Punched Hathaway for Elle.

"You too sick for school?" my mom asks.

"Yeah." I fake a cough. "Already texted Tuck and told him not to pick me up."

"Do you need me to stay home?"

"*No.*" I say it too quickly, and she frowns again. "I mean, no thanks. I'll be fine."

I grab a glass out of the cabinet and fill it with water.

"I'm going back to bed."

"Okay," she calls after me. "Text me if you need me to come home."

"I will. Thanks, Mom."

I exhale a long breath once I'm back in my room, then check my phone for texts. I have two new messages.

TUCKER: That sucks, man. Feel better.

PHOENIX: Ten a.m.

I down the water and then flop on my bed.

Nothing from Elle, which piles on to the stress I'm already experiencing. Everything her dad and Archer and Cruz said about us yesterday has wiggled its way into my brain. Stuff I already knew, yet sounds different spoken aloud.

We haven't even discussed if we're actually dating. In some ways, our relationship feels so much maturer than it did freshman year. In others, it's just as juvenile. We fool around and we flirt.

I love her. There's no doubt in my mind about that.

But my mom loved my dad, and that didn't get her anywhere.

Elle's going to college. She toured Dartmouth yesterday, a school I have no chance of going to. It's about two hours from here, which isn't terrible if I ever get my car running. But will Elle want me visiting when she's off living a new life? If I asked her now, I know she'd say yes. But that's different from the reality of her going places and me going nowhere. If I leave Fernwood after graduation for a fresh start somewhere else, I'd be abandoning one of the few things we have in common.

"You're a fucking game to her, you know."

Hathaway's toxic words circle my head.

He's wrong.

But I'm not as certain I'm not a phase Elle will outgrow. Change is inevitable and unpredictable.

I doze off eventually, my sleepless night catching up with me. I'm woken by the buzz of my phone.

ELLE: Where are you?

RYDER: Sick day. Woke up not feeling well.

I feel shitty about lying to her. But I don't want her close to any of this. I told Elle I'd keep Phoenix away from her. I told Elle I didn't owe any favors.

And I promised her I wouldn't touch Archer.

I should be there today, not just to offer explanations. To make sure Hathaway stays the hell away from her.

I miss her. I haven't seen her since Friday night, and I spent most of that time attempting to exhale my anger.

ELLE: I'll bring you some soup after cheer.

I smile.

RYDER: Best girlfriend ever.

It feels good to use the title, even if it's just over text. I've never used it before. Never wanted to. With Elle, my hesitation has never been uncertainty. More fear.

You can't lose what you never really had.

Three dots appear and disappear twice before Elle sends a reply.

ELLE: Girlfriend?

It's impossible to read her tone over text.

RYDER: We can pretend that was a typo.

ELLE: For what? Garland? Grandchild?

I snort and shake my head, mildly impressed she managed to come up with two similar words so quickly. Then drag a palm down my face. I'm totally fumbling this exchange.

RYDER: I just meant I'm not making assumptions.

RYDER: About us.

I glance at the clock. Two minutes until the start of first period. She's probably already in Mr. Anderson's classroom.

RYDER: I hope this isn't too smooth for you.

ELLE: Just awkward enough.

ELLE: You should make more assumptions.

ELLE: Boyfriend.

The tightness in my cheeks tells me I'm grinning wide.

RYDER: I love you.

ELLE: You're growing on me too.

ELLE: See you tonight.

I toss my phone onto the mattress, stand, and stretch. Tug a clean T-shirt on and take a seat at the small desk that barely fits in my room.

I'm too anxious to focus on much, but I manage to get some homework done while nervously watching the minutes tick by. Vacuum and do some dishes to help my mom out.

Finally, ten a.m. arrives.

I head outside to sit on the steps, my knee bouncing as I scan the street.

"Shouldn't you be in school?"

I glance over at Mrs. Nelson, our next-door neighbor. She's dressed in one of her typical flashy outfits. The yellow shade of her top is making my retinas burn.

"Sick day," I reply.

"You look fine to me," she comments, continuing to water the stalks that used to have flowers attached to them.

I'm not sure why she's bothering. They won't bloom again until next spring. But it hasn't rained in a couple of weeks, so maybe she feels like it's necessary to keep the plants alive.

"I'm feeling better."

Mrs. Nelson harrumphs in a way that makes it clear she doesn't believe I was under the weather at all, then heads into her trailer right as I spot a white sedan approaching.

I stand, my palms sweaty, as it stops right in front of me. Two guys climb out. The first one is huge, his biceps the same circumference of my thigh, and the second one is covered in tattoos.

"You Ryder?" the tattooed one asks gruffly.

I swallow as I walk toward them, trying to act like I have some control of this situation. I've seen more of Cruz's operation than I ever wanted to, but never this part. "Yeah."

The buff guy nods to his right. "Trunk."

I walk around to the back of the car and open it. Two black duffel bags sit in the trunk. I hoist one in each hand.

"Aren't you going to check it's all there?"

"No," I reply.

Tattooed guy shrugs. "Fine. Tell Cruz that Corey wants this moved fast. He's behind this month."

Delivering that message to Cruz is one of the last things I want to do. But I do want these guys gone, so I just nod, hoping it'll speed along their departure.

"Let's go." The muscular guy slams the trunk of the sedan shut.

"Gage?"

I glance at the tattooed guy—Gage. He's staring down the street, the look on his face chilling my blood.

"I told you we had a fucking tail," he spits.

Everything around me slows. Muffled, like I'm underwater. My gaze follows Gage's.

Two black SUVs are racing up the road, a huge cloud of dust trailing them.

A loud swear, followed by an even louder slam. The white sedan takes off, leaving a spray of dirt behind.

I'm expecting the SUVs to chase the sedan. They stop in front of me instead, brakes squealing and sirens blaring.

I'm stunned still, my brain numb with shock.

And then … I remember what's inside the two bags I'm holding.

27
NOW

Elle

"**Y**ou're playing tic-tac-toe by yourself?"

I glance toward the unfamiliar voice. There's a boy standing in the open doorway, staring at me.

My arm twitches with the strong urge to cover the folder I'm doodling on, hiding the evidence. Something about the way he's looking at me makes me feel self-conscious.

I don't know him, but I recognize him. Ryder James. He's one of the kids from the trailer park. I've never agreed with the division in town, but I've always gone along with it. Never spoken to anyone who lived in the section of town with a different zip code. The Twos.

"I'm winning," I tell him.

Ryder laughs. He has a nice laugh, deep and husky. "Of course you are, Elle."

Warmth pools in my stomach, and a flush spreads across my skin. I'm reacting to the way he said my name. To the fact that he knew my name. To the way he's focused on me, giving me his complete attention.

"Are you here because you're running for student council president too?"

Ryder laughs again, but this one is different. Short and dry. "Nah. Detention."

"Oh."

I have no idea what to say to that. I've never had detention before.

Ryder ambles deeper into the room, taking the desk beside mine. "What does student council do this early?"

"I have to collect signatures. Mrs. Scott is my faculty adviser. She told me to meet her here so she can give me the papers I need."

"Student council sounds like a lot of work."

"It's not supposed to be easy," I reply. "And I might not even win."

"You'll win." Ryder sounds very certain of that outcome. He leans over to look at my tic-tac-toe board. "It's a cat's game."

"What does that mean?"

"No winner. Or two losers." He settles back into his seat. "You got another piece of paper?"

"Yeah. Sure."

I tear a clean sheet out from my notebook, then hand it to him. Our fingers brush, and I stiffen like I was just electrocuted.

My heart begins racing, and a strange fluttering sensation appears in my chest. I don't know Ryder. All I know is that he lives in the trailer park my friends make fun of and that my chest always feels too tight when I look at him. Whenever he's nearby, I notice. My palms get sweaty.

I have a crush on him, I think.

And I didn't think he even knew who I was. I'm still reeling from the revelation that he does.

I wet my dry lips with my tongue. "What are you doing?"

"Staying out of trouble." He's flipping and folding the paper I gave him, twin lines wrinkled between his eyes as he concentrates. "I'm Ryder, by the way."

"I know," I blurt.

When I gather up the courage to glance over, he's looking at me. One corner of his mouth is curved up, and it sets off a series of fizzy fireworks in my chest. He doesn't say anything, just nods and then looks back down.

"Ryder? What are you doing in here?" Mrs. Scott has appeared, her expression confused as she glances between me and Ryder.

"Lady in the office sent me this way," he replies.

Mrs. Scott sighs. "Morning detention is in the cafeteria. Head down there, please."

"Yes, ma'am." Ryder stands and walks toward the door. He doesn't look at me as he passes by, but there's a flutter of white that flashes in the air and then lands on my desk.

He folded me a flower.

"Was he bothering you?" Mrs. Scott asks as soon as Ryder disappears.

"No," I say, then slip the flower off my desk very carefully.

My eyes fly wide open, the darkened surroundings of my bedroom registering gradually. I'm not fourteen, inside Fernwood High School. I'm twenty-five—almost twenty-six—and in my bed.

I sit up, the sheets pooling around my waist as I scrub both hands across my face.

I miss Ryder.

I miss him even though I shouldn't. Even though I don't *want* to miss him.

Part of me has missed him ever since that morning he wandered into the classroom where I was waiting—our first conversation. Like some alchemy took place during that brief conversation and changed me forever. Like there was a me *before* Ryder and a me *after* Ryder. And no matter how much time passes or what else changes in my life, I'm stuck with whatever shift took place that moment he spoke to me, crossing the imaginary line between us up until that point.

Groggy and sad and still stuck in the head of my younger self falling in love for the first time, I open the drawer beside my bed.

The eleven-year-old origami flower has held up remarkably well. This flimsy piece of notebook paper fared a lot better than our relationship did.

I twirl the stem between two fingers, attempting to muster the urge to destroy it in some way.

Protecting this piece of the past is unhealthy. Makes me a masochist.

Eleven years. That's how long it's been since I met Ryder James. It feels like a lifetime.

And the longer I stare at the flower, the more certain I become that I'll never get rid of it.

I hate the ending. But I love our story.

I grab my phone off the bedside table with my free hand, giving my alarm clock a cursory glance.

3:07 a.m.

I tap his name and then hold the phone up to my ear to listen to it ring, not caring it's the middle of the night.

Ryder answers on the third ring. "Hi."

That's all he says. He doesn't ask why I'm calling or mention how late it is. He doesn't bring up any part of our last—loud—conversation.

I say nothing at all. This was about actions, not words. Wanting to call him. Wondering if he'd answer.

Eventually, I lie back down and tug the sheets up my chest, listening to the silence on his end. Staring at the paper flower.

There's so much between us. An ocean of love and hate and giddiness and resentment.

It feels too vast to even approach. I don't know where to wade in.

I'm mad at him about so much. Yet no matter how much anger builds or burns, he's still the one person I want to talk to in the middle of the night.

"Sixteen," Ryder says.

"What?"

"You took sixteen breaths in the last minute."

"Oh. Is that … normal?"

Probably not because I'm not. He made me different.

"No idea. Considering there's sixty seconds in a minute, that's about a breath every four seconds—that sounds about right."

"How many breaths do you take in a minute?" I ask.

"No idea." He sounds … amused. "I was staring at a clock, and all I could hear was you breathing, so I just … counted."

We revert to silence.

Once upon a time, I imagined this would be every night. That talking to him at three a.m. would simply require rolling over and facing the pillow next to mine. I don't know how to say that—I shouldn't say that—so I just soak in this moment. Right now, talking to Ryder is just a matter of opening my mouth. This is my alternative reality—a brief chance to experience part of how I hoped my life might turn out.

Maybe he gets that.

Maybe he doesn't know what to say to me.

"You answered."

Ryder doesn't reply right away. Finally, he says, "You called."

"I wanted to know if you'd answer." Better than admitting I wanted to listen to silence with him.

"*You* called," he repeats.

This time, he emphasizes *you*. Makes it sound like that makes a difference. Like *my* call matters, and I resent the implication—that he has any investment in communicating with me after years of ensuring all means of contact were sealed off.

"I couldn't call for *seven years*. You made it so I couldn't even *talk* to you, Ryder."

I'm mad at him about a lot. I'm maddest about that. How easily he tossed me aside.

I heard what Tucker told me. But it doesn't feel like enough of an explanation. Ryder loved me so much that he wouldn't let me see him? He loved me so much that he broke my heart ... again? How could he not consider—not appreciate—that I would have done anything to see him? That him shutting me out was a spectacular sort of torture?

Another long pause.

Then, "I know."

"That's all you have to say?"

"That, and I'm sorry."

"I don't want your apology."

"What do you want then?" The question is sincere, not exasperated.

You. Pride and common sense keep that syllable from slipping out of my mouth.

We're over. We've been over. We'll stay over.

I wanted this to feel wrong. To be awkward. For hearing his voice to not help. But the silence where my answer should be isn't uncomfortable. It's just noticeable. Heavy.

"I have everything I want," I lie. "My life is great."

I could go anywhere I want. Be anyone I want.

And I'd still choose to be lying here, listening to Ryder breathe.

It's my favorite sound in the world, I think. It means he's near.

Alive.

"You don't have to pretend around me, Elle."

He's wrong. He's who I have to pretend around the most.

"I'm really sorry about your mom," I whisper.

He sighs heavily. "Me too."

"Good night, Ryder."

I hang up and roll over. Fling the paper flower on the floor.

Goodbye has always felt like too small of a word when it comes to Ryder. Too minimal and inconsequential and common.

If seven years of silence wasn't enough closure, I don't think any one word will manage it.

I stare at the white spot on the hardwood for several minutes.

Scout loves to chew up paper. He's in his crate downstairs right now, but he'll start whining to go outside around six thirty.

I sigh before slipping out of bed and picking up the flower. I set it in the drawer carefully, slide it shut, then climb back into bed.

It takes me a long time to fall back asleep. By the time I do, my pillow is damp, and my cheeks are stiff with salt.

28
THEN

Elle

English ends with a reminder from Ms. Hill that our essays on *The Great Gatsby* are due on Friday. I shove my binder in my backpack, standing as soon as the bell rings.

"Are we meeting on Wednesday or Thursday?" Kinsley asks, falling into step beside me as we walk into the hallway.

"Wednesday, because we might have to meet Thursday too," I tell her. "There's still a ton to do before homecoming."

"Clear entire after-school schedule this week. Got it."

I laugh. "You're the best VP ever."

Kinsley grins. "I know. I'll see you at lunch."

"See you," I say, then head for my locker.

I pull out my phone as I walk, disappointed there's no new message from Ryder. Hopefully, that doesn't mean he's feeling worse and won't want me to come over later.

I miss him. I haven't seen him since I showed up at the garage on Friday night and that evening was tainted by what happened with Archer. Saturday was overtaken by volunteering with my mom, and yesterday was a long day spent touring college campuses.

I reach my locker, swapping out the textbooks and binders in my backpack for the ones for my afternoon classes. I'm struggling to zip my bag back up when I spot Keira and Juliet walking toward me.

"Hey," I greet them, tugging harder at the zipper. I overfilled my backpack, but I need everything in it.

"Did you hear?" Keira asks me.

"Hear what?" I ask. The zipper finally cooperates, closing. I smile triumphantly.

"About Ryder."

I glance at Keira, confused by the worried look on her face. Juliet appears uncharacteristically somber as well.

"That he's sick? Yeah, he texted me earlier."

Keira shakes her head, her expression turning sympathetic. "No. That cops showed up to the trailer park. I can't get ahold of Tuck—he left as soon as he heard the rumors."

"What rumors?"

"Lindsey Davenport was in my French class last period. She said …" Keira glances at Juliet. "She said Ryder was arrested."

Lindsey's father is Fernwood's chief of police.

My heavy backpack hits the floor. "For *what*?"

Keira shrugs. "I don't know. Have you heard anything from Ryder recently?"

I don't reply. I grab my phone out again and call him. We're not supposed to make phone calls in school, but I couldn't care less about following rules right now.

It rings and rings, then eventually hits voice mail.

Panic is starting to spread across my skin, a frantic, impatient buzzing that makes me want to run or scream.

This is crazy. Wrong. Something—someone—is wrong.

And then I see Archer.

He's standing by the entrance to Mrs. Scott's classroom, right where I know his locker is, talking to Perry. He looks up, spots me, and goes still. I haven't seen or talked to him since fleeing Maddie's bedroom on Friday night.

The underneath of his left eye is bruised, like he hasn't slept for a year. The skin next to it is swollen, a large Band-Aid partially covering his cheek.

Archer might have an inflated sense of self, but he holds a lot of power in this school. The Hathaways are one of the most influential families in town. Archer's father's company insures most of it.

I can only think of one person who would be brave enough—who would be *stupid* enough—to punch Archer in the face.

He promised.

I'm pissed at Ryder for breaking that promise.

But it's nothing compared to the fury I'm experiencing toward Archer as he looks away and breaks eye contact. Dismisses me, the same way he disregarded me in Maddie's bedroom.

Perry sees me approaching first, his grin of greeting growing confused when he gets a good look at my face.

"You *fucking* asshole. What did you do?" I shove Archer into the lockers as hard as I can.

He's surprised enough that I'm effective, but the *smack* of his body hitting metal isn't very satisfying. It's just noise that adds to the growing commotion surrounding me.

Perry is saying something.

Other students are whispering.

I'm fully focused on Archer, the noise around me dulling to a low buzz in the background.

"What. Did. You. Do?"

"*Nothing!*" He straightens, tugging his shirt down so it hangs properly again. "I don't know what the hell you're talking about, Elle. And you're acting insane."

His bravado is weak at best. Archer won't look me in the eye.

"Ryder came after you, didn't he? And you had him *arrested*?"

Archer finally meets my gaze, blinking blankly. I don't know what the source of his shock is, and I don't care.

"Tell me! Admit it!" I shove him again. "What the *fuck* did you do?"

"Nothing!" Archer shouts back, his infamous temper flaring. If he feels any remorse about Friday night, it's been overwhelmed by annoyance about the scene that I'm making. "Christ, Elle. Calm down. If that Two got arrested, then I'm sure he deserved it."

I slap him, the stinging in my palm as shocking to me as it is to Archer. I'm not a violent person. But I'm not me right now. I'm witnessing this scene take place like an outside observer, surrounded by a haziness as to what's happening. It's like I'm trapped in a nightmare and can't wake up.

Archer glares at me as he rubs the red spot on his cheek.

"You know why he hit you," I hiss. "And you called the cops?"

"I didn't call the cops! I threatened to, yeah. But I didn't."

"I don't believe you."

"I don't give a shit what you believe," Archer snaps. "That psychopath is wearing off on you."

"*That psychopath* wasn't the one who held me down on a bed."

His face goes pale beneath the remnants of his summer tan. "That wasn't—"

"Wasn't what?" I shove him for a third time.

Archer's expecting it. He barely moves, and it makes me madder. Reminds me of when I could barely move.

"Whatever you did, I will *never* forgive you."

"Miss Clarke!"

There aren't just students in the hallway anymore. I step away from Archer, registering some of my surroundings again.

Shocked faces. *So* many shocked faces.

Students. Teachers. Principal Walker, who I was supposed to meet with after school about the Spirit Week schedule.

"My office, Elle," he tells me, his expression more serious than I've ever seen it.

I swallow, then follow him that way. My gaze falls to the floor, not meeting any of the eyes I can feel on me.

I should be panicked about what's about to happen. Me, who's never gotten a tardy or a detention, getting sent to the principal's office for attacking another student. I can't imagine what my friends will say. What my *parents* will say.

I *should* be panicked about what's about to happen.

But all I can think about is Ryder. Pray that Keira was wrong and Archer wasn't lying.

Ryder

A long, low whistle makes me turn around. I toss an old cabinet that got torn out of the kitchen yesterday onto the junk pile, then walk toward the front path that was redone two days ago.

"This is the place, huh?"

"This is the place," I reply.

"It's nice, man. Really nice."

"It still needs a lot of work."

"I mean, duh." Cormac toes the pile of mulch waiting to be spread in the flower beds.

The debris that littered the lawn is almost gone, the weeds removed and the grass neatly mowed. It's starting to match the exterior of the house, which was freshly painted.

"You wanna tour?" I ask.

"Sure, yeah. That'd be cool."

I nod and drop the hammer I was using to pry loose nails out.

"No internship today?" I ask as we approach the front door.

I always leave the trailer before Cormac, so it's harder to keep up with his schedule.

"Nah. They gave us a couple of extra days off because of the Fourth this weekend." He glances at me. "You still going to Martha's Vineyard?"

"Yeah." I'm not sure if I should, but I am. I promised Reese—and Tuck. "You got any plans for it?"

"Actually, yeah. I have a date."

I stop walking, blinking at my brother. "A date?"

Cormac's smile is wry as he tucks his hands into his pockets. "That hard to believe, huh?"

"No. No, not at all. It's just ..."

Just that he's still a thirteen-year-old kid in my head. Semi-regular visits for seven years weren't enough for me to fully catch up. To hear about girls and crushes and dances and realize my little brother wasn't so little anymore.

"That's awesome, dude," I finish.

Cormac rocks back on his heels. "I, uh, I'm not sure what to do for it. Where to take her."

There's an unspoken question at the end, and I realize he's asking for my input. For my advice.

I rub the back of my neck, Elle's angry words running through my head again.

"Man, I'm the last person you should be asking for relationship advice." Cormac knows enough of the past to get what I mean. "But, uh, food is usually a good idea. She from Boston?"

Cormac shakes his head. "Columbus, Ohio. She's just here for the summer. For an internship. I met her at a happy hour."

"Does she like sports?"

"I think so? She played soccer in college."

"Take her to a Sox game," I suggest. "Show her around Fenway, then take her out to dinner."

"Yeah?"

I shrug. "That's what I would do."

"Elle would have liked that?"

There's a tentativeness to Cormac's voice as he says her name, like he's reluctant to bring her up. But she's the only girl he's seen me with. My one relationship metric.

"Dunno," I answer.

"Well, where did you take her?" Cormac asks. "Brynn comes from money," he adds.

"We didn't really … we hung out at home. Or the garage. Sometimes parties."

Cormac's forehead creases. "You never took her out on a date?"

Silently, I add that to the long list of things I should've done differently.

"It was high school," I say defensively.

"Sure." Cormac snorts, then keeps walking. "This porch new?"

"Partially. We had to extend it, so there was direct access to the screened section on the side."

"Screened porch is cool. Short season to use it though."

I smile. Sometimes, I can't believe Cormac and I have the same mom and shared mostly the same upbringing. We're different in many ways. But right now, I see it.

That's the same thing I said when Elle showed me her drawing.

"We appreciate things more when we know they're temporary," I say, opening the door that leads from the screened porch into the living room.

The fireplace on one wall is the only thing to look at in this space.

The walls have been ripped down to their studs, the floor covered with plastic to protect the hardwood that was already sanded and stained.

"Yeah, it still needs work," Cormac comments, glancing around.

I chuckle. "Yeah."

"Will it be done in time for Mom to see it?"

I swallow, hard, amusement immediately evaporating. "Has … has Mom said anything to you about her health?"

My instinct is to protect Cormac. But I can't shield him from this.

He shakes his head slowly. "No. Since she told me she was sick, she's avoided talking about it every chance."

I sigh.

"She won't discuss it with you?"

I shake my head. "Not without …"

"Without …"

I rub at the back of my neck. "Without making her feelings on other topics known."

Cormac nods once. "Elle."

"Right. When I try to have a discussion with her, she turns it around on me."

"Simple. Fix your shit, then bug Mom about hers." He keeps walking deeper into the house. "This the dining room?"

I follow him. "Yeah. Chandelier got replaced last week."

The walls in here have been painted, and the floor is partially exposed. There's a path of cardboard that connects the living room and the kitchen to protect the finished floors. Afternoon sun filters in through the bay windows that overlook the backyard.

"Nice," Cormac comments.

He walks toward the stairs, and I trail behind like I'm the one taking this tour.

"It's not simple shit to fix," I say when we reach the landing.

Cormac barks out a laugh. "Obviously. Elle won't even come over when you're home."

I grimace, not appreciating the reminder.

It makes me wonder about the timing of this visit. If he showed up here while Elle was at the trailer, visiting with my mom, on purpose.

Cormac turns when he reaches the top of the stairs. I pause a few steps lower. For the first time in my life, my little brother is looking down at me. He might be grown up, but I still have a couple of inches on him.

"You love her, Ry. That's fairly obvious to anyone who knows you. And she sure hasn't forgotten about you. You lost seven years. You really want to waste more time?"

I'm frozen. I was expecting a cliché about anything worthwhile being difficult. Not for him to lay it out so ... bluntly.

"She's better off without me."

I've said that in my head so many times; it's a relief to speak it aloud.

Cormac shakes his head. "Bullshit. But if she decides that, at least you'll have the closure."

He continues down the hallway, and I follow.

"How many bedrooms does this place have?"

"Five," I answer.

Cormac whistles, long and low. "Wow."

He looks through all five, which are in various stages of completion. Some have been painted; some haven't. Some still need repairs; some don't.

"This place is awesome," he tells me. "Can't believe you've done all this."

"Hasn't just been me," I reply. "There's usually a big crew of guys here. Tuck pulled them off for another project today."

"With how much time you've spent here, no way you've contributed nothing." Cormac runs a finger along the trim surrounding one of the doorways. We've preserved as much of the original house as possible. Everything that wasn't rotted or warped. "Be nice to live in a place like this one day. I've always wondered what it would be like."

I nod, not sure what else to say.

I'm so focused on making it through the present that I haven't given any thought to the future. I have no idea what I'll do or where I'll go after my mom passes away. There's a wistful note to Cormac's voice that makes me think he's given it more thought.

Downstairs, I hear the front door open and close.

"Ryder?" a familiar voice calls. "You here?"

"That's Tuck," I tell Cormac, heading for the stairs.

Tuck grins when we reach downstairs and he sees my brother. "Hey! James Jr. How's it going, Cormac?"

"Pretty good," Cormac replies, bumping Tuck's fist. "House looks good."

"Can't take much credit. I'm usually busy with other jobs. Whereas Ryder is *always* here." Tucker glances at me and grins. "Man, you have the day off. What the hell are you doing here?"

"He got kicked out of the trailer," Cormac says unhelpfully. "Elle's visiting."

I glare at my brother. Tucker's been careful not to mention Elle around me since he, Keira, and Keira's friends overheard our shouting match in the kitchen. He probably regrets insisting I come to the beach house this weekend. No one's confirmed Elle will be there, but if she is …

She'll have the letter by then, the one my mom might be handing her right this second.

It was supposed to make everything better. Resolved. But it could also make everything worse.

"What are *you* doing here?" I ask Tuck, cutting through the uncomfortable pause that's lingering.

"Tile delivery," he tells me. "For the master bath. It was today or two weeks from now." Tuck glances at his watch. "Guy's supposed to be here at four."

"Want me to wait for it?" I offer.

"Nah, you don't need to do that."

"Tuck, seriously. Get out of here. I know you have tons of other shit to do."

"You certain?" he asks.

"Positive."

"All right. Thanks, man. I'll see you tomorrow? We should leave by ten to catch the eleven-thirty ferry."

I nod. "I'll be ready."

Keira left for Martha's Vineyard yesterday. Tuck and I are going tomorrow. Then, everyone else is supposed to arrive Saturday.

"Great." Tuck looks at Cormac. "Should've offered this sooner, but you're welcome to come, too, James Jr., if you don't mind hanging out with us old folk."

I roll my eyes.

Cormac doesn't quite manage to hide his grin as he tucks his hands into his pockets. "Can't. I've got plans. But thanks."

"He's got a date," I say, smiling.

"Oh, yeah? Nice going, Romeo."

"Where did you take Keira on your first date?" I ask.

I missed most of their early story, busy wrapped up in my own shit or absent entirely.

Tuck smirks. "The pond. I cooked a bunch of stuff and brought it in a picnic basket. Then, we went and got ice cream."

"She liked that?" Cormac asks dubiously.

"I'm marrying her, aren't I? Total success story."

I roll my eyes again.

Tuck's phone rings. He pulls it out and glances at the screen. "I should take this. See you guys later. Thanks again, Ry."

"No problem," I respond.

"I should get going too," Cormac says. "Told Mav I'd come over for a bit."

"Sounds good," I reply. "Glad you stopped by."

"Yeah. Me too." He glances around. "Really, bro, I'm impressed."

I don't deflect this time. I just swallow and say, "Thanks."

It's been a while since I did anything anyone was proud of. Since I felt like I deserved any pride.

"You should get Mom over here to see it."

I nod. "Yeah, I will. I was just waiting … I will."

I don't know what I'm waiting for. She's mentioned—usually at dinner, right when I get home—that she wants to come to the worksite. And I put her off every time, wanting it to be more when she sees it. Wanting there to be something ahead to look forward to. But if I wait too long, I'll run out of time.

"Have fun waiting for tiles." Cormac heads for the door.

"Cor … wait." I walk toward him, pulling my wallet out of my pocket, then hold out a thick wad of twenties.

I've just been cashing my paychecks so far, putting off setting up bank accounts. Hank paid us under the table, and that was the only real job I had before now. And my expenses are practically nonexistent, living with my mom.

"No, Ry," he says, looking at the cash. "I'm not taking your money."

"Yeah, you are," I reply, holding it closer. "I missed a lot of birthdays. Take it. Spend it this weekend, on whatever you want."

"You don't need to—that's not why I was asking."

"I know."

I keep holding the money out, and he finally takes it.

I'm not expecting the hug. It catches me off guard. My family has never been the overly affectionate kind. We show our love in subtler ways.

"Thanks, man," Cormac tells me, tapping my back twice with his fist.

"Don't mention it."

I mean that literally. This is already more thanks than I needed.

"I'll see you at home?"

"Yeah. I'll be back around dinner."

" 'Kay. Cool." He continues walking.

"Cormac," I call after him.

He pauses and spins back around to face me.

"She won't care," I tell him. "If she's the right girl, she won't care where you take her or how much money you spend on her. Okay?"

Cormac nods. "Thanks, Ry."

30
THEN

Elle

An unsmiling Cormac opens the door. He looks different. Serious. Older, like he's aged a couple of years since I last saw him.

I know the feeling.

I stretch my mouth into a smile. "Hi, Cormac. Remember me?"

He nods. "You heard, right? Ryder isn't here. He won't be home for a long time."

That last sentence makes me want to sink down and sob. It's so simple. So final.

But it feels like all I've done is cry recently. I'm here so I can stop.

"I-I know," I answer. "I wanted to talk to your mom. Is she home?"

"Yeah," Cormac says dully. "Come in."

I step inside the trailer, my chest squeezing painfully as I glance around the familiar kitchen, knowing I won't see Ryder here. It's still the closest I've felt to him in three weeks. He's never been in my house. I go to a different school now. The places where we spent the most time together—they're all *his* places. The auto garage and this trailer are all I have left of him.

"Mom's back in her bedroom. I'll grab her."

Cormac leaves, providing me with the perfect opening for the real reason I'm here. I reach for the woman's purse hanging off one of the kitchen chairs without hesitating, pulling out a pack of cigarettes and a hair clip before finding a pink wallet. I slip the driver's license out from behind the protective plastic and slide it into the back pocket of my jeans, my heartbeat a guilty thud in my ears as I quickly replace everything else in the purse.

When I went to the prison last week, they wouldn't let me see Ryder. They told me I wasn't an approved visitor. They'll let family in though—I hope. I have no idea if this crazy, desperate plot I've hatched will work, but it's all I have.

"You're a long way from home."

I spin to face Ryder's mother. Her first name is Nina, according to her ID. Nina James.

She's stunning. Long, dark hair. Delicate features. Willowy frame. She could pass for thirty—the only signs of her age are the raspy tone of a frequent smoker and the crow's-feet in the corners of her eyes.

"I'm adventurous," I reply, not sure what else to say.

This isn't how I wanted to meet Ryder's mom. I want her to like me, and I'm already certain she doesn't.

Her lips purse. "What can I help you with?"

"That's what I wanted to ask you. I'm a … friend of Ryder's, and I just wanted to—"

"There's nothing you can do."

The same thing everyone keeps telling me. *He accepted a plea deal. He's in prison. It's over.*

But giving up isn't an option.

I swallow. "There must be something—"

"Go home, Elle."

I stare at Nina, belatedly realizing I never introduced myself.

"Go home," she repeats a little more gently. "Ryder made his choices. You need to accept them. Move on."

She makes it sound so simple. Two words—move on.

Forgive.

Forget.

Let go.

None of those are easy. They're all hard.

But I have what I came here for, so I nod instead of pointing that out. "Nice to meet you."

Nina appraises me with an inscrutable expression as I head toward the door and step back outside. Down the steps and toward my car.

Two hours later, I'm perched on a metal folding chair, my hands anxiously fiddling with each other. Trying not to jump at each buzz or every clang. Trying not to stare at anyone passing by. Trying not to draw attention to myself.

This is further than I made it last time, which gives me hope. The guard at the entrance nodded when I gave my name—Nina's name—after checking a computer. Gave me a box to store my phone and a long list of forbidden items. I had to go through a metal detector and ended up here, in a small waiting room that smells like stale coffee and bleach.

"Nina James!"

It takes me a few seconds to react. To remember that's the name I was waiting for, not Elodie Clarke.

I walk up to the window. My heart is pounding so loudly that

I can't hear anything else. This is illegal. This is dumb. This is … necessary.

Because I'm stubborn and loyal, and I'm in love with Ryder James. I *need* to see him. Need it like air. There are so many questions that only he can answer.

"Nina James?"

"Y-yes." I steel my spine, trying to inject some confidence into my voice. I'm used to being catered to, as spoiled as that sounds. To teachers paying me extra attention and friends' parents telling me what a great influence I am. Authority figures normally adore me. But I'm so far from my comfort zone I can't see it, so I sound like a scared little kid.

"ID?"

Trembling fingers slide Nina's driver's license across the laminated counter. My heart ricochets against my rib cage.

A phone behind the plastic barrier begins to ring. The guard barely glances at Nina's driver's license before shoving it back toward me.

The door buzzes open a few seconds later.

I'm so shocked it's opening—so stunned that it worked—that once again, it takes a few seconds for my muscles to unfreeze and move. I grab the ID and then rush inside.

The room I walk into reminds me of a cafeteria. It's three times the size of the waiting area, filled with metal tables that have connected chairs. The floor is checkered linoleum, and the walls are a drab gray that might have originally been white.

I take a seat at an empty table, clasping my hands together in my lap. No one told me what this process would be like, and I was too nervous to draw attention to myself by asking any questions.

The prisoners in the room stand out—the orange jumpsuits they're wearing obnoxious splashes of color against the neutral backdrop. I scan each face quickly, confirming Ryder isn't in here.

None of the men look dangerous. Most of them look … defeated.

I unclasp my hands to rub my sweaty palms against my jeans.

Then, the far door opens, and I see him.

I freeze once again, my entire body going still. I knew seeing him here would be awful. But I wasn't totally prepared. I don't think I could have been.

Ryder's scanning the room as he walks. A stern-looking guard follows a couple of feet behind, the gun attached to his belt in obvious view.

It takes Ryder about thirty seconds to spot me. When he does, he halts. I see the moment it registers that I'm really here, that he's not imagining anything. Just like I catch the split second he considers turning and walking away.

And I know—I just know—that he's going to make this difficult.

That the past three weeks of silence were a choice. Were *his* choice.

The Ryder that walks toward me isn't the guy who folded me a flower or licked icing off my leg. He's … hard, his face all harsh lines and sharp angles. He looks older too.

"What are you doing here, Elle?" He takes the seat across from mine.

Unlike most of the men here, the air around him crackles with energy. With anger.

"I came to see you." I leave the *duh* off, but it comes through loud and clear.

"Why?"

I stare at him. *Why?* An hour and a half drive and a stolen driver's license. Weeks of worry and tears. And all I get is, *Why?*

"Here's a why for you." I lean closer, the cold metal of the table digging into my stomach. "Why are you here, Ryder?"

His jawline tightens, already straight lines pulling taut. "You must know. I'm sure the whole town is talking about it."

"You told me you didn't deal drugs. That you weren't involved with any of that."

"Shit happened."

"Shit happened," I repeat. "Did *shit happen* when you attacked Archer too?"

"*Attacked* is a stretch. I punched him once."

I haven't seen Archer since that day in the hallway. But there was a recent picture of him in the paper from the football team's senior night. The bruising and swelling on his face are gone, but he has a scar that will last forever.

Kinda impressive that Ryder did that with one swing.

"You promised me you wouldn't."

He says nothing, just stares at me.

He's so cold. So distant. So different from the Ryder I know. From the boy I love.

I'm relieved when he breaks the silence. Horrified by what he says.

"Is that all?"

"All?" The frostiness radiating off Ryder is affecting me too. Chilling me. It feels like I'm five steps behind and I can't catch up.

"Yeah. I've got a busy rest of the day." His voice is mocking, a tone I've never heard him use before. Bitter and brutal.

I pull my hands from my lap and rest them on the table. My fingers are so pale, like they're lacking any blood at all. I reach for Ryder, and he pulls away.

"No touching!" one of the guards barks.

I blink back tears. "You don't belong here, Ry."

"I was always going to end up stuck somewhere," he tells me. "Just like you were always going to attend a prestigious college and marry a guy who's nothing like me."

"Don't say that. You're wrong."

"I'm realistic, Elle. We were fun. We were never serious, and we sure as hell were never going to last. Everyone knew it."

I shake my head. "No. We—you're just saying that because you're here. But you can appeal. I'll ask my dad to—"

Ryder rests his forearms on the table. The more upset I get, the calmer he appears. "I'm guilty. I had the shit. I took the deal. There's nothing to be done."

My hands are trembling again. "Eight years for possession is crazy. There's no way that—"

"How did you get in here?" he asks.

I swallow. "I used your mom's name. Stole her ID. They-they wouldn't let me see you otherwise."

"You can't take a hint, can you?"

I stare at him, taken aback. "What?"

"They let us see friends and family to try to keep us from reoffending. An incentive to stay in line, get out of here as soon as possible. *I* decide who can visit me, Elle. You weren't supposed to get in here."

"You … don't want me to visit?"

I'm so confused. If I can't see him here, I can't see him at all. And not for weeks or months. For *years*.

"No."

I search Ryder's grave face for a sign he's lying. Find none.

"You said you loved me," I whisper.

"I got caught up in the moment," he says quietly.

My eyes begin to burn, and I know I'm close to crying.

I refuse to do that here, to let Ryder see how deeply he's cutting me.

I bite the inside of my cheek until I taste blood. The flare of physical pain slices through the emotional agony, centering me. "I forgave you for breaking my heart once. I won't do it again."

Ryder nods, no trace of regret on his face. "I know."

Then, he stands and walks away.

I keep waiting for him to look back, but he never does.

He disappears from sight, and my heart cracks in half.

31
NOW

Elle

Mrs. Nelson is reclining in her beach chair when I step out of my convertible, a wrapped book tucked under one arm. There's no sign of Nina's car, but I think—hope—that just means Ryder isn't home. I'm not prepared to see him, following the call I made in the middle of the night.

I'll have to get ready soon, before I board a ferry to Martha's Vineyard tomorrow. Keira checked—three times—that I was okay with Ryder coming. I assured her I was, and I'm not sure if it was a lie or not.

"It's not Saturday," Mrs. Nelson tells me, shading her eyes as she peers up at me. No flower sunglasses today.

"My schedule switched around a little," I tell her. "After graduating."

She nods, then says, "You let that boy's return chase you off."

I guess I know why Mrs. Nelson never asked why I visited Nina each month. She made her own—correct—assumptions about my motives.

"That's one way of looking at it," I reply, glancing at Nina's trailer.

The railing has been replaced since I was here last. An air conditioner unit whirs in the kitchen window. All the bushes have been pruned.

Mrs. Nelson takes a sip of what appears to be straight whiskey. "There haven't been any other young ladies climbing in his window, if you were wondering."

My cheeks burn. "I wasn't."

But I'm more than a little embarrassed she saw me sneaking into Ryder's bedroom during a rainstorm.

And … that's nice to know. Not that I think Ryder would bring a woman back to the trailer with Cormac and Nina sleeping down the hall. He'd go back to her place or fuck her in a bar restroom.

Not that I've given it any thought.

"Elle!"

For the first time, Nina didn't wait for me to make it to the door. She waves from the doorway, beckoning me toward her trailer.

I'm relieved—so, so relieved—that she looks the same as the last time I saw her. No sign of sickness.

Silently pray that means she has more time than the doctors predicted.

"Nice to see you, Mrs. Nelson," I say.

She hums in answer, taking another sip from her cup as I head for Nina.

Nina hugs me when I reach her, which is another surprise. One that makes me glad I didn't listen to her request to stay away. Didn't let Ryder chase me off for good, as Mrs. Nelson so delicately put it.

"It's so good to see you," she tells me.

I nod, trying hard not to get too emotional as she breaks our embrace and steps aside so I can enter the kitchen. Being back here feels so normal. So natural. But also different, seeing the *Franklin Construction* ball cap hung on the arm of the couch and the three plates dripping in the drain rack.

Ryder's no longer a ghost here. He *is* here.

"So good to see you too," I say, heading toward the table where the teapot is waiting, steam curling toward the ceiling. I set the book I brought Nina down beside it.

"Joanna has been extra chatty this week," Nina tells me, taking her usual seat across from me. "Her daughter and granddaughter were supposed to be visiting from Florida, but they got stuck down there because of a hurricane that passed through."

"That's awful," I say. I hardly know Mrs. Nelson—didn't even know her first name until now—but it feels like she's a part of my world after years of visits here.

I hadn't heard about the hurricane, which is also upsetting. That there are enough tragedies happening daily that we can't keep up with them all.

"It is. They're coming in August instead."

"Does-does Ryder's father still live in Jacksonville?"

Nina's hand stalls midair, halfway to the teapot's handle.

She's asked who I'm dating over the years, but we've never discussed her romantic past. Either of her sons' fathers. I know little about Ryder's dad and nothing about Cormac's, except that Ryder didn't get along with him.

Ryder has always been a taboo topic between us. One neither of us has brought up, not since I came here a week after sneaking into the prison, bringing her ID and a succulent. I dropped her ID loose in her purse, hoping she'd think she'd simply misplaced it. The plant died years ago, but the pot it came in still sits on the windowsill above the kitchen sink.

"No," Nina answers, recovering. "Last I knew, he was in Denver. Dax is hard to pin down, to keep track of. He shows up when he wants to, not when you need him."

I nod. That tracks with everything Ryder told me about his father.

"Not many hurricanes in Colorado."

Nina's lips twitch. "No, there aren't."

She pours the tea, filling the air with the scent of jasmine, and then pushes one cup closer to me.

"Thank you."

"Of course. Thank you for the new flavors you sent. I've sampled all of them. Been drinking a lot of tea recently. The boys have tried some too." She runs a finger around the rim of the teacup. "The pomegranate hibiscus is Ryder's favorite."

Her tone is tentative. She's not sure if she should mention him.

"Good for summer," is all I can come up with to say.

I'm still adjusting to this. To discussing Ryder with Nina so casually, like he's been a part of our conversations all along. Like she's his mother, not just my friend.

"I wasn't planning to say anything," Nina tells me. "About your visits. He saw the tea … put it together pretty fast."

"It's fine," I say. "I probably should have told him myself. He, uh … it was just hard to reach him for a while."

Nina half smiles sadly. "It was."

I blow at the steam. "He-he wouldn't let me see him," I say impulsively. "It wasn't that I didn't want to."

"I know."

I glance up. "He told you he kept me from visiting?"

Nina nods. "Yes. A few days ago."

I'm relieved. Part of me has always felt she must have judged me for giving up on Ryder, even though she'd told me to.

"He didn't give me a choice. Didn't listen to me. Just shut me out. I wanted to see him, to talk to him. Even if we weren't together anymore … I needed him. I don't know how to forgive him for that."

"There was a lot going on," Nina reminds me gently.

I huff. "That's not good enough."

"Fair enough."

I shake my head. "I'm sorry. I shouldn't be talking to you about this. You're his mom, and—"

Nina reaches out and covers my hand. "I care about you too, Elle. If you want to talk, I'm always here."

I swallow the lump in my throat. "He let you visit him. Cormac. I'm sure Tucker did too. And me … I had to steal your ID and sneak in, just to see him *once*."

Nina's eyebrows rise.

"Sorry," I murmur.

Her smile is unexpected. "Ryder didn't share that part of the story."

"It was dumb."

"I'd call it brave. We should all be lucky enough to be loved that fiercely."

I stare down into my tea, saying nothing. I've already shared too much.

Everyone else has moved on. I need to stop dragging the past into the present.

"Elle," Nina says softly, "I don't have any answers or explanations. But I want you to consider something. It's our nature to shield the people we love from pain and suffering. If I could have passed away peacefully without telling my boys about this disease that's going to kill me slowly, I would have. You think Ryder allowing others to visit him means he cared about you less? Have you ever considered that it was because he loved you more?"

Almost exactly what Tucker told me.

"Loved me so much that he refused to see me for seven years? That he let me spend seven years thinking ..." I exhale.

"I don't think he thought you'd spend seven years thinking anything." The words are quiet. Kind.

Ryder thought I'd forget about him. It's not an unreasonable assumption to make about seven years. For most people—for normal people—that should have been plenty of time to heal and move on.

Just not me.

And, logical or not, I'm offended he thought so little of me. Of us.

Nina reaches, flipping through a stack of mail and pulling out a white envelope.

She pushes it across the table toward me. "Ryder asked me to give this to you."

I already realized it was from him. I trace the familiar scrawl of his handwriting, feeling the indentations in the paper where he slashed the two L's in my name.

I'm dying to read it ... and also terrified to.

We're a tightrope, and I'm never sure which side I'll fall on.

"Thank you," I say.

Nina nods, then sips her tea. "How's Scout doing?"

Neither of us mentions Ryder for the rest of my visit.

32
THEN

Elle

Ryder,

It's been five months since I saw you. I promised I wouldn't come back, and I keep my promises. one of us should.

I got the last of my college letters today. Acceptances, every single one. you'd probably tease me about that. call me a nerd or a know-it-all.

I'm so ready to leave. It doesn't feel like it matters, where I go.

There's no way for me to tell if you're getting these letters, but I think that you are. I've been making excuses for why you're not responding, but I'm running out of them.

I hope you're okay. I'm sure it's hard, where you are.

And I hope it haunts you, how you ended things. If that's terrible for me to say, I don't really care. you broke my heart. so, here's another promise: you never will again.

you got your wish. we're over. I guess we're a cat's game.

Elle

33
NOW

Elle

Elle,

I promised I wouldn't write.

You're right, that I've broken promises. This one I intended to keep. If you're reading this, it's another way I let you down.

I know you're mad.

I know you hate me.

I made some mistakes. Little ones. Big ones. Add in some shitty luck, and I ended up here.

I'm stuck here. You're not. And the only way I'm going to get through this, the only way I can live with the consequences, is knowing you're out there, living.

You're going to accomplish amazing things, Elodie Clarke. If I know one thing, it's that. I feel lucky to have met you.

Since I'm writing this for selfish reasons, here are a few more things I want you to know:

I love you.

I miss you.
I'll never forget you.
Maybe in another life.
Ryder

Salty air blows my hair straight out of my face. By the time the ferry hits shore, it'll be a tangled mess.

I don't care.

I stare out at the white-capped waves, my stomach tumbling with each rise and rock of the boat. Scout is on high alert by my side, focused on the other passengers walking past and the seagulls sailing by.

Some ocean spray splashes over the railing and onto my arm. The July air is warm enough that the sprinkle feels good, but the water is colder than I expected. Maybe I won't be swimming this weekend after all. I was hoping the temperature would have risen since my May visit.

Twenty minutes later, we disembark from the ferry.

There are three figures waiting alongside the vintage green Land Rover instead of the one I was looking for. I decided not to bother bringing my convertible this trip, so Keira was planning to pick me up.

I shade my eyes and dig through my bag for my sunglasses as best I can while juggling Scout's leash and my luggage. The sun is sinking straight into golden hour. The ferry I just stepped off was the second to last of the day.

Scout barks as we approach the group. He's happy to be on solid land again. But he's straining toward one silhouette in particular.

It irks me that my dog likes Ryder. Likes him a noticeable amount, not just his normal friendliness.

It makes me wonder about all those silly things I decided were myths a long time ago—like destiny and fate and kismet. If there were forces that pushed me and Ryder together, not just pulled us apart.

"Here. Let me take him." Ryder's fingers are warm and calloused as he takes the leash from me. My shoulder is suddenly free from the weight of my weekend bag too.

I glance down at a wiggling Scout trying desperately to get Ryder's attention. "He remembers you."

"I'm hard to forget."

My eyes flash up to his.

I wasn't anticipating that response. Or the teasing smile on Ryder's face before he leans down to pet Scout. This is the most relaxed I've seen him since he's been back. Some of the careful mask has fallen away, allowing a glimpse at the ease behind it.

The last two times we talked were both heavy. Yelling in the kitchen. Breathing on the phone.

Then, there's the letter, tucked carefully in the bag Ryder's carrying for me.

He must know I have it. That I read it. Right?

"Yay! You're here," Keira exclaims, and I realize the only person I've greeted is Ryder. I give her a big hug, and she squeezes me back tightly. "And you are in some desperate need of sun, girl." She pokes my pale arm, the color of my skin not changing at all.

"I've been studying," I say.

The bar exam is only two weeks away.

"You also have a backyard," she reminds me.

"I wear sunscreen."

Keira links our elbows and pulls me toward the car. "Seriously, how have you been? Aside from vitamin D–deprived."

"I'm good," I say, glancing back over one shoulder.

Tucker and Ryder are trailing ten feet behind us. Scout is trotting along with the boys happily.

"You look good," Keira tells me.

"I thought I looked pale," I tease.

"Pale and gorgeous."

I smile. "So, what's the evening plan?"

"I was thinking of going out for drinks, then heading back to the cottage for dinner? Tucker got steaks to grill. We'll be too big of a group for fancy food tomorrow night. I just bought a bunch of hot dogs to roast."

"How big of a group are we tonight?" I ask.

"It's just the four of us." Keira glances at me, testing my reaction to that response.

My smile isn't forced. "Okay."

It's a surprise. I just assumed more guests would arrive before tomorrow. Not an unpleasant one, but a surprise.

The guys reach the car a few seconds later. Keira insists on riding in the back seat with me and Scout, who spends the short drive straining to stick his head out the window. Tucker and Ryder talk baseball as I stare out at the scenery passing by and avoid getting a mouthful of fur.

It's even more beautiful here now than it was back in May. Hydrangeas have bloomed. Houses are all inhabited, each clamshell driveway we pass occupied by multiple cars.

Ten minutes later, we stop in front of the Parkers' house.

"Wow. Nice decorating," I compliment, studying the exterior.

Keira beams as she climbs out of the back seat. "Thank you."

Tiny flags have been spaced along the path that leads to the front door. Red, white, and blue lanterns hang from the porch railing. And the pastel pillows on the swing have been replaced by star-and-stripe patterns.

"You should see the inside," Tucker says. "Took her most of yesterday. And it only required one emergency bookshelf repair that took me all afternoon."

Keira sticks her tongue out at her fiancé. "How was I supposed to know it would break?"

"Maybe because it's a *bookshelf*, not a ladder?"

Ryder is grinning behind Tucker, making me think Keira and Tucker have had this argument a couple of times already today. Our gazes meet, and I look away quickly, feeling weirdly … shy.

Lines from the letter he wrote me run through my head. It was dated six years ago, meaning he wrote it a full year after breaking up with me. Meaning he didn't let go quickly or easily, the way I always assumed.

Keira and Tucker are still bickering about the bookshelf as we walk inside.

The red, white, and blue color scheme has definitely spread indoors. Everywhere I look, there's something patriotic.

"Are you up for going out for drinks?" Keira asks me.

"Yeah. Definitely. Just let me get Scout settled and get changed."

"You're in the same room as before." Keira takes my bag from Tucker, who carried it inside for me, and heads for the stairs hung with bunting.

Scout trots after us once I whistle for him.

"You spoil me," I say as soon as we reach it. "No way this room doesn't have the best view."

"It does. But it's also where my parents stay when they're here, so ..." She smirks. "Basically, you taking this room is helping my sex life."

I wrinkle my nose. "You could have just said, *It's yours because you're my best friend and you showed up before Juliet.*"

"It's yours because you're my best friend and you showed up before Juliet."

I roll my eyes as I walk toward the doors leading out to the balcony, eager to take in the view I know is waiting. "Too late."

"Come down whenever you're ready," Keira says. "No rush." She shuts the door behind her.

I stand out on the balcony for a few more minutes, then feed Scout his dinner.

My hair is the disaster I knew it'd be. It takes me a good ten minutes to get the strands unknotted, then change my clothes.

My mom drove into the city last week for a shopping trip. She took the news of my breakup with Prescott better than I had expected, although I'm positive part of her muted reaction was because my dad had already told her. Still, it was one of the nicer afternoons we'd had together in a while. And in addition to more professional clothes, I bought a few fun sundresses, like the blue one I'm wearing tonight.

There's a knock on the door as I'm debating whether to pull my hair up or leave it down. I walk to answer it, holding the strands up with one hand.

Keira whistles when she sees me. "Damn. New dress?"

"Uh-huh. Frances and I went shopping." I drop my hair, then gather the strands off my neck again. "Up or down?"

"Down. Here." Keira hands me a glass that I take a tentative sniff of. Vodka, I think. "It was an early wedding gift from my liquor supplier. You wouldn't believe what it costs a bottle."

"It's going to be that kind of night, huh?" I ask before swallowing the shot.

It's good. Ice cold and smooth. Only stings once it hits my empty stomach.

Keira quirks a brow. "You tell me."

She doesn't bother to hide the burning curiosity on her face. The last time she saw me in person, I was holding back tears on her front steps.

"He had Nina give me a letter," I tell her.

"Nina?"

"His mom," I explain.

"You met her?"

I nod. "I … visit her. I've visited her for years."

"You have? Why?"

"Because …" I tuck my hair behind one ear. "Because I couldn't let go."

Keira nods slowly. "What did the letter say?"

"It explained some things. Why he ended our relationship. What he was thinking."

"In a *really sorry I broke your heart* kind of way? Or an *I'll love you forever* kind of way?"

I swallow. "Both. The second one more."

"Wow. I mean, I'm not that surprised. The way he acted at the bar when you … panicked. Waking up early to exercise your dog. The tension with Prescott? Not to mention what happened when he came over … it's clear he still has serious feelings for you."

"Maybe."

"He turned down Ophelia. And Tuck swears he isn't seeing anyone."

"He spends a lot of time at Reese's," I say.

Keira shakes her head. "I asked Tuck about it. He swears Ryder and Reese are just friends. And Reese's kid is always there."

"She has a kid?"

"Yeah. A son. They're coming tomorrow." She takes a step closer to the door. "You ready to go?"

"Yeah."

I flick the overhead light off, leaving a lamp on for Scout. He's finished his food, and he's curled up in one corner of the crate Keira—or Tucker—left out for him. The Parkers used to have a Lab they'd bring here when Keira and her brother were younger.

Tucker and Ryder are waiting next to the front door. They've both changed as well.

Tucker is wearing a pressed button-down that makes Keira's influence on his wardrobe obvious. I usually see him in T-shirts, like the navy one Ryder is wearing. Paired with khaki shorts, it's actually one of the fancier outfits I've ever seen Ryder wear.

I feel Ryder's eyes on me, so I avoid his gaze.

The same shyness from earlier has reappeared, a single shot of vodka not enough to banish it.

"Truck will be a tight squeeze," Tucker says. "Let's take the Rover again?"

"I can drive," I volunteer. That'll give me something to focus on besides Ryder.

Tucker nods and hands me the keys.

"It's a tank compared to your car," Ryder comments.

Finally, I look at him. "Are you calling me a bad driver?"

"There's a dent in the rear bumper of your convertible."

"When were you *inspecting* my car?" I ask.

"I *noticed* it the last time you were here," Ryder replies. One corner of his mouth has curved up, like he knows I'm not really annoyed, just flustered.

"I can handle driving to the bar."

"Uh-huh. Sure."

"I was trying to be *nice*."

Ryder smirks. "By offering to drive one way again? You sucked down the margaritas at this place like they were water last time, Clarke."

He's goading me. Teasing me. I'm not sure why, and I'm enjoying it too much to analyze it right now. I'm at the edge of the cliff again, the thrill consuming.

I gasp. "The fuck I did."

Had another guy mentioned the night I had a panic attack, I'd be a stiff board right now. But that's Ryder's magic. The effect he's always had on me. He doesn't wash the darkness away. But he changes the light. He makes the hard moments look brighter. Appear livable.

Keira and Tucker exchange a glance that reminds me that Ryder and I spent most of our happy moments as a couple alone.

"Give me the keys, Lo." He steps closer, holding out a hand.

I grin. "No."

"You're already drunk, huh?"

I guess he's close enough to smell my breath.

"I had *one* shot. And Keira made me."

"Hey! Leave me out of this … drama." Keira waves a hand between me and Ryder.

Her expression is alight with a feverish intrigue I know the source of. She'll have more questions later.

When he wants to be, Ryder is electric. When I'm around him,

I'm someone different.

"I'm driving, Elle. Give me the keys."

His insistence sparks a memory. He's only driven me around once before.

"How'd you get home that night?" I say. I've always wondered. Never asked. Gave up on getting answers.

Ryder stares at me. I can't tell if he's annoyed I'm bringing up the past or just taken aback.

"I walked," he finally answers.

"That's a long way to walk."

"I had a lot to think about that night."

I start toward the driver's side.

Ryder heaves a sigh out. "Don't hit anything."

He gets in the passenger side while Keira and Tucker climb into the back seat.

"If I do, you can just fix it."

"Haven't done that in a while," he says, some of the teasing leaving his tone.

I slant a glance in his direction before I start driving.

The garage where he worked in high school went out of business a few years ago. If it hadn't, I think he'd be working there instead of in construction.

Ryder seems content to be a passenger now that we're moving, and it confuses me even more. It's almost like he picked a fight just to argue with me, and I have no idea what to make of that.

I suggest going to the same bar as last time, ignoring the concerned looks aimed my way. The worry is why I want to go back—to prove that I can.

Ryder agrees first, and Keira and Tucker follow his lead.

The bar—Beachcombers, I notice it's called this time—is even more crowded than it was last time we visited. It's a good thing we're a smaller group.

There's no glimmer of panic as I push past people. No claustrophobia. No crush of confinement. I'm annoyed mostly by the slow progress toward the bar.

Several minutes later, we reach an open spot. Keira and I decide on mojitos while Tucker and Ryder order beers.

We cheers, me painfully aware of Ryder's arm pressed against mine. It's so packed in here that loss of personal space is an inevitability. But it's still so overwhelming, being this close to him.

"Oh, hey!" Tuck says. "The signed Williams jersey. You never saw it last time, right?"

Ryder shakes his head.

"Come on. We'll be right back, guys."

Tucker and Ryder disappear into the crowd.

"Who?" I ask Keira.

"He's a famous Red Sox player," she tells me.

I lift an eyebrow, surprised she knows that. I guess her influence on Tucker hasn't been one-sided.

"Keira?" a male voice says.

Keira and I both turn to face the man who spoke.

"Cash!" Keira exclaims. "It's so nice to see you."

"You too." He gives her a quick hug.

Keira glances at me. "Oh, Elle! You remember Cash, don't you?"

"I think so," I say, shaking his offered hand. I don't, not really. I must have met him when I was in college, and I'm guessing I was drunk at the time.

Cash flashes a wide smile at me, the sight almost blinding. "I definitely remember Elle." His grin turns flirtatious. "Nice to see you again."

"You too," I reply.

"You ladies headed to the fireworks tomorrow night?"

"Of course," Keira tells him.

"I've got a prime spot staked out. Right by the pier. You can't beat the view over the water. Make sure you come check it out."

"We'll be a big group," Keira warns.

"Everyone is welcome," Cash assures her. "Plenty of space."

"All right then. We'll be there."

"Here you guys are." Tucker appears.

"Hey. I'm Cash."

"Tucker." Tucker shakes his hand.

"Where's Ryder?" I blurt.

Everyone looks at me.

Tucker looks over his shoulder. "Dunno. I thought he was right behind me. I'll text him." He pulls out his phone and starts typing.

I set down my drink. "I'll be right back. Bathroom."

But rather than push toward the restrooms sign that hangs above the back hallway, I walk out the same side door I did last time.

The porch is empty, no sign of anyone. But I keep walking, around the corner to the back of the bar. Two giant dumpsters take up most of the small paved section. But past them is an unobstructed view of the water, so the area seems much more open.

Ryder's leaning against the shingles, smoking. There's a sexy nostalgia to the sight, but I mostly hate it.

"You said you'd stop." I pause a couple of feet away, staring at him. Waiting for him to look at me.

He doesn't. "I say a lot of things."

I cross my arms. "Not to me you don't."

A quiet scoff before he exhales a cloud of smoke.

"Your mom is dying of lung cancer."

"Don't need the reminder, Elle, thanks."

The next time he lowers the cigarette to exhale, I take it from him and toss it on the ground. Ryder sighs, then takes a swig from the beer bottle he's holding loosely in his left hand.

"What are you doing out here?" I ask.

"I *was* smoking."

"Well, stop."

His jaw works as he stares straight ahead at the water.

"I don't understand." I hate how young my voice sounds. How lost. "I thought we were …"

"Were what?"

"Good," I conclude lamely. "I thought we were good."

I thought we'd talk and laugh and drink with our best friends tonight. I thought he was done avoiding me.

"I just needed a minute."

"You got seven years of minutes, Ryder. And you're still avoiding me."

His fingers flex on the bottle. "Wasn't in the mood to watch another rich prick pant after you, okay?"

My exhale is more of a huff. "This is about *Cash*? Are you fucking kidding me?"

"Cash." Ryder snorts. "Fitting name."

"At least those *rich pricks* have the balls to pursue me, Ryder. They don't sulk outside, alone, poisoning their lungs."

He makes a sound in the back of his throat that's basically a growl. "Go inside, Elle."

"No."

One second, I'm standing and scowling at him. And the next, my spine is pressed against the hard ridges of the weathered wooden shingles that cover the exterior of the building, and Ryder is kissing me.

I'm so stunned that it takes my lips a minute to unfreeze and relax.

There's a rush of heat and urgency. An avalanche of unfamiliar sensation. It's been so long since I was kissed like this. So long since *Ryder* kissed me.

I melt into him, not putting up the slightest fight, and there's a noticeable stutter in Ryder's movements as my willingness registers. When he realizes I want this. How *bad* I want this.

He kissed me as a punishment. As a consequence for staying out here and not letting him run away.

He pushed, expecting me to pull away and abandon him. Forgetting that last time, he forced me to.

So, I call his bluff. I reach for the waistband of his shorts, groaning when my fingers brush the hot, taut skin between his hips.

Ryder tenses even more when I touch him, but he doesn't pull away. His mouth presses harder against mine, exerting enough pressure that I feel it everywhere.

I run a finger along the elasticized band of his boxer briefs, smiling when I feel him react.

Ryder can lie to me. His body can't.

He wants me.

My hand explores lower, finding the hard length of his cock. Ryder grunts as my fingers tighten, tugging his erection free from his clothes.

My lips move to his neck. I graze the soft skin there with my teeth. "Fuck me."

His breathing is heavy, his heartbeat racing against my palm. My other hand is still wrapped around his cock, barely moving. Just fisting enough to tease.

If he turns me down right now, I'm not sure we'll ever recover. I need him to fight. Need him to care in other ways than old letters and new apologies.

"Right now?" His hand skates up my thigh, slipping under the skirt of my dress. "What if someone comes out here? Do you want them to see perfect Elle Clarke getting fucked against the side of this bar like a slut?"

I whimper. His words are crude and rude and raw. And they only strengthen the storm building inside of me. That's what Ryder does. He amplifies everything. Pain ... anger ... *lust*. The power of it is devastating.

I have to grip his shoulders for support when his hand reaches my underwear.

My knees are useless, buckling beneath my weight, as he strokes two fingers back and forth before tugging the flimsy lace to one side. My fingernails dig deep into the cotton of his shirt, scoring half-moons in the skin beneath. His touch inflames me, igniting that deep, forbidden place only Ryder has ever been able to reach.

I've blamed Archer and that awful night in Maddie's bedroom for most of my hang-ups about sex. But it's really Ryder's fault. He ruined me, showing me what this is supposed to be like and then taking it away. Leaving me to try to find it somewhere else, only to fail miserably over and over again.

"Fuck, you're soaked," he tells me. "Has it been a while, Elle?"

I don't respond to his taunting tone. I like that he's jealous, thinking about me with other men. And I have absolutely no idea how he'd react to the truth—I've only ever been with him.

I reach for his cock. He's so hard that the skin looks shiny, the heat radiating from his substantial length searing into my palm.

He makes a strangled noise when I guide the head of his dick to the place where I need him. I'm nothing but nerve endings, all of them focused on that point of contact.

Ryder's eyes are fixed on the same spot.

Then they dart up to meet mine.

Ryder regards me in that way only he ever has. Like he can see my soul. Like he understands me on a cellular level.

Then, he thrusts inside of me in one confident stroke.

I cry out, the sudden stretch hitting like a euphoric shot of adrenaline. I forgot how *good* this feels. How primal and overwhelming. Like finally scratching an itch you've been struggling to reach.

Immediate relief.

Ryder's breathing is harsh as he slides out and then shoves right back in, creating that delicious friction my body is craving.

I slump against the wall, an unintelligible flurry of noises tumbling out of my mouth carelessly. I don't care about anything, except that Ryder keeps filling me. Keeps stoking the heat that's steadily building.

His fingers dig into the soft flesh of my thigh as he lifts one leg higher, hitting a spot deep inside of me that makes black dots dance in the corners of my vision.

"*Ryder.*" That's all I can manage to say that's an actual word. Just his name, on repeat.

I never ever want this feeling to end. Yet I'm so, so desperate for the release that's approaching.

"God, you look good taking my cock." His voice is low and

husky and intimate as his hips pump into me. His pace is quickening, sending tingles skittering across the surface of my skin.

All I can manage in response is a moan.

It's too much. Too overwhelming. Too consuming. He's like the devastating strength of a riptide, pulling me under. I couldn't stop it even if I wanted to.

A hot rush of pure pleasure floods my body, the same weightless sensation of flying off a cliff tumbling through me as my muscles tremble and quiver and pulse.

Everything around me blurs. I couldn't tell you the name of this bar. The day of the week. Where I went to college.

But Ryder's face is crystal clear. The focal point turning my world. He never takes his eyes off of me, those gray irises missing nothing. Watching like he's memorizing this moment too.

Once I've stopped shuddering, he withdraws. Takes a step back. Immediately, I miss the heat of his body.

My arms drop to my sides, my nails digging into the wood behind me as I watch him tuck his dick back into his shorts and zip them up.

My dress is half bunched around my thighs, but covering the essentials. And my underwear is still on. All he did was pull it to the side.

We both look disheveled. But no more so than you would following a windy walk on the beach.

The salty breeze blows a few strands of my hair into my face, and it's like the past few minutes never happened.

And I'm confused. I'm *always* confused, it feels like. Ryder hasn't mentioned the letter he wrote me, and I haven't brought it up either. We're stuck in this perpetual cycle of uncertainty.

I freeze suddenly, the foreign sensation of warm stickiness soaking my underwear breaking through the blissful haze of my stunned brain.

Fuck.

"We should head back in," I blurt, then turn and rush toward the porch before Ryder can say anything.

Or ask if I'm on birth control.

"I have to run to the store," I tell Keira. "Do you mind if I borrow the car?"

"The store?"

She gives me a weird look. The same one I got at Beachcombers, starting when I found her and Tucker in the crowd again. We're back at the cottage now, making dinner. Keira's in the middle of chopping cucumbers for the salad.

"Yeah. I forgot to bring toothpaste."

"We have toothpaste here, you know."

"I know. But there's a specific brand I like. Some kinds ... bother my gums."

Keira raises a single eyebrow. Maybe if we were alone, I'd be honest.

But Ryder is only a screen door away, grilling with Tucker outside, so honesty isn't an option right now. If I hurry, I can be back before dinner is ready. They just started the meat a few minutes ago, and I found a pharmacy online that's only a couple of miles away.

"O ... kay." Keira still looks confused. "I mean, yeah, of course you can borrow the car. Do you want me to ... come with you?"

"No. Thanks. I'll be right back."

There's a soft hiss as the screen door slides open.

"Right back?"

"Elle is running to the store." Keira answers Ryder so I can continue avoiding his gaze.

"I'll go with you," Ryder offers.

"You guys are grilling," I reply without looking at him, fiddling with the car keys Keira handed to me. "I just need one thing. I'll be right back."

"I don't mind."

I swallow the swear that wants to come out. "Fine."

There's no teasing about driving this time.

Ryder climbs into the passenger seat silently as I start the car. The radio is still on from our drive home. Tucker turned it on, noticing the tension between me and Ryder, same as Keira.

I'm tempted to swear again when Ryder climbs out of the car once I park at the pharmacy. I was really hoping he'd decide to stay in the car.

I browse the toothpaste aisle first to keep my cover.

After randomly picking a brand, I keep walking. I've never bought an emergency contraceptive before. My best guess is, it's by the tampons and pads, but there's no sign of what I'm looking for there.

Ryder's expression is carefully neutral as he follows me back down the aisle. I'm going to have to ask someone.

The only store employee I can find is the teenager working behind the counter. He's ringing up a woman with diamonds the size of quarters hanging from her ears. She must be close to my mom's age, but she checks Ryder out pretty obviously.

"Did you find everything you were looking for?" the guy asks as I set the toothpaste on the counter. His name is Cyrus, according to the white name tag on his chest.

"Uh, no, actually. I also need a morning-after pill. I didn't see it in the aisle."

Twin splotches of red color Cyrus's cheeks. "We keep that back in the pharmacy. I'll have someone bring one up here."

"Great. Thank you." My eyes stay straight ahead, studiously avoiding the gray gaze I can feel on me.

Cyrus picks up a walkie-talkie. "Hey, Frank?"

A garbled, "Yeah?" comes through thirty-two seconds later. I count them, just for something to do.

"Could you bring a box of Plan B up to register two?"

More static. "Bring what?"

"*Plan. B.* The morning-after pill."

It's shocking I'm not a puddle of embarrassment on the carpet right now.

"Oh. Yeah. Give me a few minutes."

Those few minutes feel like several hours. Finally, another teenage guy appears with a purple box.

Cyrus scans it, then announces, "That'll be seventy-six forty-two."

Way more than I was expecting. But I nod, opening my wallet and pulling out my credit card. When I glance up, Cyrus is already holding cash. We all wait in excruciating silence for him to count the change, which he hands to Ryder.

My stomach squeezes when I register his stony expression.

"Have a great night," Cyrus says.

Doubtful.

"You too," I reply. I aim a forced smile at the teenager, then head for the automatic doors.

Ryder's footsteps follow me in an ominous rhythm.

As soon as we're outside, I expect him to say something. But he's silent as I set the plastic bag in the back seat and then climb into the driver's side. When I turn on the car and snap my seat belt into place.

It's not until the car's headlights are sweeping the dark, sand-lined road that he speaks.

"You didn't want to take any chances?"

"I'm not on birth control."

Another long beat of silence follows. I tighten my grip on the steering wheel, forcing my eyes to remain on the street ahead.

"Why didn't you tell me?" he finally asks.

"I thought you'd freak out."

"No. Before."

Because I wanted it. Because I needed it. Because rational thoughts disappear when he's touching me. It didn't even occur to me we'd had unprotected sex until I felt his cum dripping out of me.

I can't say any of that.

"Got caught up in the moment, I guess."

Ryder's hands form fists in his lap, and I don't think I'm the only one who recognizes those words from our breakup.

I couldn't tell he was lying then. And I can't tell if he believes me now.

"I'm sorry, Elle. I should have … asked."

I close my eyes for as long as I dare to while driving. I hate his apologies. They're just empty words, following broken promises.

He might as well have just said he regrets having sex with me.

"There's no chance I gave you anything," he tells me. "Just so you know."

I nod.

Neither of us says anything else for the rest of the drive. Or for most of dinner.

34
NOW

Ryder

I overslept. I realize it as soon as my eyes open. It's too loud downstairs.

Shit, is my second thought.

This was not the morning to sleep in. This was the morning to get up early, exercise Elle's dog for her, and be waiting with a cup of coffee when she got up.

I scramble out of bed, using the bathroom and then getting dressed as fast as humanly possible. I'm already on my way toward the stairs when I remember to swerve back around and head to my room where I slept last night. There's a bed shortage tonight with all the extra guests Keira and Tucker invited. Reese and Knox are taking my room tonight.

I move my stuff to the small office down the hall, then finally make it downstairs.

"Morning, man," Tuck greets. He's standing at the stove, flipping bacon.

"Hey, sleepyhead," Mario, one of the guys from Tuck's crew, calls from his spot at the kitchen table.

Bowen, one of the painters, is seated across from him. Tucker invited every guy who works for him, but they were the only two—aside from me—who accepted.

"You sleep this late every morning you have off?" Mario grins before refocusing on his breakfast.

I roll my eyes as I help myself to some of the coffee that's been brewed.

There's just four of us in the kitchen, but there's a huge crowd gathered out on the deck. I recognize about half of them—Keira, Ophelia, Avery, and Juliet. Elle.

"Full house," I comment to Tuck between long sips of coffee. I still feel tired despite sleeping in. Groggy, like I just woke up from hibernation.

"Yep," he replies. "Dinner should be a lot noisier tonight."

I know exactly what he's referring to. "Long day. I was tired."

Elle and I did *not* make the greatest of dinner companions last night. As soon as we got back from the pharmacy, she headed upstairs for a few minutes. Tucker and Keira carried the dinner conversation, mostly talking to each other with limited input from us.

"Don't bullshit me, Ry. If you don't want to talk about it, just say so."

I lean back against the marble counter. I *do* want to talk to him. Advice is something I desperately need.

No matter what I do, I mess up.

Removing myself from Elle's life felt like the only option after I was arrested. If we saw each other after I was released—which felt like a big *if* at the time—I assumed she'd be happy. Figured I'd be so far in her past that she'd barely remember me. Hardly recognize me.

She wasn't supposed to remember or care. She wasn't supposed to visit my mom or bond with my brother.

She wasn't supposed to spray me with a hose. To call me in the middle of the night like she just wanted to hear my voice. To blush when I look at her or smile the same way she used to. To kiss me back last night like she needed my lips more than oxygen. To moan my name like she wanted my dick, not just sex.

It's all messing with my head. Making me wonder if there's a chance I *do* have something to offer her.

I can't seem to get it right though, always saying or doing the wrong thing. Good intentions have gotten me nowhere.

Before I can figure out how to share any of that with Tucker, the doorbell rings, echoing through the house.

"Mind answering that?" Tuck asks me, ripping open another package of bacon.

I shake my head, shoving away from the counter and heading for the entryway.

Reese is standing on the front porch, a suitcase on one side and Knox on her other, her eyes huge as she looks around. "I thought we had the wrong address."

I grin. "Crazy, right? Tuck invited me to a cottage the first time he mentioned this place. I thought we'd end up at some shack five miles from the water."

Reese shakes her head. "Ones."

"Here, let me take that." I reach for her suitcase's handle. "Tuck said he was picking you guys up later."

"Knox woke up early, so we decided to take an earlier ferry," Reese explains, stepping inside. Her eyes widen even more, taking in the central staircase and the expensive furnishings.

"Hey, Knox." I hold out a fist, and he knocks knuckles with me. "Good to see you, buddy."

"Did you bring the football?" he asks eagerly.

"I sure did," I reply. "It's upstairs."

I've spent a handful of evenings at Reese's, mowing her lawn or installing an air conditioner. Tuck and I built Knox a bigger bed. Knox is a quiet kid, but he's warmed up to me slowly. Our shared interest in football has helped. Reese was right; he's better at football than basketball. When he gets to high school, Fernwood might finally have a shot at a state title.

"I'll put this upstairs," I say. "And grab the football. You'll see the kitchen as soon as you walk around the fireplace. Tuck's cooking bacon."

Reese sniffs the air. "Yeah, I can smell it."

"Most people are on the deck."

"Most people? How many did Tuck invite?"

"Probably about fifty more than showed up. You know Tuck."

She nods. "I do."

He's the social butterfly of our trio. Reese and I are more lone wolves.

Last I heard, the guest list for his wedding was about five hundred people.

I walk upstairs, turning into the room where I slept last night. Keira's leaning over the bed, changing the sheets.

"Can I help?" I ask.

She glances over her shoulder, watching as I set Reese's suitcase down next to the dresser. "I got it, thanks."

"Okay." I smile, then turn to go.

"Ryder?"

I pause. "Yeah?"

Keira fiddles with the pillowcase she's holding, looking nervous. "It's none of my business, obviously. But … is something going on between you and Reese? Are you guys … *extra* friendly? Because Tuck told me you aren't, so that's what I told Elle, but after last night, I just …" She chews on her bottom lip. "I feel bad that I've put her in … awkward situations recently. I want to avoid any more."

My mind is racing. Elle never really let me explain that night when she called while I was over at Reese's, installing her air conditioner. I couldn't tell if she hung up because she was mad about the comment I made about her boyfriend or if she was jealous.

"There's nothing going on between me and Reese," I tell Keira. "We're just friends."

Maybe if I'd never met Elle Clarke, that would be different. Reese and I are similar in so many ways. She understands a lot about me, things I've never had to explain. She has rough edges, just like me. I wouldn't worry about ruining her life.

"Are you and Elle just friends?"

"We were never just friends," I reply, leaning against the wall. "We were always more."

I wanted all of Elle, not just part of her. And I never thought she'd look twice at me. Part of me is still stunned that she did. Is still that fumbling fourteen-year-old, folding a paper flower and trying to come up with something clever to say to the most popular girl in school.

"She tell you what happened last night?" I ask.

Keira shakes her head. "No."

I swallow, glancing down at the blue-and-white-striped rug on the floor. "I messed up—again. I just … I can't figure out what she wants."

When I look up, Keira appears incredulous. "Don't take this the wrong way, but are you *dumb*? She wants *you*, Ryder. She's always wanted you."

"I didn't think she'd wait," I say. "If I saw her again, I thought she'd have a massive diamond on her finger. Maybe have a kid on the way."

"Well, she's not engaged or married, and she's definitely not pregnant."

She could be. We had unprotected sex last night, and I have no idea how effective the medicine she took is.

"She deserves better," I say. "I can't give her … anything."

"Do you really think Elle doesn't know you're broke? Again, no offense. I've known her for a long time. Longer than you. She's been rich her whole life. I was there when she got her convertible and when her parents gave her diamond earrings at her college graduation. And I've never seen her light up the way she did when you two were arguing about who was going to drive last night. Or when you were washing her dog. I've met every guy she's ever dated. Yeah, most of them were wealthy. She didn't look at any of them the way she looks at you. So, if you're holding back because you think she doesn't love you or is better off without you, you're wrong. So, fucking *do* something, Ryder, before it's too late."

I stare at Keira, processing.

"Again, none of my business."

"She's mad at me," I say. "It might already be too late."

"She hooked up with you outside a bar last night, Ryder. Unless the sex was bad—which it wasn't, based on your face—it's not too late."

"I thought she didn't tell you what happened?"

Keira smirks. "Lucky guess. Her hair was down when you two disappeared and up when she came back."

I shake my head. "Okay. Uh, thanks."

"If you could not mention this chat to Tuck, that would be great. I kinda promised him I'd stay out of it."

"What chat?"

She smiles. "Thanks."

I nod, then continue toward the office where I'm staying now to retrieve the football I brought.

When I get back downstairs, the kitchen is crowded, and the deck is empty. Everyone's grabbing plates or serving food. My eyes find Elle, standing by the fridge, talking to Juliet.

No matter how long I stare, she doesn't look this way. Her focus seems purposeful, and I start to second-guess some of what Keira just said.

She couldn't get away from me fast enough after we had sex. Shut down during the drive to and from the pharmacy, then barely looked at me during dinner.

And she hasn't mentioned my letter, which is starting to give me a complex. I know she got it. Did she not read it? Burn it? Hate it?

I eat breakfast standing up by the sink since there's a shortage of chairs. Ophelia comes over to say hi, but Reese and Knox are the only other people who talk to me. Tuck is busy cooking, and Elle continues to pretend I don't exist.

As soon as I finish eating, Knox asks if we can play football on the beach. I can't say no to his excited expression, and Reese approves the outing.

Knox and I head toward the deck doors, the football I brought tucked under one of Knox's skinny biceps. Scout's been prowling the kitchen floor for scraps, but he follows me over to the door and whines when I reach for the handle.

Elle's sitting on one of the island stools, five feet away, laughing at something Avery said.

"Elle."

Her eyes flash to my face the second I say her name, not as oblivious as she was acting. Elle says nothing, just raises one eyebrow expectantly.

"Can Scout go outside?" I ask.

She glances at Knox, holding a football, then the dog at my feet. Nods.

Then looks away again.

X 💔 X

We head to the nearby lighthouse, mid-afternoon. It's a beautiful day, sunny and hot, and it's a scenic walk along the dunes, dotted with waving beach grass. Barely any traffic passes by, and the salty air smells like freshly cut grass and sunscreen and barbecue smoke.

It feels like summer.

I walk with Mario and Bowen. We talk at the jobsite, but usually about lunch orders or potential drywall problems. During the twenty-minute trip, I learn Mario is saving up to move to California and start his own vegetable farm. Bowen has a girlfriend in New York he's planning to propose to soon.

The lighthouse turns out to be a popular tourist attraction. Swarms of people fill the grass surrounding the tall, straight structure. I've seen the lighthouse before, from the ferry and from driving around the island. It's much, much bigger up close, towering over us.

Which is the whole point, I suppose. You're supposed to be able to see it.

The top half is painted red, the bottom half white. Against the blue backdrop of the clear sky, it appears as purposefully decorated for today as Keira's house.

Signs are scattered along the path that winds to a door at the lighthouse's base. I pause to read a couple of them, skimming paragraphs about the construction and the upkeep and the lost souls saved at sea by the sight of the structure's lights.

The door opens into a small gift shop. Juliet is standing right inside the opening, spinning the carousel of postcards. She glances up at me and offers a small smile, which I return. Of Elle's two best friends, I've gotten to know Keira better. Mostly because of her relationship with Tuck.

There's a display of flashing keychains by the register. And one simple metal one that's shaped like a lighthouse. I buy it impulsively.

Elle's birthday is tomorrow, and I've had no idea what to get her. A keychain isn't a car or diamond earrings, but it's better than nothing. Representative of this place we've only been to together as adults.

A winding staircase leads upstairs to the lookout. As I go up, the circles seem endless, and my lungs and calves are burning by the time I reach the top. I'm in decent shape from lifting lumber and all the other construction work I've been doing lately, but it's been a long time since I did any cardio.

It's less crowded up here, most people choosing the view from the grass over the one from up here. They're missing out. It's stunning, looking out at the water. An endless spread of shimmering blue, spots of white foam appearing and then disappearing.

But the view has nothing on Elle. Her dark hair is being blown in a wild halo around her face, but she seems oblivious as she looks out at the ocean.

My lungs feel tight again, and it has nothing to do with the exertion of climbing what felt like a few hundred stairs.

I've been dying to talk to her all day. I'm also dreading it. Because once this conversation takes place, I won't be able to go back and redo it.

"Hi," is the super-original greeting I come up with.

Elle doesn't glance over as I take the spot beside her. She keeps staring straight at the sea. "Hi."

"Nice view."

She hums an agreement, I think. It's hard to hear over the other noise around us. Not only the surf and the wind, but also the guy on my other side, who's holding a screaming toddler.

"Are you okay?" I ask.

"I'm fine," Elle replies.

Nothing in her voice says she wants to keep talking to me. But I forge ahead anyway. "Are *we* okay?"

"Yeah." She glances at me carelessly, like it's an obligation she only needs a few seconds to fulfill. Her eyes are back on the waves before I can even react, refocused on the horizon.

My fingers tighten on the railing. "Do you … regret it?"

Elle doesn't answer right away. But I can feel her deliberating, the air around us gaining a new charge of awareness. She wasn't sure if I'd bring last night up, I think.

"No," she finally says. "Maybe it needed to happen. Clear the air some."

I snort. I can't help it. "You think last night *cleared the air*?"

She stays stubbornly silent, watching the ocean like something about the sight is going to change sometime soon.

"Did you read the letter?" I ask. I can't hold the question in any longer.

"Yes."

That's *all* she says. *Yes.*

"And?" I prompt.

"It was nice. Thanks."

I want to shout. To shake her. Possibly cry because Keira got my hopes up and it feels like they're dying a slow death.

"Do you think I could make it to the water from here?" I ask.

She's still—so still—beside me. We're two statues, staring at the sea.

"I don't know what you think bringing that up is—"

"I'm *trying*, Elle. I'm trying, and I can't tell if you want me to. I can't tell what you want. I need you to tell me, the way I told you in that letter."

"The one you wrote six years ago?"

"I could have written it yesterday. I wouldn't have changed a word. Yeah, I hurt you on purpose. I wish I'd had other options, but I didn't. I did what I thought was best for you, and you don't get to tell me that's wrong. *I* was the one in prison, not you. I did what I had to, to get through it, and I can't change the past. You're mad I never gave you a choice? You have one now. You said you'd never forgive me, and I never expected you to. But I *am* in love with you."

Elle's inhale is loud enough that I catch it over the commotion around us.

"If you want me, I'm yours. But if you can't get past everything that happened, if the *air has been cleared*—whatever the hell that means—I'll get it. I just need you to tell me what you *want* from me, so we can both move forward."

At least I broke through the indifference. Shock is all I can read on Elle's face as she stares at me.

"Elle! Oh good, I was worried I wouldn't be able to find you up here. Keira wants to take a photo with her bridesmaids, down by the water." Avery glances at me. Smiles. "Hey, Ryder."

"Hey," I reply.

Ophelia wanders over to us. "Isn't the view up here insane?"

Knox and Reese join us a few seconds later. Knox is proudly showing off a rock he got in the gift shop.

That's the end of our private conversation, obviously.

And I'm not sure if it's a good or bad thing that Elle will have more time to think about everything I just said to her.

Elle

I swallow the final bite of hot dog, then snuggle into the oversize sweatshirt I'm wearing. It's chilly now that the sun has disappeared and the breeze blowing off the water isn't tempered by its heat.

The bonfire Tucker and Bowen built to roast the hot dogs is functional, not just pretty to look at.

I remember the beauty of the blue flames from other visits. But it doesn't compare to seeing it in person again, the flicker of aqua mixed in with orange a mystical sight.

We just got back from the pier, where we watched the fireworks. They set them off as soon as it was dark out because there's a chance of rain later in the evening, so we waited to eat dinner until afterward.

"Can you roast me another one?"

"Yeah," I hear Ryder reply. "You're sure you don't want to try?"

"I'm sure," Knox says. "I lit the last one on fire."

Ryder's chuckle is low, and it wreaks havoc on my insides. I watch him out of the corner of my eye as he carefully roasts Reese's son a hot dog, seemingly oblivious to the hero worship being aimed his way. It's obvious Knox reveres Ryder. Aside from his mom, Ryder is the one adult I've heard him talk to.

He'll make a good dad.

It's not the first time I've thought that about Ryder. It's a little less scary as an adult instead of a seventeen-year-old, but not by much.

Unlike me, Ryder hasn't bundled up. The flex of his forearm is visible in the warm glow of the fire as he rotates his arm.

I finish off the hard seltzer I've been sipping on and stand, planning to head up to the house to use the bathroom.

"Tuck, can you grab the s'mores stuff?" Keira asks.

"I can get it," I volunteer. "I'm headed up to use the bathroom anyway."

"Thanks, Elle."

I nod, then continue walking through the sand. I attempt to brush it off my feet before climbing the deck steps, but I don't do a great job.

Reese is standing at the island, pouring water into a glass, when I enter the kitchen.

"Hey," I say, sending a small smile her way.

I've always been aware she didn't like me. I'm no longer worried she and Ryder are in a relationship, but that doesn't mean Reese doesn't have feelings for him. Or maybe she just dislikes me because I'll always be a One to her.

"Hi," Reese replies. Her tone is polite. Cool.

I walk over to the cabinet, searching for the s'mores ingredients.

"Weird that we're both here, huh?"

"Not *that* weird," I say. "I'm glad you and Knox could come."

"I didn't want to. Tuck insisted, and Ryder promised he would be here."

I find the marshmallows and chocolate, then keep searching for the graham crackers. "Well, it seemed to work out. Tucker is a good friend to have."

"Keira is lucky to have him. He's not marrying up."

I grab the box of graham crackers then turn around to face her. "No one said that he is. But he's lucky to have Keira too."

I don't care if Reese's prejudice is a product of her upbringing. Of the hierarchy I'm too familiar with. If she wants to insult my best friend in front of me, we're going to have a problem.

Reese tilts her head to study me. "I was never jealous of you, you know. Everyone was. Everyone talked about you. All the girls were jealous of your flashy car and your big house and your expensive clothes and your perfect hair. And all the guys had a crush on you. But I thought your life looked a little … empty. *Too* perfect, you know?"

I cross my arms and raise an eyebrow. "Do I know what *my* life is like? Yeah, I do."

"I was never jealous of you … until that day at the pond. I'd seen Ryder stare at you, but I figured he was just checking you out. But the way he talked to you, I'd never seen him act like that with anyone before. And I was *so* jealous. I'm not now. I have Knox, and Ryder and I will always be friends. He's never once looked at me the way he's been looking at you all day. So … what are you doing?"

"I—what?"

"What are you doing? Why aren't you and Ryder together?"

"We're … it's complicated."

Reese shakes her head. "Is it?"

Is it?

"If you want me, I'm yours."

I told Ryder I'd never forgive him for breaking my heart again. But forgetting him has been the problem. Seven years, and I haven't figured out how to forget him.

"I'll bring those out." Reese reaches for the s'mores supplies sitting on the counter.

"Thanks," I say.

I'm not sure exactly what I'm thanking her for. Reese doesn't either, based on the flash of uncertainty in her expression.

But she nods and says, "You're welcome," before walking out onto the deck.

I use the downstairs bathroom, then head back outside.

Tucker has pulled a guitar out from somewhere. I had no idea he played guitar, and it turns out, he actually *can't*. He just strums random strings as a laughing Keira records him on her phone.

I don't walk back to my empty seat. I approach Ryder, who's still sitting next to Knox.

He glances over when I'm still a few feet away, watching me near him. My stomach flips, catching the apprehension on his face. The bob of his Adam's apple as he swallows.

My fingers twist nervously, and I'm glad the long hems of my sleeves cover my hands. "Hey."

"Hey," Ryder responds.

"I was, uh … you wanna take a walk? With me?"

He stands so fast that I take an automatic step back. "Yeah."

"Okay."

I walk ahead of him, mindful of the curious stares following us. Ryder catches up to me after a few feet, but says nothing. We pass a few strangers, but it's mostly an empty stretch of sand. Our group decided to skip the barbecue and concert downtown. I'm guessing that's where most people are tonight.

The bonfire is barely a pinprick of light down the beach by the time I stop. If I were out here alone, I'd be nervous.

"Want to sit?" I suggest.

"Sure."

"You're really agreeable tonight," I tell him. "It's weird."

One corner of his mouth lifts. "You want me to argue with you?"

"Sometimes."

"Noted." He takes a seat on the sand, close to the water, but not so near that there's a risk of getting wet.

"Room there?" I point to the spot between his legs.

A flash of surprise appears. "Uh-huh."

He widens the V, and I step into it before sinking down into the sand.

I lean back against his chest, and his arms wrap around me naturally.

I shiver, both from the cold and from the thrill of him touching me. His body heat soaks into me slowly, like a sponge meeting water.

"I'm sorry," I say.

Ryder stiffens slightly, betraying the surprise I hear in his tone a second later. "For what?"

"I handled today … terribly. I wasn't … I don't …" I exhale. "Last night was a lot."

I relax, so he's supporting all of my weight. Rest my hands on his thighs and slide them down until they're stretched straight, brushing his kneecaps.

"I know it was."

"Not just that we didn't use protection. That we had sex at all. It'd been a long time. For me."

Ryder is silent, and I start to regret this choice of position. It would be nice to be able to see some of his face right now. Staring at the sea isn't offering any insight into what he's thinking.

"It'd been a long time for me too," he finally says. "Surprised I lasted longer than thirty seconds."

I smile even though he can't see me. I want to be honest with him about this. I'm no longer scared of him knowing how much I care. "I'm talking about a *long time*, Ryder. Like back when we were together."

"I'm talking about that long too."

I twist so I can see some of his face. Basically just his jaw, but better than nothing. "What?"

"I've never been with anyone but you."

If possible, I'm even more shocked now. "What-what are you talking about?"

Ryder never said so, but I assumed he wasn't a virgin our first time. He seemed so confident and experienced. And I figured there were lots of girls in Florida. Assumed one of the first things he did after getting out of prison was get laid.

"I never wanted anyone else," he says. "Not the way I wanted you."

I trace a circle on his leg with my pointer finger. "I need to know if you're going to keep running, Ry. Because I can't go through it all again. Our whole pattern. It has to … it has to have a different ending this time. You can't disappear to avoid saying goodbye. You can't decide shutting me out is what is best for me. You can't break my heart again."

He exhales heavily enough that I rise and fall against his chest. "My plan was to leave, Lo. Before I found out about my mom's cancer, all I wanted was a fresh start."

"More than you want me?" I ask.

"No. There's nothing I want more than you. I just … I have no idea what to do with the rest of my life."

"Me neither," I reply.

Ryder scoffs. "You went to Harvard Law, Elle. I have no degree and a criminal record. It's not the same."

"I didn't say it was."

"You asked me to be honest. And I'm trying to be realistic about what my life will look like."

I tilt my head again, trying to see his face. It's too shadowed to see much more than the outline of his profile. "You seriously think I care about what you do for work?"

"*I* care. I want to be able to offer you something. Don't you get that?"

I turn fully, swinging my legs over his thighs so I'm straddling him. "I want *you*, Ryder. I can't be around you and not want you. You told me you didn't want me, and I still wanted you. I showed up at your trailer to have tea with your mom for seven years, just so I could be in a place where you existed. I wrote you letters you never responded to because one-sided communication was better than none at all. I still have that paper flower you made me in the drawer next to my bed. I've sabotaged every relationship I've ever been in because those guys never made me feel the way that you do. And parts of that are humiliating, but it's all *real*. It's real, and it's exhausting. I'm so *tired*, tired of choosing you and it never being the happy ending. Of picking myself back up and having to keep going alone."

"Lo …" His voice sounds choked as he swipes away my tears with his thumbs. "You've always been my only choice, okay? I've never picked anyone else."

He kisses me first, the collision of our mouths sloppy and urgent and frenzied. Real. Reality, not a fairy tale. A little imperfect, just like us.

"Fuck," Ryder groans as I grind on his lap. "*Elle*, you can't keep doing that."

"Or what?"

"I don't have anything," he says, leaning forward to kiss my collarbone.

My nipples pebble as shivers run down my spine. This time, they have nothing to do with the chilly wind coming off the waves.

"Dude, we were *just* at a pharmacy."

He chuckles, low and wry. "It didn't seem like the right time to suggest a repeat performance."

"Might have made dinner last night less awkward."

"Or you might have stabbed me with a steak knife."

I shiver again, this time from the cold. "That really would have freaked Tucker and Keira out."

"I think they find us entertaining."

"Does that mean you also got the *what's going on with you guys* talk?"

"Sort of," he replies. "You?"

"Yeah. From Reese actually."

"Really?"

"Uh-huh."

Ryder's stomach grumbles. He rubs his jaw, his smile sheepish. "Feel like a s'more? I'm still hungry."

"Only if I can eat it off your abs."

His laugh sounds kind of pained. "Lo, *seriously*. Stop talking about your tongue on any part of my body."

I giggle as he stands, pulling me upright with him.

And we start back toward the beach house, following the pair of footprints in the sand that led us here.

Running when the raindrops begin to fall, our hands swinging between us like the lovesick kids we used to be.

36
NOW

Ryder

Elle rolls over, her nose scrunching adorably and her hair a wild tangle, spread across the pillow like seaweed. She yawns, then smiles. "How long have you been up for?"

An hour and twelve minutes.

I didn't wake up in the middle of the night for the first time since I've been outside the four walls of Leavenworth Penitentiary, and it's amazing how much a solid stretch of sleep helps you feel wide awake. I'm used to waking up with dry, gritty eyes and often a pounding head, forcing myself to roll out of bed and chug enough coffee to get me to work.

When I woke up seventy-two minutes ago, I just stared at Elle. That's all I've been doing for the past hour-plus.

"Ry?"

"Not long," I reply.

She rolls over so she's facing me, tucking her hands beneath her cheek. Stares at me like she likes the sight—me in her bed.

"I like waking up to you," I say.

Elle blushes, and it's a beautiful sight. We've known each other since we were fourteen. I love that I can still make her blush.

I reach out and carefully place the lighthouse keychain that's been folded in my palm since I woke up. It wobbles on the mattress, but rights itself.

She glances at it.

"Happy birthday. It reminded me of you."

"Tall and striped?"

I laugh. "No. Brave. Standing alone, facing storms. You don't need me for that. You never did."

Her face softens as she rubs a finger against the top tip of the lighthouse. The cupola, as I learned yesterday. "I love it. Thank you."

"Also got you this." I grab the condom off the bedside table and toss it to her.

Elle picks it up. She's blushing again. Or still. "Gee, thanks."

I grin. "Found a box of them in one of the bathroom drawers."

She makes a face. "Keira told me this is the room her parents stay in."

"That doesn't mean it's defective."

Elle sits up, swinging her legs off the mattress. We fooled around last night, but she put pajamas on before falling asleep. I watch her walk across the bedroom in the matching set, one arm tucked behind my head.

"Where are you going?" I ask.

Not the response I was hoping for to the *let's have sex* suggestion.

"To brush my teeth."

I groan a laugh. "Elle, I don't care."

"I do. Also … I need to shave."

"Don't care about that either," I call out.

"Well, *I do.* Can you take Scout out while I get ready?"

"Yep." I climb out of bed.

I've been hard since I woke up, and waking up in bed with Elle didn't help. I pull on a pair of basketball shorts that do a decent job of hiding my erection, glad I remembered to grab my bag out of the office before sneaking into Elle's room last night.

Scout jumps all over me the second I let him out of his crate. I slip his collar on, but don't bother attaching his leash. I take it though, just in case, peeking out into the hallway before we exit Elle's room. It's empty.

A few remnants of last night's festivities—leftover hot dog buns and a few extra chocolate bars and some empty beer bottles—litter the counter as I pass through the kitchen.

As soon as I open the sliding door, Scout sprints down the steps to sniff around in the beach grass.

Two of the deck chairs are occupied.

"Hey, guys."

"Morning, Ryder," Keira replies.

"Hey, man," Tuck greets. "Couch treat you okay last night? I feel bad you got stuck in the office." He looks at Keira. "We have too many friends."

She scoffs, then sips her coffee.

"Don't worry about it. Couch was more comfortable than the twin in the trailer," I say.

Tuck winces. "I can't believe you're still sleeping on that."

"You get used to it," I say.

I won't move out of the trailer and leave my mom. But I'm hopeful, after last night and this morning, that I might be spending more nights in Boston soon. I'm positive Elle doesn't sleep in a twin.

"Are you taking Scout for another run?" Keira asks.

I glance at the dog, who's still sniffing. I wish he were a human I could tell to hurry up. I'm dying to get back upstairs to fuck Elle in an actual bed for the first time in forever.

"Uh, no," I respond. "Just a bathroom break."

"Huh," Keira says. "That's funny—that you're the one taking out Elle's dog."

"Yeah," Tuck chimes in with. "Almost as funny as the way you never answered when I knocked on the office door earlier to see if you wanted to go surfing."

I look at Scout, who's continuing to take his time.

"You're blushing, Ry," Tuck teases. "Tops of your ears are red."

"For fuck's sake, mind your own business, man."

"Good morning." Reese steps out onto the deck. "Wow, this view is insane." She looks at me next. "Did you sleep okay on the couch?"

"The question is, was he *on* the couch?" Tuck says.

"Fifty bucks he wasn't," Reese comments. "They looked cozy at the fire last night."

"Yeah, but you didn't see them at dinner the night before. Elle wouldn't even look at him and—"

"That's it," I say, setting Scout's leash on the railing and walking toward the sliding door. "Can one of you please keep an eye on the dog?"

"Can't get enough of that couch, huh?" Tuck calls after me.

Reese's and Keira's laughter follows me inside.

Elle's waiting, naked, when I slip back into her room. She rises up on her elbows when I shut the door, and I groan audibly at the view of her sprawled on the white sheets before ducking into the bathroom.

"What are you doing?" she calls out.

I grab her toothbrush off the sink, squeeze some toothpaste on it, and then step back into the bedroom.

"You're using my toothbrush?"

"I forgot mine in the other bathroom. I'm not going to have morning breath while you taste like a Crest commercial. Besides …" I smirk. "We're about to have sex, and you're concerned about mouth germs?"

Elle doesn't reply, just lies back down.

I scrub at my teeth as quickly as possible, spit, and glance in the mirror. God, I'm … nervous. Terrified this is going to get screwed up somehow. Whenever things go well in my life, it's always been temporary. My dad left, or my mom moved us to live with a shitty boyfriend, or I got arrested. I'm scared to be happy, as sad and pathetic as that sounds. I wasn't just protecting Elle, removing myself from her life. You can't lose what you don't have.

"Ryder?"

"Coming," I reply, shoving away from the counter and walking back into the bedroom.

I pull off my T-shirt, step out of my shorts, and then slip into the warm heaven of smooth sheets and soft skin that smells like jasmine.

Elle rolls into me immediately, tangling our legs together. "Where's Scout?"

"Keira and Tuck offered to watch him."

"Meaning they saw you with him?"

"Yeah. You care that they know?"

Old insecurities flicker to the surface. Not just about the fact that I'm poor and she's rich, or that she's a lawyer and I'm an ex-con. Elle's a good person, and I've done more than my share of destructive shit that speaks to the contrary. In nearly every way, we're uneven.

"Of course not," she answers before I can spiral too far. "I'm just going to have a lot of questions to answer later."

"*You* are? Tuck is the nosiest person I know."

She giggles, her right hand landing on my chest and journeying south in a way that's *very* distracting. "You have more muscles."

"Had a lot of time to work out."

Her hand pauses, playing with the strip of hair that points straight at my dick. "I've never heard you ... talk about it."

"There's not much to say," I reply. "And then, other times, way too much."

"I want to listen," Elle whispers.

My immediate instinct is to push back. To tell her there's no way I'm filling her head with the dark shit I saw and experienced. But then I look at her, focused on me with the most earnest, tentative expression I've ever seen.

I shut her out before. Long before I slammed the door closed on us, I was always so careful with how much I shared of my life. I gave her *me*, but I kept the rest of my world as separate as I could.

Elle's tough. Stronger than most people give her credit for. I don't know many people who would have stolen an ID to sneak into a state prison.

So, I say, "Okay," and mean it.

Her smile is so wide that I feel like my heart is going to explode.

"Right now, I'd rather fuck you than talk to you though."

"Right now, I'd rather get fucked than listen to you talk," she replies.

I grin. "Glad we're on the same page."

Fucking finally.

Our mouths collide in a desperate, messy kiss.

I planned to draw this out. To kiss my way down her chest and play with her breasts. To lick her pussy and suck her clit. To savor every second of this in a way I couldn't against the side of a busy bar.

But I'm also impatient. It feels like I've waited my entire life for this moment, and I want to be as close to her as possible. And every time I move my mouth to her jaw or her neck, Elle adjusts so my lips land on hers again.

She's as needy as I am.

And she's the one who fists my dick, rubbing the tip of my cock through her wet heat.

She's never been with anyone else. I was shocked when she told me last night, and I'm still stunned by it now. Elle's playing my body like a maestro. Squeezing the sensitive head of my dick and then rubbing the sensitive spot behind my balls. My control is slipping, which seems to be exactly what she wants. My muscles are tensed and burning, resisting the urge to thrust deep.

I pull away long enough to ask, "Where's the condom?"

"I don't know," Elle replies cheekily. "You had it."

I search around the sheets until I find the foil packet. Elle's as unhelpful as possible, running her hands over every inch of my skin she can reach.

I roll the condom on as fast as I can, then settle over her again. The position is deliberate. I want to be able to see her face.

She moans when my penis brushes against her swollen pussy. I tease her a little, rubbing up, down, and around.

Elle lifts her hips, trying to take me. "*Please.*"

"What do you want, Elle?" I ask.

"You," she breathes. "I want you."

I give her an inch.

She arches her back, a rosy flush spreading across her chest. I grab her knee and hook it around my hip, pressing another inch deeper.

She's tight. Wet. *So* tight and *so* wet, and somehow, this is better than every other time we've had sex.

There's a feeling of permanence I've never felt before. I'm not terrified I'll never get to touch her again. It feels like we'll do this every day for the rest of our lives.

"*Fuck*, Ryder. More. I need more."

Elle's nails dig into my back, cutting deep enough to leave marks and break skin. I've always been hers, so it feels like a fitting brand.

I give her two inches this time. Maybe three. The snug clasp of her cunt is shredding what little remains of my willpower and blurring my focus. It's taking all of my resolve to keep from pounding into her like an animal.

But Elle comes first. Always.

She wraps both legs around my waist. It shifts the angle, the head of my cock hitting a deeper spot, and she moans loudly.

I glance down, the sight of her spread around my cock making my dick swell even more. I knew I was her first. But knowing she's never done this with anyone but me … that I'm the only one who's ever seen her like this, who's been inside of her … fuck, it messes with my head in the best way. Strips me down to all these possessive, primal urges.

I'd kill for this girl. Would lie or cheat or steal or beg or borrow for anything she needed.

I think I knew she was it for me the first time I saw her playing tic-tac-toe by herself. But I realize it all over again right now.

She takes the rest of me with a loud whimper of want, her hands sliding down my back to grip my ass as I pump into her. The breathy sounds she's making are slowly driving me insane. Flames lick down my spine as pressure builds at the base of it.

"*Harder*, Ry," she begs. "I'm so close."

Thank God.

I wasn't kidding about the thirty seconds last night. Feeling her beneath me, hearing her moan my name, smelling the arousal in the air? I'm *barely* hanging on right now.

I speed up my thrusts, slipping a hand between our bodies and finding the sensitive bundle of nerves right above where I'm stretching her.

Her cunt contracts, squeezing my cock so tightly that I can barely breathe from the acute pleasure. I grunt as my dick jerks, filling the condom. A hot wave of pleasure surges through me, the force of it staggering.

The relief is more than physical. There's a lot of happiness mixing with the sexual satisfaction.

We're both breathing heavily as I pull out of her, grabbing a tissue off the bedside table and using it to wrap it around the condom. I toss it toward the trash can, relieved when it lands right.

"Nice shot."

I grin over at her. Elle's cheeks are pink, her expression a little dazed. She looks sated and sexy and so gorgeous it makes my chest hurt. "Thanks. I've been playing some with Knox."

"I'm sure he loves that."

"Yeah. His dad isn't around, so …" I reach a hand out, the few inches between our bodies too much.

She bites her bottom lip when I cup her left breast, my thumb rubbing the mark I left there last night. "There are more condoms, right?"

I chuckle. "Yeah. But this was supposed to be about you. I had this whole plan …" I lean over, swirling my tongue around her belly button and then kissing a line up the center of her stomach.

Elle's hands weave into my hair, and she yanks my head up to hers. She kisses me again, just as eagerly as before, sucking on my tongue.

I'm getting hard again.

I can't get enough of her. I don't think I ever will.

"You taste like mint," she comments.

I grin. "Back at you."

"Do you want kids?" Elle blurts. Then drops a hand from my hair and moves it to cover most of her face. "Forget I asked that. Just … thinking out loud."

I tug her hand down. "You can ask me anything, Lo."

"I didn't mean to ask that. I mean, we're not even …"

"We're not even what?"

"I-I don't know what we are."

"We're everything," I tell her.

Elle smiles, and I think she's recalling the same conversation I am. When she told me we were nothing and I countered with we were something.

"Most people would probably call it dating," I say.

"Most people would say you have to go out on a date to be dating."

I smirk. "You asking me out, Clarke?"

She rolls her eyes. "I just … you didn't freak out at the pharmacy the way I thought you might."

"I wouldn't freak out," I tell her, running my fingers through her hair. Planned or not, I'd be thrilled. But we're talking about the hypothetical, I think. "I've never really thought about kids. But I could definitely get on board with the idea."

"I was watching you with Knox last night. You're a natural."

"Well, I sure didn't learn it." I continue playing with her hair. "I wouldn't hate that part of it either."

"What part?"

"Getting to be the dad I wish I had."

Elle's silent for a moment. "Have you talked to him lately?"

"He's called a couple of times. I answered once."

"Sorry."

"S'okay."

And it is. I have my mom and Cormac. Tucker. Reese. And Elle. They're all the family I need. The people who have been there for me.

Her hand slides down my chest, tracing the ridges of my abdomen and then moving lower.

I groan, all the blood in my body following the path of her hand.

"Guess I didn't kill the mood, talking about babies and your dad?" Elle's voice is light, on the cusp of laughter.

I sit up, forcing her hand to fall away. "Nope. But you're getting another birthday gift first."

She gasps. "Keys to go with my keychain?"

The keychain in question is set carefully on the bedside table, closer to Elle's side, out of harm's way.

I smirk as I grip her knees, pulling them apart until her legs are flat on the bed and her pussy is fully exposed. "You're about to feel really bad about mocking my gifts," I tell her.

Then lower my head.

37
NOW

Ryder

"We're eating in Fernwood?" Elle's voice is all surprise as she glances over at me.

"Is that okay?"

"Of course. I just ... didn't think you'd want to."

People will stare, she means. The whole town will talk. Gossip about me. About us.

And ... I don't care.

The important people in our lives—our family and friends—all know about and accept our relationship. *Accept* might be a stretch in the case of Elle's parents. She told me they're happy for her, for *us*, but I wouldn't put it past her to be lying to protect my feelings. I've still never met her mom, and my one meeting with her dad didn't go great. Me getting arrested for drug possession the next day probably didn't improve his opinion of me.

"I've never eaten at The Franklin," I tell her. "I wanted to try it."

"You know if you hate the food, you have to pretend to like it, right?" Elle tells me.

"Why would I hate it?" I ask.

"It's … fancy. Caviar and oysters and truffles."

"Lobster?"

I tried lobster for the first time at the clam shack Tuck took me to. It was good, a lot better than I had expected. The clam fritters were decent, too, but it doesn't sound like this place serves much fried food.

"They might," Elle replies.

"Great. I like lobster."

I spot a parking space right in front of the restaurant and take it. Climb out of the car quickly and frown when I see Elle already has her door open.

"You were supposed to wait for me to open it," I grumble.

This is our first date. I'm trying to do everything right.

Elle smirks.

"I'll be right back," I tell her, jogging toward the closest meter.

This night does *not* need a parking ticket.

I'm waiting for the paper for the dashboard to print when I hear, "James."

I glance away from the meter, stilling when I realize who's walking toward me. I haven't seen Zane in years, not since the fateful night I accepted Phoenix's offer of a ride to Hathaway's party.

"Hi, Zane," I say carefully.

"I heard you were out. Nice to see you, man."

I nod, knocking the fist he offers.

He glances past me, his smile widening when he spots Elle waiting by her car. Whistles. "*Damn*. Elle Clarke. I guess things kinda worked out for you, huh?"

My guard goes up. "What do you want, Zane?"

He lifts his hand in a placating gesture. "Nothing. I'm out of all that shit. Have been for years. I just saw you and wanted to say hello. Always felt bad you got the short stick with none of the perks."

"You keep in touch with Phoenix?" I ask. More for Reese than myself.

Zane shakes his head. "Haven't talked to him in years. He was in California, last I heard."

"With Cruz?"

He shrugs. "No clue."

"He set me up?" I ask.

That's always been a nagging uncertainty in the back of my head. It seemed too … convenient, how the one time Cruz's suppliers were tailed were when they delivered to my trailer, not his.

"If he did, he didn't tell me," Zane replies. "Wasn't much of a democracy, but he didn't usually keep us in the dark."

My nod is slow. Maybe it was just shitty luck. "You still live around here?"

"Nah. Just visiting. Not a bad place, in certain circles." He glances at Elle again. "Guess you know that." His gaze lands back on me. "I'll see you around, maybe."

I nod.

Zane continues walking, right past Elle.

I finish paying the meter, then head back toward her. "Ready?"

"Who was that?" she asks.

"Just a guy I used to know."

"A guy you used to deal drugs with?"

I swallow. "It's all in the past, Elle. Let's leave it there, please."

Elle crosses her arms. "It's not in the past if you were *just* talking to him." She hesitates, then asks, "Are you … dealing again?"

"No! *No.* I've never—" I exhale, running a hand through my hair and then belatedly remembering I tried to style it earlier. "Can we talk about this later at least?"

"You went to prison for dealing drugs, Ryder."

My jaw tightens. "I remember."

"So, tell me what you were talking to him about."

I glance around, wishing we weren't having this conversation on a sidewalk. "When I moved back here, senior year, I could've joined Cruz's crew. But I didn't."

A wrinkle appears between Elle's eyes.

"When you asked me if I was involved, I was honest. But then …" I swallow. "I owed Cruz a favor. He asked me to receive a shipment. I was supposed to store it for a couple of hours. That's it. Thirty seconds after the guys dropped it off, the cops showed up. It was all just … terrible timing."

"But … why wouldn't you tell the police that?"

"What does anyone say when they're caught with a bunch of coke? *It's not mine* isn't *innocent*, Elle. I had it in my possession—*a lot* of it in my possession—and that's all they needed. If it had gone to trial, I would have risked more than eight years. So, I took the deal. If I'd snitched on Cruz, who knows what he would have done."

"Why didn't you tell me all of that when I visited you?"

"Because it wouldn't have changed anything. There was nothing you could have done."

Elle's lips press tightly together. She's annoyed. Probably hurt. And she has a right to feel both those things. But at some point, we'll have to move past all this. Or else … we won't.

"What was the favor?"

"What?" I play dumb. I *am* dumb, for mentioning it.

"Why would you get involved? What was the favor?"

"Elle …"

She hears the hesitation in my voice. "What aren't you telling me, Ryder?"

I sigh. "Cormac called me from a party the night before, needing a ride. The party turned out to be Hathaway's. When we got there, he said some shit, and I lost my temper. I punched him, and Cruz got spooked, thinking Hathaway was going to call the cops or mess with his business. Me getting that shipment was supposed to make up for it."

"Did Cruz set you up?"

I exhale. "I don't know."

Elle gnaws her bottom lip. "What did Archer say?"

Another question I don't want to answer.

And I don't have to. She reads the truth on my face.

"It was about me. You went to prison … because of me."

"*No*. No, Elle. I made my own decisions, and I made the mess. None of it was your fault."

She nods, but her expression is still unsettled.

I grab her hand and tug her toward her convertible. "Come on."

"What—where are we going? We just got here."

"We'll come back. I want to show you something first."

Elle frowns, but she climbs into the passenger seat after I open the door for her.

I back out of the parking space, then start on the route that's so familiar by now that I could travel it blindfolded.

Elle keeps glancing over, the confusion on her face growing more pronounced as I drive through town toward Fernwood's most exclusive neighborhoods.

"What's going on?"

"You'll see."

She huffs, but stops asking questions.

Five minutes later, I park in front of the old Warren house. The blue dumpster in the driveway ruins some of the effect, but the exterior still looks pretty good. Way better than when we started.

I wasn't sure if she'd see it. Get it. But one glance at her face, and I know she does.

I climb out first, walking around to open her door.

"Ryder …" Elle's wide eyes are glued to the house.

"You remember?"

"I … *how*? How did you do this?"

I shrug. "Easy. Tuck trusts my vision as his main contractor. I made suggestions; he signed off on everything. Thinks I'm some sort of design genius."

"No, I mean, how did you remember everything? The color, the brick walk, the porch swing?"

"There's a screened porch too," I tell her.

Elle looks away from the house for the first time. "You said that was impractical."

"The convertible grew on me too. Want to see the inside?"

She nods.

"It's a lot rougher in here," I warn her as we approach the front door. "Another few months of work at least."

I fish the house keys out of my pocket, smiling when my fingers brush the little lighthouse attached to Elle's car keys.

"Wow. It's …"

"Empty?"

Elle rolls her eyes. "I was going to say beautiful."

"This is the entryway, obviously. Living room is here, to the left.

Screened porch can be accessed through here or the front porch. And then this is the dining room. Those built-ins are new, just got installed this week. The kitchen is back here. Appliances are in the garage, waiting for the countertop guy to get those installed."

Elle follows behind me, peering closely at each room.

The drawing she showed me of her dream house was just the exterior, so there are no special details inside. Just the original woodwork and a whole lot of labor. I know every inch of this house as well as my mom's tiny trailer by this point.

"Want to see upstairs?"

"Maybe later." Elle looks away from the trim she was inspecting, her attention all on me.

I watch her walk toward me, a secretive smile on her lips, not sure if this is headed where I think it is.

Elle had the bar exam this week, so I haven't seen her since last weekend. She's been in Boston, and I've been in Fernwood. Tonight—our first official date—was supposed to end with us going back to her place in the city.

I don't think we'll make it that far.

She closes the small distance between us in seconds, her hands landing on my belt.

"I like the house," she tells me.

"Good."

The word turns into a groan when she sinks to her knees. At least the floors in here are clean. The crew has kept out of the kitchen since all that's left to do in here is install the countertops and hook up the appliances.

Golden sunlight spills across the varnished surface as sunset approaches, bathing the room in an ethereal glow.

I can barely hear the rasp of the zipper lowering over my harsh breaths. My hands clench into fists.

Elle teases me, running the warm tip of her tongue around the flared head of my cock. Her hand moves along my shaft, squeezing, pulling a hoarse grunt out of my mouth.

She knows exactly what I like. Information she's using to her advantage.

She sucks a couple of inches into her mouth, then releases me with a wet pop. Blows on the dampness. My hips jerk forward, seeking. Begging.

"Lo …" The syllable is thick with desire. Overwhelmed by lust.

Elle smirks, then takes me into her mouth again. Deep, until the tip hits the back of her throat. Her grip tightens on the remaining inches, her throat contracting as she struggles to take more.

I hold still, fighting the urge to thrust, giving her a chance to adjust. She swallows, and my legs go numb from the flood of endorphins.

She's on her knees, bringing me to mine. I could come from the sight of her lips stretched around my erection, let alone the sensation of her sucking.

Elle's hands land on my thighs, and then she moves one to cup my balls. They're throbbing, heavy and tight. Desperate to fill her mouth.

I groan, the urge to touch her too strong to ignore. Her hair is pulled back in a fancy twist I don't want to mess up. I cup Elle's face instead, rubbing my thumb against her cheek. Her eyes hood as her hand leaves my balls to grip the base of my cock, rubbing the tip along the outline of her lips before starting suction again.

I'm transfixed, watching her touch me. Completely mesmerized.

Someone could light this house I've poured blood and sweat into on fire, and I wouldn't move unless Elle was in danger. I'm entirely at her mercy right now.

I warn Elle when I'm close. Rather than move away, she sucks me harder. I come a few seconds later, the bob of Elle's throat swallowing as erotic as the sight of her pink lips wrapped around my dick.

I tug her to her feet and kiss her hard. Tasting my own cum is strange, but some primitive part of me likes that she tastes like me.

Elle's sucking on my tongue the same way she just sucked my dick. I pull a condom out of my pocket, one I stashed there earlier, hoping this would take place at some point tonight.

I wasn't expecting us to hook up *here*, but maybe there's some cosmic poetry to us having sex in this house, the one I tried to turn into her dream home.

I glance around the kitchen. Options are very limited in terms of a stable surface to have sex on. The only tables in here are constructed from sawhorses, and the cheap plywood serving as temporary counters is guaranteed to have splinters.

Elle realizes the dilemma and solves it.

"Sit," she tells me, reaching for the hem of her dress.

I don't argue.

She tugs the dress over her head and lets it fall in a pink puddle on the floor. Her bra disappears next, her nipples pebbled and pointed straight toward me. Her thong goes last, the view as I look up and she stands over me obscene. Her pussy is glistening and swollen, aroused from blowing me.

I toss the empty condom wrapper away, reaching for her.

We both groan when she straddles me and our hips align. My hands coast up her back and down her sides, attempting to touch as much exposed skin as possible. It feels like a privilege, seeing her naked. I think it always will.

"You're so beautiful," I murmur.

Elle blushes, the shy color in her cheeks a contrast to the confident way she moves my dick to her opening and then sinks down.

"*Fuck.*" I exhale, feeling her heat only for a second before it starts to surround me.

Elle's greedy for more, bearing down hard as I watch her opening stretch to accommodate my penis. My hands slide up her stomach and cover her breasts as she undulates over me.

"You feel so fucking good," she tells me, scratching at my shoulders as I replace my hands with my mouth. "So thick and hard and—" I bite gently. "*Ry!*"

She's close. I can feel her inner muscles rippling around me.

Elle reaches up. A few bobby pins fall to the floor as she undoes her hair, dark strands curtaining her rapturous expression. She leans back, miles of smooth skin spread in front of me. We're still fucking, and I'm already ready to start all over again.

She shifts again, grinding our pelvises together.

My hands move to her hips, working my cock in and out of her. I'm starting to sweat from all the lust burning through me. Nothing affects me like Elle. When we're touching, she has more control over my body than I do.

Elle grabs my right hand and guides it lower. As soon as my fingers touch her clit, she's coming, breathy moans and loud cries filling the kitchen as her pussy pulses around me.

Elle doesn't move away, even after both of our bodies have stilled. She rests her forehead against my shoulder, her fingers playing with the ends of my hair.

"I'm sorry, Ry," she whispers, her voice slightly muffled by my skin. "So sorry for everything that happened to you."

My hold on her tightens. "I'm not. I'd do it all over again, Lo, every shitty second, if I knew it meant we'd be here, having sex in houses we don't own."

She laughs. "This is the best first date ever."

I chuckle too. "Just wait until you try the oysters and caviar at this restaurant."

38
NOW

Ryder

Applause explodes throughout the ballroom as Keira and Tucker appear as Mr. and Mrs. Franklin for the first time.

Elle is beaming as she leans against me, watching her best friend and mine walk toward the open section of the floor for their first dance.

"When are the speeches again?" I whisper to Elle.

"Not until after dinner," she replies.

I reach up to fiddle with the knot of my bow tie.

I'm nervous, not only about speaking in front of the hundreds of people Tuck invited to his wedding, but also about what I wrote.

Tucker is more than my best friend. We're as close as brothers. Closer maybe since I've shared things with him that I felt like I needed to shield Cormac from.

My little brother doesn't look like he needs protecting though. He's seated at the next table over, between our mom and his girlfriend, Brynn. Cormac had his doubts about how their relationship might fare after she returned to Ohio, but I'd say her coming all this way to be a plus-one at a wedding bodes pretty damn well. Not to mention, she's sleeping in my lumpy twin bed this weekend while I stay with Elle.

She *must* love him, if she's willing to endure that.

My mom glances over and catches me looking their way. With her hair styled and a full face of makeup, you can hardly tell she's sick. There are starting to be some signs though. She's lost weight, and she coughs frequently. The imaginary clock is ticking even if we can't always hear it.

Her gaze bounces to Elle beside me, then back to me. She beams.

If there's one person happier about us being back together than Elle and me, it's my mom. It's the best gift I ever could have given her. She sees Elle as a daughter, and she's thrilled my life is finally moving forward in a positive direction.

Elle's parents, who are seated right by the dance floor and were invited because they're good friends with Keira's parents, are much harder to read. I've had dinner at their house twice in the two months Elle and I have been officially dating. Both were awkward meals of polite, forced small talk. They obviously have no idea what to make of me—the guy with no college degree and a criminal record, the opposite of everything they ever wanted for their little girl. And they were clearly taken aback by Elle, noticing the same thing it had taken me a lot longer than a few hours to realize—Elle's different around me. She's less stiff and polished, more relaxed and playful.

Like now, her hand is dangerously close to my dick under the table.

"Don't you dare," I murmur to her.

"You'd be less nervous about your speech."

I'd also be wondering if anyone could see the wet spot in my pants for the rest of the night. At my best friend's wedding, an event her parents and my mom are attending.

I lean over to kiss her shoulder. "Later."

The first dance ends, and everyone claps. Uniformed waiters start to move through the room, carrying trays covered with glasses of champagne and different appetizers. Hopefully, Tuck had some input on the menu. I didn't *dislike* the food at The Franklin when Elle and I ate there, but Keira and I definitely have different culinary tastes.

People stand and start to mingle. The band is still playing, and some other couples are dancing now that Keira and Tuck have cleared the floor.

I talk to a few of the guys from the construction crew, plus some familiar faces from high school, then ask my mom to dance.

She protests, saying I should dance with Elle if I have "happy feet," but gives up the closer we get to the dance floor. I promise her I will dance with Elle later.

"What a beautiful wedding," she says, looking around the ballroom at the flower arrangements and the twinkling lights.

"It is," I agree. "Do you ever regret not having one?"

She never married my dad. Or Cormac's. Gave both of us her last name instead.

"Regret? No. If I had gotten married, it would have been a mistake."

"Because you don't believe in it?"

"Because I do. You get married when you're sure it's going to work out. Not because you're not sure if it will. It's not a repair or a solution."

"I'm not sure when I'll ask Elle," I say. "I don't know if she's ready, if I am. I don't know where we'll live ... what I'll do for work ..."

"It's okay, Ry. It's enough for me, seeing you like this." My mom glances at her table, where Cormac is sitting with Brynn. He has one arm slung around the back of her chair as he sips at champagne. "Seeing both you boys happy—that's all I've ever wanted."

"I want you to be there." The words are soft, a statement I'm not sure I should share with her. It alludes to the dark cloud I want to pretend doesn't exist today.

For the most part, I've abided by her wishes. I've stopped suggesting treatment. Stopped asking questions after her doctor's appointments. I go with her and sit in the waiting room, and then we leave. Sometimes, we stop for lunch somewhere. Once, we drove into Boston to visit Cormac on campus.

She squeezes my shoulder. "I will be, Ryder. No matter what, I'll be there."

My throat is too thick to say anything else. We sway until the song ends, and then I walk my mom back to her table. We pass Reese, who's dancing with Keira's older brother. I raise my eyebrows at her, and she smiles at me.

I guess she's over her aversion to Ones. Or maybe it just helps if they're male and good-looking.

After leaving my mom at her table, I grab some food and talk to Tuck's dad for a while. He's full of praise about the Warren house project, boasting that Tuck is going to sell the place for several million. I'm no real estate agent, but I hope he's right. We've never talked about it, but I'd be shocked if Tuck has never thought about the same financial disparity with Keira that I'm aware of with Elle.

Not that you need to each have the same amount of money to be in a relationship, but it's a strange balance when it's so lopsided. It comes up at random times, whenever you see a movie or get ice cream or go out to dinner. It's always a conversation.

After talking with Tuck's dad, I head back to my table. Tuck intercepts me midway, giving me a huge hug. I've seen him since the ceremony, but there were tons of other people around. The rest of the wedding party, photographers, family members. This is the first moment we've had, just the two of us.

"So?" I ask. "How does it feel?"

Tuck's grin is bigger than I've ever seen it. "Good, man. It feels really good." He leans closer and whispers, "Can I tell you something?"

"Uh, sure?"

He snorts. "Reassuring. Anyway, Keira's pregnant, and I've been terrified her folks were going to find out before the wedding. They're stuck with me now, right?"

"Congrats, man. That's awesome. And, yep, that's great thinking with the in-laws. No way they'll do the math."

"If you knock up Elle soon, our kids could be the same age," Tuck tells me. "Raise hell at Fernwood High together, just like we did."

"Raise hell? What was the craziest thing you did in high school, Tuck? Go to a One party?"

"Hey! I was crazy."

"Uh-huh. Ask Reese. She'll back me up. Your kids will be baseball or softball stars with great grades, trust me."

Tuck's giant grin appears again. "God, I can't wait to play ball in the yard with my kid."

I clap his shoulder. "Really happy for you, man."

"Thanks. And don't tell anyone I told you, okay? Keira wants to— hey, Elle."

"Hi, Tuck." Elle pauses beside me, glancing between me and Tuck, who shoots me a nervous look. I'm not sure how much of our conversation Elle heard. "I came to ask you to dance," she tells me.

"Thank goodness," I say. "My mom was *so* worried we wouldn't get to."

"Ha. I saw you two out there. Come on." She grabs my hand.

"See ya," I say to Tuck, then let Elle pull me away.

"How much did you hear?" I ask once we're swaying on the dance floor.

"Enough to know Tuck told you a secret," she replies.

"I'm not supposed to tell anyone."

She rolls her eyes. "You can stop worrying about choosing between your guilty conscience and me being mad at you. Keira isn't drinking, and her boobs barely fit in her wedding dress. She's pregnant. I'm right, right?"

I nod. If Tuck asks, I can swear I never said a word.

"I'm so happy for them."

"Yeah, me too."

We sway in silence for a few minutes, just enjoying the moment.

"Do you want to get married?" I ask.

After my conversation with my mom, I'm realizing I don't know her answer to that. I just assumed it was something she wanted—the diamond ring and a fancy wedding like this one.

Beneath my palms, Elle's spine stiffens. She pulls back a couple of inches, her blue eyes wide as she glances up at me. "Is this your idea of a proposal?"

I laugh. "No. I'm more romantic than that."

She relaxes a little, but continues staring at me. "Then, why are you asking?"

"Because I don't know the answer. We're at a wedding. I was just wondering if this is something you want. If it's something you've thought about."

"With you or just in general?"

I pinch the side of her ribs.

Elle smirks.

"I'm not talking *that* hypothetically," I answer. "With me."

"I wondered if a bigger commitment would have made it harder for you to end things," she tells me. "We weren't even dating back then really."

Her honesty is what I always want, but I still wince. She's right. Technically, we had our first date about seven weeks ago.

Elle notices. "Sorry."

"Don't apologize. I asked."

"I also used to practice writing *Elodie James* in all of my high school notebooks. I've got four years' worth of a fake signature."

I smile. "Yeah?"

"Yeah." Her hands slide up to the back of my neck, tracing circles there. "With lots of flourishes."

She's not drawing circles, I realize. She's writing it on my skin.

"I thought this would be us," she whispers. "Before everything happened ... it felt inevitable. I love Keira, and I'm so happy for her, but ..." She lifts a shoulder, then lets it drop.

"It felt inevitable to me too," I tell her. "I didn't believe in much. But I believed in us."

Her hands pause. "Do you still?"

"More than ever," I reply, hoping she can hear the sincerity in the words.

"Then, you should ask me."

"I'm going to."

"When?"

"That's for me to know and for you to find out."

Elle pouts. "No fair."

"Well, I'm the one asking the question. That's the scary part."

"Not when you already know my answer."

"Don't spoil it," I say. "Keep me on my toes."

"That's a good idea," Elle says, pressing closer against me. Her hands leave my neck and run down my back as her breasts rub against my chest.

"Lo ..." I groan.

"What?"

"You know what."

"People have sex at weddings all the time, Ry," she tells me. "It's a great place to meet single people."

"That's great." I tighten my grip on her hips. "You're not single."

Her giggle makes me smile and my slacks even more uncomfortable. She whispers, "Prove it," and I know I will.

Because there isn't anything I wouldn't do for this girl.

39
NOW

Elle

As soon as I step out of the conference room, my phone buzzes with an incoming call.

"I'm on my way down," I say. "Two minutes."

"Okay," Ryder replies. "I'm parked right in front."

"Okay." I hang up, adjust the folders tucked under one arm, and then hurry toward the elevator bank.

Two men are standing and talking in the small lobby on this floor of the firm. I pass them and press the down arrow, my foot tapping impatiently as I wait.

"Elle?"

I spin around. Prescott is walking toward me, the man he was talking to remaining by the chairs.

"Oh. Hi." I blink twice, making sure it's really him.

Prescott tucks his hands into his pockets. "I wondered if I might run into you here. Just stopping by for a lunch meeting."

I force a smile. "Here I am."

"How've you been?" he asks.

"Good," I respond. "Busy, you know."

"Yeah, I sure do." He chuckles. "I thought law school was supposed to be the worst part."

"Lies to get through it," I tell him.

"Yeah. Right. Aside from work, you're good?"

I nod. "Yeah. I am."

"That's great." He pulls one hand out of his pocket to scratch at the scruff on his cheek. The stubble suits him. "Jenny and I started dating a few months ago."

"I'm happy for you guys."

Prescott peers a little closer. "You already knew, huh?"

This time, the smile comes easily. "Krista might have mentioned you two left her New Year's party together."

"Right." The tops of his ears turn red, which makes my smile grow. "I hope you didn't *not* show at that because of me."

"No, no."

He lifts an eyebrow.

"Well, maybe I avoided the group at first," I admit. "But I had a conflict that night."

The elevator arrives, dinging as the doors open.

"It was really nice to see you," I say, holding my hand out to keep them open. "But I-I've got to go."

His smile is good-natured. "Sure."

"No, really, I do. It's a, uh, memorial service."

Prescott's rueful expression immediately transforms to serious. "I'm so sorry for your loss."

"Thank you." I step inside the elevator. "Next time everyone gets together, I'll be there."

I catch his nod before the doors slide shut.

As soon as the elevator starts to descend, I slump against the wall and pull the clip out of my hair. I wish I had time to go home and change, but I don't. We're driving to the Cape to spread Nina's ashes with Cormac, then driving back to Fernwood to have dinner with my parents. I'm guessing we'll spend the night at the trailer rather than drive back to Boston.

My mom was insistent about doing dinner on this date, for some reason, and Cormac picked up Nina's ashes from the funeral home yesterday. She died a week ago. Back in February, she'd had to be hospitalized for a few days, but she was able to pass away in her own bed, at home with her boys, the way she'd wanted.

I got to say goodbye to her. She got to see me and Ryder together.

Those are the things I've tried to cling to since we lost her.

Ryder leans over to kiss me as soon as I climb into the car, but he doesn't say much as we drive through the city and merge onto the highway.

"Work go okay?"

"Yeah. I saw Prescott actually."

"Oh, yeah? He good?"

There's no trace of jealousy in Ryder's voice, and I'm not expecting to hear it.

"He seemed it."

"Good." Ryder pulls his phone out of his jacket pocket and hands it to me. "Can you text Cormac, let him know that we'll be there in about an hour? I forgot to before we left."

"Yeah, of course."

I message Cormac, then relax against the seat to look out the window for the rest of the drive.

Cormac is there, waiting, when Ryder pulls off into the gravel parking lot that only contains two other cars. This is a public beach, but it's the beginning of April. No tourists around yet.

Cormac hugs his brother, then me.

"How are you?" I ask, squeezing his arm.

He offers me a sad smile. "I'm okay. Good moments and bad moments, you know?"

I nod. I do know.

"Brynn still coming to visit next month?"

"Yeah. She wanted to come this week, but I told her not to. I just need some time, you know?"

Again, I nod. "Time helps. Not a lot, but it does."

"Anyway …" Cormac reaches into his car and returns holding a plastic bag filled with what looks like gray grit. "They gave me a cardboard box, too, but that didn't seem necessary. Lady definitely judged me for not buying an urn, but I didn't know what we'd do with it … after." He glances at Ryder. "Figured you wouldn't want it."

Ryder half smiles. "You figured right."

We walk across the sand in a single line, not stopping until we reach the water's edge. It's *cold*, wind whipping my hair around and making my eyes water. I should have worn a warmer coat.

Cormac goes first, grabbing a large handful of Nina's ashes and tossing them toward the waves. "Bye, Mom."

I go next. Before I reach into the bag, I grab the jasmine leaves out of my pocket. I stuffed them in there this morning. I toss the handful of tea toward the water, the wind picking up most of it and carrying it to the destination. Then, I reach into the ashes and fling them toward the sea too.

"Goodbye, Nina," I whisper. "Thank you. For Ryder, for being there, for everything."

Ryder goes last, scooping up the rest of the ashes. It's strange, how a whole person can be decimated to so little.

"I hope you are watching, Mom," he says. "I hope you'll be there, like you promised."

The last of Nina's remains disappear beneath a whitecap.

Silently, we linger for a few minutes longer, then head back toward the cars without saying anything else.

Ryder and I say somber goodbyes to Cormac, then get back on the road.

"You're sure about tonight?" I ask. "I can still cancel."

"I'm sure, Elle. I'm fine."

I'm not sure he is, but I know arguing about it won't help. I'm mourning Nina myself, but I'm also concerned about how Ryder is handling losing his mom. He knew it was coming, but I don't think that helps at all. It might be worse, honestly. He mourned her dying, and now, he's grieving her death.

We stop by my brownstone so I can change and to pick up Scout, then continue toward Fernwood.

My parents are out in front of the house, standing by the stone fountain, when we pull into the driveway. I frown as I climb out of the car. Scout sneaks out, rushing off to sniff as much of the yard as he can.

"Hi, Mom. Hi, Dad. What's, uh, what's going on?"

"Get back in the car," my mom tells me.

"What?"

"Get back in the car," she repeats. "We have something to show you." She glances at Ryder. "To show both of you."

"Um, okay."

I whistle for Scout. He bounds over, but is much less thrilled about getting back in the car. Finally, I manage to wrangle him, then climb in myself.

"This is weird," I tell Ryder, buckling my seat belt. "Right?"

"Your parents do weird stuff. Remember the last time we were over, your mom had bought an outdoor pizza oven just because I'd mentioned it was my favorite food the time before?"

"Yeah, but that was at their house at least."

"Maybe they're taking us out to dinner."

"Then I should have left Scout at their house! He hates getting stuck in the car."

Ryder sighs. "If we are going to a restaurant, I'll drop you off and then drive him back to their house, okay?"

"I don't think we're going to a restaurant," I say, peering out the window.

My dad's car is headed in the opposite direction from downtown, deeper into the nearby neighborhoods.

Five minutes later, his sedan stops in front of the old Warren house.

"Okay," Ryder says. "This *is* weird."

"They know you work for Tucker's construction company. Maybe they found out you'd worked on this property? Wanted to see it?"

"I don't have the keys anymore. It sold. We can't go inside."

I step out of the car. My parents are already waiting, standing on the sidewalk.

"What's going on?" I ask.

My mom points toward the house. "Welcome home!"

I stop mid-stride, my gaze bouncing between her finger and the house. "What?"

"We know you both have your own places. You don't need to

move in right away. But it's so rare that anything comes on the market around here, and this was such a beautiful renovation. I couldn't resist."

She stares at me expectantly. Both my parents are.

The manners they drilled into me kick in.

"Thank you," I say, gesturing toward the house. "This is ... wow."

I glance at Ryder, who looks too stunned to speak.

Or maybe he's mad. They didn't even *ask* us.

I'm less surprised than he must be. No part of me expected this, but it's so typical of my parents. They have enough money that a purchase this size is moderate in their eyes. Like how most people might see splurging for an in-ground swimming pool. A significant expense, but not a big one.

And ... this is their way of giving me the life they want for me. They always assumed—hoped—I'd end up with a wealthy guy from their world and settle down in Fernwood to raise my kids. They're accepting Ryder on their terms. They're making sure I live in the mansion, five minutes from them, regardless of who I'm in a relationship with.

My dad holds out keys to me. "Here are the keys. I've got the deed and all the paperwork in my office." He glances at Ryder. "It's in Elle's name. Just simpler since you two aren't married, but this is a gift to the both of you. I want to make sure that's clear."

"Thank you," Ryder manages.

"Well, we should get going," my mom says.

"Going?" I ask.

"We have a dinner at the Parkers' to get to," she explains.

"I thought *we* were having dinner."

"Oh, that was just a cover for the surprise. I'm sure you two want to look around, enjoy some time to yourselves. We'll do dinner a different night. I'll send you some dates of when your father and I are free."

"Uh … okay," I reply, not sure what else to say.

I'm a little numb. Between the busy morning at work, emotional goodbye at the beach, and now *this*, I'm totally drained.

My mom kisses my cheek. "I have *so* many design ideas," she whispers to me. "The space is gorgeous. And there's a screened porch! I've always wanted one."

I don't dare look at Ryder.

"We'll see you next Sunday?" my dad asks.

"Yes," I reply. "I'll be there."

My voice is somber, reflective of the occasion. It's the anniversary of Rose's death.

"You'll join us, Ryder?"

Ryder nods. His expression is grave, too, and I realize he remembers the date. He knows my father is inviting him to a cemetery. "Of course, sir."

My father puffs up with a little importance. He'd never admit it, but he loves that Ryder calls him *sir*. Most of the guys I've dated took the chummy approach, referring to him as Michael and discussing the best golf club brands. I think Ryder's *moxie* is growing on him too. That he respects how Ryder holds his ground whenever they disagree. That Ryder refuses to go golfing or drink his expensive cognac, sticking to football and beer.

My mom is harder to crack. But if Ryder ever proposes and she gets to plan the wedding, I think she'll totally come around.

They see how happy Ryder makes me. And for all their faults, I know that's what they want for me. They just had different ideas about what would make me happy.

My parents leave.

Ryder and I remain on the sidewalk, staring at the house. It's even more beautiful now, fully finished, than it was the first time I saw it.

"Do you want to go inside?" I ask.

He glances over. "Can we come back tomorrow? I'd love to change, if we're not doing dinner with your parents."

"Yeah, of course."

I'm relieved, honestly. There's a big conversation looming, and it feels like leaving the house will avoid it—at least for now.

We stop to pick up a pizza, then drive to Nina's—Ryder's—trailer. She left it to both her sons, but I can't picture Cormac ever living here. He only has one full year of college left and already has a job lined up in the city, working for the same company he interned for last summer.

Dinner is mostly silent, both of us lost in our own thoughts. I walk Scout up and down the road, stopping to say hi to Reese, who's outside with Knox, and get ready for bed as soon as I'm back at the trailer. Scout makes himself comfortable on the couch, and I'm too tired to enforce the *no furniture* rule. He doesn't have a crate here, so I can't enforce it really.

Ryder heads into the bathroom as soon as I finish.

By silent agreement, we head into Ryder's bedroom. Nina's room is bigger, and all the medical equipment was removed, but it feels too strange to be in there with her gone.

"Going to be a tight fit," he says, staring at the twin mattress.

"Heard that before," I quip. "We always make it work."

Ryder grins, but it collapses quickly. He climbs into bed first, so I crawl over his body, wedging mine against the wall. I end up half on his chest, the sheets pulled up to my chin.

"I love you."

He kisses the top of my head. "Love you too, Lo."

I relax into him, closing my eyes and trying to shut off my brain. I must succeed at some point because it's a surprise when I wake up in bed, alone.

I roll over, squinting in the dark. It's late. Or very early.

Eventually, my eyes focus on the figure by the window.

I slip out of bed, padding over to a still Ryder. He's staring out the window, rolling an unlit cigarette between two fingers.

"Need a lighter?" I ask, resting my chin on his shoulder.

His arm wraps around my waist, pulling me tight to his side, but he doesn't look away from the window. It's not much of a view, grass that could use a mow and a stretch of vinyl fencing, but I know that's not the point.

"No." The syllable comes out raspy and thick. Ryder clears his throat. "No. I'm not going to smoke it."

"Couldn't sleep?"

"Not really. Sorry if I woke you."

"You didn't."

"Do you want the house?" he asks.

I blow out a long breath. I knew the question was coming, but I wasn't expecting it yet. "We don't have to talk about that right now."

"I want to," he insists. "Do you want the house, Elle?"

"Only if you do."

"It's huge," Ryder reminds me. "Five bedrooms."

"I remember. I looked through them all, after we christened the kitchen."

He glances over, scanning my expression.

I'm not sure how much of my face he can actually see in the dim light.

"The house is a gift, but there's upkeep, utilities, furniture, taxes …"

"We can afford it."

"*You* can afford it." His tone is matter-of-fact, so similar to Nina's that it makes my eyes burn.

"Does that mean you've changed your mind about getting married?" A question I've put off asking because I'm intimidated by the answer.

He hasn't brought marriage up since Keira and Tucker's wedding last fall, which seems like a bad sign. I know he's committed to me, but if he no longer wants that … it'll feel like losing momentum.

"No, I haven't," he tells me, sounding sure enough that I wish I'd asked sooner.

I could have saved myself some stress.

"But married or not, everyone will know where the money is coming from, Elle. That's embarrassing for me. Don't you get that?"

"Do you think Tuck should be embarrassed? Keira has more money than he does. Or would you care if I had no trust fund and you did?"

His head turns back toward the window, his thumb stroking the strip of skin exposed above my sleep shorts.

"I want to quit my job. Parts of working for Tuck are great, but I miss having him just be my best friend and not my boss too. I've been thinking about buying Hank's old garage, reopening it. I was way better at working on cars than I am at construction." He swallows. "Haven't had much luck getting a loan. I don't have much in the way of savings. I might have a shot now with the cut I'll get from the house's sale as part of the crew. But that …" He shakes his head.

"Turns out, that's your money too."

"You earned that money, Ryder. You did a job, and you got paid for it. That's how the world works."

"They bought that place because they knew it was the only way you'd live in a house like that. That I'd never be able to afford it for you."

I reach out and run my fingers along his temple. His eyes flutter shut for a few seconds.

"I grew up in a house like that, and I was miserable most of the time. I don't need to own a mansion to be happy. My favorite thing about that house is that you made it look like the drawing I had shown you. Not how big it is or how much money it's worth. That it reminds me of *us*. But that can be anywhere we're together. It doesn't have to be here."

Ryder exhales, his thumb still moving against my skin.

"I wanted it to be a perfect moment," he says. "That's the only reason I haven't asked you. I wasn't sure what I was doing for work, and everything with my mom ... I wasn't second-guessing us. I swear."

I twist my head so that my cheek is pressed against his neck. His hold on me tightens even more.

"You asking me *is* the perfect moment, Ry."

We stand like that for a few minutes before his arms drop.

"I'll be right back."

I watch him leave with raised eyebrows, hearing the low murmur of his voice as he talks to Scout in the living room. And then he's back, holding a small black box in one hand, solving the mystery of what he went to get.

I thought I was prepared for this moment. Lying awake at night, I wondered why it hadn't happened yet. Worried the fairy tale was still going to fall apart. Planned out what I would say if he ever did ask.

Turns out, I wasn't ready.

Salty tears slip down my cheeks as he walks toward me.

"Elle." His voice is overwhelmingly tender as I continue to cry, the intimate tone settling around my shoulders like a warm blanket. "Lo, it's okay."

"I know," I blubber.

This is the second time I've sobbed today, but these tears feel very different from the ones at the beach. These are relief, not sadness. For so long, I was so certain we'd never have this moment.

And I'm imagining Nina looking down at this, one of her rare smiles appearing.

"I've never seen you look so thrilled," he jokes.

I choke out a watery laugh. "I'm happy. *So* happy. Just … overwhelmed. It took a while to get here, you know?"

"I know," he says.

He does. He's the only other person who knows exactly how long.

"I want the house, Elle. I want to see you sit on that screened porch for the three months it'll be usable. I want to fill up those four bedrooms with kids. For them to go to the high school where I fell in love with you. For them to grow up with Keira and Tuck's son. I want Scout to get to play in that big yard. With you, I want it all. As long as you do too."

I'm crying harder now, but Ryder no longer looks concerned. More amused.

I'm not a crier normally. Since Rose's funeral, every time I've cried, it has been connected to him in some way.

Around him, I just care more. And I think that's a good thing, especially now that it's no longer breaking my heart.

"Lo?"

"I want it," I tell him. "All of it."

He sinks down onto one knee. I swipe at my eyes, trying to clear my vision so I don't miss anything about this moment.

"Elodie Lily Clarke, will you marry me?"

I gasp when he opens the little black box. I was expecting—well, I hadn't even considered what the ring would look like, honestly. I didn't even know Ryder had bought me one.

He smirks. "Yeah, this is why I have no savings."

"You didn't have to—"

He shakes his head once. "Yeah, I did. You'll wear this for the rest of your life. I wanted it to be perfect."

"It *is* perfect." I touch the diamond gently.

"You haven't answered," he reminds me.

"Oh, right. Yes!"

"*Oh, right. Yes?* How romantic," Ryder says as he slips the ring onto my left finger, then stands.

I laugh. Maybe it's not romantic, but it's us. And he knew my answer already. I feel like I've known it since I met him.

"Shut up and kiss me."

I rise up onto my tippy-toes before he can lean down, wrapping my arms around his neck. Holding tight, knowing I never want to let go.

My heart beats in my chest, warm and whole.

We finally got our different ending.

Our happy ending.

THE END

ACKNOWLEDGMENTS

Some stories just stick with you more than others. Elle and Ryder's journey will always be one of those for me. The books that hurt the most are always the hardest, yet satisfying ones to finish.

To the amazing crew who helped create *Come Break My Heart Again*:

Mel, our conversations are always my favorite part of what's often a grueling drafting process. So grateful for your thorough feedback and thoughtful insight.

Jovana, your attention to detail is unparalleled. Thank you for another wonderful edit.

Tiffany, I wouldn't know how to release a book without you at this point and wouldn't want to. I feel lucky to get to work with you.

Britt, thank you for your polish and especially for your comments. They're the best boost of confidence before sending a book out into the world.

Julie and the team at Books and Moods, I could not love this cover more. It's perfect for Elle and Ryder's story.

Valentine and the team at Valentine PR, I'm so appreciative of all the work you do to help promote my books.

And finally, thank YOU, for reading. You're making my dreams come true.

ABOUT THE AUTHOR

C.W. Farnsworth is the author of numerous adult and young adult romance novels featuring sports, strong female leads, and happy endings.

Charlotte lives in Rhode Island and when she isn't writing spends her free time reading, at the beach, or snuggling with her Australian Shepherd.

Check out her website www.authorcwfarnsworth.com for news about upcoming releases!

ALSO BY C.W. FARNSWORTH

Standalones
Four Months, Three Words
Winning Mr. Wrong
Back Where We Began
Like I Never Said
Fly Bye
Serve
Heartbreak for Two
Pretty Ugly Promises
Six Summers to Fall
King of Country

Rival Love
Kiss Now, Lie Later
For Now, Not Forever

The Kensingtons
Fake Empire
Real Regrets

Truth and Lies
Friday Night Lies
Tuesday Night Truths

Kluvberg
First Flight, Final Fall
All The Wrong Plays

Holt Hockey
Famous Last Words
Against All Odds

From Now On

Made in the USA
Coppell, TX
18 November 2024